THE CAPTURE

ALSO BY TOM ISBELL
The Prey

THE CAPTURE

TOM ISBELL

HARPER TEEN
An Imprint of HarperCollins Publishers

HarperTeen is an imprint of HarperCollins Publishers.

The Capture
Copyright © 2016 by Tom Isbell
www.epicreads.com

Library of Congress Cataloging-in-Publication Data
Isbell, Tom, date, author.
  The capture ; Tom Isbell. — First edition
    pages cm
  Summary: "Fourteen escaped and found their way to a new territory, but Book, Hope, and Cat can't settle into their new free life knowing the rest of the Less Thans and Sisters are still imprisoned. Now the teens must retrace their steps to save the others and destroy the compound. But the path back is filled with even more heart-pounding danger—as motives are questioned and relationships tested"— Provided by publisher.
  ISBN 978-0-06-221605-2 (hardback)
  1. Science fiction. 2. Survival—Fiction. 3. Orphans—Fiction. 4. Twins—Fiction. 5. Sisters—Fiction. [1. Action & Adventure—Survival Stories. 2. Science Fiction.] I. Title.
PZ7.1.I83 Cap 2016   2015006008
[Fic]—dc23   CIP
                                                                         AC

Typography by Joel Tippie
15 16 17 18 19   PC/RRDH   10 9 8 7 6 5 4 3 2 1

First Edition

To Joy, Sue, Jim~
Family

PART ONE
THE ROAD BACK

When men take up arms to set other men free,
there is something sacred and holy in the warfare.
—President Woodrow Wilson

PROLOGUE

HE WALKS THROUGH THE valley of shadows, surviving fire and flood, flames and torrents. Marching across the barren wilderness, he carries in his heart the faint memory of those who went before him. In his veins runs the blood of warriors, the pulse of poets.

Pursuing him are those who will not rest. Like lions, they track him, chasing him across the smoke-filled prairies, the desolate hills, the sun-stroked plains. The rivers shall turn against him, as shall the fields and forests.

Though he gathers friends, there are those who will betray him. Friend will become foe and foe become friend.

But my beloved fears not. He shall mount up with

wings like the birds of the air, shall burrow beneath the earth like creatures of the dark, shall carry great loads like beasts of prey, shall run and not grow weary.

My beloved, in whom I am well pleased.

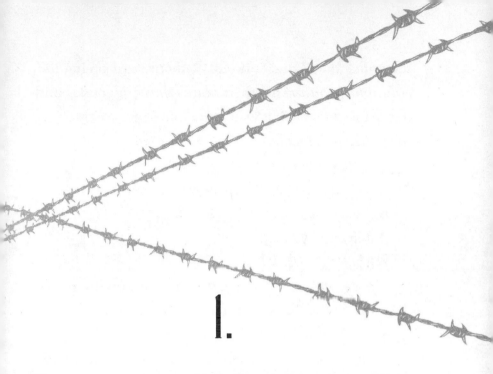

1.

THEY LOOKED AT ME with hollow, vacant stares—their sunken cheeks more like ghosts' than human beings'. Festering sores tattooed their bodies, and their pleading eyes cut circles in the black.

Please, their expressions said, as they strained against the chains that pinned them to the bunker walls. *Get us out of here.*

There were a dozen of them, boys my age, and the more I took in their emaciated bodies—the bones pushing against skin, the bloodshot eyes and skull-like faces—the more I realized I didn't know how to help them. I had no idea, no solution for unlocking their shackles and setting them free.

You must, one of them said, as if I'd voiced my

thoughts aloud, and soon all of them were saying it—
You must, you must—their voices growing louder and
more insistent until it was a kind of song, a raspy chant
from begging faces.

You must. Help us.

"But I can't. I don't know how. . . ."

You must help us.

"I don't know how!"

YOU MUST HELP US!

I woke with a start, my T-shirt damp with sweat.
With trembling hands I tried to rub the sleep from my
eyes . . . and the image from my mind.

"Same one?" Cat asked. He was hunkered in the
shadows, his long knife scraping the edge of a cedar
branch.

Every night it was the same: dreaming of those
Less Thans shackled in the bunker beneath the tennis
court. I couldn't let it go. As bad as the memory was, my
dreams only made it worse, distorting the boys' bodies
until they were more skeletons than living, breathing
human beings.

It was why we had to get back to Camp Liberty. Why
we had to free those Less Thans.

I lifted my head and looked around. Orange light
from the campfire flickered across the faces of the
others. With the exception of Cat and me, the others huddled around the fire and shared stories and

laughter. Three squirrels roasted on spits; the grease sizzled in the flames. On the surface, at least, everything seemed fine.

Just one week earlier, twenty-six of us had crossed into the other territory—the Heartland. Eleven had stayed over there; fifteen had decided to return. Seven Less Thans, eight Sisters. For the past seven days we'd been gathering food, carving bows and arrows, setting up an archery range and firing till our fingers bled. Still, I wondered: Were we up for this? Could we really pull it off?

"Do you think it's a mistake?" I pulled myself over to the log where Cat was sitting.

At first he didn't respond. No surprise there—his least favorite thing was conversation. "Do I think *what's* a mistake?" His knife dug into the wood. Cedar shavings whispered in the air.

"Going back?"

He thought a moment. His glinting blade stripped off a layer of bark as effortlessly as peeling a banana. "Nah, it's definitely the right thing." Then he added, "We don't stand a snowball's chance in hell, but it's definitely the right thing."

I couldn't argue with him. Who were we to take on Brown Shirts and Crazies, Skull People and wolves? What made us think we could even make it back to Camp Liberty, let alone free the Less Thans there?

What on earth were we thinking?

"If the odds are so bad, why're you going back?" I asked.

Cat shrugged. "Like I said at the fence, it'll be the adventure of a lifetime."

I got the feeling there was more to it than that, but there was no point asking. Cat would tell me only when he was good and ready.

Laughter erupted from the far side of the campfire—Flush and Twitch bickering like an old married couple. Tweedledum and Tweedlesmart. The oddest set of friends I'd ever come across. Twitch was tall and supersmart. Flush was short and, well, not as smart as Twitch.

"How about the others?" I asked. "Think they'll be in it for the long haul?"

"Most of 'em," he said, his sandy hair catching a sliver of moonlight.

"Not all?"

"Most," he repeated.

I wondered who wasn't committed. Flush or Twitch? Red or Dozer? Or was he referring to the Sisters? For obvious reasons I didn't count Four Fingers. Ever since his head injury back in the Brown Forest, he'd been wildly out of it. On most days he was lucky to remember his name.

As my eyes passed over the others, it struck me how much we'd changed. The sun had weathered our skin.

The baby fat had burned away. And we moved and spoke with a kind of quiet confidence. All this despite the fact that our clothes were nothing more than rags, dotted and shredded with holes, singed from fire, bleached from sun. After the inferno in the Brown Forest, all we'd managed to salvage were the essentials: the clothes on our backs, some canteens, a few weapons. The good side of that was that nothing was weighing us down.

Well, not physically.

Argos lifted his head and gave a soft moan. He came padding to my side. I reached over and petted him, the ends of my fingers disappearing into his fur. I was careful to avoid the burns from the fire. The wound from the wolves. The gimpy leg. He was no longer the cute little puppy stuffed in a backpack. He'd been to hell and back like the rest of us.

Cat's knife bit into the branch—and then stopped. He opened his mouth to speak, but just as he began to talk, Flush set himself down squarely between us.

"Would you please tell Twitch I wasn't the only one who ate the maggots?" he said. "Red did, too."

Everyone's gaze was directed toward us, waiting for a response. It figured: one of the few times Cat was actually going to start a conversation, and we were interrupted. Whatever he was going to tell me would have to wait.

"As I remember," I answered, loud enough for the others to hear, "Red had the good sense not to like it.

9

You enjoyed your maggots."

That brought on a roar of laughter. Even though Flush pretended to be irritated, I got the impression he enjoyed being the center of attention.

As I prepared for bed that night, constructing a mattress out of pine needles, my thoughts returned to where they always went: Hope. She was the very last of the Sisters to join us—only reluctantly crossing from the other side of the fence.

Things were different between us now. We'd kissed that day after surviving the fire, but ever since, we'd been so busy—just trying to survive—that it was like we didn't know how to act around each other. What I *wanted* was to take her hand, to hold her, to go back to the way we were . . . but I never had the chance.

So I contented myself with fleeting looks. Stolen glances.

There was something else, too. Something I couldn't figure out. Her expression. It had changed these past seven days—it was no longer just the haunted appearance she shared with all the Sisters. It was something more. A kind of grim determination I couldn't quite decipher.

And I saw the way she looked at Cat, her enormous brown eyes lingering on him a moment longer than they needed to. I couldn't help it. Maybe it was my imagination, but then again, maybe it wasn't.

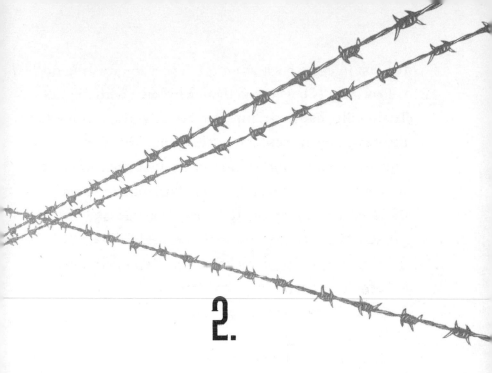

2.

IT'S JUST BEFORE SUNUP when Hope and Cat tiptoe back to camp.

The two of them waited till the others were asleep before sneaking off, the dull red glow of the fire's embers their only illumination. It's been the same each night since they crawled back from the fence. Seven nights, seven silent journeys. So far, with the exception of Argos, no one seems to notice.

The next morning the rains begin, and with the change of weather comes a change of mood. Despite the fact that it's now the height of summer, the showers are icy cold and soak the fifteen travelers to the bone. They spend much of the day sloshing through mud.

For Hope, it's impossible not to sense the resentment from some of the other Sisters. Although she was the last to cross back from the fence, she was the one who originally convinced them to join up with the Less Thans. She can only imagine the questions running through their minds. After all their hard work, after digging a tunnel under Camp Freedom itself, why are they throwing it all away to head back into the heart of the Western Federation Territory? For the sake of saving some Less Thans they've never met?

When they stop to make camp, Hope drifts off to look for firewood, happy for the chance to be alone. The rain has stopped. There is birdsong.

"You all right?" a voice asks. It's Book.

"Why wouldn't I be?" Hope says.

"Don't know. Just curious." Then he says, "I woke up last night and didn't see you."

Hope feels a stab of panic. She wonders what Book knows, what he *saw*. Even as she picks up a large, unwieldy branch, she tries to make a joke of it. "You're not stalking me, are you?"

"No, just happened to look over. Didn't see you."

"Right, well, answering a call of nature."

"Seemed like you were gone a long time."

"Now I *know* you're stalking me." She laughs and snaps the branch in two. "Plus I couldn't sleep, so I just, you know, walked around."

"In the dark?"

"I think better that way."

"Right."

"Can't say no to thinking."

"Nope."

Hope can hear the pathetic nature of her lies. They're so obvious, so blatant. *So bad.* She tries to change the subject.

"I hear there are Skull People between here and your camp," she says.

"That's what we've heard."

"You never saw them?"

Book shakes his head. "Hunters. Brown Shirts. Wolves. Crazies. No Skull People."

"Consider yourself lucky."

Her father once pointed out a camp of Skull People to Hope and her sister, Faith. With their painted skin and helmets made of animal skulls, they were the most frightening sight Hope had ever seen in her life. They were terrifying.

"How do we avoid them?" Book asks.

"Any way we can." She means it as a joke, but Book doesn't laugh. Doesn't even smile.

"What happens after?" Hope asks.

"After?"

"Once we free your friends?"

"Head back to the Heartland. Get everyone to safety." He studies her expression. "Why, you have something different in mind?"

"No, just, you know . . . curious."

"Oh."

They continue to scrounge, their boots squishing in mud.

"Good luck sleeping," Book finally says, and heads back to camp with an armful of branches. Hope's face burns crimson.

He was right, of course. She *does* have something in mind—but she's not ready to share it. Not with Book. Not with anyone.

As for what she and Cat do each night, well, she wants to break that to Book as well. She does. But there are some things she just doesn't know how to say.

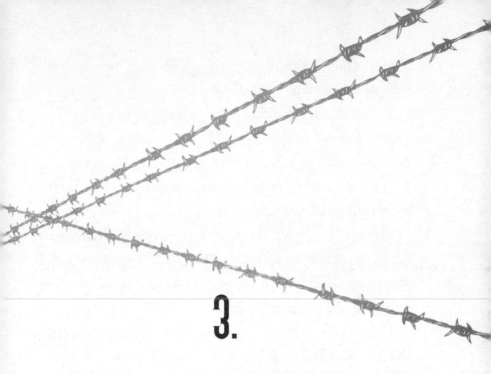

3.

I SLOGGED BACK TO camp and released the branches from my arms. They clattered on the pile with all the rest. If Hope wouldn't tell me what was really going on with her, maybe her friends would.

Of the seven other Sisters, Hope was close to three. Diana was tall and willowy, terrific with a crossbow, and never afraid to speak her mind. Then there was Scylla, who had never uttered a single word in all the weeks I'd known her. I wondered if she was even capable of talking. She was short and compact and basically all muscle—not someone you wanted to meet in a dark alley late at night.

The third friend was Helen, who was frail and shy and seemed always on the verge of being blown away by a gust of wind. Small in stature with strawberry-blond hair, she looked at Hope with adoring eyes.

It was Helen I decided to approach.

She was sitting on a log, fletching arrows. Next to her was a pile of goose feathers.

"I can't believe you're able to attach those tiny feathers with just animal guts," I said.

She smiled shyly. "Sinew. Once it dries, it's there forever." She expertly split a quill in half, then wrapped a short thread of dried animal gut around the base of the quill and the arrow's shaft.

I sat on a nearby rock. "Helen, can I ask you something?" She flinched slightly but said nothing. "Are you okay with heading back into the territory?"

"If it's the right thing to do, then we should do it."

"And your friends? They feel the same?"

"I think so."

Her voice had a sudden wariness to it. Like Argos detecting an unfamiliar scent. I realized I was in dangerous territory here.

"Everyone's on board?" I asked. "Everything's normal?"

"Yes. . . ."

"And Hope? She's fine with all this?"

Helen's body shrank in on itself, and I suddenly realized I'd crossed the line. I was asking about the very people she was closest to. Helen nodded quickly, her fingers deftly wrapping the animal gut around the top of the fletching. She placed the finished arrow in a pile.

"You're close to Hope, aren't you?" I asked.

"She saved my life."

"Then you and I have something in common."

I pushed myself up and walked away. Although I needed to know what was going on with Hope, it felt somehow traitorous to ask about her behind her back.

But I was still convinced that she was up to something—I just didn't know what.

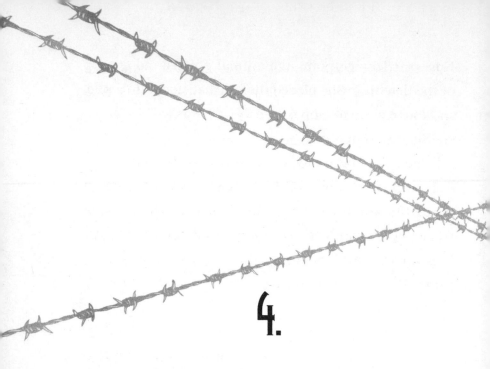

4.

THE AIR IS MOIST and heavy, and Hope's breath frosts with each exhalation.

Cat's does too, as he walks beside her.

They glide through the damp, dark woods, easing around trees, stepping over stones, hurrying away from camp—the pale light of the moon their only illumination. Hope's heart beats with a kind of feverish anticipation, and every so often Cat's arm brushes against her own. A cadence of crickets accompanies their every step.

They're not more than a mile from camp when they hear the creak of a branch. The sound is unmistakable, and they freeze. Something's out there.

Some*one* is out there.

Cat doesn't need to motion her to stay silent; she knows the drill. She was brought up in the woods. She and her dad and Faith were on the run for ten years. She knows what it is to go from hunter to prey.

As Cat reaches into his quiver and nocks an arrow, Hope readies the grip on her spear and finds the balance point. They stand there, poised to strike, their breathing shallow. There are footsteps now, scuffing through twigs and leaves. The snap of a stick.

"Don't move!" Hope shouts.

The figure stops in place.

Hope and Cat approach from different sides, weapons poised, ready to cast their spear and arrow. The lone figure stands there, hands raised.

It's Book.

"What the hell," Hope says, and Cat rolls his eyes. They each release their grip on their weapons. "You coulda gotten yourself killed."

"I didn't know it was dangerous to follow your friends," Book says.

"It is if it's the middle of the night and your friends don't know you're following them."

Book doesn't respond, and Hope realizes he's waiting for an explanation. She has no intention of giving one.

Cat's gaze shifts uncomfortably between the two. He slips the arrow back into the quiver and lowers his bow.

"See you back at camp," he mutters, disappearing

into the woods, swallowed by the black. Hope turns to Book.

"So you *are* stalking me!" she says.

"Not stalking. Following."

"Forgive me for not seeing the difference."

"The difference is you lied to me. The difference is you said you went to the woods alone."

"That was last night, and who says I wasn't alone?"

"Were you?"

Hope averts her eyes. She wants to lie again . . . but she can't. "No," she says beneath her breath.

Book takes a step back as though he's been punched. "That's why I followed you—to see what you were up to."

"And what'd you find out?"

"You tell me."

Their eyes lock. Again, it seems that Book is expecting an explanation. Again, she doesn't give one.

"Look," he says, "you can do whatever you like with whoever you want—"

"We weren't *doing* anything."

"—but don't tell me one thing and do something else. Don't—"

He stops himself midsentence, but Hope knows exactly what he was going to say. *Don't kiss me one moment and then ignore me the next.*

She wants to respond—wants to tell him

everything—but she doesn't know how, and before she knows it, the silence stretches to something long and awkward and painfully uncomfortable. When she does open her mouth to speak, she's interrupted by a sound—something mechanical. A growling engine.

Hope and Book immediately slip into hunter mode. They crouch low to the forest floor and bend their ears to the sound, determining direction, speed, object. Hope takes off first, Book right on her heels—two runners skirting the darkened landscape like ghosts.

Alder thickets slow them to a crawl, the thick brush tugging at their clothes. The sound grows louder, and suddenly it's doubled. Not just one engine, but two.

They reach the edge of the thicket and stop. A pair of headlights carves tiny holes in the dark, snaking around a bend. And from the other direction: another set of headlights. The vehicles are headed right for each other on the same small road. Even in the black night, it's possible to see the plumes of gravel that follow.

Hope realizes she hasn't seen actual cars outside camp since the day she and Faith were captured.

Faith. Which makes her think of Dad. And Mom.

She shakes her head and grips the spear. Her fingers shine white.

The two vehicles slow, then come to a grinding stop. Book and Hope share a grim look.

The headlights of each illuminate the other vehicle,

and Hope sees they're both Humvees. Pure military. Car doors open and slam, the hollow sound echoing toward them.

Feet crunch on gravel, and for the first time Hope can make out two figures walking toward each other. When they step forward and headlights wreathe their silhouettes, Hope gives an audible gasp. She recognizes those silhouettes—she'd know them anywhere. The woman with the ankle-length coat draped around her shoulders; the obese man waddling forward.

Chancellor Maddox and Dr. Gallingham.

They meet between their vehicles, too far away for Hope and Book to hear the conversation. Dr. Gallingham deposits a gleaming steel box on the ground. It's cubical in shape, and the metal glimmers in the light. He undoes a series of clasps, reaches into the bowels of the box, and removes . . . something. His body blocks Hope's view and she can't see. Whatever the object is, it makes an impression on Chancellor Maddox. Her beauty-queen smile flashes white, cutting through the dark like a sharp knife.

What could it possibly be? Hope wonders, darkness clouding her thoughts.

Whatever the answer, Gallingham returns it to the bottom of the box, fastens and reattaches all the clasps, and presents the steel box itself to the chancellor like a Wise Man presenting frankincense or myrrh.

Chancellor Maddox takes it, walks back to her vehicle, and climbs inside. Both Humvees return in the direction from which they came, the sound of gravel crunching beneath the tires growing more and more faint until, at last, the night returns to silence.

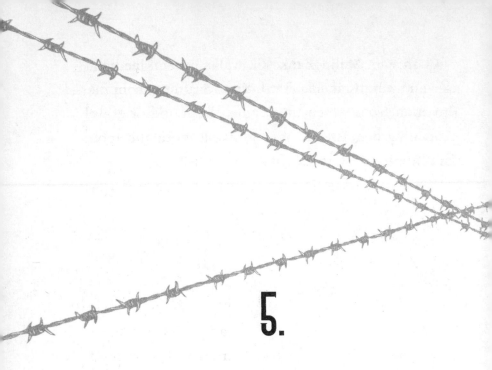

5.

WE MADE OUR WAY back without speaking. Although a part of me wanted to know where we stood . . . another part absolutely didn't. The woods slipped by without a word between us.

When we stepped into camp, we woke the others. Everyone moaned as they rubbed the sleep from their eyes, but once we told them what we'd seen, they woke up in a hurry. The Less Thans had had little contact with Chancellor Maddox, but we'd heard about her— our friend Frank in the mountains had told us she was a beauty queen turned congresswoman turned leader of the Western Federation. According to him, it was her idea to scrap the Constitution. Her idea to label us Less Thans.

As for Dr. Gallingham, once Hope mentioned his name, I swear I could see the blood draining from the Sisters' faces.

"What was it, Book?" Twitch asked. "What'd he give the chancellor?"

"We couldn't see. But you could tell from the way they handled it that it was valuable."

People threw out guesses, but Hope and I just shrugged. We could only speculate like the rest.

"What do we do now?" Flush asked.

I could feel the others' stares directed toward me. After all, it had been my bright idea to cross back from the other side of the fence. If it hadn't been for me, we'd all be safe and sound in the Heartland. It was my job to get this group to Camp Liberty and back.

"We need to leave. Tonight." A few people grumbled, but I kept going. "It's not safe being this close to a road. We've got enough food and weapons for a while, right?"

I gave a glance to those who'd been carving arrows and drying jerky, and they returned my look with unenthusiastic nods.

"All right," I said. "Let's pack up and get out of here."

People were just beginning to step away when four shadows drifted in my direction. Dozer, Red, and two of the Sisters: Angela and Lacey.

"What makes you think we can t-t-take on the

Brown Shirts?" Red asked, with his tendency to stutter. "They've got g-g-guns."

The question startled me in its bluntness. We'd been here a whole week and there'd been no discussion like this at all. I got the feeling these four had been talking.

"Red's right," Dozer said, and it was obvious he was the instigator. Dozer lived to stir up trouble. "And not just the Brown Shirts. How can we hope to fend off the Hunters with these?" He gestured to the primitive slingshots, the clumsy crossbows, the recently whittled arrows.

I understood his point. It took little effort to remember the armor plating on the Hunters' souped-up ATVs, the Kevlar vests, the M4s.

We had long ago made the decision to stick with what we knew: crossbows, spears, slingshots, bows and arrows. Not only were we proficient with those weapons, but they were quiet and light and allowed us a stealth that heavier automatic rifles wouldn't. Also, we could make our own ammunition for slingshots and bows and arrows. Not so with M4s.

"We don't need their weapons," I said. "We didn't in the Brown Forest, and we don't now."

Dozer took a bullying step toward me.

"Okay, then what I want to know is how're we gonna release those Less Thans. Even if we do make it to Liberty—which is doubtful—how're we gonna spring 'em?"

Everyone was quiet now. Even the crickets and frogs. I longed for Cat to back me up, but his eyes were fixed on the ground. I had no idea what was running through his mind.

"I don't have a strategy just yet," I said.

Dozer's eyes widened in surprise. "No strategy at all? Great plan, Book *Worm*," he scoffed. "That explains a lot."

He looked around at the others. A couple of them obliged with laughter. I felt my face burning red.

"You agreed to go back to Liberty," I said. "You didn't have to."

"That's when I thought you had a plan. Now I know otherwise."

"All I know is we have to do this." Despite my efforts, I could feel my chest tightening.

"Oh we do, do we? And why is that?"

"Because it's the right thing."

Dozer laughed. A loud, mocking laugh. "And killing us in the process? Is that the 'right thing'?"

My fists clenched, and Dozer leaned forward until our noses were actually touching.

"Well?" he asked. I nearly gagged from his sour breath.

I turned to move away, but his meaty hand grabbed my shoulder and whipped me back around. *"Well?"* he asked again.

Although I wanted nothing more than to take a swipe at him, I knew I wouldn't stand a chance. Dozer was a big, barrel-chested guy with a thick neck, and even though one of his arms was slightly withered from radiation, he more than compensated with his other. If I attacked him, it'd only prove his point that I was reckless and not a real leader.

So I did nothing, said nothing, just turned and walked away. Behind me, I heard Dozer making clucking sounds.

There wasn't anything I could do about Dozer. I'd just have to live with the situation—and him.

We marched through the night and into the morning, as the sun chased away the stars and made invisible the moon. There was little conversation, and Hope and I kept more distance between us than ever. She didn't want to talk to me, and I had no desire to talk to her.

But it hurt to lose her. Cat, too. Ever since I'd snuck up on them, he'd avoided looking at me. I felt betrayed, as though someone had taken a shot to my gut and I hadn't seen it coming.

I tried to focus on other things. Like what on earth had we witnessed between Dr. Gallingham and Chancellor Maddox? What was so precious that it had to be exchanged in a secret meeting in the middle of the night? We were utterly exhausted by the time we set up camp the next evening, but I was craving conversation. No, not just conversation: *companionship*. I needed a friend.

I found Twitch sitting cross-legged on the ground, his tall, gangly form folded in on itself. If there was ever a person who reminded me of a stork, it was Twitch.

He didn't seem to notice when I sat down next to him. His fingers gripped a stick as though it was a pencil, sketching a series of loops and lines and mathematical equations in the dirt.

"Oh, hey," he said, when he finally saw me, his cheek rising and falling in a facial tic. Even though Omega happened a good four years before we were born, the radiation from the bombs had done a number on his central nervous system. Of course, at this point, his twitches were just a part of him. Like my limp. Or Four Fingers's missing finger.

"What do you think about our decision to return?" I asked. After last night's confrontation with Dozer, I couldn't help but feel that it was me versus everyone else. All the excitement we'd first experienced after crossing back from the fence seemed a thing of some distant past.

Twitch took a bite of squirrel jerky and chewed a moment. He was the kind of guy who liked to consider an issue fully before voicing an opinion—unlike his counterpart, Flush, who blurted out whatever popped into his head at any given moment.

"On the one hand, Dozer's right," he said. "It's the most foolish decision we've made." His facial features jerked as he chewed.

"But?" I prompted.

He finished chewing and swallowed. "We need to rescue those Less Thans. And that trumps logic."

Without meaning to, I sighed in relief. All day, I'd had the feeling I was waging an uphill battle against the others.

"Not that that means we'll succeed," he added, and my happiness evaporated.

"You don't think we'll make it?"

"Are you kidding? We don't stand a chance."

I looked at him in disbelief. "But you're willing to go along anyway?"

He shrugged. "No one else is going to rescue those Less Thans—might as well be us. And who wants to miss out on that?"

I loved Twitch for that—that he knew the odds were stacked against us but was willing to go along anyway.

I pointed to the drawings in the dirt. "What's all this?"

His eyes lit up. "Ever heard of a zip line?" When I gave my head a shake, he used the stick to walk me through the drawings, telling me how—in pre-Omega days—people used to stretch out long wires and ride them down mountains. *For fun.*

"Where'd you hear this?"

"Read about it in some old science magazines."

Figured. "So what're you saying?" I asked.

"The enemy's always coming at us from the ground, right? So I say we build our own zip line and attack them from the air."

The point of his stick landed on a series of lines and semicircles, and he told me all about inertia and acceleration and other things I only partly understood. As he spoke, his facial tics decreased. It was as though the more passionate he became, the less his face twitched.

It seemed impossible, of course, finding the materials to build such a line, but I loved his enthusiasm. He would do his best to make this work, even though we had "no chance" of succeeding.

Now if I could only convince the rest of them.

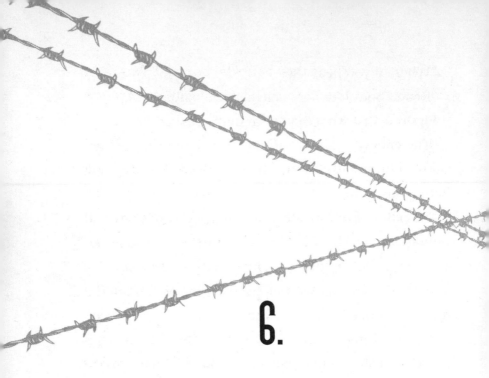

6.

THEY SHIVER THEIR WAY westward, sloshing through ankle-deep mud under leaden skies.

Hope's mind is a million places at once, darting back and forth between Book and Cat and what they witnessed on the darkened road . . . and her own past.

Just seeing Dr. Gallingham brought it all back, and it's as if the injections are happening all over again. Her body goes clammy, perspiration dots her forehead.

I'm not sick, she has to tell herself. *I am* not *sick.*

It feels like just yesterday that she and Faith were submerged in vats of ice, their body temperatures lowered some twenty degrees. It was a long forever before Hope recovered. Faith never did. Hope can still see her face, blue and lifeless, her unseeing eyes cutting into Hope's soul.

The tears press against her eyes, but she's damned if she's going to give in to them. *Live today, tears tomorrow,* her father always said.

Her father.

Dr. Gallingham claimed they'd worked together, that her father had somehow been involved in those experiments. Known as the Butcher of the West. Ludicrous to even think about.

And yet the notion lingers. Something Hope needs to find out for herself. It's one of the reasons she crawled under the fence and joined the others. A search for truth.

She is woken from her reverie when a herd of deer goes bounding past. Everyone looks up and watches them go, their white tails raised as they gallop away. It's a beautiful sight.

Then a flock of birds flies past, the flap of their wings making ripples in the air. Hope begins to wonder. When a dozen chattering squirrels leap through the trees above, the wonder turns to alarm.

"Cool," Flush says, admiring the nature parade.

But Hope knows animals don't just run in herds— *at full speed, in the same direction*—for the fun of it. Something's going on.

An instant later they hear a booming crash that shakes the ground beneath their feet. They stand there listening, afraid to speak. There's another crash. The earth trembles.

"What is it?" Flush asks. His voice is barely a whisper.

"Whatever it is," Twitch answers, "it's coming from over there." He points to the north.

The noises come regularly now: thunderous, splintering booms that rattle the ground. Hope clutches her spear and races forward, the others right behind her. They dart through the woods, ducking beneath branches, skipping over a carpet of dead leaves.

They come to a sudden stop when they spy the crown of a tree swaying forward and backward as though pushed by a violent wind. And then it comes crashing to the earth. *Whoompf!* They feel the vibration from where they stand. The throaty rumble radiates up their feet.

A moment later, another tree does the same, wobbling in one direction, then the other, before arcing through the air and slamming to the ground. *Thwump!*

What's going on? Hope wonders, her body rigid with fear. *How can a forest be collapsing on itself? What could be ripping trees from the earth?*

All at once, they hear another sound: engines. But different than the Humvees from the other night: louder, gravelly, hulking. And now the biting smell of diesel.

Cat motions them forward, and at the top of a ridge they look down and see a sight they can't quite believe: enormous bulldozers knocking down trees, clearing out a swath of forest, creating an ugly, barren scar in the middle of the wilderness.

On the sides of the vehicles is a symbol they know too well: three inverted triangles. The insignia of the Republic of the True America. And the drivers of the bulldozers are none other than Brown Shirts, clad in their customary black jackboots, dark pants, and brown shirts.

The Sisters and Less Thans watch, mesmerized. A building project—*in the middle of nowhere!* It makes no sense. As trees tumble to the ground and great shovelfuls of dirt are ripped from the earth, the Less Thans and Sisters can't begin to understand it.

What are they building? And why here?

When they finally tear themselves away, Hope feels her heart hammering against her chest. She knew they'd run into soldiers—she just didn't think it would be so soon. But it's more than that. It's the mystery of not knowing what they're up to that disturbs her most.

"Come on," Cat says. "Let's get the hell out of here."

They march the rest of that afternoon and evening, sleep little, and march all the next day, trying to put as much distance as possible between them and the Brown Shirts. When they stop the following night, the few words they speak are colored by exhaustion and anxiety.

"Are we safe here?" Helen asks.

"Should be," Hope answers. "That wasn't a search

party. It was a construction project."

"For what?"

She shrugs.

"Whatever it is," Twitch says, "they want it hidden."

"Great job leading us to safety," Dozer says to Book, magnifying an eye roll. A few others laugh in support.

They drift away and prepare for sleep, and Hope and Cat exchange a glance. *Not tonight*, her expression says.

As Hope lies down on a bed of weeds and pine needles, she remembers her conversation with Book—about what they intend to do after freeing the Less Thans. What she didn't tell him was that, yes, she does have something in mind. In fact, it's the other reason she didn't stay in the Heartland. She has unfinished business—that she knows for certain.

Colonel Thorason. Chancellor Maddox. Dr. Gallingham.

The camp overseer. The ruler of the territory. The sadistic doctor.

She doesn't care what order; she doesn't care how it happens. But she will see to it that they pay for what they did to her sister.

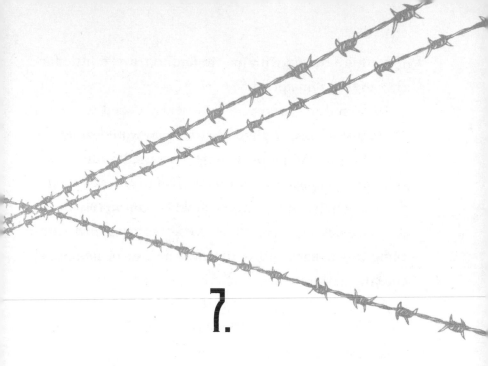

7.

THE NIGHTMARE WAS THE same: the hollow, vacant stares of Less Thans imprisoned in the bunker. They gazed at me with oozing sores and pleading eyes and begged me to do something. To free them. To get them out of there.

They reached for me with their bony fingers and I jerked awake. But it wasn't the dream that woke me, it was sound. I'd heard something.

I lifted my head and looked around. Everyone was fast asleep . . . except a lone figure tiptoeing through the woods. I couldn't tell who it was—just a fuzzy silhouette in passing moonlight—but I figured it was probably someone going off to take a leak. Guys did it all the time in the middle of the night, and now that

there were Sisters with us, we had to travel a little farther to find some privacy.

I lowered my head and had nearly dozed off again
when it suddenly occurred to me: who would be *tiptoeing*? Who was that considerate? Normally, when guys
had to whiz, they just tromped off into the woods, did
their business, and tromped back. No one *tiptoed*.

I sat back up. Argos was awake, a low growl rumbling in the back of his throat. The two of us peered
into the dark.

A moment later I saw fireflies, tiny white dots etching circles in the black. They hovered and swooped and
I was mesmerized by their movements.

But as they grew closer I realized they weren't fireflies at all—and my heart nearly exploded from my
chest. At the very top of my lungs I yelled the first and
only word that came to mind.

"Ambush!"

We scrambled to our feet, simultaneously grabbing
weapons and shouting questions.

"What's going on?"

"What do you see?"

"Who is it?"

It was like we'd never been in a battle before. Cat
was the smoothest of all, of course, nocking an arrow
before the rest of us were even standing.

In no time, bullets were whistling past our ears, the headlamps poking through the woods. Headed straight in our direction.

A flare rocketed skyward, bathing the night in eerie luminescence, and I got my first glimpse of the attackers. There had to have been at least fifty of them. Two bullets bit the earth at my feet. I did a little dance and stumbled to the ground.

I was just pulling myself up when I heard a sharp whistling sound, growing steadily louder. A moment later there was a huge explosion. Dirt and rocks and shrapnel sailed through air, throwing everyone off their feet. Whoever was standing next to me went flying, as if some giant hand had swatted him aside.

More mortars followed, but even scarier than that was the sight of Brown Shirts, surging toward us like a tidal wave. The flare's green light made their silhouettes flicker like monsters'.

"Douse the fire!" I yelled. As long as there were even smoldering coals, the soldiers would have no trouble picking us off. Someone threw the contents of their canteen on the embers, and white smoke billowed up.

I scrambled to find the person who'd been hit. His moans led me to him, and even by weak moonlight it was clear who I was looking at.

Cat.

His left arm was like spaghetti, an explosion of red

sinews and dangling muscles. He'd already lost a ton of blood and was barely conscious. At the sight of it—his limp arm and ashen face—I grew suddenly clammy. The horizon tilted. It was all I could do to keep from passing out.

I felt a pull and realized Flush was tugging at my shirt. "What do we do?!" he shouted.

I squeezed my eyes shut and tried to calm myself. Steady breaths. Steady. And suddenly it wasn't Cat I saw, but the woman from my dreams—the one with the long black hair. She was kneeling on prairie grass, hands atop my shoulders, her eyes locked with mine.

"Book!" Flush screamed, and my eyes popped open. *"What do we do?"*

Flares exploded in the sky and mortars exploded on the ground. These Brown Shirts meant to kill us then and there.

Meanwhile, the Less Thans stood in a half circle staring down at Cat, their expressions vacant and disbelieving. The sight of him gasping for breath stopped us in our tracks. It was as if we'd lost the power to act. Lost even the ability to think straight.

Without knowing what I was saying or why I was saying it, I began barking out commands. "Twitch and Dozer, lay cover with your arrows. Hope, spread out your best shooters and hammer the Brown Shirts from the sides. Red and Flush, pound them with rocks. The rest of you, get back up that ridge ASAP."

Everyone went into motion.

"Who's got Cat?" Twitch asked, nocking his first arrow.

"Me," I said, and before anyone could object, I grabbed Cat's good arm, hoisted him over my shoulder, and began carrying him up the hill.

It made no sense, of course. I was the weakest of the bunch with a permanent limp, but at that particular moment I could've lifted *all* the LTs. After all, it was Cat—my friend Cat. Sure, I didn't know what he was doing with Hope behind my back, but I knew it was up to me to save his life.

It was a mad scramble up the steep slope, every-one making for the woods at the crest. Bullets zinged around us, digging up the earth and embedding them-selves into trees. Adding to the chaos were the flares washing the night in shades of eerie green, turning the world into a lurid nightmare—as vivid and terrifying as hell itself.

"Twitch, get out of there!" I yelled.

He nodded but didn't stop firing, pulling one arrow from his quiver after another. It was like he was a man possessed, and I saw at least three Brown Shirts lying on the ground, arrows protruding from their bellies like flags. Twitch had done his job, and then some. Frank would've been proud.

"Twitch!" I yelled again.

But too late. A mortar screamed from the heavens, landing not far from where he knelt. The explosion catapulted him into the air. Red and Flush raced to his side and grabbed ahold of his hands. They began dragging him up the hill.

The only thing that saved us was the dark. Each time the flares faded, the soldiers were shooting at shadows.

"Drop me," Cat moaned.

"Like hell," I said.

By the time we made it into the trees, I was breathing so hard I thought my lungs might explode. I lowered Cat to the ground and examined his wound. It was bad. His left forearm was a shredded mess of tissue and muscle, skin hanging like a loose flap. I ripped off my belt and tied a tourniquet above his elbow. Then I tore off his shirt and pressed it on the wound, trying to stanch the flow of blood. I hated that I was getting good at this.

I noticed everyone had made it to the trees, including the two guys with Twitch. They hovered over him frantically.

"They're a hundred yards away!" Dozer cried.

A flare hissed and sizzled, illuminating Brown Shirts tromping on our campsite.

I looked down at Cat's face; it was growing paler by the minute. He was mumbling incoherently.

Red appeared by my side. "T-T-Twitch can't see," he said.

I looked over and saw Flush crouched by Twitch's side. He was wrapping a strip of fabric around his good friend's face. Four Fingers hugged himself and rocked back and forth, keening wildly, a string of drool rubber-banding from his mouth.

"Twitch!" he cried to the stars. "Twiiiiiiiitch!"

Everything was happening too fast—it was all out of control. Bullets whistling, mortars screaming, flares hissing. And now the Brown Shirts were making their way up the hill, their shadows dancing like ghosts in the green light of the flares.

"Spread out!" I yelled, but even as I said it, I knew it was useless. Though the Sisters were bringing down their share of Brown Shirts with crossbows, we didn't stand a chance. Not with so few of us. Not without Cat. Not against fifty.

My hands were a sticky mess. The balled-up shirt was a sopping, bloody sponge. Cat's face was ashen.

"Come on," I begged him. "Stay with me!" Both a prayer and a command.

I jammed the soggy shirt into the wound. But even if I managed to stop the flow, what then? Without any medical supplies, the situation was hopeless.

I cursed the woman with the long black hair. She'd led us here. If I hadn't listened to those damn dreams, we'd all be safe and sound in the other territory. But it was too late. We were about to be captured . . . or shot dead on the spot.

"They're getting closer!" Dozer shouted.

The soldiers kept advancing. There was nothing stopping them. A hail of bullets snapped small saplings in two.

Hope whistled sharply and the Sisters regrouped, dropping to one knee. With an icy calmness, they readied their crossbows and released their bolts. A half dozen Brown Shirts crumpled to the ground.

But still the soldiers came, marching up the hill, now joined by other soldiers who'd been trailing them all along. It was no longer fifty Brown Shirts, more like a hundred. Maybe more.

I looked down at Cat. His chest was unnaturally still, his face clammy.

"What do we do?" Flush cried out in a panic. Even the Sisters, so calm at first, showed signs of alarm. Their eyes were wide with terror as they reloaded their crossbows.

The Brown Shirts strode effortlessly up the hill, their M16s strobing the black, peppering tree trunks until it rained pine bark. The smell of gunpowder mixed with vanilla pine—a bittersweet concoction.

"Well?" Dozer asked. He nocked an arrow and sent it squirting into the black. "Any bright ideas, genius?"

For the longest time, I didn't answer. When I did, it

was almost as if I couldn't believe what I was telling them.

"Retreat," I said, my voice barely audible.

"Who's gonna get Cat?"

"No one. We're gonna leave him behind."

Cat.

The sandy-haired boy we'd rescued one day at the edge of the No Water. The one who showed us the Hunters and told us what LT *really* stood for: Less Than. From the moment we found him, our destiny was changed. On more than one occasion he had saved our lives.

And now here he was, pale and delirious, blood seeping from his arm.

"What're you talking about?" Flush yelled, near tears. "We can't leave him."

I understood his desperation. This was *Cat*. The thought of losing him was beyond comprehension. Still, if we stayed, we'd all be killed. And if we tried to take him with us, he'd die for sure. This was the only choice.

"Go!" I yelled.

Most of the Sisters obeyed immediately. They fired their crossbows even as they took giant strides backward. The Less Thans weren't as easily convinced.

"It ain't right," Dozer said. He sent an arrow into the black, then turned and ran.

Hope was the last of the girls to leave. I saw her stare at Cat for what seemed like forever. What was in that look I couldn't tell. Then she gave me a glance, as if questioning my decision.

"I'll catch up," I said.

Her enormous brown eyes danced back and forth between Cat and me . . . and then she went.

Flush and Red just stood there, not moving. *Unable* to move.

"What're you waiting for?" I screamed at them. "You'll die if you stay here."

"We can't leave Cat," Flush said. His eyes were red.

"I don't want to either, but we don't have a choice. Now get out of here!"

Reluctantly, they grabbed hold of Twitch and ran, guiding him through the woods.

I reached down and squeezed Cat's hand. Was it my imagination or was he trying to squeeze back? His eyes were closed, his face an unnatural shade of gray. It seemed not even remotely possible to see him this way. This was Cat—who survived a walk through the No Water, the most barren, inhospitable landscape imaginable, and lived to talk about it. Who led us up Skeleton Ridge and across the Flats and through the Brown Forest and took out the propane tank with a single bullet.

"This is just for now," I said, choking back tears. "You haven't seen the last of us."

I waited as long as I dared, hoping—*praying*—he might respond. He didn't.

I gave his hand a final squeeze, jumped to my feet, and dashed off into the woods, bullets chasing me like angry hornets. As I ran, tears spewed from my eyes and raced down my cheeks.

What have I done? I asked myself. *What on earth have I done?*

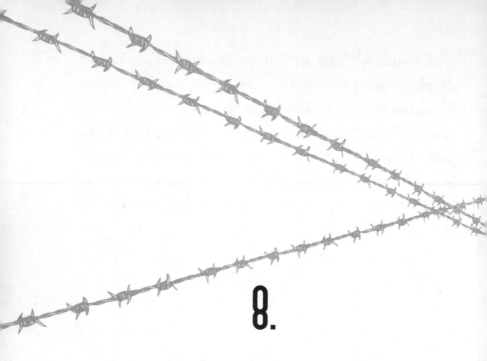

8.

HOPE LEADS THE WAY, cutting through the deepest part of the forest. Far behind her she can see the soldiers' headlamps bouncing through the woods, splashing tree trunks with miniature white spotlights.

They run through the night. As the sky brightens from black to gray, Hope thinks of Book, trying to reconcile these very different pictures she has of him. The one who kissed her so passionately. The one who stalks her at night. The one who's leaving Cat behind. They're like pieces of a puzzle that don't quite fit.

And what's the real reason he abandoned his friend? Could it have anything to do with jealousy?

They speed down a hill and come to a skidding stop. Below them is a raging river—all these days of rain have swollen it past its banks. Dead trees are swept downstream in a muddy froth of spewing rapids. There is no way to get across.

At that same moment, the soldiers crest the hill behind them, half a mile back. They kneel and fire. Bullets whisper overhead. Some pockmark the earth like hailstones. The Sisters and Less Thans crouch on the riverbank.

"Well?" Dozer demands. "What now?"

Hope looks into the river. It's pure white water, pounding the rocks and cutting away at the banks. She pities anyone who falls into it.

As they're about to do.

"As soon as you hit the water, pull your knees up to your chin," she instructs. "Don't try to swim—just float. Face forward and use your feet as springs."

Eyebrows arch in surprise.

"Wait a minute," Flush says. "We're not going to jump in there, are we?"

She doesn't bother to reply. Sometimes it's better just to demonstrate a thing than explain it.

She leaps to the very middle of the stream and the current sucks her under, tumbling her head over heels until she is completely upside down, disoriented. Her arms take her to the bottom of the river, where her fingers scrape a thick layer of silt and mud. The murky current throws her against a boulder, and what little air she has in her lungs is pushed out. Stars blink.

It's the flooded tunnel all over again.

Sunlight sparkles on the water and Hope reaches for it, following a trail of silver bubbles and straining for the sky itself. She breaks the surface and gasps for air. She's gotten only a small breath before the river pulls her back under, dumping huge mouthfuls of water down her throat. She rises back up, hacking and sputtering and retching until her lungs are on fire.

But she's on the surface.

She brings her knees to her chest, and her feet bounce off one boulder after another like a marble in a maze. The Sisters and Less Thans are still on the riverbank, paralyzed with fear. A bullet catches a Sister in the back, and she crumples to the earth.

Book and Argos jump into the raging river, then all the others. In no time, thirteen bobbing heads poke above the surface.

The water is icy cold, and Hope's feet and fingers grow numb. She flails her arms to get some circulation going. When the river widens and slows, she paddles, both to warm herself and to put even more distance between her and the Brown Shirts. Then the river narrows, sluicing through tight gorges in a rush of whitewater. It's just Hope and the water and the towering canyons.

She bobs along like a cork for hours, the river taking

her farther and farther south. Finally, it widens for good. Green grasslands lie on either side, and a sandbar juts in front of her. Her feet find the pebbly riverbed and she stands up. Her legs are stiff from cold, and it's all she can do to lurch toward shore.

The first to join her is Book. They barely look each other in the eye.

"Are you okay?" he asks.

She nods. "Just cold. You?"

"Same."

An awkward silence follows. "Look, about what happened," he starts to say, but soon the others appear.

They drag themselves out of the river on frozen limbs, trembling from cold, their lips icy blue. Argos gives his fur a shake. The Sisters' dresses cling to their bodies like a second layer of skin.

"Why'd you do it?" Dozer demands, emerging from the water like some Creature from the Black Lagoon. "Why'd you kill our friend?"

"He was my friend, too," Book replies.

"So why'd you kill him?"

"I was trying to save him. He would've died otherwise."

Dozer weighs a good fifty pounds more than Book, and when he grabs Book's shirt with his two meaty fists, there's no way Book can squirm free. "Cat could've lived. All we had to do was bring him with us."

"I'm telling you, he wouldn't've made it if we'd carried him."

"And I'm telling *you*, you don't know what you're talking about. Now he's gonna die for sure."

Book opens his mouth to speak, then thinks better of it.

"So now what, Limp?"

"Same as before," Book says. "Return to Camp Liberty and free those Less Thans."

"You really think we can get past Hunters and Brown Shirts with *slingshots and arrows*? After what just happened?"

"We don't have a choice."

Dozer spits and shakes his head from side to side.

It occurs to Hope they should be relieved. They survived an ambush from the Brown Shirts. But a single glance makes it clear they're stuck in the middle of a barren wilderness—far to the south from where they want to be. And they don't have Cat.

"Let's get a fire going and dry off," Hope says. "We can talk about this later."

Dozer's gaze flicks between Hope and Book, as though he can't decide if they're crazy or just plain idiots. Then he turns and calls out to the others, "Let's get a fire going and dry off!" Like it was his idea all along. He begins digging a pit in the sand.

"Not on shore," Hope points out. "Somewhere hidden

behind a hill, so the Brown Shirts can't spot us."

Dozer stares her up and down. "Whatever you say, *Last Hope*."

As he walks away, he mutters to Red, "First this crazy Camp Liberty plan, then abandoning Cat, then jumpin' in that river. I'm tellin' ya, these two are dangerous."

The more Hope surveys her surroundings, the more she realizes how dire their situation is. There's not a single tree in sight. It's bald savannah for as far as they can see. Thin grass bending under a blazing sun. No trees. No shade. Just undulating grasslands beneath sky, sky, and more sky.

As Flush puts it, "This place is as bare as my butt."

Because of the endless acres of dry grass, tinder is no problem, and they're able to get a flame going fairly easily, propped up with driftwood. Hope is surprised to see a separate fire fifty yards away: Dozer and three others. Perhaps it makes sense. Twelve is too many to crowd around a single flame.

That's their new number now: twelve. In addition to losing Cat, two Sisters died as well. Rosa was shot down by Brown Shirts, and Taran drowned. So even though six Less Thans and six Sisters have made it, there is a somber atmosphere throughout camp. Survivor's guilt. Hope knows it well.

They huddle around the meager fire, drying out wet

and ragged clothes. No one speaks, their eyes lost in the waving flames. Hope feels responsible for the two Sisters' deaths. She didn't protect them.

It's not the first time she's felt this way.

She moves away from the fire, offering as an excuse that she's going to find more wood. The river beckons her, and she walks its barren shore deep in thought. It bends and winds like a slithering snake, sand squishing between her toes.

She is grateful for the solitude, and surprised when she spies someone else looking for wood.

Book.

At first they work in silence. Just the river lapping against the bank, the breeze tugging at Hope's hair. She tucks what little there is behind an ear. When she looks up, Book is studying her.

"What?" she asks.

"Sorry about your friends," he says. "I know you lost two back there and—"

"I'm fine." Hope regrets that her tone is so brusque, but she can't help herself. The fact is: she *isn't* fine— not by a long shot. She misses Faith. And her dad. And mom. And now Book abandoned Cat and she's leading her Sisters to some camp way on the other side of the Western Federation Territory. No, she's not remotely fine.

If he's offended, he doesn't show it. "That was a good

call," he says, "jumping in the river."

"You think so? We lost two girls back there."

"We would've *all* been lost if we hadn't done it. If you hadn't jumped in first."

Something softens her. Maybe it's his kindness. Maybe it's the quiet of the dusk. The river gurgles and coos, and a fish breaks the surface and plops back down into the murky depths. An indigo haze settles on the riverbanks. The sense of peace is like an actual warmth spreading through her chest.

She sits back on her haunches and for a brief instant, their eyes catch . . . and then they return to scrounging for wood. Their palms and knees are damp from sand.

"Can I ask you something?" she says.

"Sure."

"Why'd you do it?"

"What?"

"Leave Cat behind." It's something she can't stop thinking about.

Book looks up. The expression on his face is stiff, and his jaw has tightened.

"Because it was the only thing to do," he says.

Hope hears the tension in his voice, but she can't help asking more. "What makes you think they won't kill him? Or let him die?"

"The Brown Shirts won't let that happen."

"Why not? You really think they're gonna stop

55

everything and take care of a wounded Less Than?" She doesn't mean it to come out as sarcastic as it does.

"Yes, that's exactly what they're going to do," Book says through gritted teeth. "Before Cat was a Less Than, he was a Young Officer. He was in training to be one of the Republic's leaders. He knows things. He knows things about *us*. He's more valuable to them alive than dead. So yes, the Brown Shirts'll do their best to revive him. I don't doubt that for a second."

It does make a certain kind of sense, but Hope's not sure if she agrees. Before she can even respond, Book grabs an armful of wood and marches off. Hope watches him go, cursing herself for pushing him away.

Why did I have to do that? Why didn't I just keep my big mouth shut?

She leans forward and buries her face in her hands.

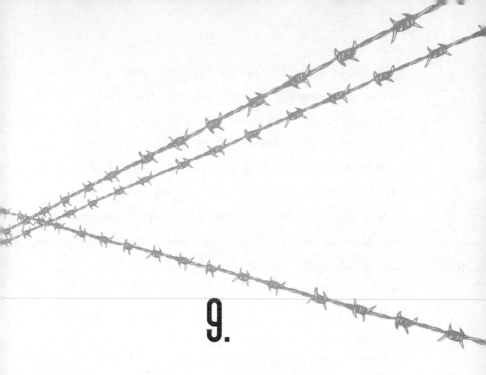

9.

I HAD NO APPETITE. Even though the Sisters carved lances from driftwood and caught a dozen brown trout feeding in the shallows, I couldn't eat. How could I put food in my stomach as long as Cat was gone? And just when I thought I was okay with my decision to leave him behind, Hope had to bring it back up.

Thanks a lot.

I sat by the fire's edge, my eyes trained on the swirling smoke. Maybe it was silly of me to be so paranoid, but I couldn't help it. It was impossible not to notice how the others regarded me. My decision to "abandon" Cat brought scorn from my fellow Less Thans, raised eyebrows from the Sisters, suspicion from *everyone*. I could just imagine what they were thinking: *Book was jealous of Cat, so he decided to leave him behind.*

And it was true: I was jealous of Cat. I saw how he and Hope looked at each other. I'd even caught them red-handed, sneaking off in the woods together.

Which hurt even more because Cat was my friend. We'd confided in each other. Told each other things we hadn't shared with anyone. My suicide attempt. The fact that Major Karsten—the most ruthless officer at Camp Liberty—was his dad. Secrets.

There was no way I'd leave him back there out of jealousy.

Was there?

Whatever my reasoning, the stark reality was that things would never be the same. We could maybe return to Camp Liberty and free those Less Thans—*maybe*—but we'd miss Cat's skills, his insights, his smarts. Him.

I remembered what he'd been telling me at the campfire that night, that not everyone was committed. What more was he trying to let me know?

I'd seen someone tiptoeing away from camp the night of the ambush. Was that same someone secretly helping out the Brown Shirts?

A million stars exploded in the sky as I marched to the other campfire, the one surrounded by Dozer, Red, Angela, and Lacey. Once the four of them caught sight of me, they cut off their conversation and eyed me in silence.

I held out some leftover trout to them.

"We don't need your pity," Dozer said, turning his back to me.

"I'm just offering some food, that's all."

"Yeah, well, we don't need it."

He threw a log into the fire. A flurry of embers exploded into the black.

I looked at the other three. One by one they met my gaze . . . and then found reasons to look away. Lacey studied her feet. Angela ran her fingers through her stringy blond hair. Red picked at the dirt beneath his fingernails with the tip of his knife.

This was going to be more difficult than I'd imagined.

Dozer's head swiveled back around. "You still here?" he asked.

"I just thought maybe we should talk."

"Now? After you made the decision to leave Cat back there, *now* you wanna talk?"

"About those Brown Shirts," I said. "How do you think they were able to ambush us?"

That got everyone's attention.

"How should I know, Limp?" Dozer said, and even in the dark I could see his eyes were blazing. "They found us and opened fire. End of story."

"But how'd they find us?"

"What do you mean *how*? We saw them earlier, we saw their bulldozers. They probably just followed us."

"Those were construction workers. It was soldiers who ambushed us."

Dozer's hand fell to his knife, and I could see the white of his knuckles as he squeezed the handle. "What're you saying, Limp? That one of us squealed?"

I took a deep breath; I didn't want to make a bad situation worse. "I'm saying it seems awfully coincidental they just happened to show up when they did. Like maybe they got help or something."

Dozer hauled himself to his feet and took a step forward. Angela and Lacey also rose, bookending him on either side.

"If you're accusing someone of something, why don't you just come out and say it instead of pussyfooting around? Unless that's what you are. Pussyfoot."

The two Sisters laughed maliciously.

"No, I'm just saying—"

"And I'm *just saying*: why don't you speak your mind? *Pussyfoot.*"

"Skip it," I said, my legs suddenly rubber. If I'd thought I could get Dozer to admit to being a traitor, I was sadly mistaken. I turned and walked away, half expecting to feel the point of his dagger somewhere between my shoulder blades.

"Hey!" Dozer yelled after me. "Next time you start accusing people, make sure you have some evidence to back you up."

Even as I strode farther and farther away, their spiteful laughter rang out in the night air.

A sharp kick to the ribs jolted me awake. I opened my eyes to find Dozer holding a torch. He was flanked by his posse of three.

"Some of us have been talking," he said. The pain in my ribs was nothing compared to the sudden knot in my stomach.

"Yeah?" I asked, rolling to a sitting position, hands pressed to my side.

"We wouldn't be in this situation if you hadn't convinced us to cross back from the other territory."

"I didn't *convince* you. I made the decision to come back; the rest of you followed."

A hiss of contempt escaped his mouth. He shook his head and spat into the coals. A glob of frothy white phlegm dribbled down a log. A number of Sisters sat up, wanting to know what was going on.

"And it goes without saying that we don't like what you did to Cat back there. So my tribe here doesn't exactly trust you, and I can't say I blame them."

I wondered how much of his "tribe" had come up with that opinion and how much they had been convinced by Dozer himself. The three torch-carrying tribe members had all the makings of a vigilante mob. All that was missing were the pitchforks.

"So what're you saying?" I asked.

"Someone sold us out to the Brown Shirts. I'm not accusing you necessarily, but someone let 'em know where we were."

I couldn't believe what I was hearing. Dozer was saying exactly what I'd told him hours earlier. It reminded me of a line from a lawyer movie we'd seen back at camp—*Inherit the Wind*. Accuse the accuser. A classic legal ploy.

"So what do you want, Dozer?"

Dozer's response was immediate. "The tribe thinks I should be the new leader."

I don't know why his statement surprised me. Maybe because it made no real sense. Why would we want a leader who made it a point to bad-mouth everyone and everything? Who had made a nuisance of himself whenever given the chance?

"Fine," I said. Truth was, I had no great desire to be the leader, and it was irrelevant to me who got us to Camp Liberty to free those Less Thans—just as long as we did it.

Dozer tried to hide his surprise. It was obvious he expected a fight. "It's not my decision," he said, trying to sound humble. "It's the others."

"I understand."

"They trust me."

"Okay."

"They know I'll be a good leader."

The only response I could have made would have been sarcastic, so I kept my mouth shut. When it was clear I wasn't going to say anything else, Dozer raised his torch high in the air like he was summoning the gods above.

"Listen up," he shouted, so that all could hear. "I'm leading this group from now on. I'm in charge. But I won't be telling you what to do. My hope is that we can make decisions as a group."

He shot me a meaningful look, as if to say Cat would still be here if we'd followed that policy before. Although I didn't expect anyone to challenge Dozer and his lackeys, I hoped someone would speak up on my behalf. But no one said a word. Not a single person. Not Flush. Not Twitch.

Not Hope.

I lay back down to sleep, knowing no nightmare could be worse than this reality. Dozer began to walk away.

"Just remember," I muttered beneath my breath. "'Uneasy lies the head that wears a crown.'"

Dozer stopped in his tracks. "What's that?" he snapped.

Me and my Shakespeare. I regretted speaking as soon as the words left my mouth. "Nothing."

He lowered the torch until the heat licked my cheeks.

"No, what'd you just say?"

"Nothing."

There was an almost gleeful expression on Dozer's face as he looked to his friends. "He said something. You heard him: he said something." Angela and Lacey nodded like a couple of puppets.

Dozer returned his stare to me. "What'd you say?"

"Nothing," I repeated, angry that I'd fallen into Dozer's trap.

"We can't have that, Book. The worst thing we can have is insurrection."

"*Insurrection?* You've been talking trash for weeks. You've been openly mocking my decisions ever since we left Camp Liberty. You freaked out in the Brown Forest and nearly killed Four Fingers. And you're accusing *me* of insurrection?"

"That's it!" he barked. "I have no choice but to place you under house arrest."

I thought for a second he was joking. "What're you talking about?"

Dozer turned to Red. "Take his knife away."

Before I knew it, Red walked to my side and ripped my knife from its sheath—all because I'd quoted a line from *Henry IV*.

I appealed silently to the others. Red. Flush. *Hope.* All averted their eyes, not wishing to meet my stare. Only Argos bristled, emitting a low growl in the back of his throat. Angela and Lacey reached for their daggers.

"No, boy," I said. I knew if he went after Dozer, they'd knife him in a second and fry him up for breakfast. Argos sat, the growl still vibrating his neck.

Dozer smiled that hyena grin of his and then turned to the others. "If anyone dares arm this Less Than, we'll have no choice but to consider it an act of treason, and they'll face similar consequences." He sounded like some medieval king meting out punishment to a peasant. "Now everyone back to sleep. We're moving out tomorrow."

"Which way are we going?" I asked, careful not to add *O powerful leader* at the end of the sentence.

"Due south," he answered.

"South?" I wasn't sure I'd heard correctly. "We're already way too south as it is, and Camp Liberty is to the northwest."

"And we're heading *south*."

"Then how can we save the Less Thans?"

"We're not saving any Less Thans. We're saving ourselves."

Dozer was daring me—or anyone—to contradict him. No one did.

As he and his minions disappeared into the black, I was consumed by a gnawing anger. Not just that we were abandoning the Less Thans, but that not one person had uttered a peep in my defense. Fine—if they wanted Dozer to be their leader, they could have him.

I'd get to Camp Liberty on my own. I was damned if I was going to let some power-hungry, lie-spewing, sour-breathed, barrel-chested bully stop me. Even if no one else believed in me, I still did.

One way or the other, I was going to make this happen.

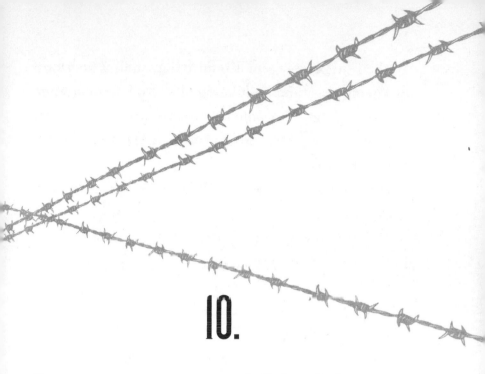

10.

THE SUN CLEARS THE eastern hills long before Dozer
even stirs. Hope waits impatiently. When they eventually break camp and begin marching south, the sun
beats down from its noontime position. They've already
missed the coolest portion of the day.

But Dozer is in charge. And he isn't going to tell them
what to do.

As for the decision to march south, he seems convinced they will eventually march out of the Western
Federation into some other territory that will take
them in. He has no evidence to support his thinking,
and when anyone asks him about it, his face twists into
a tight snarl. For someone who is supposedly interested in what others have to say, he seems remarkably
*un*interested.

The land before them is prairie flat: endless horizons of waving grass and undulating hills. No lake or stream or creek in sight. No water anywhere.

Still, Dozer is in charge. And he isn't going to tell them what to do.

Hope adjusts her pace until she's walking side by side with Book.

"What're you going to do now?" she asks. They haven't spoken since the river.

Book shrugs.

"You still planning on getting to Camp Liberty?"

He shrugs again.

"Do you still hope to free those Less Thans?"

"I don't know, Hope. If I free them, I'm afraid I might accidentally kill them, just like Cat."

Hope recoils at his words. "I didn't say that."

"You didn't need to."

They march silently through the grass, the blades making swishing sounds against their legs. Hope carries the spear in her hand like a walking stick.

"Look," she finally says, "I'm sorry I didn't stand up to Dozer last night, but—"

"Save it."

She drifts back into line, angry that he's too stubborn to listen to reason, that if she had tried to come to his defense last night, it only would have made things worse. But Book doesn't want to hear that.

The prairie stretches forever with no end in sight. Sweat bubbles from their faces. Lips split and bleed. If they don't find water soon, they'll never make it to another territory.

They set up camp that night as lightning flickers on the far horizon. Four Fingers begins to cry. "Storm!" he whimpers, his body jerking and spasming.

"Will somebody shut that moron up?" Dozer shouts. When no one does, he grabs his walking stick and whacks Four Fingers on the legs. "Shut up, I said!"

He wallops him a second time for good measure.

Four Fingers whimpers in pain.

Once Dozer returns to his bed, Book moves to Four Fingers's side. "It's just heat lightning, Four," he whispers. "Not a storm at all. Just heat lightning." It's a good hour before Four Fingers falls asleep.

The next day they march beneath an enormous dome of sky, no one uttering a word. Even the normally talkative Flush, guiding his blind friend Twitch, doesn't say a word.

That night, Hope and her fellow Sisters dig in the ground, scratching at the earth with knives and fingernails. Several feet down a brown ooze seeps up, and they scoop heaping globs of the slimy mud and strain it through a T-shirt. A murky liquid drips into a pot, which is then placed over a fire and boiled. They drink it before it cools. Hot, gritty mud water is better than none at all. They fill every canteen to the brim.

Sometime the next day, with the sun blazing hot and yellow, Dozer takes a long swig from his canteen . . . then immediately spits it out.

"This tastes like crap," he says. "How can you drink this shit?" He turns the canteen upside down and a trail of sludge plops out, landing on the ground like bird droppings.

Instead of answering him, Twitch says, "We could always turn east toward the river." Even though he can't see, he's well aware of the direction they're traveling.

Dozer gives his head a violent shake. "Nuh-uh. We're heading south."

"But the river's a water source."

Dozer leans into Twitch. "Listen, Blind Man, when you're in charge, you can make the decisions. But unless you want to be under house arrest like your friend Book here, I'd keep your piehole shut." Then he turns to the rest of the group. "There's water out here. We just have to do a better job of straining it."

He says this loud enough so the Sisters can hear, then turns and resumes marching. The others follow, fingers of dust trailing them like shadows.

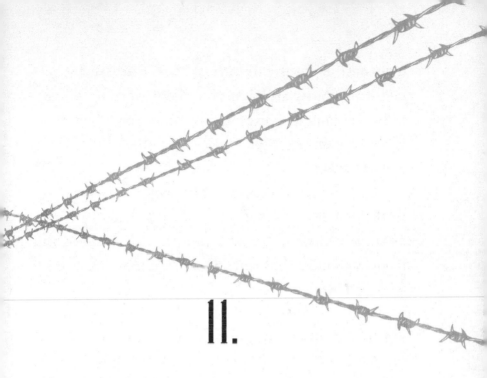

11.

THAT EVENING, I WATCHED as Hope poured huge pan-
fuls of brown slop onto a T-shirt. At one point, after she
and Scylla shared a glance, Scylla pulled the strainer
aside, allowing pure sludge to make it into the pot. An
instant later, the T-shirt was back in place. When Hope
saw me watching her, she looked away.

Later, over a dinner of cooked grasshoppers, Dozer
spat out the water like a drowning man.

"What is this crap? Is anyone else drinking this shit?"

"Mine's pretty bad, too," Red said.

"Mine too," said Angela, who pretty much copied
everything Red and Dozer did.

Dozer eyed Hope and Scylla suspiciously.

"It's that way for all of us," I blurted out, although to

be honest, my water didn't taste half bad. Murky, yes, and with a bitter aftertaste, but there was no grit in it.

Dozer planted his eyes squarely on Hope. "Tomorrow you all better do a neater job of straining or there'll be hell to pay."

Hope crunched a charred grasshopper between her teeth.

Midafternoon of the next day, the sun was hot and the wind hotter. The prairie was unending. Hope's voice broke me from my reverie.

"Hey."

I didn't answer. It had been a good hour since I'd produced enough saliva to even swallow, and I was in no mood to waste it on idle conversation.

"What if I said I'd help you free those Less Thans?" she asked.

"Where were you three nights ago?"

"Do you want my help or not?"

"Of course, but I don't know how the two of us are going to take down a whole camp and free a hundred Less Thans. Especially since I'm so untrustworthy—I'm the one who left Cat behind, remember?"

She ignored my sarcasm. "What if I said others will join us?"

"Who?"

"Uh-uh. No names. Not yet."

"Then how—"

"You have to trust me."

Despite myself, I felt my heart beating faster.

"So are you interested or not?" she asked.

"Sure, but—"

"Good. But there's one condition."

What is it? I wondered. *She makes all the decisions? I never speak to her again?*

"We rescue the Sisters from Camp Freedom," she said. "You help us. We help you."

"But the two aren't the same at all," I sputtered. "Your camp has fences. Barbed wire. Guard towers. Liberty has none of that."

"So yes or no?"

I thought for a moment. "How many girls are back there?"

"A hundred and twenty-five."

"And you think it's possible? To free them all?"

"It won't be easy, but yes."

Even though I was still angry with Hope and knew the odds were stacked against us, there was something in her voice that made me believe. It was like when I'd first laid eyes on her, back at Camp Freedom. She was walking with a group of others, and it was apparent— *even from a single glance*—that she was different. Not just her beauty, but something else. Something I could never put my finger on. Something I just *knew*.

"Okay," I said.

Before I could say another word, she moved up the column and began talking to her friends.

The next day was hot and windy—a furnace blast straight from hell.

Dozer looked downright green by the time he stumbled from his bed. Twice we waited while he puked his guts out.

It was late afternoon when a small rise appeared, extending left and right as far as the horizon allowed. Was it a dam? A wall? A barrier?

Flush was the first one to get there.

"Train tracks," he said, disappointed. We had hoped it was some kind of levee with a sparkling blue lake on the other side. No such luck.

Dozer walked across the tracks without even looking down.

"Wait," Hope said. "Maybe we can catch a train instead of walking."

Everyone stopped and turned. Even in a sickened state, Dozer still managed an air of belligerence. "You telling me what to do?"

"No, just trying to make sure we get out of here alive."

"You don't think I am?"

Dozer looked around; it was vast prairie for as far as the eye could see. The wind flapped his T-shirt. "Who says these tracks are even used anymore?" he asked.

"Look at 'em," she said. Although knee-high weeds

poked up from the gravel bed, there were places where the rails glinted from friction. Sometime in the recent past—a week? a month? a year?—a train had come through.

"But the tracks head east and west," Dozer said. "We want to go south."

"We'll get off at the first water source, then head south from there."

Dozer considered this. He was never the deepest of thinkers, and sometimes you could practically hear the squeak of wheels turning in his head.

I knew the reason for his indecision: it was someone else's plan. Someone had an idea for saving us—and it wasn't him.

"It's what you told us you wanted all along," I said. "The quickest way to a water source."

He'd never said any such thing, of course, but I was counting on the fact that he was so dazed from barfing his guts out that he barely knew up from down.

"*I* said that?" he asked.

I nodded vigorously. "On more than one occasion."

His eyes gave a woozy acknowledgment of his genius. Then, in a voice like John Wayne, he called out, "Set up camp. We'll catch the next train that comes through."

"So that was your plan?" I asked Hope that night, when no one else was within earshot. "Make him drink dirt until he'll do anything you say?"

"I have no idea what you're talking about," she said. I was pretty sure I detected a glimmer of a smile.

Later, a far-off thundering woke us from our sleep, and we spied a small, wavering star just above the eastern horizon—a freight train's distant headlight. We stuffed our rucksacks and crouched at the base of the tracks. The train's rumbling shook the earth, bouncing our bodies like popcorn.

Once the locomotive passed, we rose to our feet and jogged alongside. The cars were ancient—the wooden planking badly weathered, the red paint chipped and faded. But there was a problem. The doors were shut tight.

"There!" Flush shouted, pointing to a single car whose wooden door was ajar.

We turned to Dozer. As the self-proclaimed leader, it was up to him to make the first move, so when the car came alongside, he raced forward, pushed off against the ground . . .

. . . and went splat against the door. He landed hard on the gravel bed.

"Damn it!" he cursed, as though it was the train's fault.

The car was moving away from us.

Hope turned to one of the Sisters and shouted, "Scylla, run! Everyone else, follow." Scylla took off and we tried to catch up. Flush did his best to guide Twitch.

76

Scylla didn't stop until she reached the engine. Then she turned and waited. When the car approached, she squatted down and jumped high enough to grab hold, landing a foot in the opening. She wedged her back against the wall and pushed against the door with all her might. It groaned open with a shriek.

One by one, the other five Sisters joined her, then the Less Thans. Finally, it came down to Four Fingers, Argos, and myself, running alongside the train.

But there was a problem. Even after watching everyone else, Four seemed confused. And I was so badly out of breath, there was no way I could force him onto the train by myself. I looked to the others for help.

Dozer glared down from the freight car opening. "Leave him," he called out, then disappeared into the shadows.

Hope and Scylla jumped down from the train, then ran until they caught up with us. Scylla grabbed Four Fingers's left arm, Hope latched onto his right. At first he resisted. Then Hope counted out loud. "One, two—"

On "three" they tossed him into the black interior of the boxcar. He staggered to a standing position and smiled.

Scylla and Hope leaped into the boxcar next, leaving only Argos and me.

"Come on, boy," I said, badly out of breath, my legs churning as fast as they could. "Your turn."

Argos soared through the air as effortlessly as if he'd been doing this his whole life. His claws scraped the wooden floor as he slid halfway across the car.

My turn. Exhausted as I was, I could do this. But then, just at that moment, Flush called out at the top of his lungs, *"BRIDGE!"*

I looked up, frantic. The train was cresting a slight rise. In the near distance, spanning a dry ravine, was a narrow bridge with metal guardrails. Once the train reached it, there'd be no room for me. If I didn't get on now, I never would.

Now that the train was heading downhill, it began to pick up speed—faster and faster, the *clickety-clack* louder and more insistent. The bridge was growing closer and I was running faster and my heart was hammering harder and it was all happening way too quickly, *clickety-clack, clickety-clack.*

The train was pounding down the incline now, getting farther and farther away. Panic swelled in my chest. I could barely breathe. Barely catch my breath at all. My legs were rubber. I wasn't going to make it.

"Come on, Book!" Flush yelled.

And then others began screaming too. "Come on!" "You can do it!" "Jump!"

The train was steaming downhill. The bridge was only forty feet away. The *clickety-clack* of wheels on rails was mesmerizing and awful, like some drumbeat leading me to my death. Louder and faster, the sound pounding in my ears.

And for that brief moment, it wasn't the train I thought about, or my exhaustion, or what would happen if I failed. What I thought about was Cat. My friend, Cat. The one who I'd abandoned, who at that moment was either being butchered by Brown Shirts . . . or already a tasty meal for wolves and worms. I shouldn't have left him behind.

Flush shouted, *"Jump!"*

With every last bit of strength, I raced forward, caught up with the car, then took off, my one good leg pushing against the earth, my hands and arms straining for the boxcar, sailing through air in a silent forever.

Thwack!

My body slammed against the side of the train, but only my torso made it inside; my lower half dangled off, feet and legs kicking blindly. Hands grabbed for me, but too late. I was slipping, and the girders of the bridge were closing fast. Once my legs slammed into those metal beams, I'd have no chance of holding on. My legs would be crushed, and I'd be ripped out of the train and hurled beneath its wheels.

The Less Thans and Sisters did their best to grab hold, but my fingers slipped, my clothing tore, and I started sliding back out of the boxcar. My legs kicked wildly, drunkenly, and I was consumed by a wild panic.

In another instant I'd be dead. Gone. Sliced in two.

Help me! I wanted to scream. *Someone, please help me!*

Good-bye to Flush and Twitch and all my friends from Liberty. Good-bye to life. Good-bye to Hope.

That's when I felt the yank on my hands. My wrists were tugged with what seemed an otherworldly strength and I was flung inside the boxcar . . . just as the girders of the bridge whooshed past.

I went sailing through air until I slammed into a crate on the opposite side of the car. Stars popped before my eyes and my head swam. I caught my breath. I was safe. I was alive. I had made it.

And when I looked up, there stood Four Fingers, a goofy smile plastering his face. He had just saved my life.

When I cast a glance at Dozer, he walked away, refusing to meet my eyes.

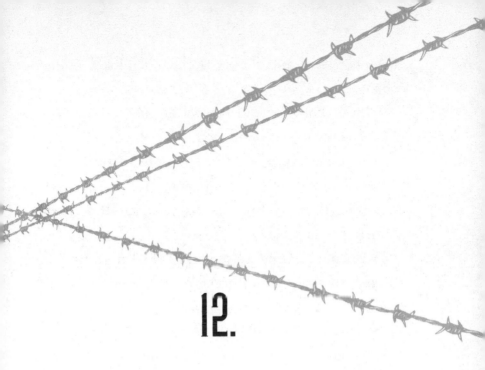

12.

THE TRAIN RUMBLES THROUGH the night. They don't know where they are, only that they're heading west, and far to the north is the Flats with its cracked mosaic of dry lake bed.

Morning brings a sharp diagonal of light slicing through the open doorway. Afraid they'll be spotted by Brown Shirts, they slide the door shut, and in no time they're dripping sweat, breathing their own stale air. They spread out as much as possible.

There's one exception: Dozer and his three pals. They huddle in a far corner with Dozer atop a crate as though it were his throne, Red, Angela, and Lacey surrounding him like obedient knights. They lean forward and speak in hushed voices. Every once in a while, Angela turns her head and shoots Hope and Book a pointed look.

"What's that about?" Hope asks Book.

"Whatever it is, it's not good."

"The sooner we get off this train, the better."

Book's brow knits in confusion. "We just got here. And weren't you the one who suggested getting on this thing in the first place?"

"Yeah, but at camp we sometimes heard trains going through the town south of us. I'm guessing this is that train."

"So that's perfect. We'll just get off there."

Hope gives her head a shake. "The town is run by Crazies."

She can see the hair rising on Book's arm. And no wonder. On the march east, they came across a band of Crazies. They were scraggly and gave off a rank smell and looked like they hadn't bothered to shave or shower since long before Omega. They'd somehow survived the bombs twenty years earlier and now lived a life of violence and squalor. A group not to be messed with.

"But now that Dozer's on this train, he won't want to get off," Book says.

"That may be true, but *we* have to."

"Should we tell some of the others?"

"Exactly what I was thinking."

Hope is just rising to her feet when a voice bellows out, "Where do you think you're going?" It's Dozer, towering over her, arms crossed like a sultan.

"Back to my friends," Hope answers. "Do you mind?"

"As a matter of fact, I do. 'Cause it's time we had us a little trial."

He nods over his shoulder, and Red, Angela, and Lacey sweep in from either side. They grab hold of Scylla, Diana, and Helen and toss them toward Hope and Book. The five of them now find themselves in the very middle of the boxcar.

"What're you doing, Dozer?" Flush asks.

"Holding a trial. What's it look like?"

"Is this because of Cat? 'Cause the others didn't have anything to do with that. Only Book."

"Perhaps," Dozer says, eyes sparkling with mischief, "but they all have something to do with treason. And if you're sticking up for them, it makes me think you're on their side, too." Just like that, Dozer grabs hold of Flush and pushes him into the middle as well.

He orders the "defendants" to sit, and everyone stares at Dozer, waiting to see what he will do next.

"On trial are these six," he announces loudly, gesturing dramatically to the group seated at his feet. "Their crime is nothing less than the act of treason."

"*Alleged* treason," Book mutters beneath his breath.

"*Treason*," Dozer corrects him. "Which I shall shortly prove." Without taking his eyes off Book, he calls out, "First witness!"

Angela steps forward. Her face is hard and flinty.

"State your name," Dozer commands. His legs bend and flex as he navigates the swaying of the train.

"Angela," she says confidently.

"And do you know these six prisoners?"

"I do."

"Who are they?"

"Hope. Diana. Helen. Scylla. Book. Flush."

"Exactly," Dozer says. "Hope, Diana, Helen, Scylla, Book, and Flush. And what did you hear when we were marching?"

"Hope was talking to some of us. Looking for volunteers."

"For what purpose?"

"To help free the Sisters from Camp Freedom."

Dozer's eyes widen in mock surprise. "And what did you say?"

"I said I'd think about it."

"But you didn't commit to helping her, did you?"

"Not in a million years, no."

"Why not?"

"Because that'd be going against you. And you're our leader."

"Exactly. And that's why you're not on trial. Thank you, Angela. You're free to go."

She shoots Hope a condescending smile as she steps away.

"Next witness!" Dozer roars, and big-boned Lacey

steps forward. She gives the same answers as Angela: Hope was recruiting volunteers, but Lacey wanted no part of it. She didn't want to do anything that would go against the wishes of their commander-in-chief.

When Dozer is done questioning, he calls Red to the stand. Red doesn't have firsthand knowledge of Hope's recruiting Sisters, but he does know that Book is too soft to be a good leader, citing his decision to leave the Heartland Territory in order to free a bunch of undeserving Less Thans.

Dozer dismisses Red with a satisfied expression and begins his summation. "So as you can see, this group of six—"

"Don't we get a chance to speak?" Book asks.

Dozer gives him a look as though a bird just shit on his head. "Huh?"

"We're the defendants. Don't we get a chance to defend ourselves?"

"Well . . ."

"Or is the prosecution afraid its case isn't strong enough?"

Dozer's nostrils flare. "Be my guest," he says.

"So I can call witnesses?"

"How can you have witnesses? You didn't even know you were on trial till a few minutes ago."

"Can I call them or not?"

Dozer's teeth clench. "Fine."

Hope gives Book a probing look; she has no idea where he's going with this.

Book stumbles to his feet and says, "I have only one witness to call."

It's impossible not to notice the smirk on Dozer's face. "Yeah, and who is that?"

"You. I call Dozer to the stand."

Although the sound of the train makes it nearly impossible to hear, Hope swears she can hear something resembling a gasp.

"Me?" Dozer asks. "Why would you call *me* to help *you*?"

"So you refuse," Book says.

"I didn't say that. I'm just surprised, that's all."

"So you'll do it?"

"I have nothing to be afraid of, if that's what you're thinking."

Dozer steps forward and Book slowly circles him as though deep in thought. Hope has to suppress a smile.

"You've accused the six of us of treason," Book begins.

"That's right."

"And what is it exactly that we did?"

"I told you."

"Tell us again."

The tendons in Dozer's neck grow taut. "The six of you conspired behind our backs. You decided to run away and free the Sisters from Camp Freedom." He nods confidently in the direction of his three supporters.

Everyone turns to Book, waiting for him to go on. Air whistles through the train's slatted walls. "Let me ask you a question," Book says. "How did we get here?"

"Huh?"

"How did we get here? We Less Thans?"

"How do you think? We crossed the mountains, the Flats, the Brown Forest . . ."

"How did we even get up Skeleton Ridge in the first place?"

"Horses. Or don't you remember?"

Red, Angela, and Lacey laugh—a little too loudly. Everyone else remains silent.

"I remember the horses," Book says, "but I can't remember how we got them."

"From the stables," Dozer says. "Where else?"

"And how'd we get to the stables?"

"What do you think, you idiot?" Dozer explodes. "We escaped from camp!"

As soon as the words pass his lips, Hope sees he regrets them.

"And this is where I don't understand the charges," Book says. "It was okay that *we* escaped, but it's not okay we help those Sisters do the same?"

"That's not what I'm saying."

"Then what *are* you saying?"

Dozer's face turns beet red. If he could get away with

wrapping his two thick hands around Book's neck, he would gladly do it.

"I'm saying that was then, this is now."

"Go on," Book says.

"That was fine that we escaped. It was the right thing, even. But now that we're on the run, we don't have time for all that."

"Freeing others?"

"Right."

"So those Sisters have to remain prisoners."

"Exactly."

"And those Less Thans at Camp Liberty?"

"Them, too."

"Why?"

Dozer looks at Book as if it's the most obvious thing in the world. "Because they're in there and we're not."

"So we deserve to be free."

"Right. 'Cause we escaped."

If it were anyone but Dozer, Hope wouldn't believe what she's hearing.

"But these other people . . ."

". . . should've had the sense to escape when they had the chance."

"Even though we didn't invite them?"

Dozer shrugs nonchalantly. "Sucks to be them, doesn't it?"

Hope has to stifle the urge to leap to her feet and take Dozer to the floor.

"So why are we being accused of treason when that same action was the very thing that got us here?"

Dozer leans in, his voice a snarling whisper. "It wasn't *treason* that got us here; it was *smarts*. And if we're going to get out of here alive, we need to work together. We can't have one group doing one thing and another group something else." In its own paranoid way, Dozer's argument makes sense. Hope hates him for it.

"But we agreed back at the border to free the Less Thans," Book says. "That's why we crawled back under the fence."

"That *was* the plan," Dozer says, "back before you got a bunch of us killed. Back before you sacrificed your friend to the enemy."

Hope can see the change in Book's face. It's like the blood drains away. He opens his mouth to speak but then thinks better of it. He stands there a moment longer, then slowly sits back down. Hope reaches out a hand and lets it rest on his forearm.

"But don't take my word for it," Dozer says, trying his best to sound humble. "Let's let *the people* decide. All those who think these six are guilty, signify by raising your hand."

Dozer raises his, and Angela and Lacey also. Red follows a moment later. That's four votes, and since the six defendants aren't allowed to vote, that leaves only two others: Four Fingers and Twitch. Even though they're on Book's side, it's not enough.

Dozer shoots Book his hyena grin. "There's your trial, Book *Worm*." He turns to his three supporters. "Tie 'em up. And make sure the knots are tight."

Before Hope knows it, ropes are flung around their wrists. Attached to the inside walls of the boxcar are big, black, metal rings for lashing cargo. Now, suddenly, the six prisoners are tied to the rings so their faces poke the wall.

Dozer shuffles over and says, "Let me know if I can get you anything, Hope *Less*." He laughs maliciously and walks away. Red, Angela, and Lacey follow in his wake.

Lashed to the metal rings and pressed against the wooden wall, Hope gives a tug, but it does no good. She's strapped in tight. They all are. There's no getting away from here, and everyone knows it.

Overcome with despair, Hope sags against the wall.

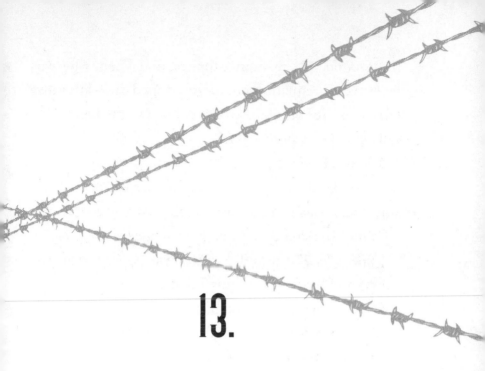

13.

THE DAY WORE ON. The temperature soared. Splinters
creased my cheek where it pressed against the wooden
planks. Once the sun set, the door was slid back open—
the fresh air washing away only a portion of the stench
of twelve sweaty bodies.

One by one, people went to sleep, even standing up,
and I gave myself over to the steady clatter of wheels on
rails and the train's gentle, swaying rhythm.

That's when I dreamed of them again: the prisoners held captive beneath the tennis courts, their hollow
eyes and sore-covered faces begging for my help.

Then the dream shifted, and it was the woman with
the long black hair. We were racing across a smoke-
covered pasture, bullets whistling, explosions rocking

the ground. The woman stopped and knelt. She was older than I remembered, more stooped, her skin more wrinkled. Her previous words echoed in my head.

You will do what's right.

You will lead the way.

I wondered what it would be this time. To my great surprise, it wasn't a sentence at all, just a single word.

"Now," she said. And then she disappeared. Vanished.

"Now *what*?" I asked, but she was gone. It was just smoke and haze and singing bullets.

"Now *what*?" I cried again.

My voice startled me awake, and there I was, hands bound, wood grain tattooing my cheek like wrinkles from a pillow. Hope was awake too. I could make out her luminous brown eyes even in the dark.

"You were dreaming," she whispered.

"Did I say anything?"

"You moaned."

There was no going back to sleep. I was far too wide-awake for that. Besides, even though I didn't know what we should do, I knew when we should do it.

Now.

Argos was sleeping in a corner, chin resting on his paws, and when I emitted a soft, low whistle, he scrambled to his feet and made his way to my side. His toenails clicked on the floor.

Way back when, Argos had been a stowaway, snuck

into a pack and carried up the mountain. He went from Less Than to Less Than, ending up with me once I'd saved him from the fire in the Brown Forest. He'd barely left my side since.

Although we were inseparable, I never trained him. Never taught him any tricks. I didn't need to, because Argos *understood*. And when I stretched away from the wall and presented my bound hands, he didn't hesitate.

Placing his front paws against the wall so he was standing on his back legs, he swung open his jaw and began gnawing, his hot breath painting my hands. The ropes vibrated and buzzed. I looked down and saw a frayed strand of rope.

"Good boy," I mouthed, but he was already onto the next strand, digging his sharp teeth into the coarse bindings. Another rope snapped in two, and I was able to squirm my hands free. My wrists were chafed and bleeding, but I was free.

I bent down and stroked Argos's head. "Thanks," I whispered, then rushed to Hope's side. The knots were cemented with dried sweat and blood, and I turned back to Argos. He shuffled over and prepared for knot number two.

At that very moment, the train snaked around a sweeping curve. I could see the engine tugging our caravan of boxcars . . . and I let out an involuntary gasp.

"What?" Hope asked.

I pointed. In the far distance, bouncing off the low-hanging clouds, was a warm amber glow: lights from a town. *Crazies.* This was what the woman with the long black hair was trying to tell me: that we had to get off the train *now*, before we reached the town.

Argos was working as fast as he could, but it wasn't fast enough. I needed a knife. Since my own had been stripped from me by Red, I needed to borrow someone else's.

Four Fingers was fast asleep, his head propped against a crate. I scrambled to his side and clamped my hand across his mouth. His eyes popped open.

"It's okay. It's just me: Book."

Once he made sense of what was going on, I could feel his smile beneath my palm, his lips stretching against my fingers. I removed my hand.

"I need to borrow your knife," I said. "Just for a little bit."

He recoiled, his hand falling across his weapon.

Ever since his accident in the Brown Forest—when Dozer had thrown him to the ground and he'd banged his head against a slab of granite—I didn't know what Four could understand and what he couldn't. But it was obvious he had no intention of parting with his knife.

"It's okay," I said. "I'll give it back."

His grip tightened on the handle.

I was getting desperate. Time was running out, and I had to free my friends.

"Hey, Four. How would you like to go on an adventure? Just a few of us."

His smile returned, his hand began to relax.

"I can't tell you where we're going yet, but if you let me borrow your knife, we can get out of here right away. And Dozer won't be coming with us."

Four Fingers seemed to consider what I was saying. He tilted his head to the side as if deep in thought. The train rounded another curve. Once more the town's amber glow came into view.

"Please?" I asked.

Four Fingers plucked the knife from his belt, presenting it to me like a general surrendering a sword. I snatched it from his hand before he had second thoughts.

I hurried back to Hope. The other prisoners were awake. Argos had made little progress in my absence, but not for lack of trying. He was panting heavily, saliva dripping from his tongue. I eased him away.

"Good dog," I said, and stroked his flanks.

Hope thrust her hands forward, and I began sawing. The coils of rope snapped. Hope was free. She took the knife and we took turns on the next four. By the time we finished, both Hope and I were each covered in a sheen of sweat.

"Now what?" Flush asked.

At the same time, Hope and I shot a glance at the open doorway.

"Now we jump."

We tiptoed through the car, avoiding sleeping bodies. Four Fingers hauled himself to his feet, and I returned his knife and guided him to the open doorway. Below us, railroad ties whooshed past. Beyond the gravel embankment stood a sea of weeds.

We were just getting ready to jump when some sixth sense prompted me to turn around. There was Red, staring right at me, his splotched face visible in the dark.

I suddenly regretted giving Four Fingers his weapon back. My mouth opened, but no words followed. What could I say? What lame excuse could I come up with?

Red's fingers curled around his dagger's handle, and I waited for his move. If I had to go at him without a weapon, so be it. It wouldn't be pretty, but what choice did I have? Nothing was going to stop us now.

But it wasn't a fight Red gave me, it was a nod. Slight. Subtle. Barely noticeable. *Go*, he seemed to be saying. *Sorry it had to end this way.*

I nodded back, releasing the breath I'd been holding.

I joined the others in the doorway. In addition to the prisoners and Four Fingers, Twitch was there also.

Flush had asked him to join us, and he was right to do so. Dozer would have little patience for a blind Less Than.

The glow of the town was closer now, lighting up a chunk of sky. Hope tapped Diana on the shoulder, and the fiery Sister tossed her backpack into the dark. She jumped out after it. Scylla and Helen followed, then Flush and Twitch. Before Hope left, she turned to me and met my eyes. I had the feeling there was something she wanted to say . . . just as I did. Something like *I'm sorry*. Maybe something more.

But neither of us spoke.

Instead, she leaned forward, kissed me on the cheek, and leaped from the train.

Now that it was just Four Fingers, Argos, and me, Four seemed suddenly afraid. He began edging away from the opening.

"No," he began saying. "No! *No!*" Even though the wind muffled his voice, it was more than loud enough to wake the others.

My mind scrambled. "You remember Frank, don't you?" I asked. "Up in the mountains? The old guy who gave his life for us, so we could be brave and do brave things for others?"

"Fraaank." He elongated the name in a way that told me he remembered. How Frank had fed us and hid us from the Brown Shirts and taught us all those skills.

How he'd invited us into his cabin and told us about his family—even given us the clothes of his dead sons.

"So now we need to jump, because that's what Frank would want us to do."

Four Fingers nodded—he seemed to suddenly understand—and without waiting a moment longer, he threw himself into the darkness. I heard the crunch of his body against the ground.

That left Argos and me.

"You ready, boy?" I said.

"He might be, but you're not."

Dozer. Before I could react, he swung his meaty arm across my shoulder. I felt the sharp blade of his knife pressing into my neck, dimpling skin.

"Where're you going?" he asked. "Or should I say, where did you *think* you were going?" He laughed, his sour breath splashing the side of my face. "The next time you wanna take off in the middle of the night, you might want to think about leaving the moron behind. He's not so good at keeping quiet."

My eyes darted to the doorway, but the knife dug in farther, a trickle of blood dribbling down my neck. "Don't even think about it, *Limp*: your life ends here."

In that fraction of a second I saw it all: our escape from Liberty and the trek to the new territory. The Less Thans held captive beneath the tennis courts. Frank in the mountains. Hope and the other Sisters. Cat. Good-bye.

As Dozer reached back to give my neck a final slice, we were both slammed to the floor with a violent thud. Dozer's knife clattered to the side. When I got my breath and turned my head, I saw Argos shaking Dozer's withered arm like it was a rat he was trying to kill.

"Get him off, get him off, get him off!" Dozer screamed, but Argos had no intention of letting go.

I stumbled to my feet. By now, the others were awake, trying to make sense of what was going on. Angela and Lacey were reaching for their knives.

"Come, Argos," I said, but for once he didn't listen. He continued to twist Dozer's arm as though snapping a wishbone.

"Argos, no!" I cried.

I should've known better.

Argos looked at me with questioning eyes, and Dozer used that opportunity to kick him in the ribs. Argos yelped and went sailing through the air, flying out of the boxcar and into the night. I heard his loud whimper as he landed in the ditch.

Anger swelled in my chest. "You shouldn't've done that," I said.

"Why? What're you gonna do about it?"

Stepping back as though about to kick a game-winning field goal, I launched my foot forward until it collided with Dozer's groin. He let out an *oomph* and doubled over, grimacing in pain.

"Don't you ever kick my dog again," I said.

I turned and threw myself out of the boxcar, landing on the edge of the rail bed and rolling hard down the gravel slope, watching as the train receded farther and farther into the distance.

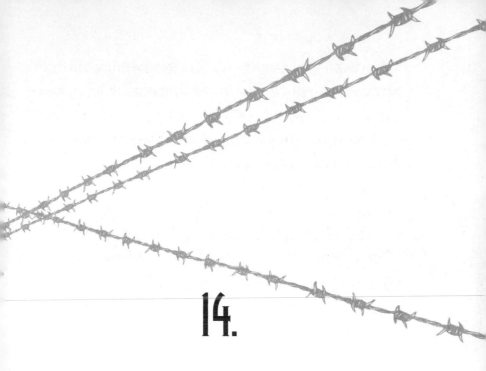

14.

HOPE WAITS ANXIOUSLY. BUT when there's no sign of Book, she can't stand there any longer, and she races alongside the track, imagining the worst. First Mom, then Dad, then Faith. She cannot add Book to that list.

When she finally catches sight of him, crouched over Argos, it takes everything in her power to stifle sobs of relief. "Are you okay?" she asks.

Book nods. "Had a little run-in with Dozer," he says, his hands shaking. Her eyes drop to Argos, who favors a back leg. When Book scratches him behind the ears, Argos pants as though everything is fine.

Hope notices a thin line of blood on Book's neck and can't help reaching for it, dabbing it with her fingertips. Book recoils slightly, and for a moment their eyes meet.

They've touched before—they've kissed—but this gesture feels profoundly intimate. Hope pulls her fingers back.

"I guess we'd better go find the others," she says. Her words sound stiff and formal, even to herself.

"I guess we'd better," Book agrees. They stay there a moment longer, alternately looking at each other and afraid to look. She feels her body leaning in. Book, too.

"Book! Hope!" a voice calls out. It's Flush, looking for them. The two of them lean back, dropping their eyes.

"Right," Hope murmurs.

They get up and follow the train tracks, walking in silence, their arms brushing slightly. Each time, Hope remembers the softness of his lips, the kindness of his eyes, the feel of his hands when they pressed against her back. She's ashamed to feel a pang of sadness when they meet up with the others.

Their friends are banged and bruised. Diana sports a long scrape on her forearm; Helen, a bump on her forehead; Flush, a gash on his leg. But Four Fingers took the worst hit of all. He rolls on the ground, grabbing the bottom of his leg.

Book kneels by his side while Helen undoes his bootlaces. A knot the size of an egg sprouts from the outside of his left ankle.

"Hey," Book says, patting him on the shoulder, "it's

all right. Just a sprain. Doesn't change anything."

"Doesn't?"

"Heck no. We'll take turns letting you lean on us. It's no big deal."

A smile spreads across Four Fingers's face, and they help him to his feet. Book can only hope he's telling the truth.

"So," Twitch says. "What now?" Remarkably he made the jump unscathed, even without sight.

"Same plan as before," Book says. "We free the Sisters, then the Less Thans after that."

Hope nods in appreciation. She has her own addition to that plan, of course, in the form of three names: Thorason, Maddox, and Gallingham. But no one knows that except her.

Scylla points to the glow of coming sunrise and they realize they need to get going. They don't want to be on the tracks when daylight hits.

"We're not going through town, right?" Flush asks. He doesn't need to mention the word *Crazies* for everyone to know exactly what he's thinking.

"Don't worry," Hope says. "We'll stay on the outskirts."

As they walk the narrow path between train tracks and cattails, Hope dwells on their new reality. Although they've escaped from Dozer and can make decisions on their own, their numbers have dwindled to just eight.

Doesn't change anything, Book said, but Hope isn't so sure.

They head north on a two-lane road, in the direction of what they hope is Camp Freedom. They come across an old sign, pitted with bullet holes.

WELCOME TO BEDFORD
Population 2,143

They skirt the far edges of town. Trudging past vine-covered houses, they realize this is less a town and more a disaster area. Weeds overwhelm the potholed streets. Trees sprout through rooftops. Debris is scattered everywhere. There's something terribly wrong about it all. How could it come to this?

But they know the answer to that. Omega. The day the bombs fell.

They're nearly past the town when Four Fingers crumples to the ground like a sack of flour. Everyone gathers around him. Even in scant light it's easy to see his face is pale, his eyes glassy. Dehydration.

"He needs water," Helen says, crouching by his side.

"Yeah, but where?" Flush asks.

Hope wants nothing more than to get out of here. Avoid the Crazies, reach Camp Freedom, worry about food and water there.

But they don't have that luxury.

"We'll find some," she says.

"Where?" Flush asks.

"Wherever they store water around here." She tries to keep her voice calm, to make it sound like it's no big deal. She knows that's far from the truth.

"I'll come with you," Book says.

"You don't have to—"

"I want to." Despite herself, Hope feels a tingle of relief.

They gather up the canteens, and Argos scrambles to Book's side. Bad leg and all, he's intent on joining them.

Just as they're about to leave, Helen reaches behind her neck and undoes the clasp of a tarnished chain. "Here," she says, presenting a locket to Hope.

Hope recognizes it, of course. It's the locket she found in her dead father's pocket. The one that contains the miniature photos of her parents. She gave it to Helen as a good-luck charm, right before they swam through the flooded tunnel during their escape from Camp Freedom.

"You might need it," Helen says.

Hope fastens it around her neck and gives Helen a quiet nod of thanks. "Come on," she says to Book. "Let's get back here before the sun comes up."

They take an anxious peek toward the east and head out.

Despite the crumbling houses and buckled roads, there is something oddly pleasing about it all. The

105

geometry of streets. The precision of intersections. Hope finds it nearly impossible to imagine what it must have been like in pre-Omega days—people strolling down sidewalks, riding bicycles, watering lawns—but it makes her think of her mother and father.

She shakes away the sentiment; no time for that now.

Live today, tears tomorrow.

Glances into the houses tell her they were ransacked years ago. Empty shelves. Cupboard doors dangling from broken hinges. No food here. No water either. They hug the shadows and move on. The eastern sky is graying.

Houses give way to shops. Then bigger shops after that. Before they know it, they're behind a brick building on what must be the main street. There are noises here: raucous laughter, whooping and hollering, the crackle of bonfires.

They come to the building's edge and peek around the corner. It's a street full of Crazies—hundreds of them—huddled around trash-can fires, cooking foul-smelling chunks of meat. The men sport long, ungainly beards and the women's hair is tangled and matted, their faces smudged with dirt. Large gaping holes in their mouths mark the absence of teeth. Even from this distance, Hope can smell their rancid stench. It's all she can do to keep from gagging.

She and Book stand pressed against the shadows,

mesmerized by chaos: Crazies gorging and drinking and belching and farting and roaring with laughter. Every so often a fight breaks out and two of them tumble to the street, trading punches. There's a sickening sound of fist on flesh.

A man who appears to be some kind of town leader steps forward toward the latest fight. He is short and compact and wears an oversize cowboy hat, and though his beard is full, it appears less greasy than those of his counterparts. Groups part as he strides forward.

"That's enough now," he says. "Break it up."

The two Crazies stand, blood streaming down their chins. They grunt and heave for breath like beasts.

"Let's find some water and get out of here," Book whispers.

Hope gives a nod as though released from a spell. They edge backward through an alley.

One street over is a pickup truck, splotched with rust. Jutting from its bed is an enormous plastic tank, cylindrical in shape, with a small spigot at one end. Above it, scrawled in black paint, is the formula H_2O.

They unsling the canteens from their shoulders, and Book begins to fill them. Hope keeps a lookout. Argos sits on his hindquarters beneath the faucet, licking stray drops straight from the asphalt.

Book has just finished filling the third canteen when they hear a thundering rumble. Book freezes, and water spills over the canteen. A growl catches in the back of Argos's throat. Hope gives them both a confused look.

"What is it?" she asks.

"Let's get out of here," he says, and starts to move away.

"But we haven't finished—"

"No time." He screws the lid on the canteen, grabs Hope's hand, and pulls her down the street.

Hope doesn't understand his sudden hurry—they have five more canteens to fill—and she's about to ask again what's going on when the drone of engines grows suddenly louder. The sidewalk trembles beneath their feet. They stop and push themselves against a building . . . and watch as ATVs go rumbling past.

Hunters. She remembers them from the Brown Forest.

Of course, that was just two dozen. This is an *army*, vehicle after vehicle, the Hunters straddling their souped-up four-wheelers. Hope has difficulty catching her breath.

The Crazies seem just as freaked. Like cockroaches caught in the light, they scramble and duck for cover and try to make themselves invisible.

At the very end of the procession is a man who wears blaze orange. He has no helmet, no Kevlar vest, just camo pants, an orange vest, and a baseball cap. One side of his face is disfigured, withered from fire. Hope remembers him from before. The leader.

The other ATVs disappear from view, but the Man in Orange loops back, stops his vehicle, and climbs off. He is greeted by a lone Crazy: the mayor with the full beard and cowboy hat. They shake hands and begin to speak. Hope and Book are too far away to make out what they're saying.

Hope looks at Book. Giant beads of perspiration dot his forehead.

"You okay?" she asks.

He nods but says nothing. At just that moment, the Man in Orange steps away from the bearded leader and swivels his head sharply to one side . . .

. . . and stares right in their direction.

Book and Hope gasp, pushing themselves against the wall. The Man in Orange continues to look their way, shielding his eyes to get a better look. It's like he knows they're there. Like he can sense their breathing. Can sense their fear.

After a short eternity, the Man in Orange smirks to himself, climbs back on his vehicle, and rides off to join his friends.

For the longest time Book and Hope seem unable to catch their breath. They only need to look at each other to know they're both thinking the same thing. *Let's get the hell out of here.*

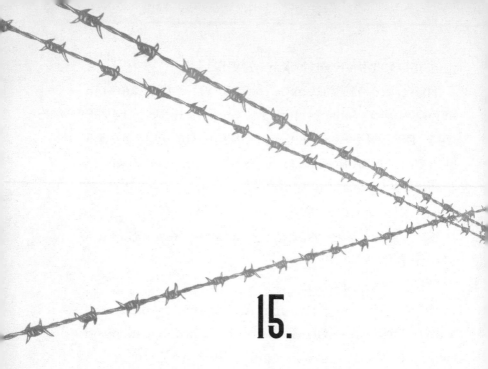

15.

WE DASHED BACK THROUGH town and met up with the others. A gravel road snaked north from town and we followed it, hugging the shoulder. Tired as I was, my mind was racing. I couldn't figure out the connection between the Hunters and the Crazies. Why were the Hunters even there? And why were their leaders speaking? It made no sense.

There was something else I wondered, too, and I hurried to Hope's side.

"How're we going to do it?" I asked.

"What?"

"Free the Sisters."

She shrugged. "How else? The tunnel."

"Even though it's flooded?"

"Guess we'll have to swim again."

"And how many Sisters did you say there were?"

"A hundred and twenty-five. Give or take." Then her gaze grew distant, her face tight. "The number was always changing."

Before I got a chance to ask her what she meant, she quickened her pace, and I was walking by myself again. That was the thing about Hope—that haunted look in her eyes never went away. I hoped to someday find out what it meant.

We took a nap late that afternoon, folding ourselves in thick blankets of underbrush. When we woke several hours later, we foraged for food. There was an eerie calm as we performed our chores, everyone focused on the coming mission: freeing over a hundred Sisters from Camp Freedom without the Brown Shirts noticing.

"We four will go into the tunnel," Hope said over a dinner of mushroom and scallion soup, pointing to the other three Sisters. "We'll sneak into camp, round up the Sisters from the other barracks, and bring them back through the tunnel."

"And us?" Flush asked.

"You four will stand watch outside camp." I was about to protest, but Hope explained. "If you went in, you'd only freak them out."

"What happens if things go wrong?" I asked.

Hope hesitated before answering. "Get away from here as fast as you can."

A quiet fell over the group.

When darkness came, we set back out, sticking to the dense shadows of the woods. We marched through the night, not stopping until guard towers cut a jagged silhouette against the purple black of the sky. Crawling to the crest of a ridge, we looked down at the camp, and I could tell the mere sight of it made Hope and the other Sisters tense.

A thin slice of red and orange announced the dawn. We lay and watched, waiting for the camp to come to life. The calm was oddly unsettling. Like a snake before it strikes.

But nothing happened. The sun rose and the sky brightened and there was no movement. None. No curling tendrils of smoke from the kitchen. No guards peering from the guard towers. No prisoners being marched from one building to another. All was silent and still.

At first we didn't speak of it, in part because we couldn't believe our eyes. *Any minute now,* I thought, *Sisters will march from the barracks to the mess hall, and from the mess hall to roll call. Just like what we saw before.*

But it didn't happen. There were no Sisters. No Brown Shirts either. It was as if they'd all mysteriously disappeared. Vanished into thin air.

I suddenly remembered the letter we'd uncovered. *Leave no trace.* My heart began to pound.

"You think they've been killed?" Flush asked.

No one had an answer to that. It seemed unlikely, if only because there were no slumped bodies, no decaying corpses strewn about the ground. Instead, everything just looked . . . empty. Utterly deserted.

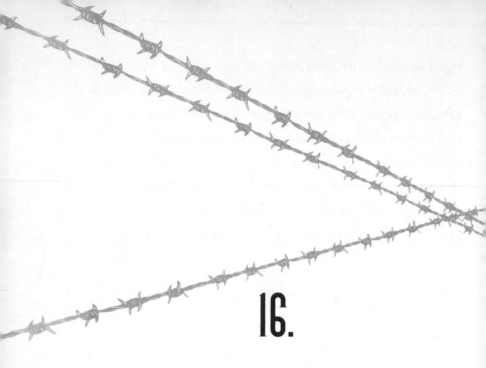

16.

THEY FIGURE THE SISTERS are hiding, so they go forward with their plans. They'll find them, then set them free.

The sun sets, and Hope leads the other seven to a pile of evergreen boughs on the far side of camp. She tosses the branches to the side, revealing the tunnel entrance.

"I'm coming with you," Book blurts out. "If they're in hiding, there's no one for me to freak out."

For the longest time they stare at each other. Then Hope looks at her three friends and they nod silently. "Fine," she says.

Book turns to Flush and Twitch. "You okay staying here with Four?"

Flush looks relieved.

The tunnel entrance swallows Hope's body. The

scent is hauntingly familiar: musty and thick with the smell of damp earth, and when her feet finally reach the ground, she's relieved to discover there's only six or so inches of water. The rest has drained away since they were last here.

Once the other four have descended, Scylla uses her knife and flint to ignite a bundle of pine needles, pressing the flame against a candle. The wick flares to life. The tunnel is as Hope remembers it: black and claustrophobic, no more than three feet high and the same in width. It seems to stretch forever: a tight, constricting hallway with sagging beams and a floor of mud and water. Still, it's miraculous to think they dug it with nothing but knives and spoons.

She leads the way, sloshing down the tunnel, her breath ballooning in front of her. A rat dog-paddles past, its greasy fur rubbing against Hope's leg. She pays it no attention.

When they reach the ladder at the far end, they huddle against the wall, their hands and knees caked with mud. Hope blows out the candle and begins to climb, the ladder groaning beneath her weight. That's when it hits her how absolutely crazy this is. They're breaking into the very camp that *imprisoned* them. The place where Dr. Gallingham murdered their sisters.

What on earth are they thinking?

She takes a deep breath, shifts the ceiling panel to

the side, and hauls herself up into the tiny closet that houses the water heater. Another deep breath later she slides through the door and into the hall. Barracks B— her former "home."

The cots are lined up in a tidy rows, the thin, ratty blankets smoothed to perfection.

But no one's here.

The other four join Hope, and they ease their way to the front window. Peering through the grimy, dirt-streaked panes, they see no one. Hear no one. Doors swing vacantly in the breeze. On the infield, where roll call used to be held each morning, debris rolls like tumbleweeds. Odd bits of paper cling to the barbed-wire fence, held there by the wind.

It's a ghost camp. Without a word, they leave Barracks B and pad quietly from one building to the next, but still, they find no one. A thin layer of dust covers everything like an extra sheet on a cold night.

Hope can't figure it out.

Whatever happened, happened quickly. In the mess hall, food sits half eaten on plates, as though the Sisters were called away midmeal. Now it's home to a million maggots and several dozen mice.

So where did the Sisters go? And why so urgently?

There is one building left to examine, but for reasons that are obvious to the four Sisters, they give it a wide berth. Hope even averts her eyes when she walks past, as if avoiding staring into a bright sun.

Book takes a step in that direction and Hope grabs his arm.

"That's the infirmary," she says. "We don't need to go there." There is a firmness in her voice that surprises Book.

He studies her face. "What do you mean?"

"It's empty."

"How do you know that?"

"I know."

"But what if there's someone in there? Someone hiding?"

"No one would hide in there." Her tone leaves no room for discussion.

"Okay," Book says, and starts to walk away, but her nails dig into his skin.

"You need to promise me something," she says. "Promise you'll never set foot in that building."

Book smiles, thinking she's kidding, and when he tries to pull his arm free, her grip tightens. "Promise me," she says again.

"Why?"

"Just promise."

Hope's attitude is matched by that of her three friends. Their faces are as set as Hope's, and it's obvious they're in complete agreement. The look of surprise on Book's face shows he has no sense of what this is all about. Of what they went through.

"Uh, sure," he stammers.

Hope leans into him—their eyes locking. "Actually promise."

"I promise," he says.

She releases his arm and motions to the Sisters. "Go get the others," she says. Scylla, Helen, and Diana exit through the unlocked front gate in the direction of the woods. Book turns to Hope.

"What's going on?" he asks.

"I don't know," she answers. "I thought the Sisters would be here."

"That's not what I mean. That building—why aren't you letting me go in there?"

She seems about to speak but then thinks better of it. "You have no idea," she says, and walks away.

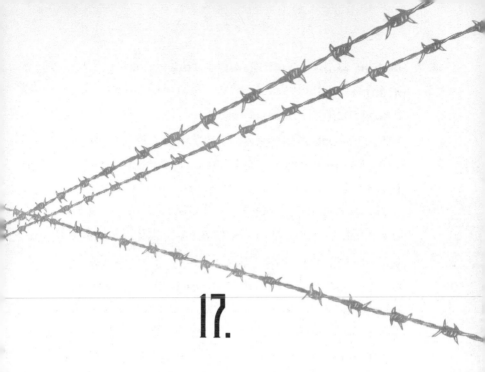

17.

YOU HAVE NO IDEA. The very words Cat said to me back at Camp Liberty, back when I didn't know a thing about the Hunters.

So what was going on? I wondered . . . and questioned if I really wanted to know.

It was Flush who had the idea to examine the kitchen. "If they were in such a hurry, maybe they didn't take everything with them."

He was right. The back pantry was a smorgasbord: dozens of gallon-sized cans of fruit cocktail, baked beans, creamed corn, chocolate pudding. A feast just waiting to be devoured. There was no electricity, and we didn't dare fire up the generators. Instead, we covered the kitchen windows with blankets, lit a small candle, and then ate straight from the cans.

We stumbled back to the tar-paper barracks and found the beds. For us four Less Thans, it was the first time we'd slept on mattresses since our escape from Liberty, months earlier. My friends began snoring before the blankets even settled on their bodies.

But I couldn't sleep. I had vowed to myself I would try to understand Hope's haunted look, and now I had a chance to do something about it.

I got up and walked across the parade ground, the air damp with summer, a million stars winking overhead. On the far side of camp a screen door banged against its frame as the breeze opened and closed it.

Slam, slam, slam, slam.

The infirmary was a plain, two-story rectangle of a building with peeling white paint and bars crisscrossing the second-story windows. Curious. Who would want to break into—or out of—a hospital?

A part of me felt oddly guilty. I had promised Hope I wouldn't do this. But at the same time I wanted to know her better. If I could understand what was going on behind those haunted eyes, maybe I could help her— just as she'd helped me when I told her about K2, the friend whose death I felt responsible for.

The infirmary knob twisted in my hand, and I eased inside. I pulled the blinds shut and lit a lantern that rested on a desk, and a yellow glow blossomed, revealing a small waiting room. A door stood on the far side.

I tugged it open. Before me was a narrow corridor with a series of rooms on either side. To my immediate right was a staircase leading up.

I inched my way down the hall, holding the lantern before me as though it was a cross to ward off vampires. The first room to my right was a doctor's office. A small desk, a chair, an examination table. The cabinet doors above the sink swung open, revealing empty shelves.

I moved to the next room. Its door was closed. I steadied my hand on the knob and turned. The door squeaked open, and the lantern's rays spilled onto the linoleum floor . . . revealing the same furnishings as the previous room. And more empty shelves.

Each room was virtually the same. I couldn't figure out why Hope had forbidden me to come here.

At the end of the hallway was another stairway leading up. A part of me wanted to get the heck out of there, maybe come back the next day when it was bright out. But I knew I had to do this now. I had to know. I took a deep breath and went up.

Each step creaked beneath me. I reached the top of the stairs, opened a set of double doors, and looked down the long hallway. It was no different from the one below. Linoleum floor. Pale institutional walls. A series of rooms on either side.

"There's nothing here," I said aloud, my voice echoing back at me.

I peeked in the first doorway—it was a simple doctor's office, just like what I'd seen below—and I was ready to step back out when I noticed something dangling from the thin mattress: two sets of leather straps with metal buckles. I'd never seen that on a hospital bed before.

The next room was stranger still. Its central feature was an enormous steel tank—something you'd see in a barn for livestock. The third room sported a metal table, splotched with rust, encircled by a gutter that drained into the floor.

An autopsy table, I realized. For dissecting dead bodies.

The next room had the same. And the next several after that. There were nearly as many rooms with autopsy tables as there were rooms with beds. As if the doctors *expected* inmates to die.

What was going on here?

The final room was a lab, flasks and beakers of every possible size, everything covered in a coating of dust. It was here that I spied a fat three-ring binder. It lay in the corner of an emptied cabinet. Whoever had cleared out the room had obviously missed it.

I set the lantern on the desk and picked up the black binder. As soon as I opened it and my eyes roamed over the contents, I realized I was looking at something I wasn't meant to see. A photo album. But without photos of smiling children or families.

These were pictures of female inmates, sporting hideous scars, gruesome wounds, festering sores. The pictures were bloody and grisly and awful, and I wished more than anything I'd never seen them.

But the photo that grabbed my attention most was absent of blood and scars. It showed two female prisoners submerged in a vat of water, ice floating all around them. Their skin had purpled and they looked moments away from death.

But worse was the fact that I recognized the prisoners: Hope and her sister, Faith. Hope's enormous brown eyes were filled with pleading, just like those of the emaciated Less Thans imprisoned in the bunker.

I slammed the binder shut, and particles of dust exploded in the air. My heart hammered against my chest and pounded in my ears, drowning out all other sounds . . . which was why I didn't hear the footsteps on the stairs and the opening and closing of the hallway door.

Sensing rather than hearing someone's arrival, I whipped my head around, shocked to see a figure standing in the open doorway—and relieved that it was Hope.

"Thank goodness," I said, breathing again. "I was afraid you were a Brown Shirt or—"

She slapped me hard across the face.

"You promised," she said. Her teeth were bared like some cornered animal's.

"I know, but I thought if I came here—"

"You promised," she said again.

"But that's what I'm trying to tell you—"

Her look cut me off, and then her eyes landed on what I was holding. With trembling hands she took the binder from me, opened it, and flipped through the pages, her eyes darting from one horrific image to another. When her gaze fell on the picture of herself and Faith, I watched as the blood drained from her face.

She put the binder down and held on to the desk so she wouldn't faint. Finally, when it seemed she'd gotten herself under control, she began backing out of the room.

"Wait!" I said.

But she was already halfway down the hallway. When I caught up with her in the first-floor waiting room, she spun around and struck me—this time not with hands or fists, but words.

"How could you?" she asked, her voice stinging with disappointment. "You said you wouldn't come here. You swore."

"But I had to," I said. "I saw those pictures, and I think I understand now. They did experiments; they did these terrible things to you, and that's how your sister died."

She crossed her arms and looked away. "You don't know."

"You're right, I don't. That's what I'm trying to figure out."

"You don't know!" she screamed again, her voice rattling the windowpanes.

"Then tell me," I said. "Please, Hope."

She opened her mouth to speak, but no words came. It was like some kind of silent scream.

"If you don't tell me," I said, "I can't help you."

Her eyes narrowed into a deathly squint. "Who says I need help?"

She turned and left, slamming the door behind her.

Hope didn't speak to me for the next two days. Her friends, too, regarded me as a kind of monster. At meals, the four Sisters ate in one part of the mess hall kitchen, the four Less Thans in the other. Only Argos bridged that wide divide, accepting scraps from both groups. He made out like a bandit.

"What's up with them?" Flush finally asked.

"A little disagreement" was all I said.

"A *disagreement*? I don't know, Book. I haven't seen that kind of stink eye since the time I accidentally peed on Sergeant Dekker's shoes."

I didn't respond. I was in no mood to talk about it.

Flush wasn't finished. "You know, if they don't go to

Liberty with us, we're screwed. The four of us and Argos can't do this on our own." He shot a look to Twitch and Four Fingers. "No offense."

"None taken," Twitch said.

"We'll make it," I said, a little more forcefully than I intended.

"Sure, I hope we do," Flush said, "but I'm just saying—"

"I know what you're saying, and I'm telling you we're going to make it. We're going to free those Less Thans."

I slammed my food down and stormed out. I was mad at myself for raising my voice at Flush, but he'd hit a nerve. Deep down I agreed with him. Without the Sisters, we didn't stand a chance.

When I woke the next morning, Hope was standing by my bed. It was the first time she'd even looked at me since our argument.

"We're leaving," she said. Behind her stood Diana, Helen, and Scylla.

I sat up and swung my legs over the edge of the bed. "Okay, let me wake the guys. Give us a minute and then we'll—"

"Not with you. Just us."

I struggled to understand. "So you're going hunting?"

She shook her head. "This is good-bye."

I realized they had their packs and crossbows. "But I thought we were going to help each other."

"We were."

"I thought you were going to Camp Liberty with us."

"We were."

"So . . . ?"

"You broke your promise." She said it like it was so obvious that nothing more needed to be said.

"You can't be serious. We need you."

"You should've thought of that earlier." She slung her knapsack over her shoulder. "We're taking some of the food, but there's plenty left."

Argos jumped down from my mattress and scampered to Hope's side. She petted him a final time.

"Where're you going?" I asked.

"To find the Sisters."

I scrambled to my feet and threw on a shirt. "We can help you."

"We don't need your help. Maybe before, but not now."

The four of them began to walk away.

"But you were going to help us free the Less Thans," I called out.

"And you were going to stay out of the infirmary." Hope turned and met my eyes. "You gave me your word, Book. I believed you. Now I don't know what to believe and who to trust."

Then they stepped into blinding sunlight and disappeared.

The rest of that day was a blur. The four of us went about our daily routine, but our hearts weren't in it. Even Argos traipsed to the screen door and let out a whimper, hoping for the Sisters' return.

It never came.

That night at dinner, Flush asked the obvious. "You still want to go through with this?"

We were sitting on the kitchen floor. I was finishing my third serving of Spam; he, Twitch, and Four Fingers had their spoons submerged in a gallon-sized can of pork and beans.

"We have to," I said.

"We don't *have* to, Book. There's no law that says we need to go back. And the truth is, once the other LTs saw us escape, they probably figured out they could do it too. Who knows, they're maybe all gone by now. Maybe they're in the Heartland."

Of all the unlikely possibilities, that seemed the unlikeliest.

I finished my Spam and slid the can to Argos. He was all too happy to lick out the can.

My gaze settled on Flush. There was no point arguing with him. He'd made up his mind, and I couldn't blame him.

"I'm going back to Camp Liberty," I said. "I have to."

"I know."

"I saw those Less Thans in that bunker. They're going to be sold off to the Hunters and massacred—just like what you and I saw up in the mountains. The slaughter of those six LTs."

"I remember."

"So I don't think I have a choice."

Flush nodded respectfully. I appreciated that he allowed me my opinion, even if it didn't match his own.

"And you?" I asked. "What're you going to do?"

He gave a glance to Twitch. "We're gonna head back to the fence and try to cross into the Heartland."

"You think that's safe?"

"Safer than what you have in mind."

He was right about that.

"And Four?" I asked.

"We'll take him with us. Maybe there's a doctor over there who can make him better."

I hated to leave my friends. Hated more to be on my own. But what was the point of arguing? There was no way I was going to convince them to come with me.

"Tomorrow then," I said. "You guys go your way; I'll go mine."

We looked away at the same time, avoiding eye contact, the silence heavy between us. But before we departed Camp Freedom for good, there was still one thing I had to do.

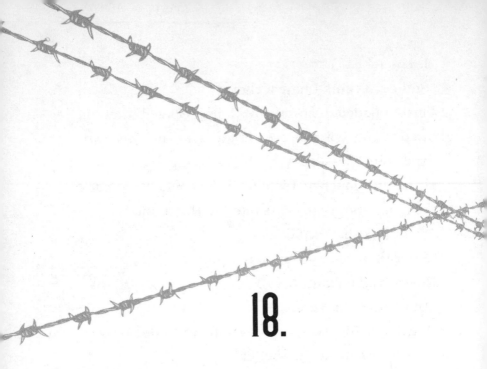

18.

SHE TRIES NOT TO think of him. There is more than enough to occupy her mind: leading the three others through deep woods, foraging for food, trying to track down more than a hundred Sisters.

But it's always Book she comes back to—the conflicting emotions swirling around her head like gnats on a summer day. Trust and doubt. Respect and contempt. Love and betrayal.

Why? Hope asks herself. *Why did he have to break his word?*

Although she tries to see it from his point of view, she keeps coming back to one thing: he made a promise . . . and he broke it. Something her father never would have done.

"Good riddance," Diana says. She's joined Hope at the front of the line. "We don't need him. We don't need any of them. We're just fine on our own."

Hope is embarrassed that Diana has read her mind.

"You can't be partners with people you don't trust," Diana says. "Period. "

Hope knows three things about Diana: she is good with a crossbow, her twin sister was murdered by Dr. Gallingham, and she is never shy about voicing her opinion.

And she's not finished. "To say one thing to your face and then go off and do another, well, it's just not right."

"I know."

"Good riddance, I say."

"I got it."

"Good flippin' riddance."

"Okay, I get it!"

Diana stops, startled. "What? I—"

"They helped us, we helped them, that's all that needs to be said." Hope is surprised by her voice's icy edge. Where did *that* come from?

Scylla and Helen watch from a respectful distance, eyes darting back and forth between Hope and Diana.

Diana shifts her weight from one leg to the other. "All I'm saying is—"

"Look, we made our decision—we left them behind— and the sooner we stop talking about them, the better."

Diana's hands rise to say, *Don't shoot me, I'm just the messenger.* "Fine," she says.

"Fine," Hope says back, then turns and resumes walking. Even as she tries to dismiss the conversation, she regrets blowing up. She knows better than that. As they march through waist-high weeds, she thinks of Book. His lopsided smile. The dark hair framing his face. The press of his lips against hers.

We did the right thing, she tries to tell herself. *It's better this way.*

Hope may have gotten angry at Diana for the way she worded things, but she was exactly right. *You can't be partners with people you don't trust.*

Period.

Hope crouches on a gravel road, her hands hovering above the rocks. Her palms and fingertips trace the grooves and indentations. She tiptoes from one side of the road to the other. The other three Sisters watch from the ditch.

"What're you looking at?" Helen asks.

"Tracks."

"Animals'?"

"People's."

If there's one thing her father taught her, it was how to track game. She's had little experience tracking people, but the concepts are the same. *Footprints tell a story; it's just a matter of knowing how to read them.*

She glances to the west, happy the sun hangs low above the horizon. That makes for the best tracking—when shadows are deepest. They might have walked across this road hours earlier and not noticed a thing.

"The other Sisters?" Diana asks.

Hope thinks so, but there are questions here. Questions without answers.

"Vehicles. At least three." She points to one side of the road. "The tracks aren't clear because they came first. The Sisters followed. Brown Shirts after that."

"Were they all together?"

"Probably. Can't say for sure."

She scrambles to the far side of the road. "Look at this."

There's a footprint in the gravel. Hope compares her own right next to it. They're nearly identical.

"Same shoe," Diana says.

"Other Sisters," Hope says.

Scylla motions to a print she's found.

"And that's a Brown Shirt's," Hope says. "Different sole entirely. Wider. More ridges. Much newer boot."

They're all looking now, identifying every tread within a hundred-foot section. In some cases, they discover footprints from bare feet. When they've finished searching, they stand up and stare down the long road.

"So these are recent?" Diana asks.

"Recent enough," Hope says.

Helen fills in the rest. "Which means they're close, doesn't it?"

Hope nods absently.

As they set off along the gravel road, they do so with a certain unease, aware they could come across the Sisters at any moment—or the Brown Shirts could come across them. Every sound is suddenly magnified; every footprint takes on a greater meaning.

But what Hope can't understand is why they find so many prints from bare feet; some of the Sisters aren't wearing shoes at all. Whatever the meaning behind it, Hope knows it can't be good.

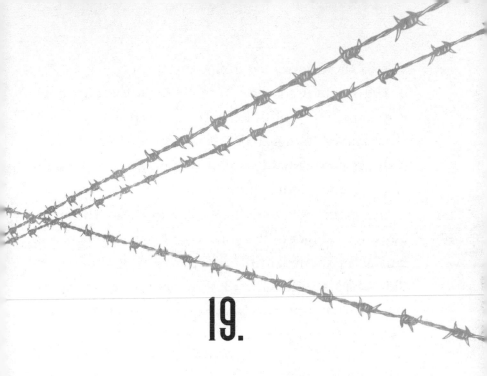

19.

CRICKETS CHIRPED AS ARGOS and I walked across the parade ground, headed for the cinder-block Administration Building. Although we'd given it a walk-through that first night, I hadn't been back since. And it seemed like forever ago when Hope and I had broken into Colonel Thorason's office and found Chancellor Maddox's letter.

The front door moaned as I pulled it open. I lit a candle, and it sputtered to life. Argos lay down on a braided rug and quickly fell asleep. He wanted no part of my search.

I'd returned here for one reason only: to find out more about Hope. Ever since I'd first laid eyes on her, I'd wondered what was behind that haunted look. The pictures in the three-ring binder told me some of the story; I was determined to find out the rest.

The sputtering candle led me down the dim hallway to the office of Colonel Thorason. It was just as I remembered it: bigger than the other offices, the furnishings more ornate . . . with a large wire wastepaper basket in the middle of the room.

One glance told me all I needed to know. The enormous file cabinet in the corner sat empty, its files now burned in the makeshift incinerator. But the Brown Shirts had been in such a hurry that they hadn't bothered to make sure everything was consumed by flames. As I began picking my way through the basket, I discovered hundreds of folders that were just charred at the edges, their contents still legible.

The files were mostly inventories, all seemingly typed with the same typewriter, the thick letters splashing gray-black on coarse white pages. Every time a new prisoner was brought to Camp Freedom, it was recorded. The name of the girl. Her height and weight. What part of the territory she came from. Everything.

But what I couldn't get over was the sheer number of prisoners. Just among the folders that hadn't burned, it was obvious that hundreds and hundreds of girls had been admitted to Freedom. Hope had spoken of only a hundred and twenty-five. So where were all the others? What had happened to them? I riffled through the wastebasket with a sudden urgency.

Forty-five minutes later, I found it: the admission records of two prisoners named Faith and Hope Samadi. Twins. There were pictures, too. Even with a freshly shaved head, Hope wasn't difficult to recognize: her luminous brown eyes, the defiant expression. Faith looked much the same as when I'd last seen her in the barracks after Hope and I survived the cave-in. But what happened to her?

I remembered Hope's words in the field the day I came back to rescue her. *Experiments. I had a sister.* More of the puzzle pieces were falling into place, but I still couldn't see the full picture.

Argos came slinking in, whimpering, his body hovering close to the ground. He nudged me with his cold nose.

"What's going on, bud?" I asked. "I'm almost done, if that's what—"

The floor began to rumble. I shared one look with Argos and realized we needed to get away.

I stuffed the pictures of Hope and Faith in my pocket, blew out the candle, and raced out of there, Argos nipping at my heels. Down the hall and out the front door, tearing across the infield. We entered the mess hall from the back.

The three other Less Thans looked up at me, just as the glasses in the cabinets began to rattle. Then the plates. Then the cups and saucers.

"What is it?" Twitch asked. "What's going on?"

I didn't know the answer, but I suspected . . . and my heart rose in my throat. Running through the mess hall, I cracked the front door so I could peer out.

A moment later they came. Headlights. Military vehicles. Dozens of them. Humvees and Jeeps, tanks and troop transport carriers. All pouring through Camp Freedom's gated entrance and circling the infield in an impressive display of military precision.

The wheels had barely ceased turning before the vehicles began disgorging Brown Shirts—all armed and spotlessly uniformed, racing for their stations like a well-practiced drill. Some scurried up the guard towers. Others stormed the buildings. Still others stood at rigid attention by their vehicles. I wanted to pull myself away, but I was hypnotized by the awful beauty of their soldierly efficiency.

When I felt a hand on my shoulder, I nearly jumped.

"We've got to get out of here," Flush said.

"Damn straight."

We tore back through the mess hall, helped Twitch and Four Fingers to their feet, and galloped out the back door. We knew the goal without having to say it: Barracks B. First to retrieve our belongings, then to sneak out through the tunnel.

In the near distance, bouncing off the barracks walls, came the sound of slamming doors, barked orders, the metallic click of weapons. As long as we stuck to the back alleyways, we'd be fine. We could make it.

At just that moment, night became day; banks of towering floodlights buzzed to life. Then the spotlights turned on with a bass *whumpf*—like the sound a fire makes as it explosively ignites—and the four guard towers sent pools of light crawling across the grounds and up the sides of buildings.

"Come on," I said, and took off. The others followed.

The going was slow. We stuck to the rear of the camp—the sheds, the smokehouse, the three-level storehouse—and each time we came to the side of a building, we stopped and waited for the searchlights to pass.

A final alley remained between us and Barracks B, and the others went before me, avoiding the oval light that splattered white on the narrow alley. My turn.

I took a peek toward the infield and froze. Streaming through the camp's front gate was a black limousine—something big and bulky and sporting two small flags just above its headlights. Even from that distance, I recognized the pennants' symbols: three inverted triangles.

The automobile rolled to a crunching stop, and Brown Shirts hurried to open the door. There was a long pause before anyone got out, and the soldiers stood at stiff attention, wreathed by headlights. The dignitary who finally exited was none other than the woman with the cheekbones and the long blond hair. Chancellor Maddox. Former beauty queen turned Midwestern congresswoman turned chancellor of the Western Federation Territory.

She was as I remembered her: tall, with crisp facial features and hair as perfectly combed as a movie star's. Even in the heat of summer she wore an ankle-length black coat that draped across her shoulders. She gripped a briefcase in her left hand; it was handcuffed to her wrist. Brown Shirts saluted her. She barely acknowledged them.

Also emerging from the limousine was Dr. Gallingham. He was so large, two soldiers had to help pull him to his feet. He popped free of the limo, found his balance, and dabbed at his eye with a handkerchief.

When Colonel Westbrook stepped forward, I inhaled so sharply at the sight of him that I nearly lost my breath. He shook hands with Maddox and Gallingham, and then their three heads bent forward in hushed conversation. Westbrook's comb-over flapped in the evening breeze.

So why was the head of the Western Federation meeting with the overseer of Camp Liberty? And why here at Camp Freedom? And what was in Maddox's briefcase that was so important? None of it made sense.

"Book!"

Flush was whispering from the other side of the alley, motioning me forward.

"Right," I said. I waited for the searchlight to pass and then tore across the gravel.

"Why'd you stop?" he asked as I pressed myself against the building.

"I'll tell you later. Let's get out of here first."

We slipped through the back door of the barracks, retrieved our few belongings, and smoothed out the blankets just as we had found them. No point leaving clues. We were moving for the back closet when we heard a series of muffled shouts. Then a gunshot. Flush had to clamp his hand across Four Fingers's mouth to keep him from screaming.

"It's okay," he said. "Nothing to be afraid of."

I moved away. Something compelled me to see what was happening.

There was a tiny window at the front of the barracks. I slid my body forward until my eyes could peek above the sill. There they stood: Colonel Westbrook, Chancellor Maddox, Dr. Gallingham, still immersed in conversation.

There was also a huddle of soldiers, their eyes focused on something I couldn't quite see. One of the soldiers lifted his rifle and slammed it down, butt end first. I heard the smack from where I stood—a sound as sickening as a melon tossed onto a hard surface.

141

The Brown Shirts shifted positions and I saw what everyone was looking at: four prisoners, one of whom had just taken a rifle butt to the head. Scylla—lying on the ground, blood seeping from her temple and purpling the gravel. Standing next to her were Diana and Helen . . . and Hope.

There was someone else as well. Dozer, dressed in the uniform of a Brown Shirt.

"We gotta get going," Flush pleaded.

I didn't want to leave the Sisters, but what could we do? We were four against many. Besides, the Sisters had left *us*, right?

I raced back between the cots and led the other three Less Thans to the back closet, where we lowered ourselves into the darkened shaft. I carried Argos down myself. We stood there in the pitch black, embraced by the sound of dripping water and fleeing rats.

"I can't see a thing," Flush said.

"Welcome to my world," Twitch answered.

I yanked a candle from its sconce and lit it using flint and paper. The tiny yellow flame shimmered atop black water, and the long, narrow passageway looked more claustrophobic than ever.

"This is it?" Flush asked. It was his first time being down there, and I could hear the panic in his voice.

"Just follow it to the end. Wait there till I come get you."

His eyes grew wide. "Don't tell me you're thinking of staying." Even when I explained what I'd seen, that didn't change his mind. "But you won't stand a chance," he said. "Didn't you see how many soldiers there were?"

"I know."

"I hate to leave those four girls as much as you, but there's nothing to be done."

"I understand."

"I mean, we've gotten out of some scrapes before, but nothing like this."

"You're right."

And yet there was no way I could leave Hope surrounded by Brown Shirts. The next muffled gunshots confirmed it.

"I'll be back as soon as I can," I said. I gave him the candle, grabbed Four Fingers's knife, and climbed back up the ladder before anyone could stop me.

I eased into the barracks and was nearly to the front door when I heard footsteps and a mutter of voices. A flashlight's narrow beam played on the front windows—a group of Brown Shirts was headed right for Barracks B.

I didn't hesitate. I launched myself out the back door, scrambled to my feet, and pressed myself against the outside wall. My heart was thudding so loudly, it felt like the whole building was shaking.

Oblongs of light spilled from the barracks's windows,

but no Brown Shirts emerged from the back door in pursuit. They hadn't seen me.

I pushed away, feet crunching on gravel. The infield had cleared out, and the few remaining Brown Shirts leaned against Humvees, puffing on cigarettes, red tips glowing. My eyes swept past the buildings. There was no jail in Camp Freedom, so where would the four Sisters be kept?

My eyes landed on the Admin Building. It was lit up like a bonfire. Light streamed from nearly every window. It seemed the natural choice.

I made it to the back of the building and crept beneath the windows, listening for the Sisters' voices.

The voice I heard instead was Chancellor Maddox's.

"And you?" she was asking. "What do you have to say for yourself?"

"We're fine." I recognized Colonel Westbrook. It was easy to imagine his coal-black eyes, his expressionless face.

"Eight escapees does not sound 'fine.'" Her voice was razor edged. There was not a hint of kindness there.

"That was months ago. Most are dead or captured. Only four unaccounted for. I'm not concerned."

"You will be if they get out of the territory." Chancellor Maddox inhaled sharply—like a north wind preparing to blow its icy gusts. "And the construction?" she asked.

"Starts this month, once we get a bulldozer there."

"You understand the Final Solution depends on this."

"I do."

There was something about the way she said *Final Solution* that made the hairs rise on my arms.

"And you?" the chancellor asked. "Is your little problem contained?"

"We've taken the appropriate steps," another man's voice answered. I wondered if this was Colonel Thorason, the overseer of Camp Freedom.

"Even though twenty escaped?" It was both a question and a put-down.

"Don't worry," Thorason said. "Dr. Gallingham's working on it now. Before the night is out, those girls will be telling us *all* their secrets." Then he added, "Unless torture makes you squeamish."

"Need I remind you about the aftermath of Omega?" Maddox said. *"Nothing* makes me squeamish." She lowered her voice and asked, "And the remaining delivery?"

"You'll get it soon enough."

I tried to piece it together. The Final Solution, the delivery, the new construction—there was so much I didn't understand. But one thing was clear: the Sisters weren't here in the Admin Building. They were in the infirmary. The closest thing to a prison—and a torture chamber—that there was in Camp Freedom. Even now, I saw a dull light glowing from a second-story window.

145

Fifty yards separated me from the Sisters. From Hope.

There were no guards posted, and it looked simple enough. All I had to do was get upstairs and steal the Sisters out of there. I might have to deal with Dr. Gallingham, but that didn't scare me. I could do this.

I pushed myself away from the building. Before I'd taken two steps, a massive hand slapped across my face and a muscled arm pulled me backward.

"Don't make a sound," a voice hissed, "or I guarantee it will be your last."

20.

SHE CAN'T WAKE UP. Her head lolls from one side of the pillow to the other, and it's as if she has no neck muscles—no muscles of any kind.

When her eyes do flutter open, flapping like the wings of a wounded moth, the world is blurry and out of focus. Only gradually does she make out the water-stained ceiling, bars crisscrossing the windows, rust-covered trays bearing syringes and scalpels. The mere sight of it all causes her to strain against the leather straps.

"Good morning, Sunshine," a man's voice says, whiny and high-pitched.

Hope's eyes land on the heavy man in the dark suit. Dr. Gallingham.

"And here I thought we'd never see you again," he

says cheerfully, his fingers intertwined across the enormous paunch of his belly.

"Wuh um uh huh?" she asks. *Why am I here?* Her tongue is as thick and heavy as an old boot.

"Because we're not done with you. Because you still haven't told us where your father is. Because you can run, but you can . . . not . . . hide." Dr. Gallingham emits a schoolboy giggle, then dabs a moist eye with his soiled hanky.

Her head is still fuzzy. She can't recall how she ended up back here.

"It was a lucky thing you were on that gravel road," the doctor says, as if reading her mind. "We might not've rescued you otherwise."

Although her memories are foggy, *rescue* is not the word she would use.

"You might be wondering what it is you're feeling, and I'm happy to tell you, because I believe in an open dialogue between doctor and patient."

He gestures to a tube that juts from a hanging vial and snakes into her arm. "A form of narcosynthesis. Looked down upon by some in pre-Omega times, but frankly, what's not to like about releasing one's inhibitions?"

He watches as a drip leaves the hanging bag and makes its slow journey down the long plastic pipeline. "Ah, sweet elixir, how do I love thee?" His round face turns toward Hope. "Sodium amytal as a base, but with a few special touches of my own. Scopolamine. Flunitrazepam. And the pièce de résistance: a touch of C_2H_6O—commonly known as ethanol. A kind of truth serum that I like to call 'Gallingham's Potion.' Kind of a fairy-tale ring, wouldn't you say?"

His words roll through her head like pebbles skittering down a hill. She is barely able to make sense of them. Her muscles have gone slack, and she feels herself sinking into the bed, like the snow angels she and Faith made as kids.

"Can you hear me?" Dr. Gallingham asks.

She has just enough strength to nod her head.

"Good. Then let's get started. Do you know who I am?"

Nod.

"Am I Colonel Thorason?"

Shake.

"Chancellor Maddox?"

Shake.

"Dr. Gallingham?"

Nod.

"Excellent. And your name is Faith, right?"

Shake.

"Oh, that's right, it's Hope."

Nod.

With each answer Dr. Gallingham makes a small notation on his clipboard.

"And you were a resident of Camp Freedom, were you not?"

Nod.

"But somehow you got out, didn't you?"

Nod.

"You escaped."

Nod.

"You and nineteen others."

Nod.

"Would you care to tell me how?"

Nod.

"Go ahead."

Hope's mouth falls open, but when she tries to speak, her lips feel clumsy, her tongue heavy and unwieldy.

The doctor bends over her to better hear. "I'm sorry, what was that?"

Again, nothing more than jumbled sounds.

With sausage fingers, Gallingham pries her eyes open and peers into them. "Can you say words?"

She gives her head a shake, and he sighs noisily, as if it's her fault she's too drugged up to speak. "I'll give you a few minutes, no more. After that, we'll get down to business."

He pats her on the leg and walks out of the room.

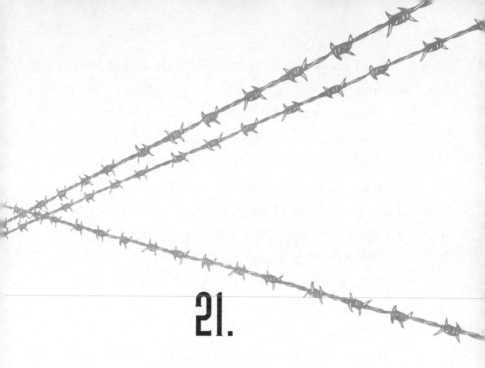

21.

THE MAN'S FINGERS WERE rough and calloused and smelled of metal.

"Don't make a sound, whatever you do," he said. "Understand?"

I nodded, and he whipped me around so fast my neck nearly snapped. My eyes grew wide when I saw who it was. Major Karsten. Cat's source. Cat's *dad*.

"Why'd you do it?" he asked. His eyes were blazing, his jaw jutting forward.

"Why'd I do what?"

"Take that Brown Shirt's weapon and shoot Cat?"

My mouth hung open. "*Me* shoot Cat?"

"And then left him to die in the middle of nowhere."

"That's not it at all. . . ."

"Not to mention abandoning those others on the train."

I tried to speak, but the words got strangled in my throat.

"Well?" Karsten asked, his scar bulging purple.

Tears pressed against my eyes, but there was no way I was going to let Major Karsten see me cry. "It's not the truth," I managed. "And I certainly didn't shoot Cat."

"So Dozer's making that up?"

"Yes, as a matter of fact."

Major Karsten's eyes narrowed. "Why don't you set me straight then," he said.

I laid it all out: the ambush, the shrapnel from the mortar, leaving Cat, Dozer taking over, jumping from the train. Major Karsten listened intently.

When I finished, he studied me long and hard. "So why are you going back to Camp Liberty?"

"To free the remaining Less Thans."

"Because you couldn't reach the other territory?"

"We *did* reach the other territory. We just decided to come back and free the others."

A long silence followed. "So she was right," he said, but it seemed like he was talking more to himself than to me.

Dr. Gallingham emerged from the infirmary, and the major pulled me into the shadows. We waited for him to waddle across the infield and into the Admin Building.

"What's going on here?" I asked. "Who're all these bigwigs?"

"A conference. The less you know about it, the better."

"And the Final Solution? What's that?"

Karsten's eyebrows arched in surprise. "Proof," he finally said.

"Of what?"

"Mankind's capacity for evil." His eyes darkened as he spoke, and he seemed to momentarily forget that I was there. "Why are you here?"

"I need to free those Sisters—get them out of here and to the next territory."

He nodded in understanding, then asked, "Just the Sisters?"

At first I didn't understand what he was getting at. But when I did, it was like a tidal wave sweeping me off my feet.

"Wait. Is Cat here?" I asked.

He nodded grimly.

"He survived?"

Again he nodded.

I couldn't believe it, and the words came gushing out. "Where is he? How's he doing? Is his wound healing? Can I see him?"

Karsten raised his hands. "The only reason he's alive is because the colonel needs to find out who else knows what he knows. Once he talks—or refuses to—they'll sell him off to the Hunters."

"Does Westbrook know you're Cat's father?"

The major peered into my face. "You know that?"

I nodded, and it seemed that Major Karsten regarded me in a new light.

"Westbrook knows Cat's a YO," he said, "and I have a feeling he suspects more. But I don't know for sure."

"So where is he?"

"That's just it—they won't tell me. I know they've brought him here because they hope to interrogate him more, but I haven't been able to find out where he is exactly." He paused and lowered his voice. "But you should know something, Book. Cat's different now. He's not the same as before. Even if you were to find him, the two of you would never get out of here alive. The best thing you can do is escape while you have the chance. Get out of this territory—and as far away from Chancellor Maddox as you can."

He gave a glance to the Admin Building. "I need to get back inside," he said.

He met my eyes. It was the first time I'd looked into his chiseled face and not feared for my life.

"Good luck, Book," he said, and disappeared into the building.

I watched him go and then took off in a mad sprint toward the infirmary. As I ran, I replayed the conversation in my head, and I kept getting stuck on one thing. When I'd told him about going back to Liberty, he'd said something under his breath. *So she was right.*

Who—and what—was he talking about?

I slipped inside the infirmary, raced up the stairs, and made my way down the dark hallway until I reached a room where three of the Sisters lay on beds. Diana, Scylla, and Helen. They were alive, but leather straps held them down. Scylla's head was wrapped in a white bandage, splotched with red. So three of them were here . . . but where was Hope?

I hurried to the next room and there she was, a bedside light casting a warm glow on her body. An IV poked into her arm, and her chest rose and fell with the drowsy rhythm of sleep. I lowered my hand to her shoulder and let it rest there.

"Hope," I whispered. "It's me: Book."

She didn't stir. I nudged her harder.

"Hope, we've got to get out of here. You need to wake up—"

Her eyes snapped open—so abruptly I stumbled backward, knocking the metal tree that held a vial that fed into her veins. My hands fumbled to silence it.

"Daddy?" she said, her voice barely audible.

"No, it's Book."

She went on as though I hadn't spoken. Her eyes were glassy and vacant. "I did my best," she mumbled. Her words were slurred and difficult to understand. "I

155

looked after Faith the best I could."

I felt compelled to respond. "I'm sure you did."

"I saw that she ate and didn't work too hard. . . ."

"You did the right thing."

". . . but I failed, Daddy. I failed." Tears slid down the far corners of her eyes. "They killed her, and I couldn't stop them."

Because her hands and arms were strapped to her sides, I sponged the tears away for her, dabbing at the moisture with my fingertips. For the first time, she seemed to notice me.

"Book," she said.

I smiled weakly. "That's right."

"Booooooook." She elongated my name like a child first learning to speak. "You came."

"I did."

"So you're my shining prince."

"I don't know about that. . . ."

"You came to slay the dragon."

"If you say so."

Her eyes locked with mine. "Kiss me."

I could feel my own eyes widen. "What?"

"Kiss me."

"Maybe now isn't exactly the best time. . . ."

"Kiss me—like you kissed me after the fire."

The truth was, I wanted nothing more than to kiss her again—had dreamed of little else. And here she was, asking me to. *Demanding* it, even. But I didn't want it to be tainted by the fact that she was higher than a kite.

"Another time," I murmured, and covered her with a blanket.

"Oh, don't be so . . . bookish." She giggled at her little joke.

I could have stood there longer, listening to her laugh, enjoying her smile, watching the light glimmer on her lips. But a voice from outside broke the spell. It was Dozer down on the parade ground, shouting to a nearby Brown Shirt.

"He's in there!" he cried, pointing in my general direction. "There's a Less Than in the infirmary!"

I ran back to the other room and fumbled with Diana's buckles. She sat up and unstrapped her ankles while I turned my attention to Helen. Then we untied Scylla together, even as we heard shouts and barked commands from outside. The four of us hurried to the next room.

"Hope, can you hear me?" Diana asked. "Do you know where you are?"

Hope's eyes were as blank and glassy as before. "The castle?"

The three Sisters looked at each other, confused.

"I'll explain later," I mumbled.

A door banged, and I knew Dozer had just gotten in

157

downstairs. Without a word, Scylla exited the room and took off down the corridor. Diana and I unbuckled Hope's straps while Helen removed the needle from her arm.

Things were spinning out of control. Scylla was gone. Dozer and his soldiers were making their way up the stairs. And when we sat Hope up, her body had the muscle control of a rag doll. Her back was slumped, her mouth hanging open.

"Kiss me," she murmured.

Diana gave me a sideways glance.

We slung Hope's arms across our shoulders and maneuvered her through the door, just barely missing Scylla, who was running full speed with a broom in her hand.

We hobbled to the rear of the building, even as Scylla came running back. Behind her, the broom jutted through the door handles, and someone was slamming against the doors. The broomstick nearly bent in half, but it held. For now, at least.

We stumbled down the back stairs. From outside, we heard sirens and barked commands. "Take my place," I said to Scylla, when we reached a reception area.

"Back to the tunnel?" Diana asked.

I shook my head. "There're troops there. We've got to find another way."

"But where? How?"

I had an idea, but I didn't dare say it out loud. It was too far-fetched. Too outlandish. Still, it was the only solution I could come up with.

A large *snap* made us jump—it was the broomstick splintering in two. Racing footsteps and raised voices followed.

"What's the tallest building in camp?" I asked.

Diana gave me a confused look. "The storehouse. . . ."

"Good. We'll meet up there."

They were just about to leave when Hope said, "Cat, why don't you kiss me?"

For a second, it felt as though someone had kicked me in the gut. So that was it. It was Cat she'd been thinking about, not me. Served me right for getting my hopes up.

I turned to the Sisters, who seemed to be waiting for me to say something more.

"Go!" I snapped.

And off they went, stealing out the back door and into the night.

In one corner of the waiting room was an old, ratty armchair. I raced to it and fell to my knees.

I sure hope this works, I thought.

With my knife, I drew a long slit in the upholstery. Big handfuls of stuffing popped out, and I fished the flint from my pocket and began making sparks. They arced in the air, landing harmlessly in the bed of white fiber like so many falling stars.

Come on, I prayed. *Catch. Catch!*

The voices from upstairs grew louder. Footsteps thundered.

A spark caught, igniting a tendril of white padding. I blew on the small flame until it became a ball of fire. I slid the burning chair across the floor so that it rested against the door. That in itself wouldn't prevent the door from opening.

But a raging fire might.

I set two more chairs on fire. Black smoke engulfed the tiny room. From the other side of the door I heard footsteps racing down the stairs and a hand turning the doorknob. A loud curse followed. The flames had turned the knob into a branding iron; someone had just tattooed their hand.

The smoke was making me dizzy and I began to cough, scrambling on hands and knees toward the door. But instead of finding the exit, I ran straight into a wall.

I began to panic, breathing deeper . . . which made me cough harder . . . which made me panic more. I hugged the floor, but there was precious little air. If I didn't get out—*fast*—I'd be a smoking ember. A piece of charcoal.

The room was ablaze. Red and orange flames raced

up the walls. Black smoke billowed, pressing against the ceiling.

I reached the far wall, hands groping for an opening . . . and there was the door! Flames followed me as I hurled myself outside and collapsed on the back stoop, coughing up half a lung.

In the near distance I heard the shouts of soldiers, sirens, vehicles whipping through the parade ground. The infirmary was in flames but I had made it out, and no one knew I was there.

I pushed myself to a standing position and was just beginning to run away when a tremendous *thwack* landed on my forehead. I hit the ground hard, pain exploding from above my eye. Blood rushed down my face.

When I managed to pry my eyes open, I saw Dozer standing over me, wielding an M16 like a baseball bat.

"Good thing for you my weapon jammed," he snarled. "Otherwise, you'd be a dead man by now." He swung again, the butt of the rifle smashing into my right side. I fell backward, grabbing my chest as though it was that easy to repair a broken rib.

"What's the matter?" Dozer asked. "Not so high and mighty without your little dog? Without your *girl-friends*?" His hyena laugh, the flames dancing behind his head—at that moment he was more devil than human being.

There was no point trying to talk Dozer out of killing me. He wouldn't listen to reason. He never had. But there was one thing I could do.

"Don't you want to know where those Sisters are?" I asked.

"I don't give a squat about them. It's you I want."

"Why? Because you sold us out?"

"I didn't sell you out. But you know what? There's more than one way to skin a cat." He smiled maliciously. "Pun intended."

"Don't you get it, Dozer? They're going to kill you when this is done."

He gave his head a shake. "Nuh-uh. I'm too valuable."

"You're not valuable. You're the village idiot."

I could see his face turning brilliant red. I kept going.

"That's why you put people down—because you know it's the only way you can pretend to be smart. The only reason you want to be a leader is so people will like you. Because let's face it: you're not terribly bright, you're not especially good with a bow and arrow, you're certainly not good-looking. In fact, there's nothing special about you at all—you're just a big, dumb, clumsy douchebag who misses his mama's tit."

I'd seen Dozer angry before, but never like this. "You little . . . ," he began, and cocked his rifle like the backswing of a baseball bat—exactly what I was hoping he'd do.

With Dozer halfway through his swing, I pulled out Four Fingers's knife and thrust it into Dozer's thigh. I felt it squish beneath my hand.

Dozer froze a moment, then let out a bloodcurdling scream that shot up to the heavens. The M16 slipped from his hands, and he crumpled to the ground. I pushed myself up and wiped the blood from my eyes. Though woozy from smoke and pain, I still had sense enough to rip the knife from Dozer's leg. There was no way I was going to leave a perfectly good weapon stuck in *him*.

With knife in hand, I turned and ran, realizing that getting out of the infirmary was the easy part. Escaping from Camp Freedom would be the true challenge.

But there was still one more thing I had to do.

There wasn't time to search all of Camp Freedom, but Dozer's comment gave me an idea.

I ran until I reached a small shack. It was an old structure, crudely constructed from pine logs, its lone door made of weathered planking. There were no other doors, no windows at all. An exhaust pipe poked through the roof.

It was the camp's smokehouse—the perfect place to "skin a cat." Although a large padlock gripped the door to the jamb, the hinge itself was old and rusty. I jammed my knife beneath the metal, and the screws squealed as they tore from rotting wood. One quick tug and the hinge flew free.

As I eased inside, the first thing that hit me was the smell: cured meat, stale wood smoke, cold ashes. Once my eyes adjusted to the gloom, I could make out the small, square room with its low wooden beams, festooned with rows of large metal hooks for hanging meat . . . and there hung Cat.

They had tied a rope around his midsection and strung him up from that, his feet dangling just above the dirt floor. He'd lost at least twenty pounds since I'd seen him last, his blue eyes were dull and vacant . . .

. . . and he was missing his left forearm. Some surgeon had cut it off just below the elbow. White gauze was wrapped around the stump, oozing blood.

"What happened to your face?" he asked. His voice was hoarse and sandpapery.

I had forgotten about my appearance. Blood was still trickling down my temple from where Dozer had clobbered me with his rifle.

"Ran into an old friend," I said.

"Dozer?"

I nodded.

"What a douchebag."

"Exactly what I told him." A stampede of footsteps pounded past the door, and I held my breath. "Come on," I said. "We're getting out of here." I began fumbling with his ropes.

Cat recoiled. "I'm not coming."

"What're you talking about?"

"I'm staying here."

"Yeah, right."

"I'm serious."

I studied his eyes to see if he was kidding. He wasn't. "But . . . they'll kill you."

"Let 'em." There was no emotion there whatsoever.

I ignored his request and reached for the ropes. He swatted my hand away.

"Not interested," he snarled.

"But I'm going to help—"

"Not interested," he said again, more forcefully.

I stepped back. Outside, sirens blared and a fire raged.

"But we need you."

A painful smile spread across his face. "You're missing one thing." He lifted what remained of his left arm. "I'm not much good to you now. Not much good to anyone."

"That's not true. You're Cat. You always find a way."

"Not this time. This time they got me. And everyone knows it."

I had heard pessimism from Cat before. Heard him doubt our chances from time to time. But I'd never heard him like this. Karsten was right; Cat had changed.

"But you'll die here."

"There are worse places to die than a girls' camp."

He attempted a smile. His eyes glanced to his stump, then just as quickly darted away—as if he had no desire to look at it. "You better get going, Book. Before they find you." Whatever hopes I'd had about rescuing him evaporated just like that.

"Just thought I'd try," I said.

"Can't blame you for that. So Dozer sold you out?"

"Something like that."

"I figured. Well, you better get going. Say hey to the gang."

"Will do. You sure I can't talk you into going?"

"I'm sure. See you, Book."

"Bye, Cat."

I turned to go, took a step toward the door, then just as quickly pivoted back around. The punch I sent flying was the hardest one I'd ever landed. It caught Cat square on the chin and snapped his head to the side. He gave me a woozy, condemning look before passing out, his body going slack. I lifted him from the meat hook and threw him over my shoulder.

There was no way in the world I was going to leave him behind.

By the time I got him to the storehouse, my legs were jelly. Diana and Scylla helped me lower him to the stoop, their eyes darting between his missing arm and my bloody face. My eyes fell on Hope. "How's she doing?"

"Still out of it," Diana said. "And soldiers are every-where. If we can't get to the tunnel, we're stuck here."

"Not necessarily." But even as I spoke, I doubted myself. What I had in mind might be possible if everyone was healthy, but two of the six of us were still passed out. Kind of a big deal.

Scylla shattered the window and we crawled in one by one, pushing and pulling Cat and Hope like two rag dolls.

"We need rope," I said. "Three-foot sections."

Diana led us to a pile of long coils on a far table, and we whipped out knives.

"Now we need lard," I said.

Diana's eyebrows arched, but she said nothing. She led the way to the foodstuffs, pointing toward a big can of shortening.

"Grease up the ropes," I instructed. "But just the middle, not the ends." They hesitated. "Now!"

While Helen and Diana greased the ropes, Scylla and I tied looped knots on the rope ends. Then we all trudged up the stairway to the third floor, stopping when we reached a small window at the far end.

"This is how we're getting out of here," I said, and the others stared at me as though I'd lost it.

An electrical wire stretched from the storehouse to a pole on the other side of the fence. If I understood the physics of what Twitch had told me about zip lines, all each of us had to do was drape the greased part of the rope over the wire, grab onto the looped ends, and fly from inside the camp to the outside. Piece of cake.

"We won't get electrocuted?" Helen asked.

I shook my head. "I doubt any current's been running through this thing for twenty years."

Diana offered to go first, and we held on to her legs as she stood on the windowsill and tucked her hands into the loops. I counted out loud. "One . . . two . . ."

We pushed on three.

She flew through the night air, the greased rope hissing like a snake. Her weight made the line droop—so much that it looked like she wouldn't clear the razor wire—but at the last moment she brought her knees to her chest and passed over the fence with a good foot to spare. She dangled a moment, let go of the rope, then dropped to the ground below. She rose from a bed of weeds and gave a thumbs-up. Success!

Scylla volunteered to carry Cat, and we wrapped his limp body around her neck like a scarf. We were just about to send them on their way when a platoon of Brown Shirts appeared in the alley beneath us. We froze. They ran by without looking up.

Once more we pushed on three. There was twice as much weight than with Diana, and the line sagged dramatically, concertina wire snagging Scylla's dress. Still, they made it free and clear.

Three down, three to go.

"You're sure you have Hope?" Helen asked.

"I've got her," I said, not sure at all. "Now go."

The frail girl was so light that when I gave her a push, the line barely bent. She had no trouble clearing the fence.

"Our turn," I said to Hope.

She was still wildly out of it, and I had to sling my hands under her armpits just to lift her from the floor. I got us to the windowsill and lashed her hands to the rope loops, but somehow, without meaning to, I gave her a nudge—just enough to send her flying. She glided away from me on the wire before I could grab her and pull her back.

Bad enough we were now separated, but because she lacked any kind of momentum, she came to a dead stop, her body hanging limply.

Oh crap oh crap oh crap.

A splintering of wood told me that Brown Shirts had just crashed open the downstairs door. There was no time for deliberations.

Only time for action.

I leaned back as far as I could and, with all the strength I could muster, pushed off against the building, sailing through air. Ahead, dangling helplessly, was Hope, her body stretching the wire into a deep sag.

The force was more than I expected, but we were moving now, two bodies connected as one, my front pressed into Hope's back. I placed my kneecaps in the crooks of her knees and lifted our legs. A razor tip snagged Hope's dress, but we sailed across the barbed wire. I loosened our knots and we fell to earth, the ground knocking what little air I had in my lungs right out of me.

But we had done it—we had escaped from Camp Freedom.

The three Sisters came running. They lifted Hope off me, and she looked at me in a kind of hazy focus, as though squinting through dense smoke.

"Cat?" she asked. "Is it you? Did you save me?"

"Yeah," I answered in a weary monotone. "Cat saved you."

She collapsed back to the ground.

22.

THEY TAKE REFUGE IN the tunnel, and for three days they crouch in ankle-deep water, breathing the cold, musty air. Only Four Fingers seems happy to be there, making mud pies from the tunnel floor and stacking them like sandbags.

Once Hope's drug-induced state wears off, her eyes land on Cat—a *one-armed* Cat—and her first thought is she's still hallucinating. He sits off to the side, tossing pebbles into the water and repeating the same few words over and over. "You shouldn't've done it, Book. You shouldn't've saved me."

At the far end is Book. He ignores Cat and seems to want nothing to do with Hope. She can't figure it out.

"So what happened?" Flush asks Cat. No one's spoken a word in hours.

"What do you mean?"

"Your arm. What'd they do?"

Cat's jaw clenches. "What do you think? The doctor chopped it off."

"So Book's strategy worked. He saved you."

"Whatever." His words ooze bitterness.

"At least you're alive. You should be grateful."

"Well, just wait," he says ominously.

If the others weren't paying attention before, they are now.

"What're you talking about?" Flush asks.

"Yeah, what do you know?" Diana demands.

For a long moment, Cat regards the eight others. Then he scatters his remaining handful of pebbles into the water. "The time may come when we'll wish we were already dead," he says, and shuts his eyes. Conversation over.

Hope remembers the final paragraph from the chancellor's letter—words she hasn't shared with the others. *A Final Solution to the question of the Less Thans and Sisters. Complete and utter annihilation. Leave no trace of their existence.* She wonders how the Republic intends to carry this out. Wonders also if that secret meeting on the road between Maddox and Gallingham is related.

After three days and nights, they ease up the ladder and hurry through the woods in scant moonlight, munching dandelions and chickweed to stem their gnawing hunger. There is no sign of Brown Shirts.

They stop at sunrise, burying themselves in thick underbrush. Hope tiptoes to a nearby brook to fill her canteen . . . only to discover that Book is already there. She unscrews the lid and lowers the canteen into the trickle of water.

After what seems like forever, Book says, "You don't have to thank me, you know, but I did risk my life for you."

"Was that before or after you lied to me?"

Book's eyebrows reach for his hairline. "You're not still thinking about that thing with the infirmary?"

"Yes, as a matter of fact, I am. 'That thing' where you promised you wouldn't step foot inside that building."

"But it's a good thing I went in there," he says. "It gave me the layout of the building. I knew where to find you. I was able to go right to where the four of you were."

She gives her head a shake. "You didn't need a special visit to find us."

"So what're you saying? I shouldn't have gone back in? I should've just left the four of you to get out on your own?"

"No . . ."

"Then what?"

"I'm saying you don't look someone in the eye and promise one thing and then do the opposite."

She finishes filling her canteen and gets up. She's done with this conversation. Done with Book. Although she's grateful he came back for her, the fact is he lied to her. There's no getting past it.

She's walking away when Book blurts out, "This is all about Faith, right?"

She stops. Dust motes dance in diagonals of light. Book reaches into his pocket and pulls out two objects. He extends them to Hope.

When she sees that they're pictures of her and Faith, something catches at the back of her throat. Her hand flies to her mouth. "Where'd you get these?" she asks.

"Your overseer's office. The night you were captured. They tried to burn everything, but they were in too much of a hurry."

Hope takes the singed pictures. Her fingers run along the outline of her sister, as if her fingertips were magic wands and the mere act of tracing could bring her back.

"So now I know a little more," Book says. "How you came to camp. *When* you came to camp. I don't know how she died, but . . ." He lets the sentence dangle before going on. "I went into the infirmary because I want to know you better—to understand you—and that was the only thing I could think of doing."

Hope's gaze never leaves the photos. She can't take her eyes off them.

174

"It's like we've had these moments—escaping the cave-in, the flooded tunnel, the fire—but I almost don't know whether I should believe them or not. Did we really kiss? Did we really hold each other like we couldn't let go? Did all that happen? Because the way you treat me sometimes . . . I don't know if I've been dreaming the whole thing or not."

Hope nods but says nothing. When she lifts her eyes from the photos and glances at Book, he is staring at her, his face radiating warmth. She has to look away. When she finally speaks, her voice is soft, hesitant, nearly a whisper.

"I don't know what to say, Book. I'm grateful you put your life on the line for me. I appreciate that. I do. And we'll go with you to your camp and free those Less Thans, because we said we would." She hesitates.

"But?"

She looks up and meets his eyes. "I don't think I can trust you ever again."

Book opens his mouth to speak, but she turns and marches away, not once glancing back.

They hike by night and sleep by day, trailing the Sisters' footprints in the gravel road. Hope marches in front of the line, Book in the rear. They sleep at opposite ends of camp. There's always a considerable distance between them.

Not that Hope doesn't think about him—she does that all the time. The press of their lips when they kissed. How their hands fit into each other when they touched. She even has a vague memory of flying through the air, Book's body holding her, protecting her, *caressing* her. But even though these memories send a tingle down her spine, there is no getting past the fact that Book lied to her.

So why does she feel a stab of regret? Why can't she stop second-guessing her decision to push him away?

One night, Hope tells everyone to hold up. The tone of her voice stops them cold. In pale moonlight, she bends down and picks something up. She turns it over in her hand. An empty shell casing. Argos gives it a sniff.

"Big deal," Flush says. "Probably pre-Omega."

"It's not," Cat says, and everyone turns, surprised to hear the sound of his voice. It's been days since he last spoke. "Too shiny."

"So who does it belong to?"

"Take your pick. Brown Shirts. Crazies. Hunters. Skull People. Does it really matter?"

Hope knows that soldiers have been here—she's been following their tread marks as much the Sisters' footprints—but the fact that one of these other groups could have been on this road raises the hair on the back of her neck.

They spread out, and it's not long before Hope notices

a break in the weeds. She and Diana creep forward, Diana with her crossbow, Hope with a spear. Flush and Book follow with slingshots. The weeds brush against their legs until they're in the middle of a large, rolling meadow. If it's an ambush they're stepping into, they're dead for sure. No place to hide at all.

Perhaps it's harmless, Hope thinks. Some soldier stepped off the road and left a narrow trail of matted-down weeds.

Crickets quiet as they approach. The only sounds are their hearts thudding against their chests. Hope's knuckles shine white from gripping the spear.

A large oak tree stands in the middle of the meadow, its twisted branches forming a wide umbrella. At first the path seems to lead straight toward it, but then it meanders in another direction. *Why?* Hope wonders. *Why leave the road and then reverse direction?*

Then she sees.

There at the trail's end, lying facedown in the tall grasses, is an inmate from Camp Freedom. A Sister . . . with a gaping hole in the back of her head.

Hope turns the body over, giving a start when she sees the eye patch over one of the girl's eyes.

"You know her?" Diana asks.

"I met her once." Hope remembers the girl giving her water in the infirmary. She was kind to Hope, even when Hope wasn't especially kind in return.

They piece it together. A Sister attempts to escape, weaving through waist-high grass. A Brown Shirt, standing on the gravel road, needs only the one bullet to bring her down.

The bigger question is: Where are the Sisters being taken?

Hope makes her way back to the road. She has just stepped onto gravel when they hear the distant thrum of an engine. When they realize it's a vehicle headed in their direction, they dive into the bushes.

A military transport carrier pulls up, and two Brown Shirts emerge. They click on flashlights, their weak beams parting the tall grasses.

"Pretty sure there's one around here somewhere," one of them says, his yellow circle of light darting from one side of the road to the other.

"Sure smells that way," the other responds. The two soldiers laugh.

When their beams land on the narrow trail, they go tromping through the weeds, returning moments later with the dead Sister in their arms. They swing her body back and forth before tossing her into the carrier. Hope notices other corpses there as well. More Sisters.

"That should be the last of them," the first Brown Shirt says.

"For now."

They both snicker, get back in the vehicle, and turn it around. It's a long forever before the red taillights vanish into black.

The Sisters and Less Thans emerge from the bushes and ease back onto the road. Their steps are hurried now, brisk, urgent. Although they come across no more corpses, they see the clues. Shell casings. Scuff marks in the gravel. Bits of discarded clothing.

They walk the rest of the night, saying little. Thoughts swirl through Hope's head like dust across a barren field, and the list in her mind becomes more definite than ever.

Thorason, Maddox, and Gallingham. Their time will come . . . or she will die trying.

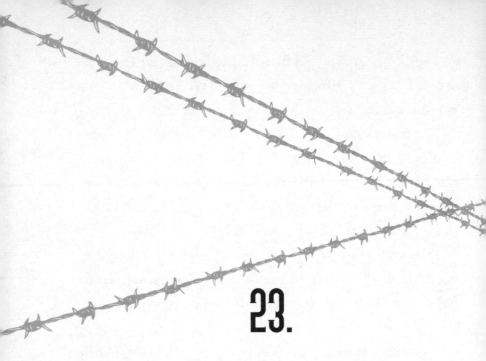

23.

I APPROACHED HOPE THE next morning while we were setting up camp.

"We need to tell them," I said. It was the first time we'd spoken in days.

"What're you talking about?"

"The letter we read in your overseer's office. We need to tell the others. No more secrets."

Her eyes shot daggers, and she seemed about to turn away until her gaze fell on Diana, Scylla, and Helen. They had stopped what they were doing and were listening to us.

Hope exhaled noisily and took a step forward. "Back before we escaped from Camp Freedom, Book and I broke into Thorason's office and found a letter. From Chancellor Maddox. It said they needed a Final Solution to the question of the Less Thans and the Sisters."

A long silence followed.

"What's 'the question' of the Less Thans and Sisters?" Diana finally asked.

"What they're going to do with us." Then Hope corrected herself. "Or what they're going to do *to* us."

"According to the letter," I said, "the government intends to kill us all. And 'leave no trace.'"

Even as sunlight crept through the trees, it felt as though all the oxygen had been sucked out of camp.

"They want to wipe us out?" Flush asked.

"Pretty much."

"Why would they do that?"

Hope shrugged. "You'd have to ask the chancellor."

"And you didn't want to tell us this before?" Diana asked.

"I thought it'd make everyone panic."

A sudden breeze rustled through the trees, smelling of dust and an approaching storm. That two individuals hoped to wipe out a whole group of people was more than we could understand. I'd known about the letter and I still couldn't quite believe it.

Flush turned to Cat. "Did you know about this?"

"No, but I'm not surprised."

"So now what?" Helen asked, her chin quivering.

"Simple," Hope said. "We have to catch up with the Sisters and free them. Before it's too late."

"And then?"

"We'll worry about that later."

She packed up her belongings and abruptly marched off, abandoning camp. The rest of us followed.

The road was littered with clothing scraps, shell casings . . . and corpses, their decomposing bodies not yet claimed by Brown Shirts. At one point we stumbled across a set of twins, their fingers intertwined like vines, as if they'd made the decision to die together.

When the rain came, it was a blessing and a curse. It soaked us to the bone and made the road a soggy mess, but it also tamped down the stench of death that hung in the air like morning fog. We sloshed through mud and gravel, each in our own private world. There was a fury building in me. I was angry at the Brown Shirts, angry at Chancellor Maddox, angry at a world that cast us as victims. I was tired of being prey. Whenever anyone tried to talk to me, I grunted and moved away. I was in no mood for conversation.

Darkness fell, but we kept going. We had to catch up with the Sisters. It was just past midnight when we first caught a glimpse of a campfire—a small orange flame cutting a hole in the black. We lowered ourselves to the ground and inched forward.

Five Brown Shirts had set up camp in a rotting barn. While they huddled around the fire just in front of the open door, behind them, lying huddled on the floor, were scores of Sisters, their withered bodies racked with shivering, their eyes sunken and hollow. A series of crisscrossing ropes created a makeshift fence that confined them to the back of the barn.

I had not seen these Sisters before, but judging by Hope's reaction, they had never been like this. Even tough Diana brought her hand to her mouth, covering it in disbelief. These captured Sisters were more like walking skeletons than actual human beings.

We retreated and laid out a plan. The five Brown Shirts had us outmanned in terms of weapons, but if we were smart, we could use the darkness as an equalizer. When Hope came to the part about "taking out Brown Shirts," I stopped her.

"What do you mean by that?" I asked.

"What do you think I mean? Kill 'em."

I gave my head a shake. "Uh-uh. We're better than that."

We'd been forced to kill in the past, it was true, but if there was any way to avoid it, I thought we should. Maybe it had something to do with not wanting to turn into the very people we were fleeing from.

"So what do you suggest?" Hope asked impatiently.

"Free the Sisters, capture the Brown Shirts. Period."

Hope rolled her eyes. "And what'll prevent the soldiers from coming after us?"

"I don't know. Tie them up, take their boots—do something so they *can't* come after us."

Hope shot a look at Diana and Scylla.

"Fine," she said. "We'll do it your way. But if things get out of hand . . ."

". . . then yes. We'll do what we have to do."

We buried ourselves in the bushes and tried to grab some sleep. An hour later, Hope woke me with a hard slap on the face. The others she gave a gentle nudge.

Cat and Helen stayed back with Twitch and Four Fingers. It was impossible for me to read Cat's expression. Was he depressed that he couldn't come with us? Or had he already given up? On us? On success? On *living*?

The rain had stopped by the time we crept forward, approaching the barn from the side. The Brown Shirts' fire had faded to embers, and four of them were sleeping just inside the rotting structure. The fifth was on watch, sitting by the dying fire.

Diana went first, crawling through the weeds. When she was in position, I launched a pebble from my slingshot, and the soldier on watch sat up, pulling a pistol from its holster. I waited a moment, then sent a second rock flying. The Brown Shirt threw himself to his feet, his 9mm aimed in the direction where the rocks had landed.

He never saw her coming. Diana sprang forward and tucked the gleaming knife edge beneath his chin. Even in the dark, we could see the enormous whites of his eyes.

"Drop it!" she hissed.

He made a move with his pistol, and she dug the knife even deeper into his neck. "Drop it!" she said again.

Reluctantly, he tossed his weapon to the ground.

We raced for the barn. Hope, Flush, Scylla, and I were each assigned a Brown Shirt, and, like Diana had, we placed our knives against their throats until the blades bit into flesh. Only Scylla's fought back, grabbing his rifle and firing off three quick rounds into the rafters. There was a great flapping of wings as pigeons scattered.

She jabbed an elbow into his nose and then disarmed him when he went to stop the flow of blood. As the gun went clattering to the side, she pressed her knife blade extra hard into his neck.

"All good?" I called out.

One by one, Diana, Hope, and Flush answered Yes. Scylla, chest heaving, gave a nod.

I breathed a sigh of relief. All things considered, it had been quick and painless. And no one had been killed in the process.

"Well done," I said to the others.

Then we heard the click of a rifle . . . and a soldier's voice cutting through the dark.

"Not so fast," he said, and I realized I'd spoken too soon.

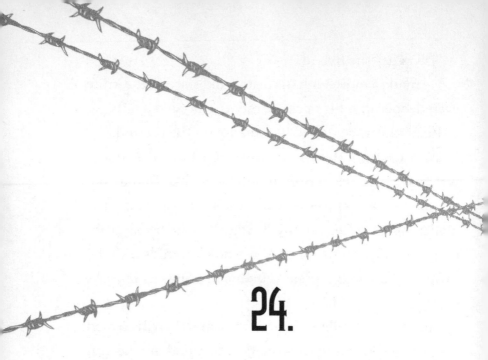

24.

THE BROWN SHIRT STANDS in the back of the barn, rifle raised.

"Why don't you all put your little knives down and step away," he says. Once he emerges from the shadows, Hope recognizes his jutting chin. He was the one who tattooed the number on her arm when she first arrived at Camp Freedom.

"Maybe you didn't hear me," he says, going right for Flush and placing the rifle barrel against his temple.

"We heard you," Hope says, "but it doesn't mean we'll listen to you." She presses her knife even farther into her captive's skin. It dimples like a plucked bird's.

Her response brings a crooked smile to Jutting Chin. "Fine with me. But remember: I'm the one with the gun."

For a long, tense moment, no one does or says anything. Even the captive Sisters, who have stumbled awake, barely move. It's a standoff. A high-stakes game of chicken. Then the Brown Shirt reaches into his back pocket and removes something black and bulky. A walkie-talkie.

"Delta Mike One calling Foxtrot Charlie—do you copy? Over."

In the seconds that follow, a dozen different scenarios run through Hope's mind: capture, return to Camp Freedom, Dr. Gallingham, experiments. Sweat pools on the back of her neck.

Jutting Chin pushes the button again. "Delta Mike One to Foxtrot Charlie, do you read? Acknowledge. Over."

A muffled voice emerges from the staticky speaker, and Hope's heart sinks. It's over. Done. No escape.

Just as she's thinking this, two gun blasts rock the barn. Sisters scream and Hope flinches, as Jutting Chin crumples to the ground, his rifle rattling to the side. Hope looks around.

Cat. Gripping the lookout soldier's pistol, a tendril of smoke curling from the barrel.

Hope doesn't hesitate. She draws her knife across her captive soldier's throat, causing an eruption of crimson. The Brown Shirt's eyes open wide before he slumps to the barn floor. Scylla does the same with her soldier; he collapses.

"No!" Book screams. "Stop!"

But they don't stop. Diana takes the pistol from Cat, lowers her knife, and shoots the lookout soldier at point-blank range.

That leaves only two Brown Shirts: the captives of Flush and Book.

"What are you doing?" Book demands.

"We said we'd do it your way," Hope replies, wiping the blood off with her dress. "Unless things got out of hand."

"But they *weren't* out of hand! Cat got the guy! We were in control!" Book is nearly screaming.

Hope gives her head a disgusted shake and motions to the two remaining soldiers. "What happens after we tie 'em up?"

"We leave 'em."

"And when they free themselves and tell Chancellor Maddox we were here? What then?"

"Like I said, we take their boots, their weapons. That way they can't follow us."

"No, but they could talk—give our location away."

At that moment there's a muffled squawk. "Delta Mike One, this is Foxtrot Charlie, do you copy? Over."

Everyone's eyes land on the walkie-talkie lying on the barn floor.

"Delta Mike One, this is Foxtrot Charlie, do you copy? Over."

At first, no one knows what to do. Then Hope walks over to the corpse of Jutting Chin, picks up his rifle, and places the barrel next to the walkie-talkie. She fires half a dozen shots until it's nothing more than a hundred pieces of smoldering black plastic. She turns to Book.

"Well?" she asks. "What're you waiting for? Tie 'em up so we can get going."

But even as she says it, she wonders if it's the right thing. Why should they show any mercy for the Brown Shirts? When did the Brown Shirts ever show any mercy for them?

The rescued Sisters are more dead than alive. Their arms and legs look more like twigs than human limbs, and pelvic bones jut against frayed dresses. Their hair is matted with mud, and oozing, pus-filled sores dot their faces. Of the hundred and twenty-five who were marched out of Camp Freedom, only sixty have survived.

Hope knows they have to get out of there fast—it won't be long before other Brown Shirts come looking. But when the Sisters shuffle forward, their bodies torque and twist like the walking dead. Outrunning the Brown Shirts is out of the question.

They leave the road and follow a stream, which empties into a large blue lake, bordered by leafy trees. On the far side are a dozen cottages. A badly faded bill-board from pre-Omega days identifies them as Dodge's Log Lodges. While they're all in various states of disre-pair, they at least have walls and roofs. The group will stop here for a day or two.

As they rip down cobwebs and sweep out cabins, Hope wants to think they're up for the challenges ahead of them. But the reality is they have no clear plan, the sick and dying far outnumber the healthy, and they can't even agree on what to do with prisoners. And now that Chancellor Maddox seems more intent than ever on implementing the Final Solution, Hope wonders if there's really any stopping her at all.

More than once she wants to break down and weep, but she cannot let herself.

Live today, tears tomorrow.

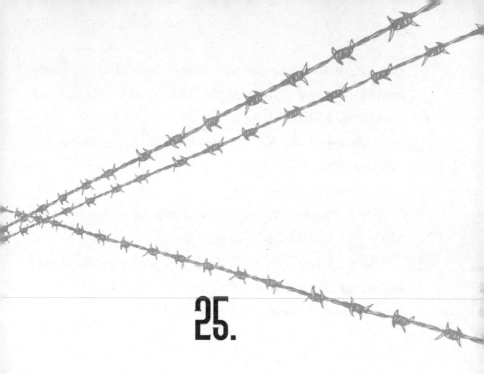

25.

WE GAVE THE CABINS to the Sisters; the Less Thans slept outside. I found a grassy area beneath a willow tree and began preparing my bed. Cat sat off to the side, throwing pebbles into the lake. *Plop.*

"You can help me if you want," I said.

Plop.

"Maybe clear out this area."

Plop.

"Or gather wood for a fire."

Plop. Plop.

I still couldn't get over it. What had happened to the *real* Cat? I wondered. The guy with a million skills and even more ideas? Even after coming to our rescue at the barn, he'd just walked away—like he wanted no part of us. To make matters worse, he had found three bottles of whiskey in a supply closet and seemed intent on getting himself drunk.

"They can't make it." Hope. I hadn't heard her come up behind us.

"Who can't make what?"

"These Sisters. They can't make it to Camp Liberty. They'd be lucky to get another mile."

I knew she was right—I did. And yet, hearing it from her so bluntly made me angrier than it should have.

"You just decided that on your own?"

"Along with the other Sisters, yeah."

"Well, thanks for asking my opinion."

I whipped the willow branches to the side. It was bad enough Hope preferred Cat over me; now she didn't even care what I had to say.

"So you think they're capable of making it there?" she asked.

"I'm not saying that."

"Then what are you saying?"

"Only that it would be nice if I was allowed to have a say in all this." I tossed the branches down on the ground.

Hope gave an exasperated sigh. "So do you disagree with the decision or not?"

"No . . ."

"Then why're you getting so upset?"

"Because you don't trust me, that's why."

"Why should I?" she said. "After you promised not to step inside—"

"I know, I know, I broke your promise. I went inside a building I wasn't supposed to go into, I'm sorry. But you never even told me *why* I wasn't supposed to go into it in the first place."

"That shouldn't matter."

"And how about you, huh? Running off with Cat in the middle of the night. Sneaking around behind my back. And then, just last night, you promised not to hurt those Brown Shirts. You think I trust *you?*"

"We made a deal. We said if things got out of hand—"

"That's just it—they weren't out of hand! Cat got the gunman! We had the others covered. There was no reason to kill them."

Hope was clenching her jaw so tightly, I thought she might crack a tooth. She glanced at Cat, but he took a long pull from his bottle, acting like we weren't even there.

"Listen," she hissed, "when you've gone through what we've gone through, maybe you'll understand. In the meantime, you have no right to judge."

"But that's just it! I don't know what you've gone through because you won't talk about it. I saw those pictures in the infirmary; I saw you and your sister; but I still don't understand. Not really."

Hope glared at me.

"You want to understand?" she said.

"Yes."

"You really want to know what happened to me?"

"Yes!"

"Fine. I had a twin sister. *All of us* had twin sisters. And the Western Federation Territory somehow thought it'd be a good idea to test out their new drugs on us, even if that meant killing a few in the process. Dr. Gallingham injected us with who knows what, and when he got tired of that, he did other things, terrible things, like yanking out our teeth and ripping off our fingernails and burning us with cigarettes, just to see how much pain we could endure. Or how much cold."

Hope's voice suddenly broke. Her nose began to run, and she wiped it angrily with the back of her hand.

"I watched Faith die and there was nothing I could do about it, even though I'd promised I'd always be there for her. When they pulled her from that ice water, I was helpless. She died, cold and alone. Now there's just one of us—me."

She looked up, her brown eyes meeting mine. Once more, it felt like her gaze penetrated my soul. "Maybe we didn't need to kill those soldiers—maybe you're right. But I know what they're capable of, and so do all the Sisters." Her eyes dropped, as if she'd said too much.

I wanted to speak, if only to say *I'm sorry*, but for some reason I couldn't find the strength. Even as Hope continued to stare at me, *expecting* me to say something, I had no words.

"As for Cat," she went on, "we *were* sneaking off in the middle of the night, but it's not what you're thinking. He was helping me search for my childhood home. My dad chose a house that was hidden in the woods, and I thought it might have been around there. I needed— well, it doesn't matter what I needed. Cat and I never found it."

My heart sank. I felt suddenly nauseous. To think I'd been jealous of her for that.

She gave her head a sad, disappointed shake. "Oh, Book, I have nothing more to say to you."

She turned and started to walk away.

"Does that mean you're not coming with us to Camp Liberty?"

She stopped. Her mouth opened wide in surprise. "Is that what you want?"

"I don't know. Is that what *you* want?"

She didn't answer—I didn't speak—and for the longest time it was just the wind rustling the leaves.

Finally, I said, "If we have nothing to say to each other, then no, I don't want you to come. We'll free those Less Thans on our own."

"Is that really what you want?"

"I just said so, didn't I?"

She opened her mouth to speak, but no words came. She turned and walked off. I looked over at Cat. He didn't say a word, just kept drinking his whiskey and tossing pebbles into the lake.

It suddenly felt like the whole world had turned against me. In a few short days I'd lost Cat and Hope both, and that realization made me sadder than anything I could possibly imagine.

We stayed there three days, long enough to catch fish, gather berries, construct some bows and arrows. When the group of us Less Thans prepared to leave one night, the Sisters gathered to see us off.

Hope was not among them.

We'd lost our bearings since rescuing the Sisters and weren't clear where we were—only that Camp Liberty was somewhere to the north of us.

Before, Twitch and Cat had guided us, using nothing but the sun and stars to get us to the Heartland. But Twitch was blind and Cat had stopped caring. He trailed along in the dark, the bottles rattling around in his backpack.

"Why didn't you just apologize?" Flush asked out of the blue. We were walking on the edge of a long-neglected field. Argos was by my side.

"Apologize for what?" I asked.

"For whatever you said to Hope. I mean, it's obvious you said or did something you shouldn't have and that's the reason she's not coming."

I felt my jaw tighten. What did Flush know about it all? And how dare he pretend to lecture *me*? "What if I don't have anything to apologize for?"

"You really don't?"

"No," I said firmly.

Flush gave a casual shrug. "I mean, I don't know much about anything, and you're a couple years older than me, but there's always something to apologize for, isn't there?"

"All I did was go into the infirmary. And she was the one who killed those Brown Shirts when we urged her not to. So, stepping inside a building versus killing some unarmed human beings. No difference there whatsoever."

"I'm not sure sarcasm becomes you."

"Well, if I can't be sarcastic, I've got nothing left."

My words wafted across the vacant field. When Flush finally responded, his voice was steady, calm, even a little quiet. I had to strain to hear him.

"I used to think we'd live forever. Even as crappy as things were back at Liberty, I just figured we'd all have long, full lives. But then we saw what the Hunters did. And Frank died. And June Bug. And those Sisters. And now I know different."

"So what's that have to do with anything?" I asked impatiently.

Flush turned to me. "I don't know about you, but I just want to make sure I make the most of my time here and don't let anything get in the way of that."

By the time I thought that through, Flush was a good ten paces ahead of me.

We marched for two straight days, and whenever we crested a hill, I took a long look behind us.

"What're you staring at?" Cat asked.

"Just making sure we're not being followed," I said.

But the truth was I was looking for Hope, longing to see her come tearing through a tangle of trees, spear in hand, ready to join up with us once again . . . even though I knew the odds were hard against it.

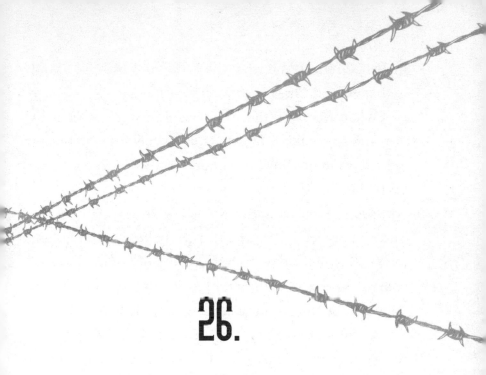

26.

IT'S BETTER THIS WAY, Hope tells herself. *I'm needed here.*

And it's true. Every healthy Sister is necessary to nurse the sick ones back to life. A few succumb to dysentery right away, and more would follow if not for the swift actions of Helen. Hope realizes it's a very different Helen from the one who relied on her sister for everything.

As for Book, Hope doesn't let herself think of him. *I've got my hands full here,* she tells herself. *Let him help his Less Thans and I'll help my Sisters.*

At least, that's what she tries to tell herself.

Then there's the other issue. If Hope can piece together where the Sisters were being taken, it will help her understand what the Territory's plan is . . . and where to find Chancellor Maddox.

"When were you told you were leaving?" Hope asks a young girl named Sarah. Hope is feeding her sips of warm broth, sliding the spoon between Sarah's trembling lips.

Sarah's body is so thin, Hope is able to watch the liquid journey from her mouth down her throat. Although Hope's instinct would be to feed her gobs of food, Helen warns against it. If they eat too much too soon, they'll actually die; their stomachs can't handle it.

"At dinner one night," Sarah says. "The guards came in and started shouting. Said we had to go on a march." She lowers her voice as she remembers. "Some girls didn't even have boots."

"And the Brown Shirts didn't care that so many were sick?"

Sarah's bony shoulders rise and drop in a shrug. "I overheard one of them say, 'Just makes our job easier.'"

Hope remembers the corpses along the side of the road. She stirs the spoon in the bowl of broth; it clanks against the edges.

"Where were you going?"

"They wouldn't tell us. 'Not long now' was all they said. Every hour, every day—'Not long now.'"

"Is your sister here?" Hope asks.

Sarah shakes her head no.

"Did you lose her on the march or before?"

"Before," Sarah answers. "Long before."

"I'm sorry. How about the others from your barracks?"

"There's no one from my barracks. I'm the only one left."

Her words cut Hope's heart in two, and she has to hurry out of the room. She finds Helen in the kitchen of one of the other cottages, cutting pieces of willow bark into small chunks. "So . . . when do we give them solid food?"

Helen barely looks up. In the other room, a half dozen Sisters lie on cots or tables—wherever there's a flat surface. Their rasping coughs punctuate the still afternoon. "Another day or two. And even then, not much."

"How soon till they can move?"

Helen measures out several teaspoons of the bark and puts it into a pot of boiling water. "Not soon."

"Days? Weeks?"

"Months," Helen answers.

Hope nods absently, watching the willow bark turn and twist in the roiling water, staining it red. She wonders how long before Brown Shirts will discover them. Wonders something else as well.

"You may as well tell me," Helen says.

"Tell you what?"

"Whatever's going through your head."

"Who says there's something—"

"Hope."

Helen gives her friend a look, and Hope knows there's no point denying it. She has an idea—an outlandishly crazy idea. And if she doesn't share it, if she doesn't act on it, she's afraid she never will . . . and then who knows where her life will lead?

She looks around to make sure no one's within earshot, grasps the locket around her neck, then leans in and begins to speak.

27.

WE HAD FINALLY EMERGED through a line of trees and found ourselves at the edge of a high limestone cliff. Far below us was a ribbon of brown—a swift, wide, muddy river. It was a good half mile wide.

"How're we supposed to get across *that*?" Flush asked.

We had managed to ford dozens of streams, even floated down one flood-swollen river, but those were nothing compared to this. This was a *river*. We watched as an enormous tree was swept down the rapids like a toothpick.

I looked at Cat, thinking he might offer a suggestion. He avoided my eyes and slurped from a bottle.

We hugged the cliff and marched north, reaching a railroad bridge an hour or so later. It was old and weathered, with huge stone pilings jutting from the river. But there was a problem: one of the metal arches had collapsed into the water, leaving a gaping chasm of about twenty feet. Gusts of hot wind keened and whistled through the twisted metal.

And then came an even stranger sound. Peals of laughter. From Cat.

"What's so funny?" I demanded.

He wobbled on the parched earth and gestured with his stump in the direction of the broken bridge. "This." As he collapsed into a fit of giggles, I felt my body stiffen. "We were safely in the other territory. *In the Heartland!* Now we can't get to Liberty and we won't make it back to the other side. Face it, Book. We're beat. We never shoulda left the other territory."

I gave Cat a hard shove. Because of his drunken state, he fell to the ground, and one of the bottles in his backpack broke, flooding the dirt with brown liquid. I jumped on top of him and began pummeling him with angry punches. It was the rainy infield back at Camp Liberty all over again—the day Cat had first told me I was a Less Than. The difference now was that I knew how to hit . . . and he was half drunk and only had one arm.

When I'd had enough, I threw myself off. Flush, Twitch, and Four Fingers stood to one side.

"Done so soon?" Cat asked. He spat out a mouthful of blood and maybe a tooth. "Why not finish me off?"

"If I had any sense, I would," I said.

"What's stopping you? I've only got one arm. I can't fight back."

"That's where you're wrong."

"Uh, in case you didn't notice . . ." He held up his bandaged stump. The gauze was black with dried blood and dirt.

"You're missing *part* of an arm," I said. "That doesn't mean you have to roll over and die."

"I'm not—"

"You *are*. You've given up. The old Cat—the Cat who shot the propane tank to save us from the Hunters—he would've fought back. He wouldn't be drinking himself to death. But you . . ." I shook my head. "You're nothing like the old Cat. You're nothing at all."

"If I was sober, I could take you."

"Fine! Take me! Fight back! Just *do* something!"

For the longest time, Cat didn't respond. No one did. Finally, Cat stared at his stump as if noticing it for the first time. "And what do I do about this?"

I pointed at my short leg, at Four Fingers's hands, at Twitch's bandaged eyes. "The same thing all of us do. Adapt. Get used to it."

I pushed myself from the ground and walked away. I didn't want anything to do with him.

Flush and Twitch came up with an idea. If there was a twenty-foot gap across the bridge, then we needed a thirty-foot span, and there were plenty of logs in the forest that would do the trick.

But there was a problem.

"How're we going to *move* it?" I asked. "I mean, it could weigh a ton." I didn't bother to state the obvious. Twitch was blind. Cat was passed out.

"Slide logs," Twitch said. While he spoke, Flush sketched a diagram in the dirt. "We place the tree on five small logs and then roll the tree forward. When we uncover the last log, we move it to the front so it becomes the lead log. We just keep rotating them."

I gave them both a glance. "Where'd you learn this?"

"It's Flush's idea." He angled his head in the direction of his friend.

Flush beamed. "And I got it from one of Twitch's science magazines. An article about the pyramids."

"You really think we can do this?"

"Do we have a choice?"

We found an old log that looked to be about thirty feet long, then cut and shaped the slide logs to go under it. The sun beat down on us, and our bodies glistened with sweat. Cat remained passed out in a bed of ferns.

Every so often I heard a rustling from the trees, but when I looked—hoping to catch some glimpse of Hope stepping through the woods—it was nothing more than a ground squirrel, curious to see what we were up to.

When we finally had the pieces in place and gave the thirty-foot log a push, nothing happened. Not on the first try or the second or the third.

Flush walked over to Cat and gave him a kick. "Come on. You're helping us."

Cat held up his stump. "I've only got one arm."

"One arm is all you need."

Cat growled and stumbled to his feet. This time, when we all leaned into it, the log moved. Just an inch or two, but still.

Flush and Twitch were beaming with pride. Four Fingers was giggling like a child. And when I looked behind me, there was Cat, his good shoulder pressed against the log's end. His heart might not have been in it, but his muscles were.

We rolled that tree all day and much of the night, rotating the slide logs, not stopping until we reached the bridge's gap. The next afternoon, Flush created a pulley system from the bridge's arches. We helped him raise the log one inch at a time, and when it was high enough, we rocked it forward and back like a pendulum. At just the right moment, Flush cut the rope and let the log fall . . . right across the missing span.

We cheered like crazy. Four Fingers was shouting, Twitch and I were screaming, Flush did a little dance, and Argos howled and howled. Only Cat was silent, chugging long swigs of his amber-tinted liquid.

After all that, shimmying to the other side was a piece of cake. Even Argos trotted across like it was the easiest thing in the world.

The train tracks led us to the middle of an enormous cornfield—the largest cultivated field we'd ever encountered. We harvested some ears, stripping off the husks and eating the corn raw. The kernels were crunchy and sweet and exploded in our mouths.

A flash of movement at the far end of the row caught my eye.

"Did you see that?" I asked.

"Probably just a fox," Flush replied, far more concerned about food than about some wild animal.

A moment later, I caught another glimpse. "How about that?"

Flush just kept on eating.

But when we heard the rustling of leaves, we tossed the corn to the ground and fumbled for weapons. I aimed my arrow first in one direction, then another. Argos growled.

"Looking for someone?"

The voice whipped me around, and I nearly released the bowstring before I saw who it was.

Hope. It was Hope. She stood in the middle of a row of corn, spear in hand. Black hair framed her face. Her eyes sparkled with sunshine. I'd never been so happy to see her in my life. At her side were Diana and Scylla.

Flush and I lowered our weapons.

"You're here," I said. After all the hours I'd spent thinking of her, those were the first words I could think of to say. "I thought you were going to stay with the others."

Hope shared a look with her two friends. "I had this crazy idea we should join you. Besides, Helen's got it under control."

"So does this mean you're going with us to Liberty?"

"We're here, aren't we?"

Just like that, Flush was screaming in my ear. "You hear that? They're going with us! They're going to help us free the LTs."

He began whooping and hollering and did another little dance, and that made Four Fingers whoop and holler and Argos bark, and even Diana and Scylla got in on the act, exchanging high fives with each of the guys. Only Cat, Hope, and I didn't join in the celebration.

I wondered what it was that had changed Hope's mind, and I felt this overwhelming urge to thank her: not just for putting her life on the line for a bunch of Less Thans she didn't even know, but for something else, too. For trusting me. For *forgiving* me. There were suddenly so many things I wanted to say to her.

But I didn't get the chance.

When the dart went whistling by our ears, all of us

turned, first at the weapon embedded in the cornstalk, then in the direction it had come from. At the far end of the row were maybe two dozen men, their clothing torn and ragged. Some were bare-chested. All wore helmets made of large animal skulls.

The men were muscled and sinewy, and streaks of brightly colored paint adorned their pale cheeks, giving their faces a devilish appearance. They grunted and made sharp yapping noises, pawing at the earth like animals ready to strike, their hands gripping bows and arrows, spears and atlatls.

One look told us who they were: Skull People. We turned and ran.

We went tearing through the field, arms slapping cornstalks, cornstalks slapping faces, arrows and darts whispering past our heads.

"No straight lines!" Hope yelled, and we dodged in and out of rows, taking turns guiding Twitch. My ears pounded with the thumping of my heart . . . and another sound, too: war cries. They were high-pitched and strangled—relentless, terrifying screams.

Before us was the end of the field, the edge of the bluff, the railroad bridge that would take us back across the river. All we had to do was get there first.

We were breathing heavily. Four Fingers was beginning to drag. Flush grabbed the back of his shirt and yelled, "Almost there, Four! No stopping now!"

"No . . . stopping," Four Fingers gasped, badly out of breath.

I could hear the footsteps gaining on us. The Skull People were fast, shrieking and screaming like a pack of rabid dogs.

Hope cleared the field first, emerging into bright sunshine. The rest of us were right behind her. Far below us was the swift, muddy river. To fall those hundreds of feet would be an instant death. The bridge was our salvation. It would lead us to safety.

Hope half ran, half tiptoed across the ties, and I was nearly to the bridge when I snuck a glance behind me. The Skull People were emerging from the field, and I could smell them now: a thick, musky scent like livestock sweat. One of the men raised his arm, and they all came to a sudden stop.

That's when I realized: They were going to let us go. They weren't going to chase us. As long as we got to the other side of the river—and *stayed there*—they weren't going to bother us. My heart lifted.

I was about to share this good news when I saw that Hope had stopped. Diana and Scylla, too. Right in the middle of the bridge!

"Keep going!" I yelled. "We've gotta get to the other side!"

But Hope turned and gave her head a simple shake. A moment later I realized why. The log we'd worked so hard to put in place was nowhere to be seen. Once the Sisters had come across it, someone had pushed it to the roiling waters below.

The Skull People weren't letting us go. They were corralling us. They were closing in for the kill.

PART TWO
CAPTURE

Woe to the vanquished.
—Titus Livius (Livy)

28.

THERE'S NO POINT FIGHTING back. Slowly, they raise their arms in surrender. The Skull People take their weapons and lash their wrists together. No one says a word.

It's early evening when their captors lead them single file along the edge of the bluff—no doubt looking for a spot where they can toss the Sisters and Less Thans over the edge, their corpses to be swept away by the swelling current.

But then the leader of the hunting party—the man who raised his arm at the edge of the cornfield—reaches a notch in the cliff . . . and disappears. The Skull Person behind him does too. And the one after that. Hope can't understand it.

Only when they stand at the very edge of the precipice do they see the steep trail that cuts into the cliff, the rocks forming a crude stairway. They creep down the incline, rocks skittering beneath their feet and sailing into the airy abyss.

It's another fifteen minutes before they reach a small ledge, obscured by scraggly pines. *This is it,* Hope thinks. *Time to be thrown to our deaths.*

Suddenly, with a mechanical *whir,* a portion of the rock face recedes, revealing a dark opening into a cave. The leader ducks his head and steps inside. As soon as the rest of them follow, the door shuts with an irrevocable *clunk.*

Hope expects to see scattered bones and rotting carcasses, but it's not like that at all. The path is paved, well tended to, with a series of torches and sconces built into the rock.

Before Hope knows it, they step into an enormous cavern, the ceiling a good thirty feet above them. And there are people everywhere! Men and women, pushing carts and pulling wagons, trading goods and carrying baskets. All this directly beneath the cornfield!

"Welcome to the Compound," the leader says flatly.

He removes his animal skull and hangs it on a peg. He is an older man, balding, with wrinkles etching his face. Despite his age, his body is taut and sinewy—not an ounce of fat on him. Without his head covering, he seems less a devil and more just a middle-aged man.

Not so different from her own father.

The prisoners are ushered into one of the side tunnels, and then another tunnel after that. People stop and stare as they trudge past.

Hope is equally curious about them. Unlike the Brown Shirts, they span a range of skin colors and body types. Their clothing, too, runs the spectrum: everything from ragged pants and shirts to animal hides to undyed wool garments with rope belts.

A bell sounds, twice—a harsh, high-pitched clang that nearly makes her jump. The Skull People come to a stop and wait, and a moment later she hears a faraway explosion. The bell clangs a final time, and the Skull People resume their activities as if there's been no interruption whatsoever.

What's going on here? Hope wonders.

Her ears are still ringing when they round a bend. There before them, at the tunnel's end, are two jail cells constructed of rebar and scrap metal. They're at right angles to each other, and the five Less Thans and Argos are put in one cell; the three Sisters in the other.

The hunting-party leader twists the key in the boys' lock until it clicks shut. He does the same with the Sisters' cell.

"I'd get some sleep if I were you," he says. "Tomorrow's your trial before the Council of Ten."

"Our *trial*?" Hope asks. "It was just a few ears of

corn. We can pay you back."

The leader shakes his head. "We don't really care about the corn."

Hope shares a confused glance with her friends. "Then I don't get it. Why're we on trial?"

"Spying for the enemy." He turns, and the Skull People walk away.

There are piles of blankets in each cell, and the prisoners go about creating beds, everyone too stunned to speak. Even after the others have gone to sleep, Hope lies there, her mind racing. If she'd just stayed back at Dodge's Log Lodges, she wouldn't be in this mess. She'd be safe and sound.

She absently fingers the locket around her neck—the so-called good-luck charm. Little good it's done her. The only luck it's brought her is bad.

Hope pushes up from the cold, damp floor and shuffles to the front of the cell. She leans against the bars. The metal is cool to the touch.

To her surprise, Book is awake as well, leaning against the bars of his cell.

"You think they'll find us guilty?" he asks, his voice a whisper.

She shrugs. The fact is, nothing much surprises her anymore.

"It's ludicrous, isn't it?" Book goes on. "I mean, who would we be spying for? Not the Brown Shirts. Or the

Crazies. Or the *Hunters*."

With each name, Hope remembers all they've gone through. They've already faced so much adversity—so much *tragedy*. So it's a wonder when a smile tickles the corner of her mouth. She tries to conceal it, but Book notices.

"What?" he asks.

"Nothing." Even as she turns away, the smile grows.

"No, what?"

"Nothing."

"Tell me."

She finally gives in. "I was just thinking . . . of what you said when we found you in the cornfield. 'You're here.'"

A flush of red creeps up Book's neck. "You're not supposed to remember that."

"Why not? It was cute."

"It was stupid. I couldn't think of anything else to say." He grins in embarrassment.

"Well, I thought it was cute." A short silence follows. The only sound is the candle's guttering flame. Then Hope says, "'You're here'?"

They share a smile—for maybe only the second time, as far as Hope can remember—and to her, there's something about the exchange as intimate as a kiss. She feels her cheeks warm. "Do *you* think they'll find us guilty?" she asks.

"All I know about the Skull People is they're the sworn enemies of the Republic. If the government's for something, they're against it."

"So maybe the Skull People will be on our side." Even as she says it, she knows that's unlikely. Why would *anyone* be on their side?

Dr. Gallingham and Chancellor Maddox certainly aren't. Her mind flashes back to their secret meeting on the country road. All Hope knows for sure is that if those two are working together, it can't be good.

Standing there, Hope contemplates their future. Their *bleak* future. Book's voice breaks her reverie.

"I just want you to know I'm sorry about our argument," he says. "I'm sorry I broke your promise and went into the infirmary. And most of all, I'm sorry about your sister. I can't even imagine . . ."

Hope has to turn her face away to hide the tears welling up. She gives a hasty nod as a fat tear rolls down her cheek.

"Thanks," she murmurs.

Neither speaks. The flame sputters in its sconce.

"You said you needed to go back to your childhood home," Book says, breaking the silence. "Why?"

"Wouldn't anyone want to visit the place where they grew up?"

"Sure. But something tells me there's more to it than that."

He's right, of course. Book always sees through her. She lets out a deep breath and tells him what happened: how when she was six years old, the soldiers came and killed her mother. How Hope and Faith survived only because they hid inside a log for two days straight. How she's never been back since.

"So you never got a chance to bury her," Book says.

"We couldn't—not then. My dad did, later on. He went back on his own." She pauses. "He never talked about it."

"So . . . you were going to visit her grave."

She nods as the tears roll down her face.

"I'm sorry," Book says. "And I'm sorry I didn't trust you."

She wants to respond, but the lump in her throat won't let her. She can't define what it is that gets to her—thinking of her mother or Book's apology or the fact that he *understands* what she's going through— so instead of talking, she pokes her hand through the grid of rebar, fingers extended. Book does the same. Because they're not standing in the very corners of their cells, their hands fall short of each other. But by pressing themselves against the bars and reaching forward, they are able to get their fingertips to brush against each other. No kiss, no squeeze of a hand, just the simple touch of fingertips. Skin against skin.

"Can I ask you something?" Book says.

"Of course."

"Based on where you and Cat were looking, I'm guessing your home was somewhere near the eastern edge of the territory, is that right?"

"I think so, yeah."

"So why didn't your family ever cross into the Heartland? You were so close."

Hope hesitates before answering. Book's question is something she's thought about before, many times, but she has no definitive answer.

"I think he didn't want to give up on this territory," she says at last. "Even though we were being chased, as long as we were here, he thought he could maybe do some good." At least, that's what she hopes the answer is. She still can't shake Dr. Gallingham's referring to her father as the Butcher of the West.

Standing there, relishing the touch of Book's fingers against her own, sensing his genuine concern, Hope has a sudden urge to express herself—to let Book know what she feels for him. She knows it would be the most courageous thing she's ever done. Far braver than fighting soldiers or digging tunnels. *She needs to tell him.*

Flush appears before she gets the chance.

"What's going on?" he asks, stepping to Book's side.

Hope jerks her hand away.

"Um, couldn't sleep," Book says.

"Me either," Hope blurts out, feeling a sudden blush creeping up her face.

222

Before they know it, nearly all of the Less Thans and Sisters are at the front of each cell, talking in hushed voices. Although their conversation focuses on the next day's trial, Hope can think of little else than the touch of Book's outstretched hand. The feel of it warms her still.

But whether she'll ever get the courage to actually tell him how she feels is something she doesn't yet know.

Breakfast is a feast: bread, hard-boiled eggs, slices of ham, plump strawberries, cold milk. Hope is savoring every delicious bite of it when she suddenly recalls something her father once told her, that convicts about to be executed were always given a big final meal. She pushes her plate away.

When the Skull People arrive, Hope barely recognizes them. They wear no animal skulls atop their heads. No streaks of color adorn their faces. Their clothes are less shredded and torn. More like togas and jeans and wrinkled khakis. They appear almost . . . normal. Whatever normal is in this post-Omega world.

As Hope and the others are exiting the cells, the leader—the same one who did the talking the day before—points a bony finger at Argos. "He stays."

Argos looks at his friends with pleading eyes and whimpers softly. "Sorry, boy," Book says. "We'll be back."

But whether that is true or not, Hope honestly doesn't know.

The guards slip bandannas around the prisoners' eyes and escort them through a maze of tunnels. When they come to a stop and the blindfolds are removed, they find themselves in an enormous chamber, far more massive than the one they passed through the day before. At one end, a shelf of limestone creates a natural dais. On it sit ten elderly Skull People—the Council of Ten, Hope assumes. They're a mix of men and women, each wearing a sheepskin pelt across their shoulders.

The guards guide the eight prisoners to the middle of a chalk circle. All around them stand a throng of spectators, several hundred in number. They whisper behind their hands and shoot the prisoners darting glances.

A man who appears to be the oldest of the Council rises and shuffles forward. His skin is like rice paper, his hair silver, his face gaunt from age. When he reaches a rock podium, the crowd quiets.

"Are you ready to proceed, Goodman Nellitch?" he says.

"I am, Mr. Chief Justice," a voice answers. Hope turns to see an older man in a radiantly white toga. What he lacks in height, he makes up for with a full beard, black and silver in color. There is something about him that is oddly familiar.

The Chief Justice of the Council shifts his gaze to the prisoners. "Is there a spokesperson for the defendants?"

The prisoners look at one another, and Hope gives Book a nod. "I guess I am," he says, stepping forward.

"What's your name, young man?" the Chief Justice asks.

"Book, sir."

"And your last name?"

"No last name. Just Book."

The crowd titters. The Chief Justice's mouth tightens. "And the charges, Goodman Nellitch, for . . . Book . . . and his friends?"

"Stealing from the state, resisting arrest"—here he pauses dramatically—"and spying for the Republic."

An excited buzz tears through the crowd.

The Chief Justice bangs a hammer against the rock, and the buzz dies down. He turns to Book. "And how do you plead?"

"We didn't do any spying, if that's what you're asking," Book says.

His Honor stares at them a long moment. Then he turns his focus to Goodman Nellitch. "And the evidence?"

Goodman Nellitch details the events in the cornfield and how the prisoners ran from the Skull People, despite being ordered to stop.

The Chief Justice narrows his eyes. "You understand,

Goodman Nellitch, that while this is certainly a transgression of the laws, it is hardly grounds for a charge of spying."

"I understand that, Your Honor."

"Well then?"

"There's more."

Hope and Book share a confused glance. What is he talking about?

Goodman Nellitch reaches into the folds of his toga and produces a flimsy piece of paper. He unfolds it twice and holds it aloft for all to see.

"And what is that?" His Honor asks.

"A map of our territory," Goodman Nellitch responds, with a glint of satisfaction in his eye. "Property of the Republic, with this location circled in red." He pauses dramatically before adding, "Found on the body of this very Less Than."

His stubby finger points in Book's direction, the spectators erupt in a chorus of angry murmurs, and Hope and Book share an urgent look. *This isn't good. This is definitely, one hundred percent, not good.*

29.

WHEN THE CROWD FINALLY settled down, the Chief
Justice turned back to me. "And how do you respond to
these charges?"

"I've never seen that map in my life," I answered.

"Even though the leader of the hunting party says he
found it on you?"

"He didn't find it on me; that's a lie."

More murmurs, topped only by Goodman Nellitch,
who spoke with a condescending smirk. "Trust me,
Your Honor. That's where the map came from. The
leader of the party told me himself."

"But that's not true!" My eyes searched the crowd
for the man who'd captured us. I couldn't find him
anywhere.

"So you deny any contact with the soldiers of the Republic?"

"I didn't say that. We've been surrounded by soldiers all our lives."

"And where was that?"

"The girls are from Camp Freedom, and we're from Camp Liberty."

The silence that descended on the chamber was immediate.

"Camp Liberty?" the Chief Justice asked. "You're from Camp Liberty?"

"Yes, sir. I mean, just us five." I motioned to the four other guys.

"So they're Less Thans," Goodman Nellitch chimed in. He said it the way one said *plague* or *evil*.

"We are," I said proudly. "And we have the markings to prove it."

All of us pulled up our sleeves to reveal the tattoos on our forearms. Some members of the crowd actually gasped.

"And may I ask how you got here?" the Chief Justice inquired.

I gave him a shortened version of our escape and journey, making it clear we not only weren't spying for the Brown Shirts, we were fleeing from them. When I finished, he stared at us a long time before conferring with the other members of the Council.

I was in a state of shock. Where had that map come

from? And why had the hunting party leader said he'd found it on me?

The Chief Justice stepped forward, tugging at his sheepskin pelt.

"While we have no evidence to deny your statement of the nature of your origins," he began, his voice echoing across the chamber, "neither do you have evidence to support it."

"But our tattoos—"

"Could have come at your own hands. And the evidence we do have is a map, found on you, indicating you are in collaboration with . . . the *Republic*."

That was all that was needed to incite another angry buzz.

Hope took a step forward. "That's not true," she said, straining to be heard above the crowd. "There was no map."

The Chief Justice glared down at her. "I will ask the defendants to refrain from speaking until judgment has been passed."

"You're not listening!" she cried out. "They're our enemies. They're the ones we're running from."

The crowd grew louder. The Chief Justice banged the rock. "Order!"

"They tortured us. And they're the ones killing us!"

Two guards rushed forward and grabbed Hope's arms. One of them stifled her mouth with his hand.

"Given the fragile nature of our post-Omega circumstances," the Chief Justice said, "there is no greater threat than spying. Therefore, the punishment we prescribe is . . . thirty years' hard labor."

He banged the rock a final time, the crowd burst into applause, and the Council members rose and began shuffling out. I turned to the others. We were in a daze.

"Thirty years?" Flush was asking, his voice barely audible above the drone of the crowd. "Is that what he said? Thirty years?"

I nodded dumbly.

"But that means"—he did the math in his head—"I'll be nearly forty-five."

We looked at each other. We were no spies. But how could we convince the Skull People of that? A glance at the prosecutor revealed his satisfied expression.

"You lied!" I yelled.

His leering smile split his face in two.

Even as the guards blindfolded us and led us back to our cells, I kept thinking over and over, *This isn't happening. This cannot be happening.*

Stuck as we were at the end of a windowless cave, it was impossible to have any true notion of day or night. All I knew for sure was that I was sleeping soundly— dreaming of Hope and the touch of her outstretched fingers—when eight guards appeared.

"Rise and shine," one of them called out. He had bright-red hair and a lean, pointy face. He ran his knife across the rebar to make a loud, clattering sound.

I rubbed the sleep from my eyes and realized this was Day One of Thirty Years. Only 10,949 days to go.

"Where's your friend?" I asked one of the guards as we shuffled through the cell doors. "The one who captured us." I wanted to know why he'd lied to Goodman Nellitch.

"Not here. I get the honor today." He said it like it was anything but.

We were led to a small chamber, where we were given new clothes. Faded gray pants, T-shirts, long-sleeved shirts over those. Not all that different from what we'd had before except actually clean, like they'd been washed a million times.

Once more we were blindfolded and led down a series of tunnels. This time, I could hear us being split up, each prisoner forking off into a different passageway. Soon, it was just me and the red-haired guard.

Farther and farther we descended into the bowels of the cave, the explosions getting louder with each step. The guard abruptly yanked me to a stop, then ripped off my bandanna. We stood on the edge of a precipice, looking down into an enormous cavern. Branching off from it, like spokes from a wheel, were at least twenty tunnels. Hundreds of workers scurried in and out like ants.

The guard turned to me. "Hope you're not afraid of hard work." He snickered and led me down the rest of the way.

My boss was a big, burly man with a thick, bushy beard. His cheek bulged with a plug of tobacco.

"So you're the spy, huh?" he said matter-of-factly.

"I'm *not* a spy," I said.

"Yeah, right," he scoffed, then turned to the side and spat. "Makes no difference to me. Labor is labor." He and the guard met eyes. "I got him from here."

The guard gave me a threatening look. "I'll be back for you at the end of the day," he said, then retreated back up the slope.

"Welcome to the Wheel, boy," my boss said, then turned to get a better look at me. "What happened to your leg?"

"Born this way. Radiation."

"Those damn politicians. Had no right firing off nuclear weapons. Had no right building them in the first place."

His candor surprised me. I'd heard only one other person speak so openly about Omega or against the government, and that was Frank.

"What's your name?" I dared to ask.

"Why do you want to know?"

"If you're my boss, I should know what to call you."

He thought a moment, then answered gruffly, "Goodman Dougherty."

"So your name is Goodman, too? Just like Goodman Nellitch?"

"All the men here are Goodman, and all the women

232

are Goodwoman. It's our way of creating equality."

"But there was a judge. . . ."

"Sure. That's his task. Chief Justice. Just as I have a task and the woman who keeps the torches going has a task and the men who plow the fields have a task. We all have our jobs; no one is greater than anyone else."

A very different structure from what we'd experienced back at Camp Liberty, where we were just Less Thans. Where we had no more identity than a number . . . and even less value.

"Enough talk. It's time we got you to work." He hawked up what sounded like a hairball and told me the basics: the Skull People were expanding the Compound, digging deeper into the earth, carving out more caves.

"Where do they lead?" I asked.

Goodman Dougherty smiled, revealing a mouth that was missing teeth. "Wouldn't you like to know?" The clanging bell sounded twice, followed by an explosion and then the final bell. "Well, don't just stand there," Dougherty said. "Go get those rocks."

He thrust two large white plastic pails into my hands—pickle buckets, he called them—and led me into a cave where the dust was just now settling. My job was to fill the buckets with rocks and dump the rocks into a cart. Simple.

But backbreaking. Within fifteen minutes I had sweat through my shirt. There was also the limestone dust coating my arms, my nostrils, the back of my throat. Even when they let us take a break and fed us lunch, I mainly tasted rock and grit and sand. Yum.

Goodman Dougherty slapped a meaty hand on my shoulder. "How's that limestone tasting?" He threw back his head and laughed.

"Is it always this way?"

"Always. Why do you think I keep a mouthful of chaw?"

He hawked up another enormous glob of black phlegm and shot it to the side. Explosions rocked the ground, my lower back ached, I was choking on dust and exhausted to the point of collapse, and even as his laughter filled the air, one looming question rattled around in my brain: how was I ever going to endure thirty years of this?

Four Fingers dug irrigation ditches, Flush tended solar panels, Hope and Scylla were assigned to the kitchen, Diana to the laundry; and Twitch was placed in a mechanic's shop, where he sorted nuts and bolts. Someone even went to the trouble to carve Cat a wooden arm so he could be placed on a painting crew. Cat did the painting, but he refused the arm.

"Don't need it," he grumbled.

"But it'd make your life easier," I said.

He just grunted and left the artificial arm lying on the cell floor.

As for Argos, he was taken away from us. They wouldn't tell us where to.

When we returned to the cells each night, we shared what we'd seen. The one thing we agreed on was that the Skull People had created a highly functioning society.

"And the thing is," Flush was saying, "these people are smart. They get all their energy from the sun and wind—and they've created a grid to store the excess. It's amazing."

All the Sisters lined up at the front of their cell, just as we were lined up at ours. All except Cat. He sat off to one side, picking at his stump.

"There's still something I don't get," I said, trying to rub the limestone off my arms. "How can these tunnels support all these people? Where do they get the oxygen?"

"That's the most incredible part. They've built these air shafts with enormous fans, so there's constant circulation."

Okay, so they were intelligent. Then why were they wearing those animal skulls the day we first encountered them?

People began drifting off to bed until it was finally just Hope and me at the front of our cells.

"Did you recognize him, too?" she asked.

"Who?"

"The prosecutor. Goodman Nellitch. He was the mayor of the Crazies back in Bedford. The one who talked to the Man in Orange."

That was it! Although he was all cleaned up and his

white toga was a far cry from the cowboy hat and boots, she was absolutely right.

"But why would a Crazy be here with Skull People?" I asked.

"Or a Skull Person with the Crazies?"

Yet more questions we had no answers to.

When we were sure no one was looking, we stretched our hands forward through the bars until our fingers touched. We let them linger there as long as possible, holding on for comfort, for reassurance, for the desperate hope of not just a future, but a future together.

By day we worked; by night we shared notes. Not only were our lives passing before our eyes, so too was any chance of rescuing those Less Thans back in Liberty. Each day meant they were one day closer to the Rite, to imprisonment in the bunker, to being sold off to Hunters and shot down like prey.

I began taking on more responsibilities at the Wheel, even assisting with the explosives. Soon I came to understand the basics of dynamite and C-4, how to use fuses and blasting caps, how to mold the explosion based on needs.

But I knew I wasn't put on this earth to help dig tunnels for the Skull People. I had to get back to Camp Liberty.

"So how're you going to stop the Brown Shirts?" I

asked my boss one day at lunch. We were seated on the ground, backs against a wall.

Goodman Dougherty gave me a funny look. "What do you mean, stop 'em?"

"I mean, what happens when you're discovered? You can't very well just pick up and move somewhere else."

He leaned to one side and spat. Bits of brown chew got stuck in his thick beard. "Don't you worry. Those soldiers ain't interested in us, and even if they were, they'll never find us, not with our camouflaged entrances."

He had a good point about the door; it had been nearly impossible to see.

"So you're fine with the Brown Shirts?" I asked.

"I didn't say that. It's just . . ." He searched for the right words. "They're like a bunch of wasps. You don't go bothering them, and they won't be bothering you."

Was it really that simple? I wondered.

"But if they did find you—"

"Which they won't."

"—how would you fight back?"

His beard pendulumed from side to side as he shook his head. "We don't fight back."

"You mean you haven't yet?"

"I mean we won't need to. That's why we got escape tunnels." He swiveled his head to me and explained, "Besides, we'd rather put our efforts into educating and feeding folks than building weapons. Just makes a lot more sense to us."

He was right, it did make sense . . . unless you had firsthand experience with the Brown Shirts.

"And you're fine with their policy?" I asked. "The Final Solution?"

He poked a couple of stubby fingers into his bushy beard and pulled out some tobacco and crumbs—from what meal I had no idea. "The final *what*?"

"The Final Solution. You know, how the Republic intends to eliminate all the Less Thans and Sisters from the face of the earth."

Goodman Dougherty looked like the kind of guy who might be a first-rate poker player—his expression veiled behind a tangle of beard and facial hair—but at that moment there was no hiding his shocked expression.

"Eliminate? What do you mean, *eliminate*?"

"Wipe out. Murder. *Kill us all.*"

He gave his head a shake. "That ain't right." He paused in disbelief. "Where'd you hear this?"

"Read it in a letter from Chancellor Maddox."

"That *beauty queen*." He spat as he said it, and we went back to our tasks.

Watching him that afternoon, I couldn't help but notice he spent much of the time engaged in hushed conversation with his friends. I had thrown the bait out there. Whether the fish would bite, I didn't yet know.

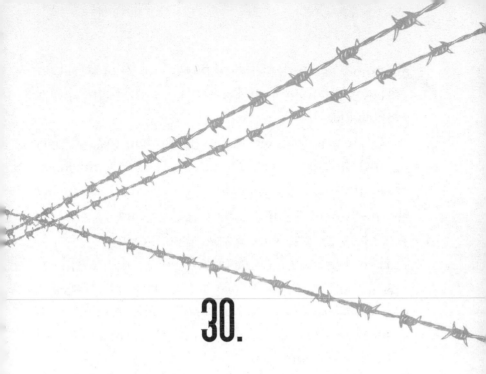

30.

HOPE LIES IN THE back corner of the cell, thinking of Book. She remembers their shared smile and can still feel the caress of his outstretched fingers. In all her life, Hope has never felt so vulnerable and so alive.

The sensation is both thrilling and scary as hell.

She daydreams and then chastises herself for it. *Why am I getting my hopes up when we're going to be separated by metal bars for the next thirty years?* Her fingers rub the tiny locket that dangles from her neck.

She hears a tiny *click* as her fingers glide along the locket's edge, and she realizes that she's accidentally opened it. She's about to snap it closed when she notices a slight bend in one of the photos—her father's—bulging his face outward.

She's not surprised. The locket's been submerged in

water, roasted by fire, baked by the sun, shot at, sat on, you name it. It only makes sense it's starting to warp and buckle.

But when she places the tip of her index finger against the photo, trying to push it flat, she finds more resistance than she expected. She sits up and pinches the photo free from its chamber . . . and sees there's something behind it. A tiny scrap of paper.

Heart pounding, she removes the folded slip. It is yellowed and tattered, with a series of permanent creases. She is careful to iron it out. The crumbled edges waft to the stone floor like snowflakes. When she's unfolded it, her breath catches.

To Faith and Hope
Dear girls. Either you get this or you won't, but if you do. Know that I love you. Know that I believe in you. Either way, your mom and I have been so proud to raise two such amazing daughters who don't give up. Remember your mother and do what's best.
Dad

Hope has to force herself to breathe. She knew nothing about this note, despite the fact it's been dangling around her neck all these months. She doesn't know when her dad wrote it, or why, or when he expected his daughters to find it.

The realization that Faith isn't around to read it brings

tears to her eyes. She tries to fight them—it was her father, after all, who taught her: *Live today, tears tomorrow.* But the tears come anyway, racing down her cheeks.

She tucks the note into its chamber and lies back down, her face away from the others. Her mind races as she picks absently at the cell's limestone wall, its grains pebbling on her fingertips.

And that's when she gets the idea.

The next night, after the guards have taken away their dinner trays, Hope announces she has a surprise. As everyone looks on, she reaches into a pants pocket and produces . . . a spoon. Its curved shape catches flickering torchlight.

"Where'd you get it?" Flush asks.

"Washing dishes."

"I don't get it. What's the big deal about a spoon?"

"Not a spoon," Hope corrects him. "A shovel."

Flush's expression shows he still doesn't understand.

"It's how we get out of here," Hope explains. She scrapes it against a wall. Granules fly.

"You're going to use that little thing to dig a tunnel?" Flush asks.

"We'll get more silverware later on, but this is where we start."

"And you really think it'll work?"

"We did it before. Why not now?" Diana and Scylla nod their support.

"But the guards? Won't they hear?"

"Not if there's noise to cover it."

As if on cue, Cat begins singing, a sea shanty he's picked up from somewhere.

> *"Come all ye young fellows that follow the sea*
> *To me, way hey, blow the man down."*

Hope looks at Book. It matters that he approves—that he wants to escape. She needs to know that he wants to be with her as much as she wants to be with him.

"What do you think?" she asks.

Book hesitates only a second. "What're you waiting for? Start digging so we can get the hell out of here."

Hope ventures a smile and begins scraping the wall as the others join Cat in song.

> *"I'm a deepwater sailor just come from Hong Kong.*
> *You give me some whiskey, I'll sing you a song."*

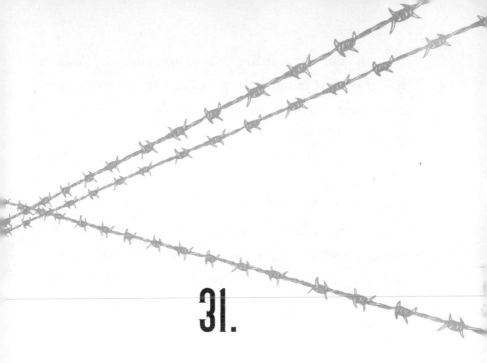

31.

I'D JUST FALLEN ASLEEP when I heard my name.

"Book."

My eyes blinked open. Two guards stood outside our cell.

"Come with us," one of them said. Nothing more.

I scrambled to my feet, casting a glance into the Sisters' cell. Hope's eyes were open, her face stroked by the orange flames of the wall candle. I felt her gaze long after the blindfold was slipped over my eyes.

As the guards led me through the tunnels, panic started to set in: Where was I being taken? Was I going to be one of those political prisoners who mysteriously "disappeared" in the middle of the night?

My blindfold was whipped off, and I found myself in

a small chamber. Sitting behind an oaken slab was the leader of the Council of Ten. I hadn't seen him since our trial, weeks earlier. The guards pushed me into a chair and marched out.

I looked around. It was a small room, maybe fifteen feet square, its only hint at opulence an enormous fireplace where flames licked the limestone black.

"It's silly, I know," the Chief Justice said, his eyes never wavering from the document he was writing, his quill pen scratching paper. "It's not for pride I requested the largest fireplace in the Compound. I just get so chilled in this subterranean world. I hope you don't mind."

Confusion overtook me as sweat trickled down my sides. *Why is he talking to me in this way?*

He slipped the pen into its holder, pushed the paper to one side, and looked up. His eyes met mine. "Book, huh?"

"That's what they call me." I wondered if he was going to get all chummy with me. Colonel Westbrook had done that back at Liberty, trying to get me to rat on my friends. Fat chance I was going to fall for that again.

"So you read?"

"I *did*."

If he picked up on my sarcasm, he ignored it. "Favorite book?"

I shrugged. Why should I confide in him? He was the reason we were imprisoned. "*A Tale of Two Cities* is good," I said.

"Ah, yes, who doesn't like a story of selflessness, even if it means one's own death in the process? And all set against a backdrop of revolution." He sat back and stared at me. "You don't like me much, do you?"

"Why should I?"

"Indeed, why should you? What convict approves of his sentencing judge?"

"We're not convicts. And we're not spies either!"

"Now, now," he said, calming me with his hands. One of the guards looked in, and the Chief Justice merely shook his head. The guard disappeared.

"Like me or not, the fact remains: you were found guilty of spying. The Council of Ten had a duty to do."

"I don't know anything about your 'Council of Ten,' but my guess is you're supposed to provide justice."

"That's right."

"Well, I assure you that we're innocent, so this is *in*justice."

"And that map you had?"

"I told you. We never saw that map before the day of the trial."

He regarded me for a long moment, absently tugging at his earlobe. A log exploded in the fireplace.

"Tell me about the Final Solution," he said.

245

So. The fish had taken the bait. "You're telling me you've heard of it?" I asked.

"That depends. There was a Final Solution many years ago, long before you were born, but I doubt that's the one you're speaking of."

I explained what I knew about Chancellor Maddox's intention to kill us all off, all the Less Thans and Sisters.

"And you saw this letter with your own eyes?"

"That's right. Me and one of the Sisters."

"You understand why I ask. The claim of genocide is nothing to be bandied about. We need actual proof."

"Like when you accuse someone of being a spy?"

He sighed wearily and steepled his fingers. "You know, Book, you may think us an ignorant, backwoods people, but in fact, many of the adults here were at one time distinguished professors. Respected scholars. Once our children started getting drafted into the army, that's when we realized we wanted nothing to do with the fascist principles of the new Republic. So we created our own society."

While what he said made a certain sense, I wasn't in the mood to hear it.

"I didn't know there was a University of Skull People."

The Chief Justice actually smiled. "Let me ask you something: before you came here, had you heard of us?"

"Of course."

246

"And what had you heard?"

"That you were the meanest, most ruthless people in the country."

"You've been around us a few weeks now. Are we really so ruthless? So mean? Cannibals who eat their young and sacrifice virgins into fiery pits?"

"Well, no . . ."

"So the branding has done its job." A pleased expression painted his face.

"You're saying your reputation is just a ploy?"

"I'm saying we want to be left alone."

I took in what he'd said. Maybe the Skull People were even smarter than I'd thought.

"Okay," I said, "if you're so open-minded, then you'll be willing to help us out."

He eyed me warily. "What do you have in mind?"

This was the moment I'd been hoping for—an audience with the head of the Skull People. I took a breath and launched into the world as I knew it—everything I knew about the slaughter of Less Thans and the medical experiments at Camp Freedom. As I spoke, his expression darkened.

When I finished, he rubbed his temples with his fingertips. "I understand your passion, I do. And your claim might very well be legitimate."

"But?"

"I'm sorry, Book. We enjoy our freedoms and the

civilized society we've constructed. For us to take sides would put all that in jeopardy. While helping the few, we would sacrifice the greater good. Surely you can understand that."

I let out an angry sigh. "All I understand is that people are going to die unless we help them, and even though you may not have heard about the Hunters, I can guarantee you they've heard of you. Especially since your head prosecutor is friends with their leader."

The Chief Justice's head snapped up. "What're you talking about?"

I explained what Hope and I had seen back in Bedford: the conversation between Goodman Nellitch and the Man in Orange.

"Now I know you're wrong," the Chief Justice said. "There's no way Goodman Nellitch would be caught dead with the Crazies. They're nothing more than an uncivilized mob."

I shrugged. "We saw what we saw."

The Chief Justice studied me with tired, blood-shot eyes. The longer he contemplated my words, the angrier I grew. What more did he want? I'd revealed to him things he had no way of knowing—Chancellor Maddox's letter, Goodman Nellitch's dealings with the Crazies—and here he was, too cowardly to act. This was the problem with the world: too many people afraid to do the right thing.

I pushed my chair back and got up. "Are we done?"

"No." He dipped the quill pen into ink. "I'm changing your work assignment." He signed the document on his desk with a flourish—the one he'd been working on when I came in. He folded the paper and sealed it with wax.

"Is this the punishment I get for speaking the truth?" I asked.

"Something like that." Then he added, "Book, we're not your enemies."

"Maybe not, but you're not our friends, either."

I took the document and exited.

The blindfolds ended the next morning. While the guards still locked us up each night, we were free to travel to work and back on our own. With one stipulation—we had to wear symbols on our clothes. A black square with an embroidered eye in the middle, as if to remind us we were always being watched. I wondered if we'd ever not be branded as somehow different.

The red-haired guard took me down an entirely different path, and my chest tightened with anxiety. Where was I being sent? To dig ditches? Clean outhouses? Haul irrigation pipes in the broiling sun?

When we came to a stop, I nearly lost my breath.

In the midst of this subterranean world, buried deep beneath the earth's surface, was a library. Hundreds—*thousands*—of volumes lined the walls. Not since

Frank's cabin had I seen anything so heartbreakingly beautiful.

I couldn't tell if the red-haired guard envied or pitied me. He stomped away without a word.

There were three others in the library—one old man and two middle-aged women—each sitting at tables and scribbling furiously. One of the women put down her pen and came over to me. She was short, with a shock of white hair and tight facial features. A tattered sweater was pulled over her faded blue dress. She took the document from my hand, sliced open the seal, and scanned it quickly.

"You're Book?" she asked.

"That's right." I expected her to comment on the appropriateness of my name.

"I'm Goodwoman Marciniak."

"Nice to meet—"

"You'll meet the others presently. In the meantime, there's work to do."

She sat me down across from the old man; if he noticed I was joining him, he didn't acknowledge it. He was stooped so far forward, his face was mere inches from the table. Goodwoman Marciniak slid four objects in front of me: a ream of paper, a quill pen, an inkstand, and a leather-bound book.

"There," she said. "We're under a deadline, so no dallying."

She began to walk away. "Wait. I don't know what you want me to do."

The look she gave me was one of pure exasperation. "You can read, can't you?"

"Yes."

"And write?"

"Of course."

"Then what're you waiting for? Copy that thing. We don't have all day."

I soon learned that while most of the books could be checked out, some of the law volumes were deemed so important that it was necessary to have multiple copies, especially for Council justices. It fell to the library scribes to create those copies.

That's what I was now: a library scribe.

And it wasn't just the four of us; apparently there were others who worked different shifts. So while I toiled over *An Exposition of Fecial Law and Procedure* by day, someone else copied it at night. The handwriting alternated, of course—mine for a few chapters, and some anonymous old geezer's for the next few—but that didn't seem to matter.

I asked if typewriters wouldn't make more sense, but Goodwoman Marciniak informed me that the Republic had confiscated them all years earlier.

For eight hours a day I sat hunched over a sheaf of papers, scribbling away. By the end of my shift, my fingers cramped, my back ached, my eyes stung from strain . . . but I was surrounded by books, breathing their heady, musty, *heavenly* smell.

Still, there was a cost. With each passing day, the Less Thans back at Camp Liberty were getting that much closer to the Rite—to their cruel imprisonment in the foul-smelling bunker, followed by their release into the wild, where they'd be hunted down like animals.

32.

HOPE AND SCYLLA ARE returning from the kitchen when they see the leader of the hunting party. It's the first time they've laid eyes on him since he escorted them to their trial.

"You go on ahead," Hope says to her friend. "There's something I need to do."

Scylla heads off, and Hope pushes herself into shadows. She lets the Skull Person get twenty yards ahead before she begins to follow.

He's an older man, his limbs lean and muscular, and wherever it is he's going, he seems in no hurry. The trail he takes is a winding one, through smaller and smaller tunnels, to a part of the Compound where Hope has never been.

When she emerges from a narrow walkway into the tiniest of chambers, she is surprised to find herself alone. He's not here. No one is.

So where did he go? she asks herself. *And how could I have lost him?*

She pivots in place, gazing down each of the tunnels. All are vacant, shrouded in dark. She kicks at the dirt floor and turns back around to retrace her steps . . .

. . . and runs smack into him.

He grabs her wrist and leans into her. "Why are you following me?" he hisses, his breath hot.

Hope tries to squirm free, but his grip is too strong. "I was just . . . trying to find my way back."

"You were following me. Why?"

The man may be old, but he is all muscle. His grip cuts off the blood to Hope's hand. Pinpricks stab her fingers.

"Let go of me and I'll tell you," she says.

"Tell me first."

"Why should I trust you?"

"Why should I trust *you*? You're the spy."

"Because I won't tell you otherwise."

The Skull Person casts her wrist away as if disgusted with it. He rests his hand on a huge knife sheathed at his waist. "You should know I'm pretty good with this."

She stares at him warily, then shakes her hand,

trying to get the blood back to it.

"Why?" he asks again.

"I wanted to speak with you."

"About what?"

"Why you lied to the Council of Ten."

"I never lied to them."

"During our trial, they said you found a map on us. You know it's not true."

His eyes flick nervously from side to side. When he speaks, his voice is lowered. "Who said that?"

"The prosecutor, Goodman Nellitch."

The Skull Person recoils slightly, eyes looking everywhere. "I don't know anything about that," he finally mumbles.

"When you arrested us, you accused us of spying."

"Sure. Everyone who's caught trespassing is accused of spying."

"But you deny telling him about the map?"

"I mean what I said: I don't know anything about it." His voice echoes back at them, and a fearful expression comes over his face. Hope wonders why he's so defensive. So jumpy.

When he speaks again, his voice is soft, urgent, *desperate*. "Why are you doing this?" he asks.

"I'm trying to get at the truth. We both know there was never any map, right? And if I can prove the prosecutor lied, then maybe they'll change our sentence. So

I'm wondering: if there was never a map, why'd that man say there was?"

"You'll have to ask him."

Hope remembers Nellitch's leering, self-satisfied smile. Fat chance he's going to tell her anything resembling the truth. "Why didn't you stay for the trial that day? Everyone else was there."

"My orders were to drop you off and go hunting. People have to eat, you know."

"Do you hunt every day?"

"Most days."

"*Every* day?"

"*Most* days."

"So who told you to hunt that particular day and not stay for the trial?"

The man's face twists into a scowl. "For your own sake, you need to drop this. Stop asking questions."

"How can I? We're imprisoned because of a lie. You're our only hope for setting the Council straight and getting us out of here."

The man seems to consider the request. Then his eyes lower and he says, "Look, I'm just trying to live my life. The last thing I need is people asking questions they shouldn't be asking."

It seems he's about to say more, but two women walk by, deep in conversation. They pass, their footsteps echoing down a narrow passageway.

"Is there something else you want to know?" he asks. His tone is all business, with no hint of kindness or understanding.

"No," Hope says, discouraged. "Just that."

"So you won't be following me anymore." It isn't a suggestion; it's a warning. His knuckles tighten on the hilt of his knife. Then he turns and strides away, swallowed by the tunnels' dark shadows.

Hope goes back the way she came, angry at him, angry at herself, angry at the world for imprisoning them deep beneath the earth when there are still three people out there she needs to teach a lesson to.

One way or the other, she vows, their time will come.

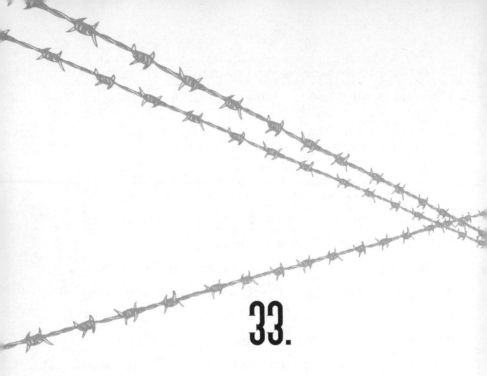

33.

WE WERE ALLOWED TO eat on our own, at a place called the Commons. But my lunch break was different from the others', so when I stepped into the large, low-ceilinged room, I didn't know a soul. And because of the black square stitched to my shirt, none of the Skull People urged me to join them. I found a wobbly table in the corner and began shoveling food into my mouth. The sooner I got out of there, the better.

Across the room sat Goodman Nellitch. He and three other men swapped stories as they inhaled that day's soup. On the surface, he was just a short man with a full beard and a big laugh. So why did I have such a bad feeling about him?

"What's the matter? You smell or something?"

A girl slid into the seat opposite me. She had pale skin and long, dark hair pulled back into a ponytail. Her gray eyes glinted with mischief, and she had one of those mouths that seem constantly on the verge of smiling.

"I, no . . ."

"There must be some reason you're sitting all alone."

"I don't know anyone," I said.

"That doesn't stop people sitting with *you*. What, you think just because you're a spy, people avoid you?"

"I'm not a—"

"Personally, I think it's something else. Probably body odor."

"What?"

"Or maybe bad breath."

"Hey, you can't—"

"I'm just teasing. I'm Miranda, by the way. Mandy to my friends." I guessed she was my age, maybe a year younger.

"Nice to meet you, Mandy. Miranda," I corrected myself.

"That's right. We're not friends yet."

"Sorry, I—"

Freckles danced as her face erupted into a smile. "I'm just joshin'. Fact is, we'll probably be friends. If you're lucky." She gave me a playful wink. My face felt suddenly warm.

"So," she went on, "how's the spying business?"

"I'm not a spy."

259

"That's what they all say. You just happened to be in the neighborhood? Just *happened* to cross that bridge and come into our fields?"

The conversation felt like a walk with Cat: I was one step behind and unable to catch up. "We were on our way back to Camp Liberty."

"Right, right, that's what you said at the trial." She tugged at her necklace—a metallic pendant that scattered shards of light. "Where're your friends?"

"Different lunch assignments."

"Too bad. Tough for spies to be effective when they're separated."

"We're not spies."

"Oh right, I keep forgetting." She smiled again, then ripped off a hunk of bread and dipped it into a mound of blueberry jam.

"How about you?" I asked, trying to regain my footing. "Where're *your* friends?"

She shrugged. "Not that many people my age in the Compound—most were snatched up by the Republic years ago. And those that are still around are usually on patrol."

"Patrol?"

"You know, keeping the Compound safe. Looking out for enemies."

"So what do you do?"

"Wouldn't you like to know?" She winked again, and

sweat ran down my temples. My face was like a river.

"I meant—"

"I know what you meant." Another wink. Another rush of blood.

"Skip it." I buried my face in my food.

"Aw, I'm just pulling your leg. You're so serious. Anyway, nice to meet you, Book."

"How'd you know my name?"

"I was at the trial, remember? I gotta run, but maybe we'll do this again."

"Uh, sure."

She rose, her now-empty tray in her hands. "By the way," she said, "you slant your *f*'s and *l*'s."

"Huh?"

"Your *f*'s and *l*'s. You slant them."

"What're you talking about?"

"Your handwriting. It's not terrible, a little erratic at times, but the main thing is, some of your letters lean. You wanna watch that."

I looked at her, dumbfounded. "How do you know?"

"I'm the other scribe working on the book." She gave her necklace one last tug and presented me with a lopsided smile. "Oh, and call me Mandy." She pranced off, her ponytail swishing from side to side.

Although I didn't see Mandy for several days, she did leave me a series of notes in the book we were copying.

261

Silly messages. Things like: *Make sure you don't leave out the* i *in "Fecial."* Or *Your* o's *are very sexy.* Or *You can cross my* t *any day of the week.*

One day, Goodman Jotson caught me reading one of the notes.

"What's that?" he asked, his voice gravelly and humorless.

"Just something from the other scribe," I stammered. "About the book. The one we're working on. Together. Whoever that person is."

I was about as good a liar as Flush.

Plus I felt oddly guilty receiving these messages. It almost felt like a betrayal of Hope, even though it was Mandy who was writing the notes, not me.

When the day shift ended and I left the library, I rounded a bend and Mandy was there. She was wearing faded dungarees, her hands tucked into her back pockets. A gray T-shirt hugged her torso.

"What're you doing here?" I asked.

"That's a nice way to greet a friend."

"No, I didn't mean . . . I never see you at dinner, is all."

"I'm just giving you a hard time." She placed her hand on my arm and let it linger there. "I'm taking you away, that's what I'm doing here." Then she slapped me playfully on the shoulder. "You don't have to look so glum about it."

"But dinner . . ."

". . . is right here." She held up a tidy bundle wrapped

in a large bandanna. "We're going to have a picnic."

"But my friends . . ."

". . . will have to have dinner without you. Or don't you want to have a picnic with me?" She stuck out her lower lip and pretended to pout.

"No, I do." I was about to say more, but Hope and Scylla strolled by. They slowed to a stop, waiting for me to join them. When I didn't, they gave Mandy a quick once-over. An awkward silence followed.

Mandy nudged me in the ribs. "Well? Aren't you going to introduce me?"

"Right. Hope, Scylla: this is Miranda. Miranda: Hope and Scylla."

Hope and Miranda said, "Nice to meet you," at the same time. Scylla was grim and silent as always.

Mandy hooked her arm through mine. "I hope you don't mind," she said to the two Sisters, "but I'm going to steal your friend for dinner."

I dropped my eyes to the ground. For whatever reason, I couldn't bear to see Hope's expression.

"You can have him for breakfast, for all I care," I heard Hope say.

"I may just take you up on that," Miranda said. "Come on, Bookie Boy."

Bookie Boy?

"Where're we going?" I asked as Mandy dragged me away. It was hard to imagine a picnic hundreds of feet beneath the surface of the earth.

"You'll see." That same Cheshire cat smile as always. We turned off into a side tunnel.

"Should we be here?" I asked. "You know I'm—"

"A spy?"

"A *prisoner.*"

"We're not leaving the Compound. We're just going to the edge of it."

Guards lined the wall. Their eyes narrowed when they caught sight of me and the embroidered eye on my shirt, but when they saw Mandy, they seemed to relax, exchanging crisp nods with her.

It was a different entrance from the one we'd first been herded through, and the door was open. Sunlight poured in through the jagged oval. I blinked, my eyes adjusting to the sudden brightness. Mandy led me outside to the edge of a precipice. Below us, looping like a writhing snake, the brown river sparkled in evening sunlight.

"Come on," she said. We picked our way among the rocks, careful not to trip and plummet down the limestone bluff. She found a spot to her liking and plopped to the ground, legs and feet dangling over the edge. I joined her.

"Nice, huh?" she asked.

Nice was an understatement. Below us lay the river; across the way, limestone cliffs jutted upward. Swallows darted in golden twilight, moving in an acrobatic frenzy. It was *spectacular.*

Mandy unwrapped the bandanna and gave me a sandwich. For the longest time we ate in silence, serenaded by the distant sound of the rushing river and the swallows' staccato chirps. The sun slid behind a bank of clouds.

"Can I ask you something?" I said.

"Sure."

"Why me? There are tons of people in the Compound. Why'd you choose me to take on a picnic?"

She shrugged. "There may be tons of people, but there aren't tons my age. Besides . . ." She hesitated a long moment. "There's something about you I trust."

"Really?" I enjoyed the compliment, especially since Hope felt just the opposite.

"Absolutely." Then she added, "And it doesn't hurt that you're kinda cute."

"But according to your Council, I'm a spy."

She smiled that mischievous smile, freckles dancing. "You and I both know you're not. You're too bad a liar for that."

I had to laugh. "How about you?" I asked.

"How about me what?"

"I know nothing about you. How long have you been here? What's your family like? You know, that kind of stuff."

She gave a small, restless sigh. "Nothing much to say, really. I was born and raised here, so this is all I know."

"And your parents?"

265

"I lost my mom when I was a kid—cancer from the radiation—so it's just my dad and me."

"What's he do?" For some reason I wondered if he was one of the men I worked with down in the Wheel. What if he was Goodman Dougherty with the bushy beard?

"He's a clerk. He does . . . clerical things, I guess. Kinda boring stuff, really." Her eyes left the winding river and landed on me. "Was what you said at the trial really true? That you all came from Camp Liberty and Camp Freedom?"

I nodded.

"That's, like, really far away."

"Tell me about it. I had the blisters to prove it."

She laughed softly, then studied me a moment. Without any warning whatsoever, she leaned forward and kissed me on the cheek.

"What's that for?" I asked.

"For making it all this way. Blisters and all."

A warmth coursed through my entire body. Without really meaning to, I said, "'Admired Miranda.'"

"Huh?"

"Oh, just a line from Shakespeare. *The Tempest*."

She smiled slyly and said, "'Indeed the top of admiration!' Ferdinand's next line."

My mouth fell open.

"You don't have to look so surprised," Mandy said.

"I've read a book or two myself. And I happen to love that play."

I couldn't think of a response, but I didn't need to. As twilight set the sky ablaze in orange and purple, Mandy leaned her head on my shoulder, resting it there as the sun dipped behind the western plateau. She kept it there long after stars began popping in the sky, and I didn't dare move. I suddenly felt incapable of it.

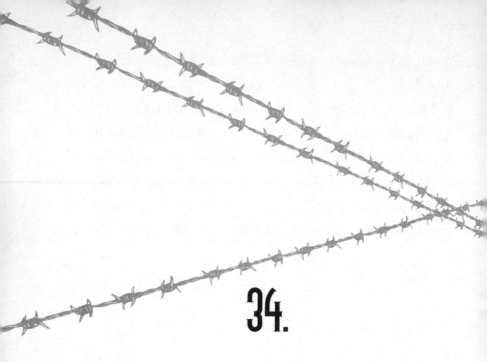

34.

HOPE IS ON HER way to work when she hears raised voices.

"Out of the way!" someone shouts, and people stand to the side.

Hope presses herself against the cave wall just as a group of men bursts through. They carry a man on a stretcher. A shaft of an arrow juts from his chest; an enormous bloodstain paints the front of his shirt.

"What happened?" someone asks.

"Hunting accident," someone else responds. The stretcher is carried past.

What grabs Hope's attention most is the patient himself: It's the man who led the hunting party. The one she spoke to in the deserted tunnel. He had been paranoid about talking to Hope that day . . . and now this has happened.

Hope feels suddenly light-headed. She tries to tell herself it's just a coincidence, that her conversation had absolutely nothing to do with this, but when she looks up, she sees Goodman Nellitch across the way. He seems to make a point of meeting her eyes . . . and giving her a little wink.

Hope feels sick to her stomach.

Later, she learns the man has died.

"What do you think?" she asks Book that night, after everyone goes to bed.

"About what?"

"The death of the guy who captured us."

"It was a hunting accident," he says.

"And you believe that?"

"I don't know enough *not* to believe it."

Hope can't figure Book out these days. He seems . . . different. He asks fewer questions, provides fewer observations. But it's more than that. It's like he can't look her in the eye. At night he no longer reaches for her fingers through the bars.

"But don't you think it's a little strange that the man who captured us—who told me he didn't know anything about the map—turns up dead? Just days after I spoke to him?"

Book gives a noncommittal shrug. "Hunting accidents happen, Hope."

He's about to turn away when Hope blurts out, "You still want to escape, right?"

"Of course I do. Why wouldn't I?"

"I don't know. You tell me."

For a long moment, their eyes lock. Book looks away when he begins to speak. "Look, I want to escape just as much as the next person. But I also want to make sure we have a plan before we do something rash, that's all. I'd hate for us to commit to something and then realize we don't know what we're doing."

"But there's no point coming up with a plan if not everyone's going to commit."

"I agree."

"So why aren't you working on a way to get us out of here?" Hope asks.

"Because at the moment I don't see one."

Hope wants to reach through the bars, shake him by the shoulders, and scream into his face, *Where's the real Book and what have you done with him?! Why don't you look me in the eye anymore? Why don't you talk to me the way you used to?*

But she asks none of it, and she is suddenly filled with a deep despair. Although she and the other two Sisters have continued to scrape away at the back wall, the hole's no bigger than a small cantaloupe, and they all seem to realize their thirty-year sentence might very well be concluded before the tunnel reaches even a few feet.

And now she's lost Book. Though she doesn't know exactly why, she can only assume it has to do with something she said. Or *didn't* say.

When she lies down that night, she buries her face against the wall so Scylla and Diana can't see the tears that tumble sideways down her cheeks, nor hear the heaving sobs that shake her body.

Two evenings later, Hope sits at dinner, absently pushing food from one corner of her plate to another. Her mood has gotten worse.

She lets the fork clatter to the table and rises from her chair.

"Done so fast?" Diana asks.

"Not hungry" is all she says, not entirely sure where she's going or what she intends to do. All she knows is that she has to get out of there. The walls are closing in, and the Compound seems more claustrophobic than ever. She needs air.

She makes her way to one of the entrances, where sunlight creeps in through the open door. Two guards perk up when they spot the embroidered black square, and point their weapons at her.

"I need to go outside," she says. "Just for a second." There's a tightness in her lungs—like a giant hand squeezing her chest.

"You're not allowed out there."

"I know that—"

"We can't let prisoners out of the Compound."

"Keep your gun on me. Shoot me if I start to run away. Mow me down. I just need a breath of fresh air. *Please.*"

The guard looks at his friend, who gives him a non-committal shrug.

"All right," he says at last. "But just for a second."

"That's all I need."

The guard escorts her through the narrow opening. Below her is the wide brown river; above her, a limitless sky. Sunlight warms her body like a flame melts wax. She takes a series of deep breaths, trying to soak it all in: the air, the sun, a blue sky above orange-painted clouds. For ten years she lived outside, in the forests and fields, and to be trapped like this, beneath the ground, is the cruelest of all punishments.

"Time's up," the guard says. "Ready to go back in?"

No, I'm not ready, she wants to say. *Not by a long shot.* But she nods her assent. Although the time outside was brief, it's what she needed. Comfort. Tranquility. A dose of happiness, even.

But as she turns to step back inside, she spies two figures farther up the trail, haloed by the setting sun. She has to shield her eyes to make them out. It's Book and Miranda. Just as she recognizes them, Miranda kisses Book on the cheek.

272

Hope feels suddenly dizzy. A wave of nausea rolls through her body. In a fraction of a second, all the tension has returned, and other feelings, too. Envy. Jealousy. Utter heartbreak.

She wheels around and races back inside. Her vision is blinded with tears; her legs are stiff and wooden. She stumbles and falls. The stone wall is cool against her back as she leans against it and tries to catch her breath.

This is stupid. Stupid!

Unaware she's even doing it, she begins banging the wall, slapping the stone with her closed fist.

Why should I care who kisses Book? What's it to me?

The wall feels suddenly damp and sticky, and when she examines it she finds a patch of sticky red. Blood. *Her* blood. From *her* fist.

Hope hears the echo of people's voices, and she curls up behind a boulder. She can't face another human being. Not at the moment. She fingers the locket around her neck as if it has healing powers.

Live today, tears tomorrow, she tries to tell herself, but her body won't even begin to listen.

She is just about to hoist herself to a standing position when Book and Miranda appear. There's a familiarity in how they walk, arms grazing, shoulders touching. They don't see Hope, and when they come to a stop, Miranda once more plants a kiss on Book's cheek.

Hope has to force herself to breathe, then watches as Book disappears down one tunnel, Miranda another.

For no good reason at all, Hope decides to follow Miranda. Maybe she'll confront Book's new girlfriend. Maybe they'll have it out. Anything's better than returning to the cells with Book.

When the tunnel empties into an enormous chamber, Hope feels a jolt of panic. These are the residences, the lodgings of the Skull People—off-limits to a convicted spy. But Hope has no intention of stopping now, so she removes the badge she's been forced to wear, the black square with the eye in the center. That's against the rules, too, but at the moment she doesn't care. Her fingers rip it from her shirt and stuff it in her pants pocket.

Some of the dwellings are carved out of caves, some built of mud and hay, all with wooden ladders and stone staircases leading from one floor to another in a dizzying arrangement of towers and pyramids that stretch all the way to the ceiling. Hope had no idea there was anything like this in the Compound.

Miranda rounds a corner and veers down a back alley. She stops at a wooden door, pushes it open, and steps inside. Hope loses sight of her, and she wonders why she felt compelled to follow Miranda in the first place. What did she expect to do? Tell her to lay off, tell her that Book is spoken for?

Hope turns to go. At just that moment, Miranda appears in a downstairs window . . . and Hope realizes she has to get a closer look. Even when Miranda climbs to the second floor of the adobe house and disappears from sight, Hope knows she can't just leave.

Miranda's house is built within a sprawling complex of houses, and there's no way Hope can sneak in there. But if she were able to climb up *opposite* the house, she'd have the perfect angle.

A cave wall looms behind her. It is jagged and sharp, hollowed out with holes. Not so difficult to climb, but more than a little suspicious for a convicted spy to be caught rock climbing across from the residences.

Still, what choice does she have?

Removing her shoes and socks, she finds a series of toeholds and begins dragging herself up. Within moments she is five feet off the ground. Then ten. Then twenty. An echo of approaching voices freezes her, and she presses herself against the rock, her body as motionless as a fly on a wall.

Three men pass without noticing.

Hope takes in the house opposite her. She now has a direct view into Miranda's house—and she can't believe what she sees.

When she has seen enough, she releases a foot and searches for the hold below. Her toes brush against a loose rock, and it bounces twice before clattering to the ground. Hope hugs the rock and prays no one heard it.

When it seems like no one did, she begins making her way back down, more carefully this time. A voice stops her cold.

"Hey! What're you doing up there?"

An old woman from across the way leans out a third-floor window, pointing a trembling finger at Hope.

Hopes doesn't think, just jumps—sailing through air and landing with a thud on the hard-packed ground. Other voices echo behind her. Shouts of confusion. Cries of alarm. People asking what the commotion is all about.

Hope grabs her shoes and socks and begins to run, tearing through the tunnel as fast as she can. The pounding of footsteps follows her.

Her feet seem to guide her, taking her on a zigzag trail from one small tunnel to the next. Her father always taught her to find escape routes, and she has done just that, cutting through one shortcut after another.

She rounds a final corner and spies the open jail cells. The Less Thans and Sisters stop what they're doing and watch, openmouthed, as she comes racing in.

"In case anyone asks," she says breathlessly, "I've been here since dinner."

Hope whips herself into the cell and rests her arms on the bars, trying to catch her breath. The others return to their tasks, feigning nonchalance so as not to arouse suspicion in case any Skull People should appear.

And they do.

Three men come racing down the long corridor, and the fact that all eight prisoners are in their cells seems to surprise them. The men drift to a stop before the metal bars. Their eyes travel from one prisoner to the next.

"All present and accounted for?" the oldest of the Skull People asks. His face is long and horse shaped.

"Count for yourself," Diana says.

Horse Face grunts. "And I suppose you've been here all evening."

"Ever since we left the Commons."

Horse Face looks down at Cat. "Is that true?"

Diana tries to intervene. "I just said—"

"I'm asking him." To Cat: "Is that true?"

There's a long moment of silence when everyone wonders what Cat will say. "Course it's true," he finally growls. "Where else would we go?"

Diana hurries to explain what they've been up to, and that's when Hope notices Flush. His eyes are wide, and it seems as though he's trying to tell her something. She wants to tell him to calm down, that he's going to give her away. His gaze travels from her face to her chest and seems to linger there. *Perv,* Hope thinks angrily.

When she realizes what he's telling her—that she's failed to put her badge back on—she panics. If these

Skull People see that, she'll be a suspect for sure.

As Diana continues talking, Hope slowly lowers a hand into her pocket, fumbling for the square patch. *This is where I put it, right?* Horse Face glances in her direction and she freezes. It's like he knows something's not right. When he returns his attention to Diana, Hope resumes searching, desperate now, breathing heavily.

Come on, where is it? Where is it?

She finally locates the badge, pinching it with her fingers. Then she raises her arm gradually, imperceptibly, afraid any quick movements will draw attention to herself. Folding her arms across her chest, she presses the black square to her shirt. It won't stay there, of course, not without stitching, so she leans slightly backward to balance it.

At just that moment, Horse Face turns to Hope.

"You sure are breathing heavy for just standing there," he says.

"Asthma," Hope says. "If you'd ever turn the heat up in this place, maybe it wouldn't be so bad."

"Not because you were running through the tunnels?"

"Why would I be running?"

"Exactly. Why *would* you be running?"

He stands there, examining her the way one studies a wild animal one intends to kill. For the longest time, nobody says anything. It seems as though all the Less Thans and Sisters have forgotten how to breathe. The man suddenly lowers his eyes.

"Your square," he says.

A surge of fear shoots through Hope. *Did it not stick? Is it lying on the ground?*

"What about it?" she asks. Her stomach has gone all jelly.

"It's crooked."

She refuses to look down at it. "So they tell me."

"Then you better get it fixed."

"If you say so."

When the man with the horse face realizes he's not going to get any more information, he gives a grunt to his two comrades. The three men wheel away. Hope waits until they've completely disappeared before allowing herself a breath.

There are nods of congratulations all around, but Hope knows they're not out of the woods. Not by a long shot. Based on everything she saw earlier this evening, she suspects they're in more danger than ever.

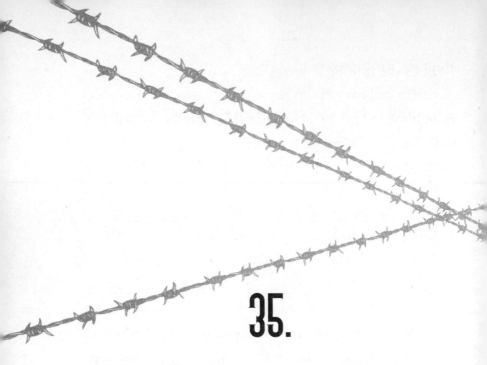

35.

MANDY AND I SAT on our ledge and shared a picnic dinner. When an enormous thunderhead exploded on the far horizon, we inhaled the dust-scented perfume of a coming storm, then hurried back inside, dodging the first fat pellets of rain.

After a long good-bye and a short kiss, a goofy smile plastered my face as I made my way back to the cell. When I rounded the bend and saw the sober faces of the other seven prisoners, the smile died on my face.

"What's going on?" I asked. "Is there a problem?"

"As a matter of fact, there is," Diana said. "You."

"I'm sorry?"

"You're the problem."

I laughed uneasily and shifted my gaze to the others.

"What's she talking about?"

Flush looked embarrassed and dropped his eyes. Twitch angled his head in another direction. It was left to Cat to ask, "What've you told her?"

"Told *who*?"

"Your girlfriend."

My body tensed. "Mandy is not my girlfriend, and I didn't tell her anything."

"You didn't tell *Mandy* anything?"

I gritted my teeth. "No more than any two people tell each other."

No one said anything. The silence lengthened.

"So how'd the guards know we were stashing silverware?" Diana asked.

"Got me. I didn't tell her that."

"You sure?"

"Positive."

"Nothing about our tunnel?"

My mind raced. "Okay, once, I might've mentioned that if we ever hoped to survive, we'd have to dig our way clear . . ."

"Book!"

". . . but I said it as a joke. And I never mentioned *how*. Or *where*. And it's not like it's any big deal—"

"The guards went through our stuff today," Diana said. "They found the silverware and cemented up the tunnel."

I looked across to the other cell, and sure enough, a moist layer of fresh cement painted the back wall. I felt like throwing up.

"You don't know that was related to her," I said.

"Seems awfully coincidental."

"So what're you saying? Miranda's a spy?" I laughed at the absurdity of it.

"Do you know who her father is?" Hope asked. She'd been silent up until now. Her expression was rigid.

"Yeah, he's a clerk. He keeps ledgers or something." Even as I said it, the pit in my stomach expanded.

"What if I said he's not?"

"Sure he is. That's what Mandy told—"

"What if I said he's the Chief Justice of the Council of Ten?"

It felt like she'd slapped me in the face. "That's not true," I managed. "He's a clerk. "

The others shook their heads as one.

"How do you know this?" I could hear the desperation in my voice.

"I followed her. After she left you."

"Wait a minute. You've been spying on me?"

"And it's a good thing. I trailed her back to the residences."

"Okay, so you saw Mandy with the Chief Justice. Big deal. I met with him too, but that doesn't make me his son."

"They live in the same house."

I was suddenly flustered. "Well, I mean, there could be reasons—"

"We asked around. They're father and daughter."

I remembered how people deferred to Mandy in the tunnels, how the guards always let her pass. "That still doesn't mean anything," I said. My words were like feet scrambling on a slope of loose gravel. "Just because she's the daughter of the Chief Justice—"

"Sounds to me like you've been played, pardner," Cat said, picking at his stump. "That's why you got assigned to the library. So you two could meet."

"There's no way you know that!" I wanted to yell, but I didn't dare raise my voice. "She's not a spy. And even if she is—*which she's not*—I didn't tell her anything."

Although the others weren't convinced, I believed in Miranda. We were friends. We liked spending time together. She brought me dinner and we watched sunsets and she kissed me on the cheek. If it'd been a setup, I could've seen through that, right?

Right?

I opened my mouth to speak, but at that very moment a blur of movement wheeled me around. It was Argos— running right for us.

"Argos!" I cried. "How'd you get out?" I knelt down and buried my face in his fur. I'd never been so happy to see him.

"Don't try to change the subject, Book," Flush said. "I'm serious. How'd he get away?"

Before anyone could answer, we heard the muffled blast of an explosion. We waited for the sound to fade away and the bell signaling the all-clear, but instead there was another muffled blast that followed. And another after that.

We looked at one another. Something wasn't right.

When the next explosion came, it was followed by horrible, bloodcurdling screams.

36.

THEY TEAR OUT OF the cells and race down the tunnel.
In no time they smell the pungent scent of a fire. Thick
coils of black smoke waft past like tumbleweeds.

"Why would there be a bonfire?" Flush asks.

No one answers, but Hope knows: this is no bonfire.

The screams are everywhere now, interspersed with
the *pop pop pop* of gunfire. Other sounds, too. Shrill
alarm bells. Blaring klaxons. It's deafening and frightening, and no one knows what's going on.

When they peek around a tunnel's edge, they see for
themselves.

Crazies.

Their shaggy beards and grease-stained clothes are
as foul as ever. But there's a difference now: they sport

gleaming pistols and spotless rifles, 9mm handguns and M16 assault rifles. Their primitive weapons are nowhere to be seen.

They round up the Skull People like livestock, shooting them at will. It doesn't matter their age or condition. Many litter the chamber floor, their blood coloring the limestone in swirls of red.

Off to the far side, Crazies feed a growing fire. Furniture, books, clothing—all tossed into the flames. The smoke that billows forth is black and acrid. The only things they appear to be saving are food, tools, and weapons.

"How'd this happen?" Flush demands.

But Hope knows. She and Book saw Goodman Nellitch conferring with the Man in Orange back in Bedford. The Skull People are being massacred by one of their own. What she doesn't know is why.

Hope gestures across the chamber. Two Crazies brandishing torches are coming their way. There is no good place for the Sisters and Less Thans to hide, and they have no weapons to defend themselves with.

"Back to the jail," Book says.

Everyone looks at him like he's crazy.

"Back to the jail!" he says again.

They turn and run. Slipping inside the boys' cell, Book pulls the door shut behind him. He motions for the Sisters to do the same.

"They don't lock without a key," Diana says.

"The Crazies don't know that."

They grip the bars and rattle them, giving the impression they're trying to flee.

"Let us out of here!" Book yells, just as the two Crazies round the corner.

The first one pauses when he lays eyes on them. When he sees the three Sisters, he actually licks his lips and shuffles forward. His gaze falls to their black squares with the eye in the middle.

"I got *eyes* for you all," he says with a smirk. "Who's looking for a husband?"

"Why're you bothering asking?" the second one says. He is round and covered in hair like a Neanderthal. "It's not like they have any say in the matter."

As if to prove his point, he reaches between the bars, wraps his filthy fingers around Hope's chin, and squeezes. He yanks her forward until her face is inches from his. Hope has no choice but to stand and take it. If she steps back, the door will swing open, and the Crazies will know they've been tricked.

"See?" the Neanderthal says to Crazy #1. "All you gotta do is tell 'em. Don't give 'em a choice."

His dirt-smudged fingers imprint themselves into Hope's cheeks, distorting her lips into an exaggerated pucker. For a long moment the two face off. Then he brings his mouth forward and presses it against Hope's.

She squirms, but the best she can do is keep her teeth clenched.

"That's it, Hank!" Crazy #1 guffaws. "Go get her!"

Book takes a step forward, but Cat puts a restraining hand on his arm.

The Neanderthal pulls away from Hope and gives her a big grin. His teeth—what few he has—are like black kernels on a dead ear of corn. "She's a fighter, I'll say that for her."

He releases his hold on her chin, then shoots his hand forward until his fingers rest on her breast. He gives it a firm squeeze. "And I *like* fighters."

Book flings off Cat's hand and pushes the cell door open. Crazy #1 can't quite believe what he's seeing, and he's slow to draw his sidearm.

"Hey, you can't—"

A swift kick to the groin cuts short his sentence. He tumbles to the floor, the 9mm clattering off to one side. Book reaches for the man's torch—just as the Neanderthal is turning to see what the commotion is all about.

"You little—"

He doesn't finish his sentence. Hope pushes the cell door forward—thick rebar smashing against his cheek. Book follows with a massive swing of the torch; the Crazy does a face-plant on the ground. Even though the man's lying there, nearly unconscious, Book tosses the torch to the side and keeps punching him, over and over and over again. Finally, Flush pulls him back.

"It's okay, Book. You got him. He's down."

Book is breathing heavily. The others tie up the two Crazies with their belts. Meanwhile, Hope is bent over, running the back of her hand across her mouth, trying to rid herself of the taste of the Crazy's mouth. When she finally lifts her head, her brown eyes are on fire. "Let's get the hell out of here," she says.

They race through the tunnels. Everywhere they look, the corpses of Skull People lie scattered on the floor, their bodies riddled with bullets. The Sisters and Less Thans tiptoe around the lifeless bodies.

Fifty yards from the entrance, they round a bend and freeze. Positioned in the very middle of one of the cave's openings, facing their direction, is a man nestled behind a wall of sandbags . . . and a .50-caliber machine gun. If anyone is foolish enough to race for the exit, they'll be gunned down long before they near it. They scramble to other entrances and it's the same: machine guns just waiting to mow down anyone trying to escape.

"Now what?" Flush asks in a fit of panic.

They look at one another dumbly. Echoing through the tunnels is a muffled mix of screams and gunshots. Black smoke drifts in the air. If they don't act fast—act *now*—they're dead for sure.

"We've gotta get outside, right?" Book asks.

"Sure," Flush says, "but there's no way we'll make it past the Crazies."

"If we stay in the tunnels, you're right. But we're not going to."

Diana grabs his sleeve. "How do we know we can trust you?" she asks, and Hope wonders the same thing.

Book looks from Diana to Hope. "I guess that's up to you." He turns and takes off at a jog.

The others look at Hope. Although she doesn't know what to make of Book and his relationship with Mandy, she has no real reason to suspect he's a traitor. She gives a nod, and they take off after him.

They stick to side passageways, cloaking themselves in shadows. After a while, Hope's sure they're all alone.

She's wrong.

"Don't move," a voice hisses from the shadows. "Hands up where we can see them."

They have no choice but to obey. Hope's heart slams hard against her chest. The body belonging to the voice emerges from darkness, the features backlit by a guttering candle. Slowly, gradually, the form takes shape. The body is a woman's.

"Goodwoman Marciniak?" Book asks, obviously shocked.

The woman cranes her head forward and squints through the gloom. "Book?"

"Yes, it's me . . . and the other prisoners."

The librarian is suddenly joined by two dozen other middle-aged women, all armed with bows and arrows. War paint, not makeup, adorns their faces.

"What're you doing here?" Goodwoman Marciniak asks.

"Trying to get out. Killing a few Crazies in the process."

Her face is set, her mouth rigid. She wears a toga ornamented with a series of belts—resting places for knives and arrows.

"You're prisoners," Marciniak says. "You shouldn't be out of jail."

"Wouldn't you rather have us fighting with you than not fighting at all?"

Suddenly they hear the thud of footsteps. Crazies. Hope's gaze falls to Goodwoman Marciniak's bow and arrow.

"We know how to use those," she says, stepping forward.

Marciniak's eyes flicker once, twice . . . but she says nothing. Then she releases her hold and extends the bow. Hope takes it before the older woman changes her mind.

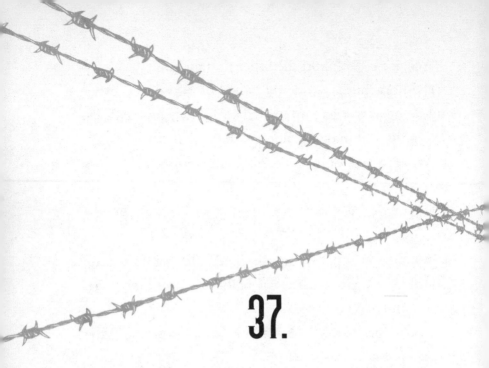

37.

WE FORMED A HURRIED line—some kneeling, others standing—with just enough time to nock our arrows.

"Draw and hold," I commanded. We waited, bowstrings taut. The sound of the approaching Crazies grew louder and louder until our heartbeats and their footfalls merged into one awful drumbeat.

"Fire!" I cried when they rounded the corner, and the arrows found their targets. Crazies fell to the ground, some firing their weapons into the ceiling, others tugging hopelessly at the shafts that protruded from their bodies.

"Again at will!" I shouted.

We released our bowstrings, and the remaining Crazies tumbled to the rock floor. It was a victory, but a temporary one.

"We need to hide the bodies," I said, "so their friends won't know something's up."

Goodwoman Marciniak led us to a secluded back corner, and we'd just managed to drag the corpses there when there were more footsteps.

"Book!" Flush yelled.

"I hear 'em."

We hurried back and reloaded. Although the next band of Crazies was smaller, they were better equipped. One fired a rocket launcher, the grenade's explosion hurling shards of rock on top of us. When the boiling smoke cleared, we were able to pick off the Crazies, but I wondered how many more attacks we could withstand.

We raced to hide the corpses. After reaching the back corner, I glanced off to an adjoining chamber. There were several women there, huddled by the side of a bed.

"What's that?" I asked Goodwoman Marciniak.

"A hospital."

My gaze swept the interior. White iron beds, clean sheets, gleaming silver trays. Only one bed was occupied.

"Our founder," Goodwoman Marciniak explained. "Not long for this world, I'm afraid." Her concern was obvious.

"May I?" I asked. I had a sudden impulse to see the originator of the Skull People. Goodwoman Marciniak nodded her assent.

When I reached the foot of the bed, I lost my breath.

Lost any ability to breathe at all. For there, lying on her back, with a thin blanket pulled up to her chin, was a woman. But not just any woman. The woman from my dreams.

The one with the long black hair.

She appeared to be sleeping, her chest rising and falling as gently as lapping waves. As soon as I came to a stop, her eyes snapped open—so suddenly I nearly lost my footing and stumbled backward.

Her eyes locked on mine. She was older than the way she appeared in my dreams, and the crow's-feet seemed to pull at the corners of her eyes. Still, there was a liveliness in those eyes, and the smile that tugged at the corners of her mouth was utterly youthful.

"There you are," she said. "You're alive."

"Yes," I managed to say.

She forced a smile. "I knew you'd come." She closed her eyes and fell into a deep sleep. I stood there, numb.

"You know this woman?" Goodwoman Marciniak asked.

I nodded dumbly. "I dream of her," I stammered. "No, that's not right. It's that I *remember* her." In stumbling sentences I told her how this woman had appeared to me for years. How the setting was always the same—the smoke-filled battlefield—but the words were different.

You will lead the way.

There you will go.

You will do what's right.

Now.

"So it's you," Goodwoman Marciniak said aloud—more to herself than me.

"So it's me what?" I asked.

Before the white-haired librarian could respond, Flush charged in. "We got all the bodies dragged back!"

"Good. Line up for the next attack." I turned back to Goodwoman Marciniak. "So it's me *what*?" I repeated.

She looked me in the eye, her face serious. "She thought you might be able to save us, to save the country."

She had to be kidding. How was that even remotely possible? I was a Less Than—a prisoner in the Compound. I wasn't even seventeen. Even if I wanted to, how could I possibly save the Republic of the True America?

And how did this woman—this *stranger*—even know about me?

Goodwoman Marciniak read my thoughts. "She's not a stranger, Book. She's your grandmother."

My knees went wobbly, and I had to sit. It felt like the walls were closing in.

"Goodwoman Olvera did her best to keep you hidden," Marciniak said. "But the Republic has ways of finding people."

Olvera. So that was her last name. But I wondered . . .

"Was she my mom's mom or my dad's?"

"Your mother's." She went on to explain. "Your mother died in childbirth. From what I understand, it was a miracle she was able to bring you to term."

I pointed to the still body of Goodwoman Olvera—my grandmother. Her eyes were closed, her breathing slow and jagged. "She raised me?"

"Until the ambush at Chimney Creek. That's when the Brown Shirts captured you. You must've been about four."

Her words meshed with my own fuzzy memory: the smoke, the soldiers, the whistling bullets. All this time I'd thought that was a dream.

"How'd she escape?"

"She let you get captured—that way they wouldn't kill you." Goodwoman Marciniak paused briefly. "She always said it was the hardest thing she ever did."

Just as I'd done with Cat.

"And she founded the Skull People?"

"Not long after that day. A way of rebelling against the new government."

There was more I wanted to ask—more I *needed to know*—but Flush came dashing in.

"We gotta get out of here," he said.

I nodded, but all of a sudden I had no desire to leave. I'd just met my grandmother—*my lone family member*—and I was in no hurry to go.

"Book!"

I gave my head a shake. "I can't leave," I whispered.

"*Book!*"

"I mean it, Flush. I've got to stay."

Things were happening too fast. I'd waited a lifetime to find out I wasn't an orphan—that I had *family*—and there was no way I was going to leave my grandmother now.

"Your friend is right," Goodwoman Marciniak said. "You need to go. You won't survive if you stay."

"But my grandmother—"

"Is too ill to even get out of bed."

"Then we could carry her. We've done it before. We know how to do it. I can't leave without her—without all of you." I was desperate, and the words came rattling out.

Goodwoman Marciniak pursed her lips. "Go, Book. We'll look after her."

"But I can't—"

"Go."

My shoulders slumped. "Okay. But we'll come back for her—for all of you." I looked up and met her eyes. "So how do we all get out of here?"

"The Crazies have sealed off all the entrances, but there's a rumor that we've been building an escape tunnel off the Wheel. The problem is it's way on the other side of the Compound."

"I might have an idea about that," I said.

Perching on the edge of my grandmother's bed, I took her hand and felt the coolness of her bony fingers. Her eyelids fluttered open.

"You're still here," she said, her voice frail and tired.

"Of course."

"Look at you. Your mother would be proud."

"Tell me about her. And my dad."

A smile creased her face. "He was a good man, treated Maria well."

"That was my mom's name? Maria?"

She nodded. "They were a hundred miles downwind from a blast site. They couldn't escape the radiation. He lived about three and a half years after, then died right before you were born."

"So he never saw me?"

She shook her head.

"And my mom?"

My grandmother's face brightened. "She was a beauty. The boys were crazy about her. Me too, of course. And then . . . Omega." She paused and took a painful swallow. "The spark went out of her, as it did for many of us. Only when she was pregnant with you did it come back. She knew that giving birth would probably kill her, but she didn't care. You were the one thing she could pass on."

I realized I was barely breathing. To hear all this—to learn about my parents for the first time and how my mother gave up her life for me—was like plunging into a pool of icy water.

"Did she?" I managed to ask. "Live long enough to see me?"

"Just barely. She was weak and only half conscious, but she insisted on holding you. She died that way. The last thing she saw on earth was you."

"Then what happened?"

"I took you. I knew once the Republic found out about you, how you had one leg shorter than the other, they would brand you a Less Than and lock you up. So I smuggled you out of the hospital and went into hiding. Just the two of us."

As she spoke, flashes of memory popped in my brain, illuminating for the briefest moment images from a dozen years earlier: tossing a ball beneath an apple tree, chasing chickens in a yard, being read to. How had I ever forgotten?

Then she extended her hand. "Let me touch your face."

"What? I . . ."

"To remember you."

I leaned forward, and she ran her fingers along my cheeks. It was like she was memorizing my face, one square inch at a time. "My beloved," she whispered, "in whom I am well pleased."

My breathing was short and rapid, my heart fluttering.

Then she said, "You have to leave."

"Okay, but we're coming back for you."

"Don't."

I recoiled in surprise. "But I have to."

"This is our home, Book. These are our friends. We can't abandon either it or them."

I looked at Goodwoman Marciniak. She was nodding her head in agreement.

"But we have to take you with us," I pleaded.

She smiled weakly and shook her head.

Flush popped back in. "Book!" he called out.

"Coming."

"They call you Book?" she asked.

"That's right."

She smiled. "It's a good name."

I don't think I was breathing. Tears were pressing against my eyes. My throat was tight and throbbing.

"And you're fighting the Brown Shirts, aren't you?" she asked.

"Yes, ma'am."

"Good for you." Then she said, "You need to keep fighting them."

While a part of me understood why she didn't think she could go, why she insisted on staying, it didn't make it any easier to accept. I couldn't bear to think of these poor women taking on the Crazies.

"Book!" Flush cried from the hallway.

"Thank you," I somehow managed to say to my grandmother. "For raising me. For guiding me all these years."

She gave her head one last gentle shake. "I haven't been guiding you, Book. You must be listening to your heart."

She shut her eyes, then lapsed into a series of slow, steady breaths. She was sound asleep. I leaned forward and kissed her on the forehead. I gave her hand a final squeeze, then rushed to join my comrades. As I ran into the hallway, ignoring the hot tears that scalded my cheeks, I realized I had neglected to ask my name. What was it my mom had called me? In the excitement of meeting my grandmother, I had forgotten to find out.

But then again, maybe it didn't matter. I was Book now, a Less Than—and would be until the day I died.

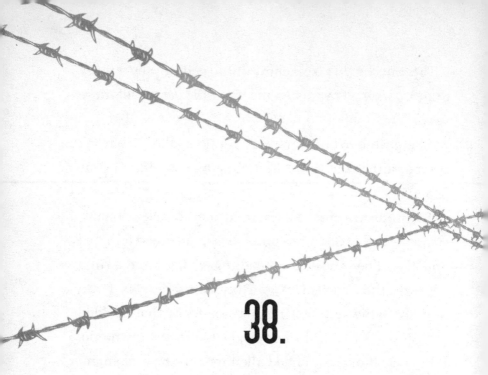

38.

GOODWOMAN MARCINIAK INSISTS THEY take the bows and arrows, and the Sisters and Less Thans hurry away. For Hope, it's as if she's in a fog. First the assault by Crazies, then the destruction of the Compound itself, and now Book's encounter with his grandmother. Like she's living out some bizarre dream.

"You know where we're going?" Cat asks.

"I know where I *want* to go," Book responds. His eyes are puffy from crying, but he seems more determined than ever.

Twice they reach dead ends and have to double back. They hear an ear-shattering explosion, and Hope can only pray it isn't Crazies firing more rocket-propelled grenades.

The black smoke grows thick and burns their lungs. The pops of semiautomatics echo off the limestone walls. The Compound has been transformed into a living, breathing hell.

Finally, they come to a stop.

"*This?*" Flush asks. It looks to be just another of the Compound's cramped rooms.

"The Chief Justice's office," Book says.

"That's great and all, but I don't see—"

"And that's the largest fireplace in the Compound."

Scylla is the first to understand what Book is getting at. She grabs a torch and rushes to the hearth, scattering blackened logs. She sticks her head up the chimney, then gives an enthusiastic nod.

"If that chimney can take all that smoke away," Book explains, "it must be wide enough to climb. And where do chimneys lead?"

Flush actually smiles. "Above ground."

They're just preparing to begin their ascent when Diana appears from a back room . . . shoving a prisoner.

"Look who I found," she says, and Hope's heart jolts to a stop.

It's the girl. Miranda. The one who kissed Book on the cheek.

Her face is smudged, her hair disheveled. Although Hope's first instinct is to slap her across the face, something prevents her. Maybe it's the flicker in Book's face—some vague expression she can't quite place.

"So it's true?" he asks.

"Of course," Miranda says, defiant.

"And the stuff about your mom dying and your dad being a lowly clerk?"

"My mom did die . . . just maybe not how I described it." Everyone waits for an explanation, but she doesn't offer one.

"Why?" Book asks.

"Why do you think? To see if you were telling the truth. You think I meant all that?"

Book looks like he's just been punched. As angry as Hope is, she's surprised that she feels a pang of pity for him as well. Miranda's words are like a razor slicing across a soft patch of skin.

"So what'd you find out?" Diana asks.

"You're not bright enough to be spies. I don't know who or what you are, but you're definitely not spies."

Diana jabs an elbow into Miranda's side.

"Oops," Diana says. "My bad."

From down the hall they hear approaching footsteps. Time is running out. If they're going to climb the chimney, they have to do it now.

Book turns to the others. "She's coming with us."

"Nuh-uh," Diana says. "No way, nohow."

"We can't leave her here. The Crazies'll kill her for sure."

"Guess she shoulda thought of that when she was lying to you." She raises her knife to Miranda's throat. "Why don't I just kill her now?"

Hope gives her head a shake and takes a step forward. "We don't do that anymore," she whispers. It's the first time she's spoken since they left the cell.

Everyone stares at her, surprised by her words. Diana lowers the knife and meets Hope's eyes.

"You sure about this?"

Hope gives a nod. "I'm sure."

The footsteps outside the chamber grow louder.

"Fine," Diana says. "But one false move and she gets it."

Hope doesn't disagree, and a part of her even wonders why she suggested sparing Miranda's life in the first place. Probably something to do with the look on Book's face and how he came to her defense against those two Crazies.

One by one they begin hoisting themselves up the soot-covered chimney. Black powder rains down. The last to go are Hope and Book. He stops her just as she's about to climb.

"Are you all right?" he asks. They both know he's talking about the Neanderthal back at the cell.

She gives a subdued nod . . . then disappears up the shaft.

Inching up blackened limestone, she reaches a

horizontal part and joins the others at an intersection of passageways. Everyone is crouched beneath the three-foot high ceiling. Book is the last to join them.

"What now?" Flush asks when everyone is there. "We'll never make it through that thing."

His eyes are trained on an enormous fan fifty feet above them. It sucks up the air and discharges it into the night sky. But he's right; there is no way they can climb the steep shaft, let alone crawl through a whirling fan without getting chopped to pieces.

"There may be another option," Book says, and turns to Miranda. "You know your way around up here?"

"Are you kidding?" she answers. "I've never been up here in my life."

"So where're we headed, Book?" Diana asks.

Everyone looks to him and waits.

"The Wheel," he says.

"What's that?"

"Either our ticket out of here or our last stand."

On hands and knees he pushes past the others and scrambles down a narrow passage.

As Hope struggles to keep up, she knows that time is running out, and her many feelings for Book—hurt, jealousy, anger, *love*—won't matter a single bit if they can't get away from the Crazies and escape the Compound.

39.

LIKE RATS IN A maze, we tried one passage after another, the shafts so narrow they scraped the skin right off our hips and shoulders. When we finally reached the Wheel, we lowered ourselves into the construction site: filthy, exhausted, covered in a black paste of soot and sweat.

There wasn't a soul in sight, but we knew it was only a matter of time before the Crazies found us. We had to hurry.

"Which way?" Flush asked.

There were dozens of tunnels, some of which I knew were miles long. If we chose the wrong one, we'd have to double back and start all over again, and by then the Crazies would have reached the Wheel. There was no time for a wrong choice. We got one shot at this.

I turned to Miranda. "Do you know?"

She shrugged and shook her head. For some reason I believed her.

Since I was the only one who'd been there before, it was up to me. I pivoted in place. A handful of guttering torches threw flickering light against the walls. The lingering aroma of their burning oil drifted to where we stood.

"Grab those torches," I said, "and go stand in front of the entryways."

My command was greeted with puzzled expressions.

"Book, there's not time to look in all the tunnels," Flush said.

"We're not looking in the tunnels. We're looking at the flames."

Scylla, Diana, and Flush each took a torch, yanking them from their sconces. They ran from one tunnel to the next, standing at the entrance and watching the torch's fire. Did the flames burn straight up, or did they bend with a breeze?

In the meantime, my eyes landed on a wooden trunk off to one side. The explosives trunk, if I wasn't mistaken. I jimmied open the lock, revealing stacks of dynamite and C-4. There was a canvas knapsack nearby, and I began stuffing them inside. Who knew when some explosives just might come in handy?

Miranda drifted to my side.

"You're wrong about one thing," she said. I didn't look up. "My father gave me the assignment of befriending you, and it's true, I didn't want it—"

"You made that clear already, thank you."

"—but it was for the safety of the Compound. We can't have spies."

I didn't bother to respond. I knew if I opened my mouth, I'd just say something sarcastic or mean. I piled coils of fuses into the canvas knapsack.

"What I didn't expect," she went on, "was that I'd like you. That wasn't an act."

I gave her a hard look. Frankly, I didn't know what to believe anymore.

"That's all fine and good," I said, "but you missed the spy right under your nose: Goodman Nellitch. We saw him in a town, meeting with Hunters and Crazies."

"That's not possible. . . ."

"So while you were writing me cute little notes, you missed the biggest danger of all."

Miranda's eyes widened in shock. "If that's true," she said, "then I've got to tell my father. Now."

"I already told him, and he didn't believe me. Too bad too, 'cause I bet Nellitch is the one who let the Crazies in."

As if on cue, muffled gunfire echoed through the tunnels. The Crazies were nearly to the Wheel.

"I'm sorry," Mandy said suddenly.

"For what?"

"For what happened between us."

"Nothing happened between us," I shot back, and started to walk away.

Then she reached beneath her shirt and pulled out a flat, square object. When she unfolded it and spread it out on the stone floor, I nearly lost my breath: it was the map of the western Republic.

"What, you're going to frame us again?" I asked.

She placed the tip of her index finger on the map—on a thin ribbon of blue in a vast expanse of nothingness. "Here's where we are. And here"—she traced her finger along the winding river—"is Camp Liberty."

Sure enough, there it was, just south of Skeleton Ridge. Some of the others gathered round.

"Follow the river upstream and veer off when you get to this fork, and then this fork after that. That's how you get back."

The river would be our guide. And the best part was that it allowed us to skip the Flats entirely.

"Why're you showing us this?" Hope asked. Her tone was hostile, threatening.

Miranda tugged at her necklace and looked Hope in the eye. "To make up for things," she said, and left it at that. She refolded the map and extended it to me.

I took it just as Flush shouted, "Found it!"

He stood in the entry of a tunnel, a breeze slapping the torch flame sideways.

"Let's go," I said, pocketing Miranda's map and slinging the canvas knapsack over my shoulder.

We had just entered the tunnel when gunshots shattered the silence. They pinged off limestone walls and dropped us to the ground. The Crazies had found the Wheel . . . but they hadn't yet found us.

"Don't fire," I hissed, even as a couple of the girls nocked their arrows. It would give away exactly where we were.

"We can't outrun 'em, Book," Cat said.

"I know."

"Even if they don't know which tunnel we're in, all they have to do is follow the sound of our footsteps."

"*I know.*"

Distant gunfire clattered off rock. We'd found the escape tunnel, but now it seemed doubtful we could make it out in time.

"What if I lead them to another tunnel?" Miranda suggested. "That'll give you a head start. Maybe time to reach the end."

I looked at her like she was crazy. "You'll never make it out alive."

"I'll find my people. They'll protect me."

"Who says there are any left?"

She acted as though she didn't hear me. "Follow the

river. That's how you get back to Liberty."

I opened my mouth to speak, but she wouldn't let me.

"Follow the river," she said again, then kissed me, not on the cheek this time but on the mouth. We watched as she ran out of the tunnel and disappeared from sight. My heart shuddered with a sadness that surprised me.

Everyone took off in a mad dash down the tunnel; only Hope and I remained. She gave me a long look, and I had no doubt her brown eyes could see to the depths of my soul. Finally, she turned and jogged after the others. I followed, Miranda's kiss on my lips still warm, its imprint as distinct as the tattoo on my arm.

40.

THE BREEZE TUGS THEM down the tunnel. Even though they're caked in sweat and grime, there's a sudden sense of optimism, of exhilaration. They're going to make it. They're going to escape the Compound.

As Hope runs, she thinks about Miranda's sacrifice and how she's risking her life for Book and a group of strangers. Hope doesn't know what to make of it. A part of her admires Miranda for it . . . and a part of her is wildly jealous.

They race on without words. It's just the scrabble of feet, muffled coughs, the occasional clatter of stones. The torches' flickering flames throw orange light on the umber-colored walls. With each bend of the cave, they expect to spy the opening and an endless field of corn. But the tunnel goes on. And on.

"Why are we going down?" Diana asks.

It's what they're all thinking. The tunnel angles down, not up. How can it deposit them in the cornfield if it keeps sloping downward? Something isn't right. Still, the breeze seems to suggest that there's an opening ahead of them.

It is scent, not sight, that alerts them to the end. A smell of dust and wet and pure night air. An intoxicating fragrance. The tunnel narrows . . . and there it is: the outside world. A rainy downpour makes a curtain across the opening. Black night presses against it from the other side.

But there's a problem: it isn't a field the tunnel empties out on, but air itself. Space. The sky. They are smack-dab in the middle of a cliff, and when lightning flashes, Hope catches a glimpse of the brown river below them. *Directly* below them. She pulls herself back, gasping for breath.

Diana steps out onto a small ledge. When she comes back in, water drips from her hair.

"There's no path," she reports flatly.

"There's gotta be," Book says. "Why build this tunnel otherwise?"

But when he goes to inspect, he sees she's right: there is no trail. They've come all this way, only to be confronted with the fact that it's nothing more than a glorified air shaft. A hole for letting fresh air in and sucking bad air out.

At just that moment, distant gunfire clatters off the walls. The Crazies—in this very tunnel. It's only a matter of time before they find the eight Sisters and Less Thans.

"This *is* an escape tunnel," Hope says.

Diana bristles. "I was just out there, Hope. There's no path."

"You didn't look directly above." Hope knows a thing or two about escape routes, like how the best way to hide one is to put the trail above the tunnel itself.

To prove her point, she steps outside. The rain comes down, not in sheets, but thick, cold, suffocating blankets. With fumbling, outstretched hands she reaches above the tunnel. Fingers curl around a jutting stone, first one hand, then another. A burst of lightning shows the river directly below her, several hundred feet down. If she loses her grip, there is nothing between her and the river. Death on impact.

"Is there a path?" Flush calls out.

It's not so much a path as it is a limestone cliff angling straight up with a series of tiny notches and indentations scattered here and there. Nothing more. And somewhere far above her the cliff plateaus out, but where that is she can't yet tell. She lowers herself back into the tunnel. Her clothes are soaked, and Diana holds

315

the torch close so Hope can steal some of its warmth. Her teeth chatter as she explains.

"I'm not sure all of us can make it," Flush says. His eyes fall on Four Fingers, on Argos, on Twitch, on Cat with his one arm.

"Don't worry about me," Cat says. "Besides, we don't have a choice." Gunfire punctuates his comment.

"We could maybe manage if we had a rope," Flush says.

Their eyes fall to the few supplies they carry. Nothing comes close to a rope.

Hope rips off her outer, long-sleeved shirt . . . and Book suddenly does the same. The others look at them as if they're out of their minds, watching Book and Hope knot the sleeve of one to the sleeve of the other. In no time, two shirts equal six feet of rope.

"What're we waiting for?" Diana asks. She rips off her outer shirt as well, and soon all of them are in their T-shirts, tying their long-sleeved shirts together. As they work, Hope's gaze returns to Book. There are times he seems to know exactly what she's thinking . . . and that makes her more nervous than she dares admit.

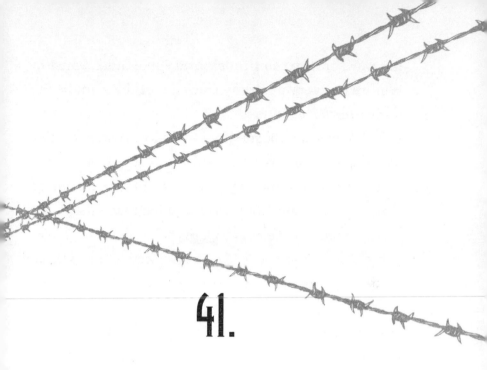

41.

HOPE WENT FIRST. WITH one end of the makeshift
rope strapped around her waist, she stepped into the
pummeling rain and began pulling herself up. Diana
followed, the rope connecting her to Hope.

A fresh burst of gunfire exploded from the tunnel.

"What're they shooting at?" Flush asked. "There's no
one there."

"They're trying to get us to fire back," I said. "To pin-
point our location."

My eyes met Scylla's. "Here. Take my knapsack and
help the others." I dropped the canvas bag at her feet,
grabbing a bow and a quiver full of arrows.

"Wait," Flush said. "Where're you going?"

I didn't answer. Darkness embraced me as I picked

my way back up the tunnel. Every so often a spurt of gunfire stopped me in my tracks. I let the sound echo away before moving on.

The Crazies' rank smell wafted in my direction like an animal's sour breath. I had to breathe through my mouth just so I wouldn't gag. And then I realized that if they were close enough for me to smell them, they were close enough for me to attack them.

I lowered myself behind a boulder and lined up three arrows in front of me. I fixed the first one to the string and drew back until the fletching tickled my cheek.

Breathe, I told myself, just as Frank had instructed us way back when. *Breathe and hold.*

Footsteps grew louder, and then the Crazies' shadows wavered on the walls like giants. It looked like there were a dozen of them. More than I'd expected.

I released the bowstring, and the arrow sliced through air. There was a muffled thud as a body fell to the ground.

"What the hell, Bobby!" one of the Crazies shouted. I recognized the voice: Goodman Nellitch. Our prosecutor.

When he saw the arrow sticking from his friend's chest, the gunfire started. It splattered the rock and ricocheted off the walls. Once the volley ceased, I released two more arrows. One hit a Crazy in the thigh; the other sailed wide.

Then I was on the move, rounding a bend so I was

out of the line of fire. I hid behind a boulder and lined up three more arrows.

The Crazies' confused shouts bounced off the limestone walls. By the time they rounded the bend, their torches showed them perfectly.

My first arrow went through the lead man's neck, the second into another's abdomen, the third into a Crazy's arm. I went racing away before gunfire erupted.

I was breathing heavily now, and my assailants had grown strangely quiet. They'd extinguished their torches and were tiptoeing forward. I could no longer see or hear them. We were all blind together.

As I waited, existing in a world of black, I prayed my friends had made it safely out of the tunnel and were making their way up the cliff.

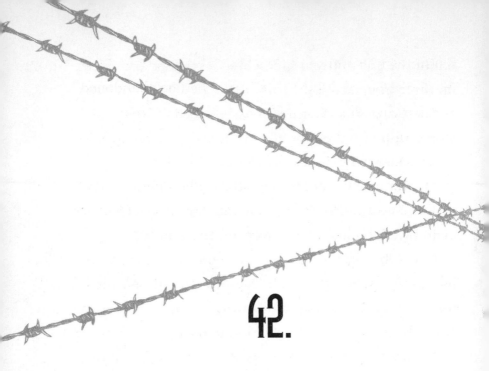

42.

Hope trembles. Whether from the ice-cold rain or straining to climb a sheer limestone wall, she can't say. Her arms and legs are shaking uncontrollably, her fingers bleed from clinging to the cliff.

The others are beneath her, connected by their rope of shirts. Each time she hears a clatter of stones, her body tenses. Although the rope strains from time to time, no one has lost their grip and plummeted to the river below.

Not yet.

Thunder rumbles, making the rocks vibrate beneath her hands. She worries about Book. The last lightning flash showed only six others beneath her. So where is he? Why hasn't he joined them? If he doesn't get here soon, he won't be able to reach the rope. He'll be completely on his own.

But why should she care if he makes it or not? First he lied to her about the infirmary, then he abandoned her for Miranda. What's it to her if he's able to join the group or not?

But just when she's convinced herself she doesn't care, she hears a burst of gunfire. She doesn't know which is worse: the sound of bullets or the silence that follows. Both make her heart shudder.

The rope has gone slack, meaning the others are caught up, even Cat, who is climbing one-handed with the rope secured tightly around his chest. Scylla has Argos draped around her neck. Diana is helping Four Fingers. Flush is guiding Twitch.

Hope shakes the rain from her face and fumbles for the next handhold, her arms and legs a series of right angles. She takes a deep breath and shifts her weight. This is how it will go, one small lizard-movement at a time, until they manage to reach the plateau—thirty to forty feet above her.

A snake's tongue of lightning strikes the opposite cliff, and she counts seven bodies beneath her. Seven! Her heart swells with hope—Book made it out! But as the lightning fades and the world is plunged back to darkness, she realizes that seventh form is just the trunk of a scrub pine jutting from the cliff. Not a person at all.

Come on, Book, she silently prays. *You can do it. You can make it.*

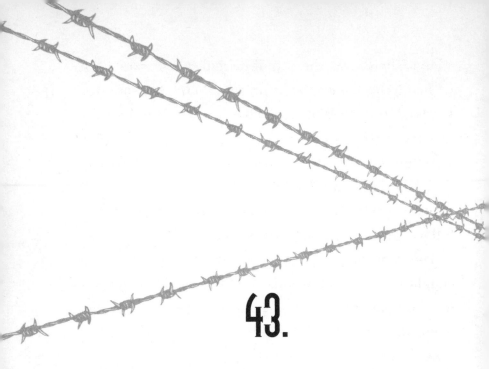

43.

Silence. The only sounds were the distant drip of water and my heart hammering against my chest.

Suddenly, the cave exploded in a flurry of gunfire and orange muzzle spits. When the bullets finally ceased and the last ricochet echoed off the narrow walls, I opened my eyes. It was as black and dark as before. My ears were ringing, but I'd survived. They hadn't gotten me, not yet.

I pulled back an arrow and stopped when I heard . . . someone's slow, steady inhalation. It wasn't just the sound that alarmed me, but where it came from: mere yards away.

So *that* was the tactic: fire at will to cover the sound of others drawing close. A high-stakes game of Red Light, Green Light. And it had worked. I was surrounded. If I took off down the tunnel, I'd run smack-dab into them.

I could stay hidden and let them pass, but then the Crazies would reach the end of the tunnel, see my friends clinging to the cliff face, and swat them down like flies.

There was no good solution.

As they walked by, I counted seven of them. They passed, and I exchanged my bow and arrow for my knife. My body unfurled to its full height and I inched forward. When I reached the trailing Crazy, my knife came whipping around his head, licking his neck.

"He's here!" he yelled, and the cave exploded in rifle fire.

I tucked myself behind him, his body rippling with every bullet he accepted. He was my shield—my only chance for survival.

"Hold your fire!" one of the Crazies called out, and the bullets stopped, the echoes faded. "Someone light a torch."

As I listened to the scraping of flint and steel, my heart raced. Once there was light, all bets were off. The Crazies would see me and that would be that. Whatever I did, I had to do it before the torch was lit.

I lowered the Crazy's lifeless body to the ground, fumbled for a rock, then threw it down the tunnel in the direction of the Wheel. It clattered off the walls. Gunfire followed it.

"He went back that way!" one of the Crazies said, and

they ran off, shooting as they went.

The Crazy with the torch remained where he was, working on the flame. I picked up my bow, nocking an arrow in darkness.

I could hear his hands fumbling with flint and steel, then the silent *whoosh* of flame as the torch caught and an orange oval of light illuminated the two of us. For the briefest of moments we locked gazes . . . and then I released the bowstring.

The arrow embedded itself in his abdomen, and his knees buckled. Before he dropped to the ground, I ripped the torch from his hand and took off running, scrambling down the passageway. Gunfire chased after me.

My guess was there were five left, and although I could outrace them to the tunnel's mouth, that wasn't good enough. Somehow I had to finish them off.

My feet slipped on loose gravel, and the ground went out from under me. I fell to the stone floor, the torch rolling to one side. It gave me an idea.

I left it there and dashed ten paces in the direction of the Wheel—*toward* the Crazies. I was now between them and the flame. I concealed myself behind a rock and readied two arrows.

The first Crazy rounded a far curve, his eyes focused on the torch's glow. He didn't expect me to be so close, and when I released the arrow, he fell to the ground with a muffled cry of surprise. My second arrow did the same to the next. I grabbed the torch and took off.

Only three Crazies were left!

Two hundreds yards later I did it again, taking down two more. That left just one. And if I wasn't mistaken, it was none other than Goodman Nellitch.

But there was a problem. The yawning black mouth of the tunnel's end was right behind me. I had run out of room. I extinguished the torch, dropped to one knee, and picked up a rock. This had to work.

It took every ounce of willpower to be patient. When Nellitch crept around a bend, I cocked my arm and hurled the rock forward. It sailed wide, clattering down the tunnel. I threw again and had the same result. Nothing.

Goodman Nellitch laughed. "Looks to me like someone's out of arrows. To which all I can say is: Sucks to be you."

He laughed and raised his body to its full height, and by then I'd nocked an arrow—my final one—and sent it flying. It landed hard in his chest, and Goodman Nellitch fell to the ground with a thud.

"Guess I had one left after all," I said. He was gasping for his last breath.

With trembling legs, I rose and stepped to the tunnel's edge. I had done it, I had taken out the enemy, and I enjoyed the moment. The cold, hard rain slapped my face, and I stared into the dark. Only when a jagged shaft of lightning split the sky could I see.

Far above me, mere ants against the rock face, were the seven others. I breathed a sigh of relief. I had delayed the Crazies long enough to let the others scale the cliff. But my friends were so far ahead of me, there was no way I could reach the rope. I'd have to do this on my own.

I began to climb. The eroding rain had sent stones plunging to the dark abyss, and I had to create new hand- and toeholds altogether. My fingers dislodged a rock and my hand flailed, grasping for something to hold on to as my body fell backward into air. Only at the last moment did my fingers squeeze into a tiny crevice and pull me toward the cliff. My heart was pounding so hard, it seemed to shake the mountainside itself.

The rain was coming down harder now, and the others were farther away than ever. How could I possibly do this on my own?

A stroke of lightning strobed the night, and a grunt of sound made me look downward. I nearly lost my breath—there was Goodman Nellitch, directly beneath me. Somehow he was still alive, the stub of my arrow poking from his chest. His shirt was red with blood, and he had a wild look in his eyes.

"Not dead yet, boy," he said, and grinned.

I needed to get up the cliff face as quickly as possible.

But when I went to move my foot, it wouldn't budge. It was somehow stuck in place. Even when I jerked and swiveled, there was no give whatsoever.

Goodman Nellitch's pudgy fingers were gripped tightly around my ankle. Rain dripped from his beard, and he seemed hardly aware of the chunk of arrow sprouting from his body. Lightning flashes showed his eyes, squinty and hard. He wasn't going to stop until he pulled me from the cliff . . . even if it meant plunging to his own death as well.

"Not so smart now, are you, *Less Than*?" he screamed, his harsh, guttural voice slicing through rain and wind.

And he was right. There was nothing I could do. I kicked and jerked my foot, but he wouldn't let go. He had me and both of us knew it. He gave a hard tug, and my foot came flying free. I was now holding on by two hands and one toehold. These were my final moments.

Nellitch laughed uproariously. "Didn't know you could do the split, did you, boy?"

Something brushed my face, and I blinked. I wanted to wipe it away, but I didn't have a free hand. Below me, the demonic sound of Goodman Nellitch's crazed laughter bounced off the canyon walls. I couldn't hold on much longer.

My face was hit a second time and I looked up. It was the rope of tied-together shirts, snaking over the edge of the cliff. My friends had made it to the top and were throwing down a lifeline.

But there was no way to grab it. Once I released

a hand, the two of us would go spiraling through air until we smacked into the river. Death would be instantaneous.

The rope was there. The Less Thans were counting on me. Nellitch was getting ready to pry my other foot from the cliff. I'd get no second chance.

This is the night
That either makes me or fordoes me quite.

Lines of Shakespeare, tugging at my thoughts. Now or never. Do or die.

My right hand slipped from the rock, and for the long forever of that moment I felt my body falling backward, felt it leave its vertical and bend toward horizontal. Felt my stomach rush upward to my throat as terror gripped my chest.

I thrust out my right hand, slapping air, waving at nothing, until—finally—it collided with the dangling shirt. I clutched it hard and my left hand joined it. Even as I was falling backward, I snapped the rope around my wrist in a hasty knot. The rope jerked to its full length, nearly yanking my shoulder from its socket.

Nellitch was pulled away from the cliff, hanging on to my ankle with his hands. I was supporting the two of us, dangling hundreds of feet above the river. Laughing maniacally, he swung drunkenly from one side to the next, pushing off against the rock like an insane rappeller, the shaft of the arrow jutting from his chest.

The rope was weak to begin with—it was just a bunch of shirts knotted together, after all—and the rain had loosened it further. I could feel it stretch even as we hung there. Somewhere up above a knot was slipping.

"No point fightin' it, Less Than," Nellitch called out. "Time for us to meet our maker." He guffawed loudly

He was right; I couldn't fight it. The weight was too much. My arm muscles were giving out.

In this final moment of living, I was consumed with a sudden urgency—there was something I needed to know.

"Why'd you do it?" I shouted, my voice fighting the rain.

"Do what?"

"Sell out the Skull People?"

He laughed a barking laugh. "Don't you know nothin', boy? After the Conclave happens, I want to be on the winning side."

I realized I never would find out what he was talking about. I could hold on a little longer, but what was the point? Why bother to extend my life an extra thirty seconds if this was what it came down to?

Then I thought of those Less Thans back at camp— the ones who'd be stuffed in a bunker on their seventeenth birthdays and sold off to the Hunters and hunted down like prey—and I did the only thing I could possibly do. Using my one free leg, I brought my boot down on Nellitch's hands and squeezed my feet together, pinching his fingers. He just laughed.

"No gettin' rid of me that easy, boy!" he shouted, having the time of his life.

The rope jerked downward. The knots were slipping, the fabric tearing.

It was at that moment that Hope's face appeared before me: black hair framing tea-colored skin, her brown eyes wide and mysterious. I remembered all we'd gone through: How I'd held her after the cave-in. How we'd kissed after the fire. How we'd caught the train and made the jump to freedom.

I was suddenly consumed with a new feeling. Not a fear of dying or even a desperation to live, but *anger*. Pure, raw anger, building inside me like floodwaters straining against a dam. How dare this crazed human being deprive me of my life? *Deprive me of Hope?*

I began kicking at his hands, at his thick, grasping fingers, one blow after another, my boot jerking and digging at his fingers. Even as he strained to hold on, I found some reserve of energy I didn't know I had, pummeling, kicking, jabbing with the toe of my boot until, finally, one of his hands slipped free.

When it was obvious he couldn't hold on, he looked

at me and hissed, "You Less Than. You're not even a normal human being."

Then his other hand let go. He hovered in midair an insanely long time as though some invisible god—or *devil*—was holding him in place, and then he plunged through night and rain, disappearing from sight.

Was it my imagination or could I hear the splash as he collided with the water?

"That's right," I answered to the dark. "I am a Less Than. And don't you ever forget it."

44.

THEY CREATE A LINE and pull Book up six inches at a time. Hope is the anchor, the final one in the row, and when the rope strains and slips, she coils it tighter around her wrist. It cuts into her skin—grows soggy with rain and crimson with blood.

Still, she will not let go.

When Book's hands finally edge the top of the cliff, Scylla and Flush grab him by the armpits and pull him up the rest of the way. He lies there motionless like a caught fish, pummeled by rain. The others bend over, hands on knees, struggling to catch their breath.

Hope watches as Book pushes himself to his feet and slowly looks around. He stumbles through the driving storm, eyes darting left and right as though in search of something lost. Something he desperately needs.

He locates Hope. Their eyes meet, stopping her heart. Her arms hang limp and lifeless by her side. Her chest heaves.

Book crosses to her.

"I'm sorry," he says, and before she can respond, he puts his arms around her and pulls her into a hug, his hands pressing against her back. Hope's first reaction is one of shock; she doesn't know what to do. Doesn't know what she *wants* to do.

Only gradually do her arms return the embrace, tentatively at first, as though Book is made of fragile glass. But soon her grip grows tight, holding him like she never wants to let him go—as if they're two colors on a painter's palette melding into one. His heart thumps in answer to her own.

They stand there, serenaded by rain. When Book releases the embrace, he presses his forehead against hers. Hope can feel the heat from his face, their mingling breaths. She begins to cry.

"*I'm* sorry," she says, the words barely manageable through choking tears.

Book shakes off her apology. "You just saved my life."

"That was all of us."

"I'm not talking about that."

He slides his hands to either side of her face, pulls her toward him, and kisses her. His lips are soft, moist with rain and the salt of her tears, and in that kiss is hunger, yearning, *need*. When at last he pulls away, Hope can barely catch her breath.

Book turns to the others. "Thank you," he says, going to each of them in turn to give them a hug and express his gratitude.

When he reaches Flush, Flush rolls his eyes and says, "Can't we all just agree we're awesome and get on with it?"

Argos barks, and everyone laughs.

"Come on," Book says. "Let's get out of here before the Crazies figure out where we are."

He bends down to undo a knot in the makeshift rope, letting his arm brush against Hope's. Neither attempts to move away.

They follow the river upstream. When the sun breaks through the morning clouds, it shines down on endless prairie. No trees, no cultivated fields, no signs of civilization. Once more they're back in vast wilderness. Sun-drenched grassland.

Every so often, a large *thwump* shakes the ground. A peek behind shows fingers of smoke rising from the cornfield.

"What's that?" Flush asks.

"They're blowing up the caves," Hope says.

More muffled blasts follow.

She feels an enormous pang of guilt for leaving those women behind. Although the Skull People were their captors, no one deserves to die at the hands of the Crazies.

Despite the blazing heat, there is pleasure in being on the move. They've been cooped up far too long, and the beating rays of sun invigorate them. Conversations pop up, up and down the line.

Hope is silent. Her mind dwells on past events: the loss of Faith, the Crazy who assaulted her, Book and Miranda. Her feelings are a confusing mass of contradictions. On the one hand, she still doesn't know whether she can trust him. And yet he keeps coming to her rescue; he keeps *protecting* her.

Then there was the kiss. The mere thought of it sends shivers down her spine.

As her feet carry her across the prairie, she dares a glance at the back of the line. Book is as silent as she is. She wonders what's going on inside his head. She wonders if she'll ever know.

A memory of Faith flashes through her mind. Although she tries to think of happy times, it's the other recollections that intrude. Faith's look of hurt before they separated. Faith's slow deterioration in camp. Faith's shivering body in the tank of ice water. Hope is filled with a terrible sadness.

And that's when she decides: no matter how drawn

she is to Book, no matter how much she longs for the touch of his embrace and the press of his lips, she dares not allow herself such feelings. The potential hurt is just too great. Bad enough to see Miranda lean her head adoringly on his shoulder; any hurt worse than that would kill her.

No, she thinks, *I won't let myself fall for him any more.*

As Hope marches along in the hot sun, silent tears spill from her eyes. The back of her hand swipes angrily at the offending moisture. Still, she knows it's better to feel this minor pain today than endure a major one tomorrow.

PART THREE
RETURN

Learn from yesterday, live for today, hope for tomorrow.
—ALBERT EINSTEIN

45.

WE MARCHED UNDER CLOUDLESS skies. When the land-scape sloped downward and brought us to the river's edge, we were suddenly afforded an unending supply of water and food: fish and crawdads, frogs and turtles. A welcome change from our diet of grasshoppers and squirrels.

As we slogged along, following the twisting, bending river, one question echoed in my mind: Why would the Hunters want to arm the Crazies? I wondered if it was somehow related to Goodman Nellitch's words before he fell to his death. *After the Conclave happens, I want to be on the winning side.* Of course, I had no idea what Conclave he was talking about, and wondered if I ever would.

Hope insisted on leading the march each day, as though trying to put as much distance between her and me as possible. I couldn't understand it. Ever since our kiss atop the cliff, she'd barely spoken to me. Couldn't even look me in the eye. It was as though I'd ceased to exist.

I assumed it had something to do with Miranda, and frankly, I didn't know what to think about her. When we had last seen her in the Compound, she'd promised to distract the Crazies so we could escape. And yet they'd found us anyway. Had she done the best she could, or just the opposite—told the Crazies exactly where we were?

Days passed. The nights grew cold. The air smelled of autumn. The first morning we woke to frost, our clothes were as stiff as boards, crinkling when we first got up. We picked up our pace. We had to get to Camp Liberty before the snow flew and winter froze us in our tracks.

The river forked and we followed the smaller tributary north, just as Miranda had instructed. At night, we made bowstrings from yucca leaves and knapped flint into arrow points. Each morning, we practiced, firing arrows until our fingers bled.

Still, it was impossible to imagine just how we were going to defeat a camp of Brown Shirts, even with a canvas knapsack full of explosives.

One night, after the others drifted off to bed, Cat remained sitting at the fire's edge, his gaze lost in the flames. I threw something at his feet.

"What's that?" he asked, not bothering to pick it up.

"Your new arm."

His eyes squinted as if I was spoiling for a fight. "I left that back at the Compound," he snapped.

"I know. I picked it up." I had stuffed it in the knapsack with the explosives.

He spat on the sand and turned away.

"I'm serious," I said.

"Yeah, well, why don't you just mind your own business?"

"Let me show you how it works." I bent down and tried to attach it to his arm. He flung my hands away.

"I said skip it, all right?"

I met his stare and didn't flinch. "You don't want to just try it?"

"Why should I?"

"You'll be able to fire an arrow again."

He scoffed. "I'll never fire an arrow like before."

"You're right. You won't fire like before. But maybe this new way will be even better."

He looked at me like I was from another planet. "You don't get it, man. I'm not who I was before. I got *this* now." He raised his stump of an arm. "I can't do the shit I used to do. I'm a . . ."

341

"What? A Less Than?"

He gave his head a long, slow shake and turned away.

"You're right," I said. "You're different now. And yeah, you'll have to make some adjustments, but you'll figure it out. You're Cat—you're still the best athlete any of us have seen."

The flames glimmered in his blue eyes, and his piercing gaze tore through me. "What if I don't want to make those changes?"

"You mean what if you just want to drink yourself to death?"

His jaw clenched.

"I don't know why you crawled back under the fence and came with us," I said. "If you want to feel sorry for yourself, go ahead. But you're alive. That's more than June Bug can say. Or Frank. So I'm going to Camp Liberty to free those Less Thans, and if you want to be a coward and stay behind, be my guest. Just don't expect me to think much of you."

I stalked off to bed, not waiting for a response.

46.

THE MEASLY TRICKLE OF the river leads them to the
far edge of Camp Liberty. To the north rests Skeleton
Ridge, already shrouded in snow. When stars begin to
pop in the sky and a full moon rises orange and bul-
bous in the east, the group comes out of hiding and
tiptoes forward.

What they see shocks them. The camp is surrounded
by a fence. It is old, rusty chain-link, obviously stripped
from some other site and set up here. It is topped with a
coil of razor wire, the jagged edges catching moonglow.
While Hope and the Sisters are used to fences, it comes
as an obvious surprise to the Less Thans.

"Why would they do that?" Flush asks.

"Maybe because of us," Book says.

A new reality sinks in. It was going to be difficult enough to rescue a hundred LTs; now it just got harder.

They circle north, reaching the firs and ponderosa pines that separate Camp Liberty from the stables. The Brown Shirts haven't bothered to stretch the fence this far, but what surprises the Less Thans is that the stables are no more. The barns and corrals have been razed to the ground. In their place are bulldozers and the beginnings of an enormous hole.

"What's all this?" Hope asks, but Book doesn't have an answer.

They inch their way to the pit, their breath frosting in the night.

"I don't get it," Flush says. "Why put up a building on the outside of camp?"

"Maybe they're not going to put a building there at all," Twitch says, "but something else." There is something about his tone that stops everyone cold.

"Like what?"

"Bodies."

Flush scoffs at the idea. "You wouldn't put bodies in a big hole."

"You would if it's a mass grave."

They hike an hour up the mountain, stopping to make camp only when the snow gets too deep. When they clear away the snow and get a small fire going, they resume the conversation.

"For burying people?" Flush asks.

"And hiding them," Twitch adds.

"So what're you saying? The Brown Shirts no longer use the cemetery?"

"That's right."

"Because it's full?"

"No, because they intend to hide the evidence."

"What evidence?"

"The fact that we've been prey for all these years."

Hope knows Twitch is right. She remembers the letter, the one from Chancellor Maddox. The Final Solution. This is what the Brown Shirts are up to.

Suddenly, the bulldozers they first witnessed in the middle of nowhere make sense. The Western Federation Territory is trying to cover up what it's been doing all these years. *Leave no trace.*

Wind *shoosh*es through pine needles, and Hope knows they're all thinking the same thing: they're the last hope for saving the Sisters, the Less Thans, the Skull People. If they don't do something, the Republic will be a nation of Brown Shirts.

Flush's hands dig at his face as though trying to rub away a bad dream. "So if we don't free those Less Thans, they'll be slaughtered and buried."

"That's right."

The problem is, how do they break into an armed

camp and sneak out a couple of hundred Less Thans? Plus, the seasons are changing fast. The aspens are golden and shimmery in the afternoon sun, but the nights are icy cold. A thick blanket of snow already covers the mountains. If they're going to free the Less Thans, they have to do it soon.

"We need those Less Thans to help us," Hope says. "They need to be our army."

"Okay," Flush says, "but how do we convince them of that?"

For the first time since their kiss, Hope's eyes fall on Book. "Someone needs to break in there and tell them."

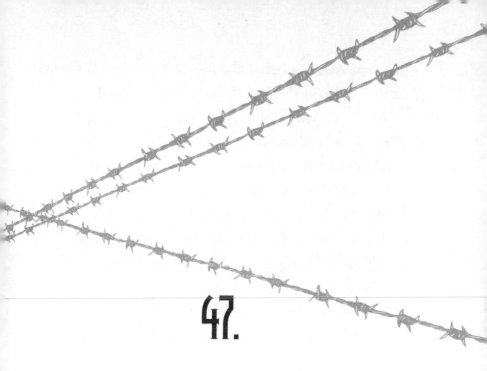

47.

It was decided that two of us would slip inside. I volunteered—in part because Hope had basically challenged me to, but also because this was my idea in the first place. I was the one who'd convinced the others to come back to Camp Liberty.

Finding a partner wasn't so easy. Flush wanted no part of it, and I couldn't really blame him. Four Fingers and Twitch weren't possibilities. The three Sisters were willing, but given that it was a camp for boys, that didn't seem the best idea.

That left Cat.

"You'll do it?" I asked.

"Do I have a choice?" His tone was surly and not the least bit cooperative.

Of the four entrances into camp, the gate on the

western edge appeared the most promising. It opened onto a series of sheds and seemed unwatched.

As we crawled through sand and tufts of matted grass, I realized we weren't all that far from where we'd first found Cat that sunny spring morning—dying of dehydration at the edge of the No Water. How everything had changed since then.

The entrance was double gated, with a thick chain and padlock holding the two frames together. There was no way to undo the lock, of course, but by tugging the one door forward and pushing the other back, we managed to create an opening maybe six inches wide. Just enough space for a couple of emaciated Less Thans like ourselves.

"Where to?" Cat asked after we slipped through.

"The barracks." We needed to recruit those LTs.

We clung to shadows as we tiptoed forward. It felt strange to be there. We'd gone to such lengths to get away, and now here we were again—by our own choice, no less. It was impossible not to feel the grip of panic.

We edged around the buildings. Although faint lights glowed from the camp's eastern edge—the Soldiers' Quarters—this section of Liberty was lit only by the moon.

The Quonset hut stood big and hulking, its high curved roof cutting into the star-spattered sky. But when I gave the front door a tug, it didn't budge. A closer inspection revealed it was locked.

We circled around to the back, hearing the snores of LTs reverberating through the walls. I couldn't wait to see their reactions when they caught sight of us. We'd have to quiet their celebrations so we wouldn't be discovered.

The back doors were locked as well. Strange.

"Guess Dekker wised up," Cat offered.

I grunted a response. It was painful just thinking of Sergeant Dekker: his oily hair, his noxious smile. *Slice Slice*, he'd called me, in honor of my failed attempt at suicide. I could well imagine his glee at locking up the LTs.

"I guess that's that," Cat said. He made to return the way we'd come.

"Not so fast," I said, grabbing the back of his shirt.

I led him around to the side of the building, to the lavatory window. It was where we'd jumped free the night of our escape. Surely they couldn't dead-bolt a window. The window was covered up with a large piece of plywood, nailed firmly to the frame. But when I ran my fingers around the edge, I found a small gap between the wood and the building. I jammed my knifepoint in and managed to separate board from window. I lowered the plywood to the ground and slid the window upward.

"Be my guest," Cat said, motioning for me to go first.

I hoisted myself in, landing with a quiet thud on the tiled floor. I remembered this floor—remembered this *room*. It was where we'd conducted more than one secret meeting . . . and where, two years earlier, I'd tried to end my life.

My body went clammy at the thought of it. *Dripping blood. Darkness closing in. My vision narrowing to a pinprick.*

I shook the thought from my head and helped Cat haul himself through the window.

We tiptoed to the door and pulled it open, easing into the bunkhouse itself.

Even before my eyes adjusted to the dark, my nose was assaulted by a strong, offensive odor. The ammonia smell of urine and the foul odor of feces . . . coming not from the lavatory but from the bunks themselves. How was that possible?

We slid forward in the black, stopping when we reached the far edge of beds. By now my eyes could make out the general shapes and forms of boys.

No, not so much boys as *bodies*—scores of them—crammed onto the wooden bunks. Alive, yes, but just barely so. More like skeletons than living, breathing human beings. So thin they lacked the strength to sit up. So weak they'd soiled themselves in their own bunks.

That's when it hit me: this was my dream—my *nightmare*. For weeks I'd been seeing this very sight, picturing the tethered Less Thans beneath the tennis courts, but it was worse than that. They were right here—*in the barracks themselves*. Carcasses wasting away to nothing. The Republic hoped to starve them to death, then toss their emaciated corpses into the pit and cover them with dirt.

Something else occurred to me, too. These LTs were far too weak to be the army we'd envisioned. Too weak to even register our presence. A far cry from what I'd expected.

I gave a glance to Cat. He was in shock like me, his jaw working back and forth.

"This ain't right," he whispered, his voice thick with emotion.

I nodded my agreement—what more was there to say? Even as I looked around and spied LTs who had bullied me in younger days, I felt no sense of victory. On the contrary, I would gladly have gone back to that time in a second.

"Book," a voice said, strangled and raspy. "Cat."

Our feet shuffled forward, pulled by the sound of our names.

"Over here," the voice said, and Cat and I shifted one aisle over.

We finally located the body, and even though my eyes

traveled up and down the thin skeleton, for the longest time I couldn't figure out who it was. Only when I saw the enormous red splotch on one side of his face did I realize.

It was Red. We were reunited once again.

"You made it," he said. His voice was weak and strained, but it was still the same old Red. I hadn't laid eyes on him since the night I'd jumped from the train.

"What's going on here?" I asked.

"They've locked us up."

I couldn't help but stare at his emaciated body. His neck was no thicker than the trunk of a sapling. He weighed maybe half as much as when I'd seen him last.

"Do they feed you?" I asked.

He tried to laugh—it sounded like he was being strangled. "A piece of moldy bread a day. A cup of water. Once a week some soup. Makes me miss those grasshoppers." He noticed Cat's missing arm. "That from the ambush?"

Cat nodded grimly.

"Sorry. At least you're alive."

Cat didn't respond. His eyes were flinty and hard.

"How'd you get here?" I asked.

"Beat you, didn't I?" Red swallowed. His Adam's apple seemed huge set against his scrawny neck. "They shipped us here."

"They?"

"Brown Shirts."

"How'd they find—?" Red's eyes flicked away, and I didn't bother to finish the question. I didn't need to.

A thin sheen of moisture covered his eyes. "After we saw the bulldozers, I snuck back and told the Brown Shirts where we were. Thought it was for the best. They promised they wouldn't sell any more Less Thans to the Hunters. Then I saw how they ambushed us, and well . . ." He trailed off.

I could scarcely believe what I was hearing. Red had sold us out. *Red.*

"Not Dozer?" I asked.

"Nah. He joined up with them later on—once he saw there was no way out. I'm the traitor."

Poor Red. I reached out and took his hand. It was bony and cold to the touch. "It's okay," I said. "You didn't know."

He nodded, but I could tell he didn't believe me.

Cat and I looked around at the living skeletons. Their mouths were stuck open in grimaces of horror. Yellow pus oozed from their eyes.

What kind of hell is this, I wanted to know, *where people starve others to death just because they're somehow different? Just because they consider them Less Thans?*

My knees went wobbly. It was all I could do to remain standing.

"Why're you here?" Red asked.

"Like we said back at the Heartland: we came to free the Less Thans."

"Good luck with that."

I understood his sarcasm. As we looked around at the skeletal bodies that lay on the bunks like so many corpses in a morgue, it was impossible to imagine how we were going to lead them to safety.

"I don't mean to discourage you," he said, "but it seems kinda, um, impossible."

I had no good response to that. Fact was, I was beginning to feel the same way.

"One good thing," he said. "It's just us. There's no nursery anymore."

"What'd they do with the kids?"

"Shipped 'em out one night. I don't think we want to know where." Then he added, "Sorry about siding with Dozer. Don't know what I was thinking."

"Don't worry about it."

I could see his decisions ate at him. I understood the feeling. I still struggled with some of the choices I'd made. Just part of life, I guess. Regrets and all.

"Hey, there's someone else here, too," Red said. "He might even have some brilliant ideas."

"Who's that?"

"Over there." Red pointed one aisle over and one row up. "You'll see."

We left Red's bunk and approached a sleeping body. The breaths were jagged and uneven, like the rusty teeth of a saw. We stood over the LT, not recognizing who it was. As his chest strained to rise and fall, my gaze settled on the skull-like face. When I saw the scar that traveled from eyebrow to chin, I had a shiver of recognition.

It was Major Karsten. Cat's father.

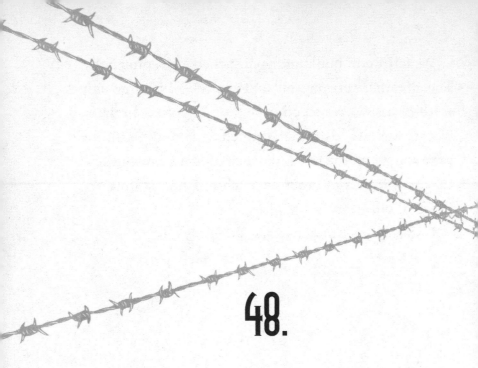

48.

THE OTHERS HAVE DRIFTED off to sleep, but Hope remains by the fire, mind racing. She wonders what Maddox and Gallingham are up to. Remembers her family. And most of all: thinks about Book. Was it just plain idiotic to think she could turn off her feelings for him?

But then she remembers Miranda—can't shake from her mind the sight of her head resting on Book's shoulder.

It's better this way, she thinks. *If I allow myself to love, I'll only get hurt.*

As her eyes gaze into the wavering flames, she absently strokes the locket around her neck. Like the Sisters and Less Thans themselves, this little charm has been through hell and back: flood and fire, blood and bullets. It's nicked and tarnished and scorched and singed, but that doesn't diminish what it means to her. She can still imagine her parents' faces through the thin metal.

And now she's discovered the note, it's not just their faraway gaze, but words of encouragement and love. It's almost like her dad is sending a message from the grave—willing her to carry on.

Hope's fingers stop and clutch the locket. What if it's more than that? What if it's more than mere words of reassurance? What if her dad was actually trying to tell her something?

With fumbling fingers, she removes the locket from around her neck and places it in her palm. She snaps it open. Her thumb and index finger pinch the picture of her father and the tiny slip of paper behind his photo. She unfolds the paper. Even though the words are seared into her brain, her eyes pore over the short paragraph.

To Faith and Hope
Dear girls. Either you get this or you won't, but if you do. Know that I love you. Know that I believe in you. Either way, your mom and I have been so proud to raise two such amazing daughters who don't give up. Remember your mother and do what's best.
Dad

Is it possible there's something there she didn't see before? Some hidden message? Some clue her father is giving her from the grave?

Hope reads the paragraph once more and a thought occurs to her: she doesn't understand the punctuation. Why are the first and second sentences separated? Or, more to the point, why is there a period after the first sentence? Why is there a period after the greeting? It makes no sense. Unless . . .

Her hands are shaking as she examines the tiny scrap of paper once again. Maybe he was doing something with the first letters. Maybe that's why he made two sentences out of one.

So *Dear* would be *D*.

Either would be *E*.

Know is *K*.

And so on, until she arrives at six letters. *D-E-K-K-E-R*.

Dekker.

A person, if she's not mistaken. She's heard the name before, but can't recall why or when. She thinks Book mentioned him once.

She scrambles over to Flush and gives him a hard nudge. He's sleeping on his side with Argos tucked against his chest. They both look up.

"Is it morning already?" Flush's words are slurred with sleep.

"Shh. I have a question. Dekker. Who is he?"

Flush tries to focus. "Sergeant Dekker? A real prick. Used to give Book shit for some reason."

Hope suddenly remembers. The cruel sergeant who pulled his pistol on Frank when she was hiding in the attic.

"Thanks," she says, patting Flush on the shoulder. "Go back to sleep."

She returns to her spot by the fire and studies the note again, her eyes landing on that final sentence. *Remember your mother and do what's best.*

What was her father telling her? That Dekker was somehow involved with her mother's death? Is that what he was getting at?

If so, Hope wonders how he knew. He returned to the house only once, to give his wife a proper burial, but he never spoke about the experience, and Faith and Hope never asked. All Hope remembers is that he came back with a hard glint in his eye.

Maybe he'd discovered more than just his wife's skeletal remains; maybe he'd discovered clues.

If so, then Hope needs to add another name to the list.

Thorason, Maddox, Gallingham . . . and Dekker.

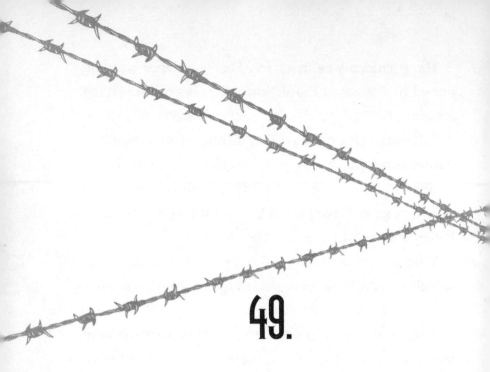

49.

ONCE THE MAJOR SENSED us standing there, his eyes slid open. I hadn't seen him since the summer, the night at Camp Freedom when he told me Cat was alive. He'd lost maybe a hundred pounds since then, and his bones pressed against his skin.

Cat fell to his knees by his father's side. "What happened?" he asked.

Karsten took a long moment to swallow before he spoke. "Westbrook," he finally croaked. "Aims to kill us all."

Cat shook his head in disbelief. "But why you? You're not a Less Than."

Karsten tried to force a smile. His teeth and gums had turned black. "Found out . . . about my son."

He turned away and coughed—a deep, gagging sound that reached the depths of his lungs. Was it my imagination or were there drops of blood on his pillow?

Cat began flexing his hand, balling it into a tight fist before straightening it out again. Karsten's eyes landed on me, his face more skull than flesh and blood.

"Remember Final Solution?" he managed.

"Of course."

He gave a sober nod.

Cat and I shared a look. Those mass graves were for real. Chancellor Maddox intended to kill everyone off, then bury them and hide the evidence. Cat's face went rigid, his eyes blazing. He reached out and took his father's hand.

"We want to free you all. Take down the Brown Shirts in the process."

"Won't . . . be easy."

"We've faced big odds before."

It was true. But never odds like this.

"All warfare . . . is based on deception," Karsten murmured.

The Art of War," I said, remembering the book from Camp Liberty. Back when I was a prisoner, someone used to leave books for me in my trunk; I never did know who.

Karsten managed the weakest of smiles. "So you got it?"

I could only imagine the shocked expression on my face. "That was you," I heard myself say.

He nodded and said, "Promised . . . I'd look out for you."

"Promised who?"

"Who else?" he asked. "Your grandmother."

My head was suddenly swimming. *He knew my grandmother?*

"How? *When?*"

Before he had a chance to answer, a coughing attack folded him in half, bending him like a pocketknife.

"Come on," Cat said. "Let's get out of here and let him sleep."

Even though I was impatient to find out more, I agreed.

We grabbed some spare coats and blankets and made our way down the long aisle. Many of the LTs were now awake. As we passed, some managed to prop themselves up on an elbow. Most remained lying on their sides, their hollow eyes wide with pleading. I wondered if they thought we were the stuff of dreams. Once-familiar ghosts come to taunt them in their sleep.

Help us get out of here, their expressions read. *Help us live.*

If only we knew how.

We returned to camp. Cat didn't utter a word. Whenever I glanced over at him, his jaw was clenched, his stare a million miles off.

After I told the others what we'd seen, looks of shock and disgust passed across their faces. Even Argos buried his snout in my side and gave a soft whimper.

"How many are left?" Hope asked.

"Seventy-five or so," I answered. "Maybe less."

"Anyone beneath the tennis courts?"

"Didn't get a chance to check. If so, they'll be in even worse shape."

"So who can help us out?" Flush asked. "Red?"

"Unlikely."

"Major Karsten?"

I shook my head. He was more skeleton than person.

"So who?"

"Maybe a dozen of 'em," I said matter-of-factly. "But that's it."

The sobering reality of the situation settled on us like the hovering smoke from the campfire. A log popped in the fire, and orange embers exploded skyward. No one said a word. Finally, Cat got up and strode angrily away. The rest of us stumbled to bed.

I woke a few short hours later when a boot nudged my chest. My eyelids fluttered open . . . and there was Cat looking down at me.

"Get up," he said sharply.

Fuzzy with sleep, I tried to make sense of the situation. Although the eastern rim of mountains glowed pale and golden, the sun had yet to rise.

"Can it wait?"

"No," he said, and walked away. I sighed and threw the blankets off.

I followed him as he went tromping through a meadow. What was so urgent that needed talking about right now? *Before the sun was up.* And why way out here? Then I noticed someone had carved a series of concentric circles on the trunk of a thick pine tree fifty yards away.

Before I could figure out what was going on, Cat bent down and retrieved something from the ground. He slapped it against my belly.

"Show me how this thing works."

It was his artificial arm from the Compound. I couldn't believe he'd kept it.

"So you gonna teach me or not?" he prodded.

"Right," I said, somewhat dazed by the fact that Cat was asking for my help.

The prosthesis was carved from oak, meant to attach to the elbow and serve as a forearm. Hammered to its base was a swatch of leather with some adjoining straps; the leather would circle the stub that was his elbow and the straps would wrap over his shoulder. It was simple, it was uncomplicated, it was primitive . . . but it would work.

"What're these things?" he asked, referring to the two curved pieces of wood that jutted from the end and tapered off to fine points.

"Pincers. They're fixed in place, but they'll act like fingers."

"They look more like claws."

"Well, they're not," I said. "They're supposed to be fingers."

He grunted but said nothing.

I helped him into the contraption and tightened the straps until his new arm was snug against his old.

"Now what?" Cat asked. It was odd hearing him ask *me* for instructions.

"Now you need to make it an extension of your arm."

He rolled his eyes and muttered something beneath his breath.

"I'm serious. If you let it remain a separate thing, you'll never master it."

"It's a piece of wood," he pointed out.

"It's your *arm*," I countered. "It's like what Frank said about an archer and his bow. There's no knowing where one ends and the other begins."

His face softened—slightly. "Now what?" he asked impatiently.

"Now you fire an arrow."

He looked at me as if judging my sanity. "Well?" he asked, eyes gesturing toward his weapon. "You gonna give it to me or what?"

"I think you can get it on your own."

365

As if to spite me, he picked up the bow with his *right* hand.

"Go on," I said.

He tried to shift it to his left, but it slipped between the pincers and clattered to the ground. When he tried it again, the same thing happened. And the next time after that.

"This ain't gonna work," he said, kicking a pinecone with his foot.

"You're right. If you give up, it's not going to work."

"I'm not giving up."

"Looks to me like you're giving up."

"I'm not giving up."

His neck and face turned beet red, and for a second I thought he was going to tackle me to the ground and beat the living hell out of me. Even though I outnumbered him two arms to one, I knew there was no way I could take him.

When I pretended to look away, he transferred the bow to his wooden fingers. Unlike before, he took his time, understanding he couldn't match his former speed. He had to learn a new quality: patience. Not in his current vocabulary.

As he worked, his tongue stuck out of one corner of his mouth. Beads of sweat popped on his forehead. Finally, the pincers managed to balance the bow's grip.

He reached for an arrow, and because it was his

right hand dealing with it, that part was as smooth and effortless as ever. He raised the bow, rotating his left arm just enough to maintain the pincer's "thumb" in the special notch I'd added to his bow. He pulled the arrow back, held the draw, and let it fly.

A piece of bark went flying as the arrow grazed one side of the tree. The woods were silent, as if all of nature was waiting to see Cat's reaction.

The expression that settled on his face was an interesting mix of emotions. He was dissatisfied he hadn't hit the bull's-eye, even more upset he hadn't hit the circles at all, but the fact he'd come close—on his *first attempt*—seemed to give him hope.

"*Maybe* this'll work," he grumbled, and then picked up another arrow. He fired, and it landed with a resounding *thwack* at the base of the tree, just inches from the circle's bottom arc. By the time he was drawing the third arrow, he had forgotten I was there. By the fifth, he was landing arrows in the circles, gaining confidence, and I was easing away, happy to know Cat was once again one of us.

50.

THE NEXT DAY THE snows come. Not dry, fluffy flakes, but the thick, heavy stuff. It piles atop their blankets, their clothes, nearly smothers the fire. While Camp Liberty gets only a dusting, where they are—farther up the mountain—it measures a good foot or two. That on top of what was already there. To make their plan work, they need to act fast.

Everyone stays busy. Cat spends countless hours at the archery range, Book and Twitch fiddle with explosives, and Hope and the others divide their time between carving arrows, constructing crossbows, and sewing. Lots and lots of sewing.

By night they huddle around their meager campfire and review their plan.

They gather for a final meal. Scylla has managed to bag four squirrels, and they roast them on a spit. They eat in silence, knowing that after tonight things will be different. They will either be dead, captured, or surrounded by grateful Less Thans.

"To freeing the Less Thans," Flush says, raising his canteen in a toast.

"To freeing the Less Thans," the others repeat.

As they pack up and collect their few belongings, everyone works in silence, surrounded by their private thoughts. Hope can't take her eyes off Book. She knows this may be the last time they'll be together.

"Hey," she says, drifting to his side.

"Hey," he says back.

Their eyes meet—and then instantly dart away. Hope may have promised herself not to fall for him, but the fact is, she wants nothing more than to run off with Book and hide far away somewhere deep within the woods. To live the life her parents lived, cut off from civilization, just the two of them, forever and ever, amen.

But that isn't possible and she knows it.

"I just want you to know," she says, "that whatever happens tonight, well, thank you."

Book seems surprised. "For what?"

"For saving us. For saving *me*."

"You saved me too," he says. "We're even."

Tears press against her eyes, so she turns her back, continuing to pack arrows into quivers. *Why did I make that silly decision to not let him into my life? What was I thinking?*

"Where will you go when we're done?" Book asks.

"Back to the Sisters," she manages to say. "I promised Helen I'd join up after we freed the Less Thans."

"I'm sure they'll be glad to see you."

"Mm."

It's true, Hope thinks. They will be glad to see her. And she'll be glad to see them. But what she really wants is for Book to convince her to stay with him. To say, *Don't go. Let's make a life together—you and me.*

But he doesn't say it. And she silently scolds herself for even imagining the possibility.

"And you?" she asks.

"Get these guys to the Heartland. Beyond that, who knows?"

She nods. The reality is they stand little to no chance of making this happen. A ragtag collection of Less Thans and Sisters up against a camp of Brown Shirts? No way they can pull this off. But they have to trick themselves into thinking they can. Why bother otherwise?

"There's one other place I'd like to go as well," Book says. "If you'll let me."

"If I *let* you? What're you talking about?"

"Your childhood home. I'd like to take you to your mom's grave."

370

Now it's not just tears, it's a lump the size of a plum lodging in her throat. Her muscles go all slack, and when she dares a glance at Book, he's staring right at her. Their eyes lock.

"Yes, I'll let you," she says.

She opens her mouth to say more, but no words come. Hope doesn't know exactly what she wants to tell Book—doesn't know what she's *able* to tell Book—but she knows exactly what she wants to happen.

She wants Book to wrap her in his arms, wants to feel his breath tickle her ear and to inhale the sweet fragrance of his musky scent, wants to feel the caress of his hands against the small of her back and her body pressed against his. Not out of sheer desire or physical longing but something else. *Need. Comfort.*

Maybe even something more—like *love.*

But neither one says or does anything. Finally, Book whispers, "For Faith."

The tears jump from Hope's eyes. "For Faith," she manages to say.

"Live today," he says.

"Tears tomorrow," Hope finishes.

She smiles gratefully . . . and turns away.

By now, everyone is packed and ready to go. They douse the fire and hike down the mountain single file, plowing through the snow. No one speaks a word, and Hope wonders if she and Book will share a moment together ever again.

They crouch in bushes and watch. Even though the hole—the mass grave—is no deeper than when they first saw it, the Brown Shirts have built a fire there, an enormous bonfire in the earthen pit. Hope wonders why. Is it to burn off the downed trees they've bull-dozed, or is it there for other reasons? Reasons having to do with incinerating corpses?

One thing she knows for sure: Dr. Gallingham is present, directing the soldiers how best to feed the flames. Just seeing him makes Hope's pulse race, and her fingers grip her spear. But she knows now is not the time.

A Humvee pulls up and Chancellor Maddox steps out. When Gallingham sees her, he retrieves a small metal box—identical to the one on that deserted country road. He opens it reverently and removes a tiny object. The chancellor takes it, placing it in her briefcase.

Hope and the others have seen enough. They circle the camp and reach the western gate, slipping through the gap in the chain-link fence. Only Twitch and Argos stay on the outside. The other seven tiptoe from one building to the next. Book leaves the group at the back of the Quonset hut; Cat separates a few moments later. Flush leads the remaining five, stopping at the back of Camp Liberty's storehouse. They wait, crouched in shadows.

Time passes. Hope tries not to worry, but the fact is

that Book is out there by himself. The thought of him fills her with a million regrets.

They hear a bird cry—three times—and Hope begins to count aloud. At ten, they hear two muffled explosions: one from the western part of camp, one from the east. Scylla throws herself against the storehouse door. The jamb splinters and they rush inside.

A siren wails, and the camp is bathed in illumination—towering banks of floodlights. Then the sounds of shouting and distant footfalls.

"Everyone good to go?" Hope asks.

The others nod. Even Four Fingers seems to understand what's expected of him.

They move quickly through the aisles, grabbing supplies. As they reach the second floor, Hope hesitates by the window; she can just make out the entrance to the Quonset hut. Three Humvees come to a sliding stop, slinging snow and dirt. Brown Shirts pour out, rifles drawn.

Scylla tugs at Hope's sleeve, but Hope can't tear herself away—because the Quonset hut is exactly where Book is. He's inside that very building.

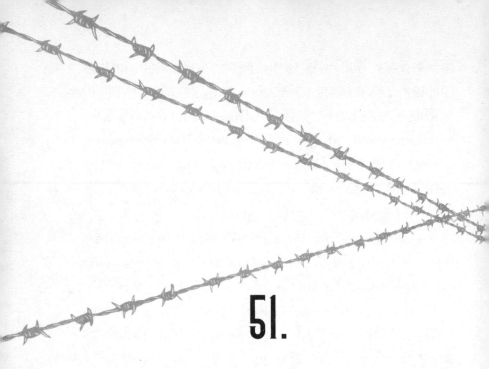

51.

I FIGURED THE EXPLOSION would rouse some Brown Shirts; I didn't think it would wake all of Camp Liberty.

The cold had made the C-4 firm, and it took far longer to mold it to the Quonset hut's back door than I had hoped. When I finished, I let out a birdcall. Three times.

The explosives popped open the door and sent up an angry cloud of black smoke. By the time the soldiers appeared, I was still in the process of ripping the door from its hinges. I had yet to sneak out a single Less Than. The soldiers bound my hands behind my back and marched me across the infield.

Colonel Westbrook sat behind his desk, his eyes as coal black as ever. Sergeant Dekker was also there.

"Slice Slice," he said, presenting an oily smile that seemed to drip grease. I couldn't turn away fast enough.

There were three others in the room as well, hunkered in shadows. Chancellor Maddox. Dr. Gallingham. Colonel Thorason. I wondered why they were all there. Was it to witness the mass burial in the open pit? The completion of the Final Solution?

"Ah, 183," Colonel Westbrook said, calling me by my old camp number. "I was hoping we'd run into each other again."

I grunted. I was in no mood to talk.

"Frankly, I'm surprised you came back. Did you really think you could free seventy-five Less Thans?"

It was hard not to agree with him—it suddenly seemed like the most ridiculous plan of all time.

"You're killing them," I said.

"They're killing themselves. We can't help it if they don't eat."

"Maybe you should try feeding them."

"I see you've been listening to the rumor mill. Let me guess. Red? Or maybe your friend's father: Major Karsten?" He leaned forward, elbows resting on the desk. "You're the one who likes to read, aren't you? How's that working out for you?"

More than anything in the world, I wanted to wipe that smug smile off his face. "You have no right to treat human beings like that."

375

"You're right. I don't. But since Less Thans aren't really human, it's not really an issue, is it?"

From the corner, Dr. Gallingham burst into schoolboy giggles.

"All part of your 'Final Solution'?" I asked through gritted teeth.

Westbrook's eyebrows arched in surprise, and Chancellor Maddox stepped from the shadows, the briefcase handcuffed to her left wrist. "What have you heard?" she asked.

"Just that you don't trust anyone who doesn't look like you."

"You're too young to understand. You don't know what it's like to watch your country change."

"You mean since Omega?"

"I mean *before* Omega." There was a smugness in her tone, an I-know-something-that-you-don't kind of tone. An attitude that drove me crazy, especially from adults.

"Too bad you're only chancellor of the territory and not president of the whole country," I said.

A smile lifted her cheeks. "That may change after the Conclave." She shot a look to the doctor.

It was the second time I'd heard the word—the first was from Goodman Nellitch before he fell to his death. "What's the Conclave?" I asked.

"Nothing that concerns you."

When I realized she wasn't going to tell me any more,

my eyes fell on Colonel Westbrook, sitting slumped in his chair. His comb-over was damp with perspiration, and it struck me that there was something supremely pathetic about him. Funny I hadn't seen it before.

"And let me guess," I said. "No place for Less Thans in this *changing* America?"

The chancellor gave me a look that was supposed to be apologetic. To me, it just looked smug. "We can't very well have a perfect civilization with the *deformed*." She said it like it was a swear word. "But we do make exceptions." She pulled open the door and gave a nod. A Brown Shirt shuffled in.

Dozer. Something about seeing him wearing the uniform of the enemy was more than I could stomach. Even though my wrists were bound behind my back, I lowered my shoulder and threw myself into his barrel chest.

"*Oomph*," he cried, and went staggering backward. His head collided with the wall, and a picture went crashing to the floor. Glass shattered.

He shook his head and came at me. His strong hand wrapped around my neck and I felt my face go purple.

Only reluctantly did Sergeant Dekker separate us. "Enough," he said to Dozer. "You'll get your time."

I was bent over at the waist, trying to catch my breath. "How could you?" I gasped. "You're a Less Than."

"*Was* a Less Than. I'm a Brown Shirt now."

Chancellor Maddox smiled all angelic-like. "You see, Book? Your friend here might be imperfect, but we accepted him into the fold."

"*Bought* him into the fold, more like it. And he's not my friend."

From outside I heard two birdcalls.

"What happens now?" I asked.

"Now we find out who else accompanied you here," the chancellor said.

"You really want to know?"

"We do."

"An army."

Dozer laughed. "You wish," he said.

"I don't need to wish; it's true."

He laughed again. Harsher, more mocking.

At just that moment a loud explosion rocked the camp, rattling the windowpanes. The electricity went out a moment later.

"What the hell was that?" Colonel Westbrook asked.

"An army," I said, "taking out your generators."

Chancellor Maddox didn't buy it. "Nothing more than parlor tricks," she said.

She fumbled for a match, lighting a candle. Another explosion followed, louder than the first. This one shook the walls. She turned to me as if studying me for the first time. Sergeant Dekker whipped out a knife and held it to my throat. A third explosion came. It was the loudest of all, followed by an enormous fireball that lit up the sky.

"The vehicle compound," Westbrook said breathlessly.

The chancellor, the two colonels, and Dr. Gallingham made for the door. "Don't lose sight of him," the colonel said to Dekker. "And if he makes any noise at all, cut his throat."

"My pleasure," Dekker said.

"Just so you know," Chancellor Maddox added before stepping outside. "I suppose you remember your friend from the Hunters. Wears orange a lot. Has a scar on the side of his face from a certain propane explosion. He'll be joining us soon. And I'm sure he would like nothing more than to see you for a final time."

She smiled her beauty-queen smile before disappearing into the hall.

I felt my breathing go short. If she was telling the truth, then there was no possible way we could make it out alive. Brown Shirts were bad enough, but Brown Shirts and Hunters together would be unbeatable.

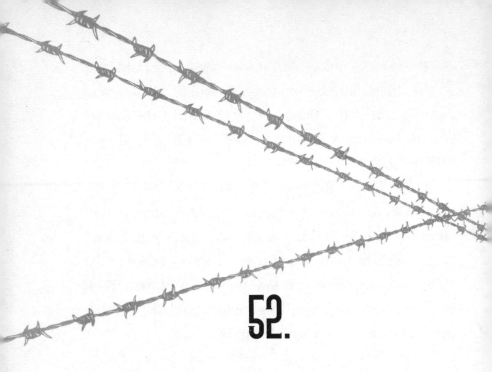

52.

HOPE AND SCYLLA ARE the last to leave the storehouse.
They step outside, clad in the baggy, ill-fitting uniforms
of Brown Shirts. Caps conceal their hair.

They carry an extension ladder to the rear of the
storehouse, digging its feet into the snow. The ladder
shrieks as they lengthen it, and they're counting on the
camp's sirens to cover the sound.

Their packs are full and heavy, and it's no easy task
climbing the ladder. Even trickier is scaling the steep
incline. Crawling on hands and knees, it's all Hope and
Scylla can do to grab vent pipes and chimneys, ascend-
ing the roof's snow-covered shingles like mountain
climbers.

They reach the ridge and catch their breath. A fire

rages to the east—the vehicle compound, courtesy of Cat. The camp is a hornet's nest of activity.

The two Sisters get to work. Moonlight is their only illumination. Removing crossbows from their packs, they line them up on the roof, one next to another, and hammer them in place. When a Humvee barrels past, they duck. No one gives a glance to the roof of the storehouse. Why would they?

As she works, Hope glances toward the headquarters, wondering about Book. Rectangles of candlelight spill from the windows. She can only imagine what the Brown Shirts are doing to him.

Her work is tedious and slow: nailing, aiming, and arming a dozen crossbows to the top of the roof. It's taking longer than Hope expected, and she and Scylla are behind schedule. They have to hurry.

A slamming door startles them both. Hope peeks above the roof's ridge to see the two camp overseers hurrying from the headquarters. They are followed by Chancellor Maddox and Dr. Gallingham. Her stomach clenches at the sight of them.

The four officials hop into an army vehicle and accelerate away, heading toward the vehicle compound. Even as Hope watches them leave, she doesn't have a good feeling about this. Everything, she fears, is going terribly wrong.

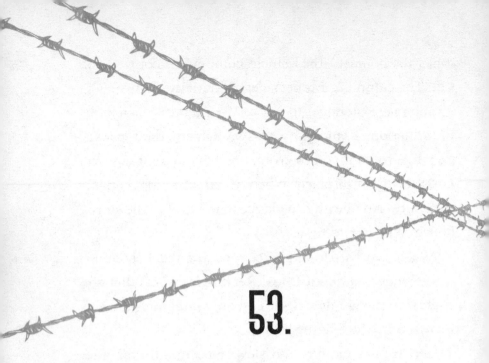

53.

Despite the blaring siren from outside, the office of
Colonel Westbrook felt deathly quiet. Just Dozer, me . . .
and Sergeant Dekker pressing a knife into my neck. A
guttering candle sputtered on the mantel.

"You are one funny dude, you know that?" Dekker
said. "An army, my ass."

He and Dozer shared a laugh. It was meant to be
manly and full of swagger, but there was something
pathetic about it.

"You happy, Dozer?" I asked.

"Course I'm happy. Why wouldn't I be?"

I shrugged. "You tell me."

"I get respect here. I got my own room. They want
me to be a leader. Sure beats running around with you

d-bags." He gave a mocking laugh.

"Maybe, but we did something, you know. We made it to the next territory."

"What good was that when we turned right around and came back?"

"Didn't you feel a sense of accomplishment?"

"For what? Eating maggots and squirrels? Yeah, that's a hell of an accomplishment." Another laugh.

"For living. For surviving. For proving we could do it."

"Don't give me that. Escaping from here was the stupidest damn thing we ever did."

I gave my head a mournful shake. There are some people in life you just can't understand, no matter how hard you try. Dozer was one of those for me.

"And it was even more stupid for you to come back here," he went on. "Did you really think we wouldn't catch you?"

I didn't answer him, and I realized—a moment too late—that I should have. I should have expressed remorse or anger or at least surprise at getting captured. But for a brief moment, I forgot my role.

"Wait a minute," Sergeant Dekker said. "You wanted this."

My heart came to a lurching stop, and I made a pathetic attempt to laugh. "What're you talking about?" I asked.

"This. Getting captured."

"Yeah, right, 'cause everyone wants to have their hands bound behind their back."

He stuck the knife deeper in my neck. I could feel a thin line of blood snaking to my collarbone. "You're too smart to use explosives in the middle of a camp. You wanted us to catch you."

"Oh sure," I scoffed. "Because I like being held at knifepoint."

"Don't BS a BSer." He leaned his face forward until it was so close, I could taste his sour breath. "The question is: why'd you want us to find you?"

"You're crazy," I said, attempting to look away.

Dekker grabbed my chin and yanked my face around. "Am I?"

I avoided his stare. Out of the corner of my eye, I saw that Dozer was watching us with curiosity. He had no idea where Sergeant Dekker was going with this.

Dekker took a step back and lowered his knife. "If I'm really crazy, then let's go back to where we found you."

Although I tried to hide it, I felt the blood emptying from my face.

"Fine," I said. "If you want to disobey the colonel's orders, be my guest."

A devilish smile pricked the corners of his lips. "He only said to keep an eye on you. He didn't say *where* I had to do it." He looked to Dozer. "You have your nine mill?"

Dozer removed the handgun from its holster.

"Good," Dekker said. "Just in case our little prisoner here gets any crazy ideas about running away."

As the three of us left the headquarters, I could feel the cold, hard stare of Dozer's pistol aimed at the center of my back. I knew with absolute certainty that if I even *thought* about running away, I'd be gunned down in an instant. Nothing in the whole wide world would make Dozer happier.

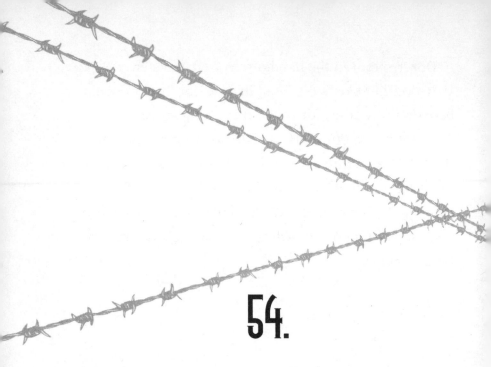

54.

THE PLAN UNRAVELS BEFORE her eyes.

Hope knows if she doesn't prevent Dozer and the other Brown Shirt from reaching the Quonset hut, the mission fails. All the Less Thans die. End of story.

"I'm going down," she mouths to Scylla, and slides down the ladder. Tugging her cap downward, she emerges from behind the storehouse and makes her way across the infield. Moonlight shadows her. Dozer glances once in her direction but thinks nothing of it. Just another Brown Shirt.

She is twenty yards behind them, stepping in their footprints. All she has to do is get Dozer's pistol. She can take out the lead soldier after that.

The cold steel of her dagger sighs as she pulls it from

its scabbard. Fifteen yards. Ten. She lifts the blade, ready to strike. . . .

"Halt!"

The lead Brown Shirt has pivoted in place, training his 9mm at a spot between Hope's eyes. She freezes, blade poised in air.

"What do we have here?" he asks, sauntering toward her. When he's close enough, he knocks Hope's cap off with the barrel of his gun.

Dozer's face lights up in recognition. "That's one of the Sisters I was telling you about."

"Well, this Sister nearly slit your throat."

He motions for her to drop the knife, and she has no choice but to do as he says. It hits the frozen earth with a muffled clank.

He steps forward and explores her face. "Hey, I think I know you," he says. "Your hair's not as long, and you don't have the wrinkles, but you look just like your mother. Same big eyes, too, although hers were a little wider the last time I saw her." He makes the sound of a firing pistol.

That's when Hope knows. This is Sergeant Dekker— the man her father wrote about. The man who killed her mother.

She suddenly finds it difficult to breathe. A stabbing pain radiates outward from her chest, and gun or no gun, she is tempted to throw herself at this Brown

Shirt, this *monster*, even if it means ending her life in the process.

"So who're you with?" Dekker asks. "A couple of your friends?"

Hope grits her teeth. "An army," she says.

Dekker's smile evaporates. "Your mother thought she was clever, too. Wouldn't tell me where her daughters were. And look where it got her. That's why I wrote my name in blood on your little porch. So you all would know not to mess with me." Dekker turns to Dozer. "Tie 'em up. Together."

Before Hope can react, Dozer whips out a rope and yanks her wrists behind her back. When her hands are bound, Dozer joins the two prisoners by lashing their hands together. Their backs press into each other's.

"Now that's what I call dancing cheek to cheek," Dekker says. "And your timing's excellent. We were just on our way to see what's going on in the barracks."

"Nothing's going on," Hope responds, a little too quickly.

Dekker gives his head a shake. "And you see? It's the fact that you both deny it so fast that makes me think just the opposite."

He traces the gun barrel across her face. The metal is cold and makes her shiver. Then he turns his attention to Book. She can no longer see the sergeant, only hear him.

"So," Dekker says, "what're you all up to?"

Book doesn't respond, and Hope hears the thud of the sergeant's fist striking Book, followed by a violent exhalation. Book struggles for air. All she can do is stand helplessly and listen.

"Stop it!" she says, her outburst provoking laughter.

"Maybe we will when you tell us what you're up to." Dekker comes around and eyes Hope, waiting for her to speak.

But it's Book who talks, not Hope. "There's an army," he manages to say.

Dekker's face turns crimson with anger. "We'll see about that."

He marches toward a Humvee, one with a .50-caliber machine gun mounted on top. He climbs in and positions himself behind the weapon, training its long, sleek barrel at the Quonset hut—where seventy-five Less Thans are currently locked in captivity.

"Last chance!" he calls out.

Hope and Book are too stunned to speak.

"Fine," Dekker says. "Then here's what I think of your 'army.'"

Book cries "No!" at the top of his lungs as Dekker pulls the trigger and the machine gun spits angry bursts of fire, shell casings arcing in the air and landing with steamy hisses in the snow. He sprays the Quonset hut with round after round, the bullets slicing through the thin metal like nails through paper, exploding and ricocheting and puncturing the walls with a thousand percussive shrieks.

Windows shatter and sparks fly, the door flies off its hinges, and the side of the barracks is tattooed in enormous, gaping holes. It doesn't take much imagination to visualize what's happened to the LTs inside, and to Hope's ears there has never been a more violent sound: the grating, jarring, slashing cacophony of bullets shredding metal as they penetrate the barracks into the sleeping quarters themselves.

Through it all, the muscles in Dekker's face are contorted in a grimace of satisfaction. *This is what you get,* his expression says. *Don't mess with the Brown Shirts.*

When, finally, he removes his finger from the trigger and leans back against the turret, smoke plumes from the rifle barrel. It glows red with heat. To one side of the Humvee rests a steaming pile of casings, like droppings from some metallic creature.

Dekker swivels his face until his eyes land on Book and Hope.

"Where's your army now?" he says. He smiles.

"You killed them," Book manages. His voice sounds disembodied. As if he's trapped in a deep, dense fog.

"They were going to die anyway. I did 'em a favor." Dekker wipes his hands, climbs down from the Humvee, and sticks out his lip in a mock pout. "Aw, is someone going to twow a tantwum? Someone going to have a wittle cwy?" He snorts with laughter and turns to Dozer. "Go check to see if anyone's left."

390

Dozer goes galumphing off toward the Quonset hut.

"What now?" Hope asks. It's taken her this long to gather words.

"Now we eliminate any remaining Less Thans, and then: bye-bye, army."

He circles his two prisoners, jabbing at them with his knife so that they stumble backward. "Whaddaya say, Slice Slice? Like a few more scars to go with the ones on your wrists?"

"Leave him alone!" Hope screams.

Dekker steps around and looks at Hope. "And why would I do that?"

"Because he didn't do anything. If you want to torture someone, torture me."

"Don't worry. I've got a whole other set of plans for you. You know what they say: like mother, like daughter."

At that moment Dozer returns, wearing a dazed expression. In his hands are clumps of dried grass and bits of shredded clothing.

"What do you got there?" Dekker barks.

"The bodies," Dozer says, not able to comprehend what he's holding.

"Huh?"

As Dozer speaks, his voice is halting, as though trying to understand a riddle. "No blood. No people. Just clothes . . . stuffed with grass."

Dekker's face tightens. "What about all the Less Thans?"

Dozer gives his head a shake. "There were none in there."

"That's impossible. There were seventy-five of 'em; they were too sick to move; they had to be in there."

"They weren't there. Just this." He raises his hands, and the weeds filter between his fingers, floating to the snow-covered ground like blowing hay.

Sergeant Dekker's look of triumph changes to outrage. His eyes land on Book . . . and then he backhands him. Book's face whips to the side. The sergeant hits him again, and Book's face reels in the other direction.

Dekker is about to hit him a third time when Hope sees something that turns her eyes to saucers.

"Duck!" she yells, jerking Book to the ground. Dekker stands there, a look of bewilderment on his face. Seconds later, a *whoosh* is heard.

The sergeant's mouth opens in surprise. Like a puppet whose strings have been cut, he collapses to his knees, then falls backward. The shaft of an arrow juts from the middle of his chest like a planted flag.

Hope's gaze travels to the far side of the infield, where Cat holds an archer's pose. He is in the process of nocking a second arrow.

Dozer stands there, stunned. He fumbles for his 9mm, accidentally firing it from its holster. A bullet nearly gets him in the foot. An arrow takes out a chunk of his shoulder. He grabs the wound with one hand, the gun with the other, then turns and runs, firing blindly as he goes.

Cat races forward, slicing through the rope that binds Hope and Book.

"Nice shot," Book says, rubbing his wrists.

"I was trying to hit Dozer," Cat says.

Book's eyes go wide. "But he was on the other side of us."

"I haven't gotten my aim down yet."

Cat is about to go to Sergeant Dekker, but Hope beats him to it. The sergeant is writhing on the ground, gasping for breath. Hope slams a foot on his chest and rips the arrow from his body.

"Do I look like my mother now?" she asks.

Grimacing, Dekker struggles for a final, gurgling breath, but Hope doesn't pay attention. She gives the arrow to Cat.

He puts it in his quiver and is about to leave when Book says, "Welcome back."

Cat looks at him a moment, nods, then runs off without another word.

"Are you okay?" Hope asks Book, raising a hand to his lower lip, which is swollen and oozes blood.

"Fine," he says. "Cuts and bruises. You?"

She gives a none-too-convincing nod. The fact is,

she's not fine. It's not just learning more about her mother's death, but what Sergeant Dekker was doing to Book . . . and how utterly helpless she felt.

Book sees she's shaking and takes her quivering hands in his. Energy courses through her body. Her breaths are jagged, halting, uneven. She can feel the heat rising from Book, mingling with her own. Her eyes land on his cuts. "We should get those cleaned," she murmurs.

"Later," he murmurs back.

Hope knows they have much to do. But more than anything, she wants to stay and bandage Book's cuts. Wants to be by his side. And when she looks at him, she can't help but feel he wants the same thing, too.

All at once, their faces lean into each other and their lips touch. The kiss is brief, fleeting, as if each is asking permission. Even so, when they pull back, Hope feels dazed.

"Go," Book says, and she knows he's right. They have work to do. She runs in one direction and Book in the other.

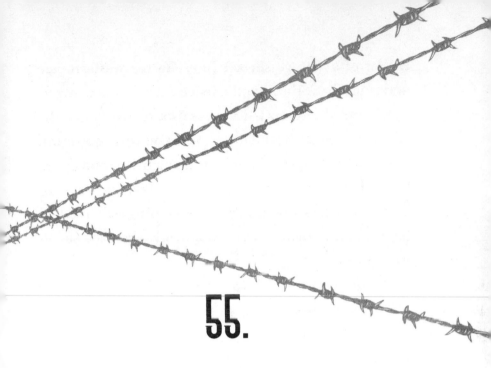

55.

My first stop was the Quonset hut, and it was a war zone. The rows and rows of bunk beds were gouged and splintered, the walls drilled with a thousand bullet holes, the air swirling with smoke and dust and pillow feathers . . . but there were no bodies. They'd all been pulled to safety.

I bent over, hands trembling as they grabbed my knees.

"Thank you," I said aloud, and a long sigh of relief left my body.

The sound of vehicles brought me to a standing position. The Brown Shirts were back. Time to get out of there.

The remaining explosives were right where I'd left them, tucked in their canvas knapsack in the back corner of a storage shed. I raced to the western gate and snuck back through the fence.

I found the seventy-five Less Thans just below the cemetery. Some were sitting, most were lying down. Flush, Four Fingers, Twitch, and Diana went from LT to LT, giving them sips of water and covering them with blankets. When Diana heard me coming, she readied her crossbow, then lowered it quickly when she saw it was me.

"Well?" I asked.

"All here," she said.

I couldn't believe it. *"Everyone?"*

She nodded.

"And just in time," Flush added. "If Hope hadn't slowed them down, they would've killed a bunch for sure."

I looked around at the emaciated bodies. They were bent over, coughing, so thin I could see each tiny expansion of their lungs.

"How'd you do it?"

Flush shrugged. There was no hint of bragging as he spoke. "Four carried the ones who couldn't move; Diana and I led the rest. And Argos made sure no one was left behind."

I looked over at my dog, licking the faces of the sickest of the bunch. The slobbering touch of his tongue seemed to revive them.

"You sure they won't discover us?" Flush asked.

"I'm not sure of anything. But once we start the next phase, they'll have their hands full."

"And we'll be safe here?"

That was the question I didn't have an answer to. Twitch turned to me. I was relying on guesses, estimates, hunches . . . and what little he had taught me about physics. "You'd be safer farther west," I said.

"What if we can't move everyone?"

"Do the best you can." I had no more answer than that. I turned and started to go. As I was walking back up the hill, I caught sight of Major Karsten, his scar visible in the moonlight. He sensed my stare, looked up, and gave me a subtle nod.

Racing around the camp, I headed back up the mountain. My breath was short and rapid. I found the fuses and fumbled for a piece of flint. My fingers were numb from cold, and because time was running out, I was hurrying faster than I should have been—all reasons I failed to see the shadow on the snow beside me.

Dozer.

Blood dribbled down his arm from where Cat's arrow had taken a small chunk out of his shoulder. If he was aware he was bleeding, he didn't show it. Or maybe he didn't care. In his hand was the 9mm pistol.

His face was fixed in a menacing snarl like some rabid dog. When he spoke, it was husky and guttural, more the growl of a beast than the voice of a human being.

"Whatever it is you had going, it's over."

Staring down the barrel of his gun, I couldn't argue with him.

"Listen," I pleaded. "I'm just trying to help those Less Thans. We're not here to harm any Brown Shirts."

His eyes were woozy and out of focus. "I saw how you looked at me. I know you'd like nothing more than to take this little pistol and shoot my brains out." He waved the gun dangerously, and it occurred to me he was half crazy from loss of blood.

"You know what?" he said, his words slurring. "It doesn't matter what you've got in mind. All that matters . . . is what *I've* got in mind." He gave a shrill little laugh and jerked the pistol to one side, indicating that I should walk. "Come on."

"Where to?" I asked.

"Where else?"

The hair rose on the nape of my neck. When I didn't move, Dozer fired a shot that came inches from my face. My ears rang.

"Unless you want me to shoot you right here," he said.

I had no choice but to ease down the trail, shuffling through the snow to where he intended to finish my life: in the spiraling flames of the fiery pit.

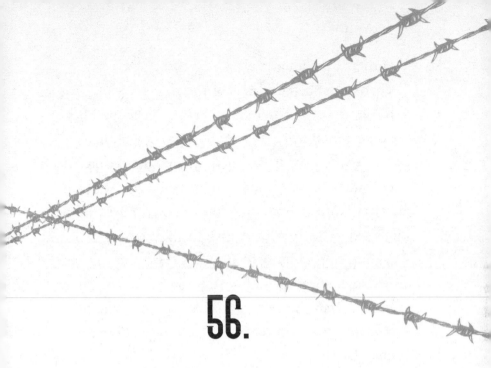

56.

HOPE AND SCYLLA FINISH arming the crossbows, then attach long strings to the triggers. They scramble down the ladder, race to another building, and arm still more. The more arrows they can throw at the Brown Shirts— and from as many different directions—the better.

Deception. It's all about deception.

As Hope joins the strings together connecting the triggers, all she can think about is Book. Although the plan was for him to get captured so they could sneak the Less Thans from the Quonset hut, everything that's followed is happening way too fast. Things are spinning out of control. Like right now, staring past the southern boundary of camp, she spies a snaking line of headlights in the desert, distant miles away. A convoy of ATVs.

Hunters, no doubt.

There must be hundreds of them.

If they make it up to Liberty before the assault begins, the Sisters and Less Thans won't stand a chance.

That's when she hears the gunshot. There have been other bullets fired tonight—many of them—but this is the first from the north side of camp, where Book is supposed to be. Her heart gives a shudder.

A couple of dozen Brown Shirts return to the camp's infield, exhausted from fighting the fire at the far edge of camp. They throw themselves to the ground, and Hope realizes that most of the camp's soldiers are now in one place.

She turns to Scylla and gives a look. They're supposed to wait for Book's signal, but they can't afford a moment's delay; they've got to start right now. Hope pinches the string, which loops around the triggers of six crossbows. Scylla does the same. On the count of three they pull . . .

. . . and twelve arrows whistle through the air.

Some clatter off the sides of vehicles. One punctures a tire. But a couple hit their marks, striking Brown Shirts in the chest. Two bodies crumple to the ground.

Hope and Scylla race to the other crossbows, tugging at the strings, firing off the arrows as they run past. From the opposite direction, Cat and Diana launch their arrows.

The night is suddenly raining arrows, and the Brown Shirts are in disarray. They form an improvised circle, backs to one another like wild beasts against an enemy, firing randomly toward the outer edges of camp.

Hope and Scylla split up. Hope reaches the back of the storehouse, and with another pull of a string, she's able to fire six more crossbows. Two more Brown Shirts hit the ground, writhing.

Soldiers squeeze the triggers of their M16s and spray the darkness with bullets. But they're shooting blindly; they can't see the enemy.

The four of them—Cat and Diana, Hope and Scylla— alternate their shots so that when two are firing, the other two reload. Just when it seems the arrows are coming from one direction, they come from the opposite way as well, flying from all four compass points. The Brown Shirts think they're surrounded.

In the midst of the chaos, Hope makes out a tall, stooped figure racing frantically across the infield, clutching his pistol and firing wildly. Colonel Thorason.

Hope removes an arrow from her quiver and nocks it to her bow, waiting for soldiers to clear so she'll have a clean shot. Her focus has never been stronger, her sight never clearer. Just before she releases the bowstring, Colonel Thorason looks her way . . . as if he knows what's coming. When the sharpened tip exits out the back of his neck, he sinks to his knees and falls face-first in the snow.

Leaving only Chancellor Maddox and Dr. Gallingham.

The plan is working—the Brown Shirts are corralled in a single place. But Hope knows there's a catch. They only have so many arrows. If Book isn't able to detonate his explosives, the soldiers will figure things out, the Hunters will arrive, and the four of them will be mowed down in seconds. Then the freed Less Thans will be executed, too.

Please, Book, tell me you're not hurt. Tell me everything's okay.

Meanwhile, the Brown Shirts are returning fire with all they have: M16s, machine guns, even RPGs. One of the grenades shatters a window and blows a small building to smithereens.

Hope gives a glance to the faraway road. The Hunters' headlights are growing closer. Another fifteen minutes and they'll be in camp. But there's still no signal from Book; time is running short.

She fingers the locket around her neck, imagining the photographs of her mother and father. That's when she decides she can wait no longer. She needs to find Book. She emerges from the shadows, fires six crossbows, then turns and runs. Just as she moves away from the building, it explodes in a swirl of flame and splintering wood, catapulting her to the ground. She gets up and darts off quickly.

Even when she rounds a corner near the Soldiers' Quarters, her ears are still ringing, which is why she neither hears nor sees Chancellor Maddox until she runs right into her. Hope fumbles for an arrow.

"Don't bother," Maddox says. To one side of her stands a Brown Shirt holding an assault rifle.

Hope has no choice but to let the bow and arrow slip through her fingers.

Chancellor Maddox smiles warmly, her rosy cheeks raised. "Going somewhere?" she asks sweetly.

Hope doesn't answer. What can she say? For all these months, she's dreamed of exacting her revenge. Instead, it's the chancellor who will get the final say.

Maddox reaches into the folds of her coat and removes a set of plastic zip ties.

"Tie her to that drainpipe," she commands.

The Brown Shirt whips Hope around and yanks her hands together. He pushes her back against the building and cuffs her to a rusted pipe that descends from the roof. Hope strains, but it only makes matters worse. She can feel the plastic cutting into her skin.

"It won't work," Hope blurts out.

"What won't work?" the chancellor asks innocently, and then her eyes glance to the briefcase attached to her wrist. "Are you referring to this? If so, you're too late. What's done is done. As for killing you, well, who'll even know? You'll be no more missed than a dead bug."

403

She smiles as though she's said something nice.

Hope has no good response—not in words, anyway—so she spits an enormous ball of phlegm onto the chancellor's cheek. The chancellor recoils as if she's been shot.

"Then consider that a bug splat," Hope says.

Chancellor Maddox reaches back to strike Hope but stops herself. "No," she says, regaining her composure and wiping away the spit with a hanky. "Give me your knife."

The Brown Shirt removes his dagger from its scabbard and presents it to her. Maddox bounces it in her hands a time or two to judge its weight.

She steps forward until a mere six inches separate the two of them. The knife is extended now, its glistening tip reaching for Hope's face. Hope leans back, her head pressing against the drainpipe. When the chancellor speaks, her voice is sugary sweet.

"I know about you and that Less Than. Book, is that his name? Your friend Dozer told us all about it. How you two formed some kind of *special bond* in the wilderness." The knife tip presses against Hope's cheek; the skin dimples.

Hope tries to turn her face away; the knife won't let her.

"I'll tell you something about boys," the chancellor whispers, as though confiding secrets to a girlfriend.

"So much depends upon appearance. They're so fickle that way. Girls are able to look past outward appearances. Boys—not so much."

By now, the blade has punctured skin. A pearl of blood stands poised between the skin and the knife tip, as if deciding which way to roll.

"Nothing turns off a boy more than—how shall I say it?—a *scarred* appearance."

Hope's muscles have gone slack; it's a miracle she is able to stand at all.

"Which is why I'm going to give you a teeny, weeny reminder of all the kind things you've done for me." Although her smile is enough to light up a room, her voice is as steely as the blade she holds.

A part of Hope wants to beg forgiveness. Wants to plead for mercy. But a larger part won't let her. She won't give Chancellor Maddox that satisfaction.

The chancellor gives her head a shake. "You're as stubborn as you are dumb."

She drags the knife slowly across Hope's cheek, first in one direction, then in the other, branding a giant X into her skin. Not content with a single tattoo, the chancellor does the same to the other cheek as well, taking her time, as though carving her initials in a tree. She steps back and admires her handiwork.

"There," she says. "Two Xs. Two *strikes*. One more and you're out." She smiles sweetly, as if the whole thing has been a pleasant game between friends.

Hope slumps forward, blood dribbling down her face, dripping from her chin as steadily as rain from a roof.

Chancellor Maddox returns the knife to the soldier and walks away, her head tossed back, her shoulders square, like a beauty queen on a runway, strutting her stuff before the judges. A moment later, Hope blacks out.

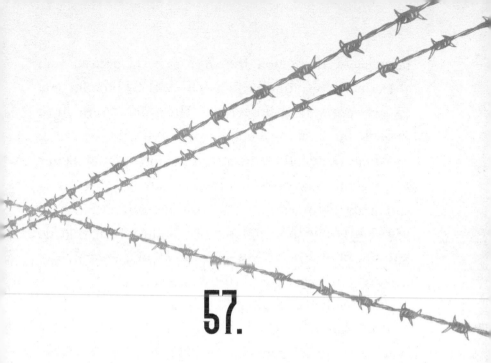

57.

I HEARD IT BEFORE I saw it—the roar of flames, the *pop*
and *crack* of burning wood—but when we reached the
edge of the fiery pit, there were no soldiers there. Just
an enormous bonfire gouging a hole in the cold and
black.

"Where is everyone?" I asked.

"Out looking for you. But I thought it might be better
if we had some alone time. You know: Brown Shirt to
Less Than."

Dozer motioned me closer to the flames, and I felt
the wall of heat. Trickles of sweat edged down my temples. He kicked a pile of wood into the growling pit.
Embers exploded upward like a volcano spouting lava.

"They tell me if it's hot enough, a body will burn

completely. If it's not, the skin does, of course, and the organs, but not all the bones. And I'd hate for you to only *partially* disintegrate." His words were lucid enough, but I got the feeling he was still wildly out of it.

Worse, I had the sickening realization that Dozer had no intention of killing me beforehand. He wanted me to burn alive.

His hyena grin oozed across his face. "So what do you say, Book *Worm*? Not so cocky all of a sudden? Not so sure how to get out of this predicament?"

"Don't you ever feel bad?" I asked.

Dozer laughed harshly. "Why should I feel bad? I got what I wanted. I'm no longer a Less Than. *I'm better than you.*"

His eyes were getting hazier by the second, and he motioned me toward the fiery furnace with his pistol. There was no good way out, and both of us knew it. I was suddenly filled with an overwhelming sorrow—not just at losing my own life, but for all the others, too. Cat and Flush and Red and Diana and Scylla. And Hope. All gone.

I was moving toward the pit when I heard my name. "Booook!" The way the word was elongated could only mean one person.

Four Fingers.

He stepped from the shadows, his face lit in a goofy grin. Dozer swung his pistol back and forth between the two of us. "What's that moron doing here?" he asked.

He must have followed me.

"It's okay, Four," I said. "You can go." I was grateful to see him, but there was no point getting the both of us killed. I had to get him out of there. Besides, maybe he could tell the others where I was.

Four Fingers was looking from me to Dozer and back again, trying to make sense of the situation.

"You heard him," Dozer said. "Get out."

Four Fingers didn't move.

"Get out!" Dozer called again. When Four still didn't budge, Dozer lowered his pistol and pulled the trigger. The slug ripped through Four Fingers's pant leg and embedded itself in his thigh.

Four Fingers made no sound. He staggered but didn't fall, staring at the stain of blood. When he looked up, it seemed as though he was regarding Dozer in an entirely new light. Like it was finally dawning on him: *He's the reason. Back in the Brown Forest, he's the one who threw me against the rock.*

He walked wooden-legged toward Dozer.

"Stay back, ya big idiot," Dozer warned, and he fired another round. Four was a big guy, and the bullet only slowed him briefly.

"I'm serious! Don't come any closer!"

Four Fingers limped forward, trailing blood. Even when Dozer fired two more shots into the Less Than's stomach, it barely slowed him.

Dozer began to panic. He was backed up against the pit, and there was nowhere for him to go. He raised the 9mm, but Four Fingers lunged forward and knocked the gun free. It clattered to the ground. As the two of them grappled, I reached for the pistol. We had Dozer where we wanted him.

"Good job, Four!"

But Four Fingers wasn't done. He spread his fingers around Dozer's thick neck and began to squeeze. Dozer clawed at Four's wrists, trying to pry them free, his face changing from red to purple. It suddenly dawned on me that Four Fingers had no intention of letting go. He was going to strangle Dozer to death.

They stumbled backward, Dozer's heels poking over the edge of the volcanic hole. He shrieked in pain as flames licked his back. Four Fingers kept pressing forward.

"It's okay, Four," I said.

But Four Fingers didn't—or wouldn't—listen.

Dozer shook his head wildly from side to side, eyes popping from their sockets, pleading for mercy. Four Fingers didn't care.

"No, Four," I said. "Stop."

I placed a hand on his shoulder, but he shrugged it away.

Dozer was bent awkwardly at the waist, feet on the

410

ground, back leaning over the fiery pit. He couldn't hold the position for long. Four Fingers realized it too—but he kept shuffling forward until both of them teetered on the edge of the leaping flames.

"No, Four!" I cried.

Their clothes were on fire now, and right before Four pushed both of them into the raging bonfire, he turned and met my eyes. In that look was gratitude and sorrow both, thanking me for looking after him, sadness that it had to end this way. A moment later the two of them disappeared into the fire, then were consumed by flames.

I made my way back up the mountain, my hands shaking as I found the coiled fuses and laid them out. Four Fingers had sacrificed himself—not only for me but for all of us. Now I had to make sure his efforts weren't in vain.

The first explosive would be the signal. Even though my friends had already started the next phase, I had to let them know what was coming. They would need the warning.

I fished out a bit of flint, managed to light a small bundle of pine needles, then set off the fuse. It sputtered and spat before crawling along the braided thread like a hissing snake. I ducked behind an outcropping of rocks.

When the dynamite went off, it sent a percussive blast rolling through the air, raining snow and dirt and felling a half dozen trees in the process. As I scrambled to the next station, I let some time pass. My friends needed to get far, far away.

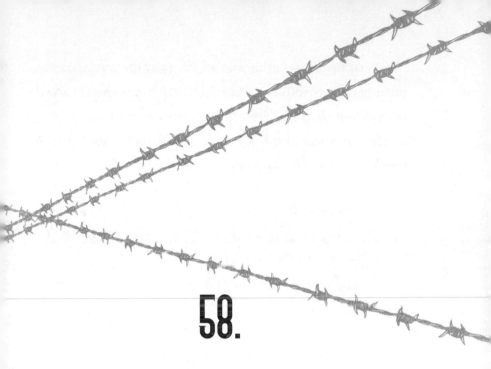

58.

Hope doesn't know how long she's been passed out. All she knows is that she's awake now, her wrists cuffed behind her back and strapped to a drainpipe. When she gives a tug, the plastic bindings cut into her flesh. She winces.

Even worse is the stinging that radiates from her cheeks. When she looks down, she sees a splattering of red on snow. Blood. So it was no dream: Chancellor Maddox really did carve up her face.

The pain is awful, the sense of violation worse. The fact that someone went to the trouble to *brand* her makes her sick, and she leans forward and retches in the snow. She lets her head hang there until the nausea passes, wiping her mouth on her shoulder.

Gunshots grab her attention. They come not from the parade ground but from the same direction as before—only closer. Is it possible Book is still alive?

She looks around. Chancellor Maddox has disappeared. So too the Brown Shirt. If she's going to escape, it has to be now.

She cranes her head. There's a place where the metal is speckled. Rust spots. The weakest part of the drainpipe.

She straightens and lifts her arms. Her shoulders pop. She gives a yank against the pipe. Nothing. She tries again. Still nothing. There's no give whatsoever. Her body slumps forward in defeat.

I can't do it, she realizes. *There's no way I can free myself.*

She resigns herself to death.

I'm coming, Mom and Dad. See you soon, Faith.

But when she thinks of Book, the tears begin, spilling from the pools of her enormous brown eyes and cascading down her cheeks, mingling with the trails of blood. The warm tears caress her lips and remind her of the kisses, Book's kisses . . . and she can't give up. She will join her parents and Faith—but not now. Not if she can help it.

Shifting her weight, she positions the plastic tie against the rust spots. She has to stand on tiptoe, and her fingers flail blindly behind her.

"Okay," she says aloud, "let's get to work."

She begins sawing through the plastic. Her arms are grotesquely twisted, and the sweat runs down her neck and back. She's making progress, but how much? How much further does she have to go?

A muffled, faraway explosion raises her head. *The signal.* Her mouth goes dry. The hairs rise on her arms.

It's too late. There's not enough time. Game over.

Her head tilts back and she releases an ear-shattering scream—a primal cry that rises from the very depths of her soul and carries with it all the sorrow and anger, all the grief and pain, the sound filling the night and rising to the heavens themselves.

Good-bye, Book, it says. *I love you. . . .*

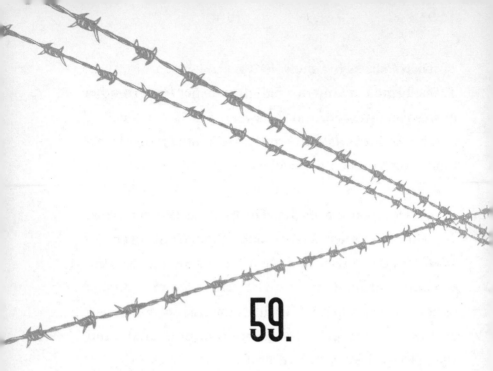

59.

THERE WERE FOUR FUSES, each heading to a separate clump of dynamite, but as I held them in my hands, I realized the problem: they weren't long enough. I could *maybe* survive the explosions . . . but definitely not the aftermath.

I glanced around me. Far off to one side was a massive red cedar—it must have stretched a good seventy feet into the air. It could possibly be my salvation, but there was no way for me to climb it. Its lowest branches were twenty feet off the ground.

Distant gunfire told me I couldn't wait, even if it meant sacrificing myself. Just as Four Fingers had sacrificed *him*self.

I nudged the flames to the fuses, and the sparks

slithered across the snow. If I remembered right, these fuses burned at a rate of ten seconds per foot. In other words: no time to waste.

I pushed myself through the snow. Any moment the fuses would reach the explosives and the world would change.

A blue spruce stood just uphill of the cedar, its boughs dipping with snow, and I began hoisting myself up—slipping, stumbling, scrambling my way up the tree. I was still a good ten feet short of where I wanted to be when I heard the first explosion. Buried in layers of snow, it gave off the sound of a muffled pop. A second explosion followed. Then a third and fourth.

And then all hell broke loose.

I heard the avalanche long before I saw it: a deep bass rumble, a sound so low and loud and *throbbing* that it took my breath away. It sounded like the planet itself was being formed, as though molten lava was spewing from the earth's core. My body shook. My teeth rattled. It took every bit of strength I had to hold on to the branches.

The snow coming down the mountain was a moving wall of sound—not just the rumble of the avalanche but also the shriek of trees as they were splintered to pieces. The snow destroyed everything in its path, wiping it clear, obliterating the landscape.

The spruce I was on snapped in two, and I went

sailing through air . . . smashing into the cedar. My hands clung to the cedar's side, clawing into the bark itself. The tree bent and swayed, vibrated and shook, but it was too thick, too massive, to be pushed over entirely. I pressed myself against it and held on for dear life.

The sound was overwhelming—like some beast letting loose the most horrible yell from the darkest corners of its miserable soul. The sliding snow created its own wind, and gusts tore at me, tugging at my clothes. All around me, trees were being toppled, either torn in two or ripped from the earth itself.

And then it wasn't just trees, but Camp Liberty as well, and new sounds: the groan of nails wrenched from walls, the violent *thwump* of buildings being flattened, and even—I was certain—the horrific screams of Brown Shirts, as a wall of white slammed into them with the force of a moving train.

Whoever was corralled in the center of camp had little chance of surviving, and I could only pray that Flush had taken the Less Thans far enough into the No Water to escape this raging tsunami of snow.

Finally, the roar ceased. All sound died away. There were a few trailing noises, of course—a tree falling to the ground, final snowballs rolling downhill, the squeak of settling snow. But the quiet that followed was the loudest silence I'd ever heard. Deafening.

Although the cedar I clung to was now leaning downhill like an old person straining to hear, it was still standing. It—and I—had managed to survive.

Now I had to find the others.

It was like walking across an ocean of snow, and I knew that buried beneath me were the shipwrecks of trees and Brown Shirts and Camp Liberty itself. Here and there, treetops or shards of buildings poked through the snowy surface like frozen waves, but in general the world was white as far as I could see.

There was one exception: the fiery pit. The volcano of flame was alive and well; plumes of steam hissed upward as though erupting from hell itself.

As we had counted on—and Twitch had calculated—the bowl-like shape of Skeleton Ridge sent the avalanche careening straight into the very middle of Camp Liberty. It was hard to imagine that everything—the barracks, the mess hall, Major Westbrook's headquarters—was all entombed beneath tons of hard-packed snow.

I veered west, and the snow grew more shallow until I was out of the snow and onto the high desert. The morning sun turned the eastern clouds bloodred.

I found the others at the base of a sandy hill, not far from where we'd first discovered Cat those many months before. The few LTs who had strength enough came running when they saw me, their faces lit with gratitude. We greeted one another with handshakes and awkward slaps on the back.

"Well?" I asked.

Cat merely nodded. "No sign of Brown Shirts."

"None of 'em?"

"If they were in the camp, they didn't stand a chance."

"And the Hunters turned back once they saw the avalanche," Flush chimed in.

The news was too good to be believed, and I felt like collapsing into the arms of my friends. Emotion tugged at me.

I told the others about Four Fingers and together, we shed a few tears.

Still, we had made our difficult return, enduring traitors and Crazies and weeks of captivity by the Skull People. And now, finally, we had achieved our goal.

We had freed the Less Thans. We had done what we set out to do. We had done what was right.

"Did any get away?" I asked.

"Too soon to know," Cat said.

But even the possibility that some might have escaped couldn't dampen my happiness.

Diana joined us, and I was about to thank her for all she'd done, when I suddenly realized . . .

"Where's Hope?" I asked.

Diana shared a look with the others. "She's not with you?"

I felt the blood drain from my face. "I haven't seen her since Cat rescued us from Dekker." I gave a panicked look to the others. "Seriously, where is she?"

"We don't know, Book."

My heart began to race; my knees went weak. "Well, where was she last?"

"She heard the gunshots and went looking for you."

A cold, firm hand gripped my heart. Hope hadn't reached me, so that meant exactly one thing: she was somewhere in the bull's-eye of the avalanche. I could imagine the lethal weight of it pressing down on her, flattening her like a leaf between the pages of a book. No way in the world to survive it.

I don't know if it was sorrow or exhaustion or a broken heart, but my legs went out from under me and I collapsed. I fell to the desert ground, convulsed by shoulder-racking sobs and a steady stream of tears. Just when it seemed the crying would stop and I could regain my breath, I remembered I'd never gotten the chance to tell her how I felt about her . . . and the weeping began again.

Although we knew it was hopeless, we formed a search party, poking through the snow with branches, hoping to make contact with a living, breathing Hope. Scylla, too, was missing, buried by the avalanche, and we spread out in a line, edging our way from one side of camp to the other. No one said a word. We were mourning Four Fingers. Mourning Scylla. Mourning Hope.

Whenever we saw part of a body wearing Brown Shirt clothing, we fell to the ground and dug with an anxious frenzy, remembering Hope and Scylla were wearing those uniforms. But in each case they were actual soldiers, dead from suffocation or arrows or maybe both. We kept searching.

We spent the entire day crisscrossing every inch of what had formerly been Camp Liberty. There were no survivors.

"Come on," Flush said, tugging at my sleeve. "You should eat."

I shook off his hand. "Just let me search a little more," I insisted.

"Okay. But not too long."

As he walked away, I realized all the others were gone and it was getting dark, an orange moon sliding up from the eastern horizon. It was just me and Argos amid a sea of snow. He let out a whimper.

"Just a little while longer," I told him.

Only later, when I collapsed on the snow—from hunger, from exhaustion, from *grief*—did I finally admit it was time to give up. No person could possibly survive this long buried beneath the snow.

Argos and I headed back to the makeshift camp. Cat brought over some food, and everyone gave me a respectful distance. They knew no words of comfort could possibly erase my pain, and they had sense enough not to try.

The next morning, it was decided to build some shelters. Although we wanted to leave immediately, we knew that wasn't possible—not until the Less Thans got their strength back.

We spent the day hauling debris to our temporary camp. I was in a daze, tugging at pieces of corrugated tin, yanking at fence posts, carrying armloads of branches back for fires. My body might have been present; my mind was somewhere else.

I blamed myself for Hope's death. If we hadn't kissed, maybe she wouldn't have come running for me. Maybe she would've gotten away.

But Hope had come running, and the avalanche swept her away and swallowed her up. I was filled with despair, with anger, with the deepest sorrow.

When I finally nodded off to sleep, I dreamed of her again—the woman with the long black hair. My grandmother.

The dream started out as it always did: running through the prairie amid whistling bullets and a gunpowdery haze, my grandmother pulling me to the ground and then—poof!—she was gone. But this time, the dream repeated itself—prairie, bullets, smoke, grandmother, prairie, bullets, smoke, grandmother—

until it wasn't a dream but a nightmare, a whirlwind of images sped up to a terrifying blur.

I startled myself awake. All around me lay the still forms of the sleeping Less Thans, their thick snores cutting through dark. As my eyes took in their emaciated bodies and hollow, sunken cheeks, it hit me.

I nudged Cat and Flush awake.

"She might be alive," I said.

Their expressions went from blank to pity as I began sketching in the sand. With a trembling index finger I traced the outline of Camp Liberty. When I finished, I drew a dotted line from the storehouse—the last place Hope had been seen—to the pit.

"What do you see?" I asked excitedly.

Flush and Cat shared a glance that I wasn't supposed to catch.

"Tell me," I insisted. *"What do you see?"*

By now, some of the others had woken as well.

"Uh, our camp," Flush said, rubbing sleep from his eyes.

"What specifically?"

"Some buildings."

"Which buildings?"

Flush bent forward to get a better look. "Well, the mess hall, and the storehouse, and the Soldiers' Quarters."

I began nodding wildly, and my finger landed in the

middle of that rectangle of buildings.

I took off before the others finished getting dressed.

A part of me knew it was hopeless, but I couldn't help myself. The odds of her surviving were flat-out terrible, but maybe, *maybe*, she had done what my grandmother always did in my dreams: vanished into thin air. And the only place in Camp Liberty where Hope could have vanished to was the hidden bunker beneath the tennis courts—the pit where the LTs were imprisoned after going through the Rite. The very place I'd been haunted by ever since I stumbled on it.

The hard part was finding the tennis courts buried under snow. There were no markers left from Camp Liberty, and it was a guess as to where things were. We walked around blindly, searching for clues, lining up our location with Skeleton Ridge.

When we had it narrowed down, we began to dig. I fell to my knees and used an old tin plate, scooping up heaping platefuls of snow, which I cast to the side. Everyone else was doing the same. The sun rose and amber rays bounced off the white surface and we kept at it.

I reached the ground—bare earth. Not a tennis court at all. I shifted fifteen feet to one side and started over. My clothes were wet with perspiration. It occurred to me I had never shown Hope the bunker, of course, only talked about it. She knew it was beneath the tennis courts . . . but that was it.

"We've got something!" Diana called out.

She had reached a patch of faded green cement. Everyone jumped to her side and began expanding the hole. When the tennis court's white lines appeared, we were able to imagine the layout, and I paced off a few feet in one direction.

"Over here," I said, and we went at it again, clearing away snow, debris, *anything* in our way. In no time, we'd created a small mountain behind us.

When we reached the court, the others stepped aside. I found the brass ring set into the cement, and my fingers—red and blistered and numb from cold—pushed away the snow and wedged themselves beneath the curve. I took a deep breath . . . and then yanked upward.

The bunker was pitch black, and even with the sun angling in from one side, painting the black walls with light, it was as dark and impenetrable as a cave. We stared down into the chasm. There were no movements, no cries of salvation—nothing to indicate a person's existence. Argos leaned in and barked, but there was no response. Just echo.

We had found the bunker, it was true, but it seemed utterly empty. With trembling legs, I lowered myself onto the metal ladder and descended into the dark.

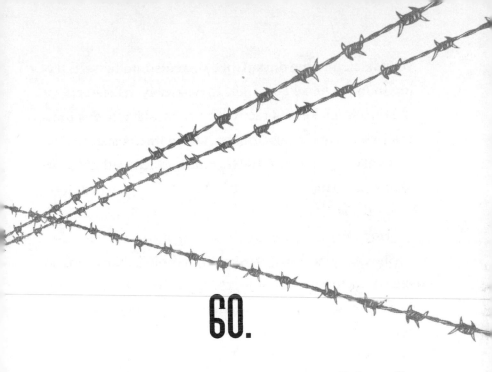

60.

"HOPE?" THE VOICE CALLS out, bouncing off the walls.

"Hope?" the voice calls again. Louder. More desperate.

Hope hears the voice . . . and recoils. It's been almost two days since she nearly lost her life. Only at the last moment did she rip through the drainpipe and stumble toward the tennis courts, falling headfirst into the bunker mere seconds before the avalanche hit. In all that time, she hasn't heard the sound of another human being. Still, she huddles in the corner, drawing her knees up to her chest.

She knows the person calling. It's Book. And she watches as he reaches the bottom of the bunker in a shaft of sunlight, inching his way forward, his eyes not

427

yet adjusted to the dark. Hope retreats into herself, trying to make herself smaller. Invisible, even.

His foot makes contact with hers and he lowers himself into a crouch, kneeling by her side without knowing he's kneeling by her side. His hands reach out, groping, stopping when they land on Hope's knee. Now it's Book who recoils.

"Hope?"

She can hear the confusion in his voice, and although she wants to respond, something prevents her. Not vanity or embarrassment. More like . . . shame. She covers her face with her hands.

Book's own hands fumble forward. "Thank God," he says, grabbing her by the shoulders and leaning into her. Although Hope wants nothing more than to return the hug, to take his face in her hands and bury him with kisses, she can't. Not now. Not ever.

Book attempts to pull her hands away from her face, but she won't let him. "Don't," she says.

"It's okay. You're safe."

Again he gives her wrists a tug. Again she stops him. "I mean it, Book, don't!"

He sits back on his haunches. "We're all here," he says. "We'll get you food and water and you can leave this place."

Hope gives her head a shake. She doesn't know what to say or how to say it. Can't possibly find the words to explain. She's grateful to be rescued—she is—but it's more than that.

"It's okay," Book whispers, and whether it's fatigue or hunger or just plain resignation, she allows him to separate her hands so he can get a shadowy glimpse of her. His eyes have adjusted to the dark, and his shocked expression mirrors what he sees: two deep Xs, outlined in blood.

"Who did this?" he gasps

At first, Hope doesn't reply. Then quietly she murmurs, "Maddox."

Book leans in and traces her wounds with the tips of his fingers, as if they were healing wands.

"Come on," he says. "Let's get you out of here and get those cleaned."

He unfolds himself to a standing position and takes her hand. Although there is something heart-achingly beautiful about the feel of his hands, she doesn't budge.

"Book," she says, struggling to find the words. "It's over."

"I know," he says. "We beat 'em. We won."

She shakes her head as if to say, *That's not what I mean*. "Us," she says.

"What're you talking about?"

"I can't anymore." She gestures vaguely to her cheeks.

"What difference does that make? You think I care about that?"

"No . . ."

"Well then?"

"It's not that. I don't really care how I look. I mean, not really."

"Then what?"

As her mouth opens, tears bubble in the corners of her eyes, and this is where she struggles most to express what she feels. "I wanted to give you more," she finally says, her voice a whisper. "I wanted to give you . . . my best."

"But you do."

She bites her lower lip and slowly rises. She'll join the others, she'll do what needs to be done to help the group, but her time with Book is done. He deserves more. He deserves better. Not . . . damaged goods.

But when she starts to walk past him for the ladder, he grabs her arm and swings her around until he faces her.

"No," he says angrily.

"What?"

"You heard me. *No.* I don't agree."

"But Book . . ."

"Don't you understand? I'm not attracted to you because you're beautiful and because you saved my life and because I could drown in your eyes. I'm attracted to you because of *who you are*. I love you, Hope. I always have, from when I first saw you outside Camp Freedom,

430

covered in mud. I saw something there—something inside you—that told me you were the most beautiful, most wonderful person I'd ever laid eyes on. And these wounds don't change any of that. They only make you more beautiful. The truth is, there is no better best than you."

"But . . . I'm damaged."

"No more than all of us." He places his hands atop her shoulders and looks her in the eye. "Do you love me?"

She shakes her head. "Oh, Book, it's not that easy—"

"Do you love me?"

"Things are different now. . . ."

"Do you love me?"

"Yes!" she cries. "Of course I love you! I've always loved you!"

The words echo off the bunker walls like a ricocheting bullet. Then Book reaches out and carefully wipes away the tears that stain Hope's cheeks. "That's all that matters," he says.

He leans forward and they kiss. Hope can feel his heartbeat racing against her own. When they draw apart, their foreheads lean into each other as though the kiss continues.

"'Better best'?" Hope says in a lightly mocking tone.

"I couldn't think of any other way to put it."

Now it's Hope's turn to smile. She bends forward and gives Book a kiss.

"We should go," she says.

"We should," he says.

They don't budge.

Finally, Book leans forward and gives her two more kisses—one on either cheek.

"Come on," he says, and leads her out of the bunker and into the light.

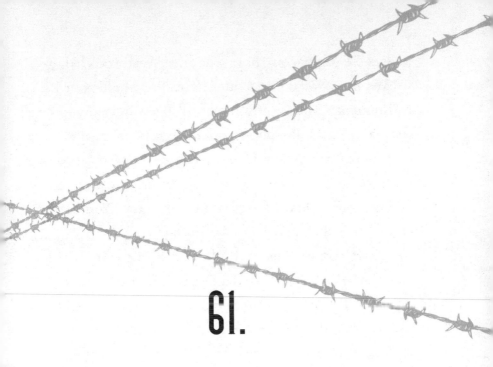

61.

WE BUILT A SHANTYTOWN—shacks of corrugated metal held up by fence posts and bits of trees, lashed together with barbed wire. Then we divided into teams. Some tended to the sick; some were in charge of salvaging materials from the former camp; still others went on hunting parties, bringing back whatever game they managed to track down.

On the surface we were happy. Joyful even. We had survived against insurmountable odds, freeing Less Thans and wiping out an army of Brown Shirts.

But there was something hanging over us, a dark cloud that shadowed us. We had survived, yes, but we were hardly free. We were still deep in the Western Federation Territory, and while we had found the bodies of Colonels Thorason and Westbrook, there was no proof we'd taken out Chancellor Maddox or Dr. Gallingham. They could have still been buried . . . or they could have somehow gotten away.

And before we could even think about migrating east, we had to nurse the sick ones back to health.

One night, Flush roused me from sleep. "You better come," he said, and took off running.

I threw on clothes and followed him to the listing shack where Major Karsten slept. A flickering candle provided the only illumination, but one glance told me everything. Pneumonia had ravaged Karsten's body, making him even more skeletal than when we'd found him in the barracks. His cheeks were so hollow, you could see the outlines of his teeth. His breath was jagged.

Kneeling by his side was Cat, and the look on his face told the rest of the story. He'd come all this way to be reunited with his father, and all he'd gotten was to watch him die.

I lowered myself to Cat's side and put my hand on his shoulder. He didn't cast it off. He even seemed to appreciate the gesture.

Hours passed while we watched Major Karsten struggle for breath.

Since the avalanche and the rescue of the Less Thans, Karsten and I had spoken only once, just long enough for him to tell me about my grandmother. They'd met a dozen or so years ago, right before the ambush and my capture, and once she discovered his true loyalties—that they were both plotting against the Brown Shirts—she'd made him promise to look out for me at Camp Liberty. I'd wanted to ask him about my birth name, if my grandmother had ever mentioned it, but it didn't seem the time.

The major's eyes stuttered open, landing first on Cat, then on me.

"Glad you made it," he rasped, his words meant for me. I wasn't sure what he was talking about, but then he slowly finished the thought. "That's why . . . carried you away."

With a jolt, I realized what he was getting at: he was the one who'd rescued me two years earlier when I'd tried to kill myself. Who'd tied a tourniquet around my arms and lifted me to safety. True to his word, he'd been looking out for me far more than I could have imagined.

The major turned his attention to Cat, giving his son's hand a squeeze with whatever little strength he had left. "Proud of you," he mumbled. "So proud."

He closed his eyes, took a final breath, and was still. Cat began to sob, and we left him to mourn his father alone.

Despite the frozen ground, we dug Major Karsten a

proper grave, working through the night, burying him the next afternoon in the cemetery west of camp, one row down from K2.

After the impromptu service, Red, Twitch, Flush, Hope, and I hung around to be with Cat, standing by the mound of freshly dug earth. For the longest time, no one spoke. We each seemed to be off in our own separate worlds.

"Do you think we can do it?" I asked.

"Do what?" Flush said.

"Everything. Survive the winter. Get to the Heartland. Save the country."

The silence stretched a long time before someone spoke up. Of all people, it was Cat.

"Everyone else seems to think so," he said. Then he turned his head to me and added, "So maybe we should, too."

I thought about my grandmother, wondered why it was she believed in me. All I knew was that I would stop at nothing to get these Less Thans to the Heartland and to prevent Chancellor Maddox from destroying the country.

Maybe that's what my grandmother knew about me—more than I even knew about myself.

The wind tugged at our clothes, and the sun eased behind a bank of purple clouds. I pulled my collar up to ward off the chill. I took Hope's hand in mine.

"There's a storm coming," Cat said, and Flush glanced to the sky. But I knew that wasn't what Cat was referring to.

"Who will it be this time?" I asked.

"Who *won't* it be?" he responded. "Brown Shirts, Hunters, Crazies—they all want us dead."

We didn't know why exactly, but it was true. Chancellor Maddox, in particular, wanted us good and gone.

"So we should get to the next territory as soon as we can," Flush suggested.

Cat, Hope, and I shared a look, and I knew what they were thinking—because I was thinking the same thing, too.

"Or just the opposite," I said.

"Huh?"

"Finish them off once and for all," Hope explained, and Cat and I nodded.

Flush swallowed. "All of them?"

"All of them," I said. "The Man in Orange. Dr. Gallingham. Chancellor Maddox."

It looked as though Flush's mouth had gone suddenly dry. "And how're we going to do that?"

"Don't know," Cat said, "but it's going to be a hell of an adventure."

I looked at him and then at Hope. Despite the circumstances, despite all the sick and injured Less Thans

437

and the fact that we barely had food and shelter for the coming winter, despite the odds against us, the three of us broke into the deepest smiles.

A whole range of emotions tugged at me: overwhelming grief for those we'd lost, utter fatigue at what we still had yet to do, but also . . . trust, gratitude, a sense of belonging. And yes, love.

We turned away from the cemetery and the shanty-town, looking out in the direction of the rest of the territory: Chancellor Maddox and Dr. Gallingham and the Man in Orange and the Crazies and the Hunters and the Brown Shirts—everyone who wanted us good and gone.

Cat was right; the storm was coming—*it had already arrived*—and we had no choice but to throw ourselves into its howling winds, its all-shaking thunder. Our freedom—our very lives—depended on it.

ACKNOWLEDGMENTS

THE CAPTURE HAS TAUGHT me many things, not least of which is that writing a second book is just as joyful an experience as writing a first . . . and just as challenging. Authors, of necessity, write for themselves, but I'm also well aware of the confidence you readers have placed in me to look after Book and Hope and Cat, and I take that trust seriously.

I'm also even more aware this second time around of all the tasks that so many people perform to bring this book to you, and I am more grateful than ever for their hard work, their contributions, and their dedication to making this the best book possible.

As always, I am indebted to my amazing agents—Victoria Sanders, Bernadette Baker-Baughman, Chris

Kepner—for their continued guidance, wisdom, *patience*, and belief in me. It is the greatest luxury to have that kind of support, and I don't for one second take it for granted. I am blessed to have you as my representatives, and I thank you more than I can ever say.

To senior editor Alyson Day and assistant editor Abbe Goldberg, copyeditors Renée Cafiero and Valerie Shea, designer Joel Tippie, marketing manager Jenna Lisanti, and publicist Lindsey Karl, and all the fantastic people at HarperCollins who tackle all the tasks of editing and copyediting and book jackets and designs and marketing and on and on and on: please know that I continue to be wowed by your artistry and smarts, and humbled by your commitment to this series.

In particular, I want to thank my editor, Alyson Day, who manages to find that delicate balance between encouragement and criticism, and who is unfailingly respectful, professional, insightful, to-the-point, and, above all, cheerful. How did I ever get so lucky as to get to work with you?

I'm also blessed to have friends who are writers, who teach me and inspire me, and who offer wise words when I'm wise enough to ask for them. Sarah Pekkanen and Joshua Bellin, thank you for all you've done, both emotionally and practically. I'm honored to call you friends; I'm honored to call you comrades. It's a great blessing to get advice—and encouragement—from such good writers.

I also want to pay tribute to all the terrific writers—and writers writing about writers—in the Duluth area: Margi Preus, Claire Kirch, Barton Sutter, Louis Jenkins, Sheila Packa, Christa Lawler, Sam Cook, Linda LeGarde Grover, Tony Dierckens, Lucie Amundson, the late Joe Maiolo, and many more. It's an inspirational time to be a writer in this town. I attribute it to the water.

Once more, I am thankful to those readers who offered early feedback and helped steer me through some dark tunnels, especially when I couldn't see the light. In particular, I want to mention Gracie Anderson, Katie Caskey, and Ryan Gallagher, who all offered wonderfully specific criticism, not all of it easy to hear, but all of it absolutely necessary.

Thank you to my students and colleagues at UMD, past and present, who inspire me, who remind me of the value of storytelling and the joy of imagination. Whenever I despair for the future, I walk into a classroom . . . and hope returns. Thank you for the gifts of inspiration, laughter, and tears. (And all the *Prey* selfies!) It's no secret why I'm crazy about you all.

I also want to thank you, dear readers, who read *The Prey* and offered your loving criticism. Your comments have lifted me, instructed me, *moved* me, and you complete this sacred triangle of Author, Story, and Reader. Without you, those first two elements would cease to exist.

I've dedicated this book to my three older siblings,

who have always loved and supported me, cheering my first steps as a baby and also as an author. Every human should be so lucky as to have such loving, living guardian angels. Just as every person should be as lucky to have the kind of parents we had, who nurtured and encouraged us and loved us unconditionally. I miss them every day.

And finally, to Pat, who is my first reader, my best reader, my true companion, who is there every step along the way, who teaches me to laugh, to mourn, to *love*, to live today and live tomorrow. I am a lucky guy to travel through life with you.